LITERARY NEW ORLEANS

LITERARY NEW ORLEANS

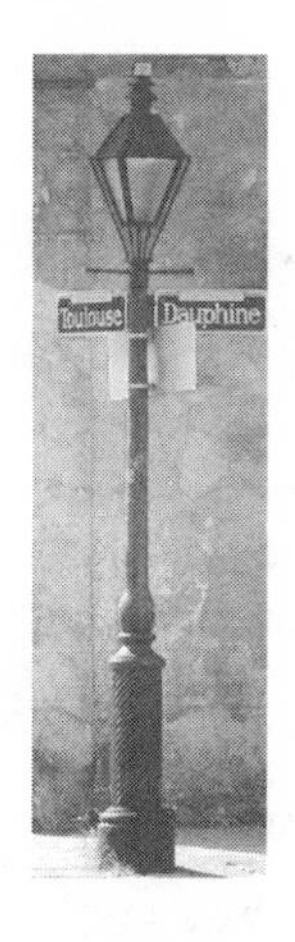

edited by

JUDY LONG

foreword by

PATRICIA BRADY

d

HILL STREET PRESS ATHENS, GEORGIA

A HILL STREET PRESS BOOK

Published in the United States of America by
HILL STREET PRESS, LLC
191 East Broad Street, Suite 209
Athens, Georgia 30601-2848 USA
706-613-7200
info@hillstreetpress.com
www.hillstreetpress.com

Hill Street Press is committed to preserving the written word. Every effort is made to print books on acid-free paper with a significant amount of post-consumer recycled content.

Text and cover design by Anne Richmond Boston.

Printed in the United States of America.

Library of Congress Catalog Card Number: 98-75331

ISBN # 1-892514-05-2

2 4 6 8 10 9 7 5 3 1

First printing

Contents

CONTENTS

Foreword

Have you ever been in New Orleans? If not you'd better go,
It's a nation of a queer place; day and night a show!
Frenchmen, Spaniards, West Indians, Creoles, Mustees,
Yankees, Kentuckians, Tennesseans, lawyers, and trustees,
Clergymen, priests, friars, nuns, women of all stains;
Negroes in purple and fine linen, and slaves in rags and chains.
Ships, arks, steamboats, robbers, pirates, alligators,
Assassins, gamblers, drunkards, and cotton speculators;
Sailors, soldiers, pretty girls, and ugly fortune-tellers;
Pimps, imps, shrimps, and all sorts of dirty fellows;
White men with black wives, et vice-versa too.
A progeny of all colors—an infernal motley crew!

Quoted in the *WPA Guide to New Orleans*, with the lines referring to loose women and interracial sex discreetly omitted, this nineteenth-century verse echoes the bemusement that New Orleans often evokes in observers. A bawdy stranger to the Puritan heritage, the city was so foreign in American eyes that a New England congressman argued in 1811 that the Union would be violently ruptured by its admission. New Orleans was indeed different, a Creole city with a rainbow population of black, white, and every shade of brown, red, tan, and yellow in between.

This is a city haunted by its past, its physical and emotional landscape still colored by colonial regimes, both French and Spanish, and an affinity for the lifestyle of its Caribbean neighbors. After the Louisiana Purchase nearly two hundred years ago (much against the will of the inhabitants), New Orleans doubled and redoubled to become one of the antebellum nation's busiest ports. An influx of Americans eager to profit from their Yankee grit, black and white Creoles fleeing the slave revolution of Saint Domingue, Napoleonic loyalists from France; and Germans, Irish, and Italians escaping successive political and economic disasters—all contributed to the city's multicultural environment, long before the term was coined. New Orleans still strikes outsiders, that is, anyone from north of Lake Pontchartrain to infinity, as the least American of all American cities.

A constant in the city from the earliest days of settlement has been a large, visible, and assertive black population. In the harshest days of slavery, free blacks here enjoyed civil, economic, and social liberties beyond the imagination of most Anglo-Americans. They owned property in all parts of town, succeeded in businesses and professions, supported private schools for their children, and numbered important musicians (whose descendants created the signature American art form—jazz), artists, and writers in their ranks. Black writers published a literary journal in the early 1840s and *Les Cenelles*, the first African American collection of poetry, in 1845. The founder of an order of black New Orleans nuns, Henriette Delille, is well on her way to sainthood. No wonder blacks in New Orleans were in the national vanguard fighting the imposition of Jim Crow through their newspapers, political action, and landmark lawsuits like *Plessy v. Ferguson*. During segregation, local black writers—Rodolphe Desdunes, Alice Dunbar-Nelson, Charles Roussève—kept their history alive.

Race relations—harmonious, tense, violent, or some combination thereof—are a central preoccupation of New Orleans life that any serious writer, not culturally tone-deaf or color-blind, must consider. Recently the *Times-Picayune* ran a weeks-long series on race, letting a spectrum of New Orleanians air their views on the good, sometimes very bad, and indifferent ways they see one another. After the series ended, letters poured in as people continued to have their say. Ignoring race here is a lot like not mentioning the alligator in the room.

Before the Civil War, New Orleans was so devoted to making money that cultural life lagged behind. The performing arts—music, dance, and theater—were those most favored. Poetry, history, folklore, and journalism were produced by local writers, but seldom reached a national audience. It was travelers, dozens of them, who interpreted the city to the world, and it was one of the mandatory stops on most literary foreigners' tours. Writers came to observe, often ever so briefly, a city that looked *up* at ships passing on the Mississippi River. Entranced or disgusted, they tended to focus on the same few sights, interpreting them according to their own tastes. They came to write, but certainly not to stay in a place where summer brought yellow fever with its nasty habit of wiping out "unacclimated" strangers.

Oddly enough, the city's long economic decline, ushered in by its surrender to a Union fleet in 1862, fostered its literary development. The world's fair of 1884, a bust at showcasing the city's return to prosperity, gave local writers a chance for publication and drew literary celebrities nationwide. Looking backward to a highly romanticized past, New Orleans appeared in late Victorian print as the exotic haunt of Creoles with bloodlines so pure they wouldn't stoop to call the king of France cousin or were conversely haunted by the possibility of mixed race.

The 1880s and 1890s set the pattern for New Orleans as a literary town which attracted writers with the ease of life here: a combination of decayed elegance, live music, friendly watering holes, and literary salons then, literary festivals now. The city became a sort of "Greenwich Village South," in Sherwood Anderson's phrase, in the 1920s, and today literary life is again hot. Despite some valiant efforts, this has never been a publishing town. Its allure for writers is as a place to live, often to write about, but not as an opportunity to hobnob with editors or publishers.

New Orleans is still unlike any other American city—charming, enraging, disappointing, tantalizing—all at the same time. Critics indignantly deny the "myth" of the city's distinctiveness, citing crime, filth, fast food joints, tee-shirt shops, chain stores, and malls (all too true), but the very frequency of the attacks smacks of protesting too much. Debunkers to the contrary, from the moment visitors are enveloped by the heat and humidity, their bodies turned languid and slow in the heavy atmosphere, they know they've arrived at a special place for better *and* worse very different from home.

People feel that powerful sense of place in their bones— or on their palates. When they move away, New Orleanians are astonished that the rest of America doesn't observe Mardi Gras, All Saints' Day, or Twelfth Night. They demand care packages of king cakes, chicory coffee, and Zapps potato chips, and carry back ice chests of fresh shrimp and crawfish. This is a city obsessed by food. Out at a restaurant, New Orleanians critique the menu (trading bites, of course), dredge up the merits and demerits of past meals, and discuss where and what to eat next.

With a New Orleans locale, writers are obliged at least to mention food (without sounding like a guidebook)—and get the details right. People still talk about the famous writer whose character snagged a bagel at Café du Monde. Look at how many of the pieces included in this book mention food or take place in a restaurant. What is the quintessentially New Orleans restaurant mentioned most often here? Galatoire's, of course.

And liquor . . . it's such a cliché. But this is a place where every event calls for cocktails—fund-raisers, literary readings, musical performances, art openings, post-funeral gatherings, and the countless outdoor festivals. Even church fairs have a cash bar, and alcohol is sold at drugstores, groceries, and gas stations. Nonstop parties can jazz up a dragging narrative, but pose a danger to the susceptible. Many a writer has sunk into an endless boozy haze here, immersed in a local scene that never gets translated into print.

The sense of place is historic as well as geographic. Buildings are identified by relationship to familiar landmarks—across the street from the Magazine bus barn, down the block from the Napoleon House, catty-cornered from Schoen's funeral home—or by predecessors in time. The Fairmont Hotel may have been in New Orleans for many years, but to diehards, it's still the Roosevelt or even the Grunwald, the hotel's previous incarnations. Newcomers who've bought a grand Garden District mansion can be made to feel like squatters in a house still invisibly populated by past owners. Genealogical head hunting is not limited to the elite; most New Orleanians know their roots and have a strong sense of the past. They even routinely trace the history of their houses: architecture and neighborhood loom large in any understanding of the city.

The lush, semitropical beauty of New Orleans is overwhelming. The relaxed Caribbean atmosphere of the French Quarter and the Faubourgs' Marigny and Tremé, the Greek Revival mansions of the Garden District, the gingerbread-festooned Victorians, shot-guns all over town, the river-view lofts of the Warehouse District—this city has more interesting buildings per square block than almost anywhere else. The walled cemeteries with their white-plastered or marble houses of the dead provide irresistible metaphors (they have, after all, appeared in just about every movie filmed in the city). And who can ignore the live oaks and cypresses, azaleas and camellias, the scents of sweet olive and jasmine, the concealing cats-claw vines?

New Orleans actually suffers from its own attractions. In some ways it is being devoured by its admirers, the real city cannibalized by the phony. Jazz funerals are staged—who needs a body?—and tour guides splatter fake blood on "haunted" sidewalks. There is even a carnival parade now in which tourists on floats throw beads to tourists on the street.

There is also the dark side of the vision—poverty, decay, crime, corruption—where writers dig into an ugly reality beneath the picturesque surface. But even the gritty underside of the city manages to sin in its own way. As politicians cynically remark, these people don't just accept corruption, they *demand* it. Maybe an easy-going tolerance of the more human vices seems less threatening than the changes in lifestyle that reform might bring.

Shades of gray are the norm here, and there's an ambiguity about many things, including sex, race, and money. The city is exuberantly home to one of the nation's largest gay communities, but there is also a certain fluidity in the sexual orientation of others—staid married people who slip over to the wild side. It takes a scorecard sometimes to guess a person's race (an artificial construct anyway). You can meet people with the same name and skin color, one black and the other white by their own self-definitions. Uptown families in splendid mansions may spend thirty, forty, fifty thousand dollars on a debut and Mardi Gras, only to declare bankruptcy shortly afterward. Things are seldom what they seem. People define and exaggerate themselves for their own and others' enjoyment.

Interpreters struggle to see and re-see the city without falling into cliché. But New Orleans is ultimately a city of the imagination, a land of dreamy dreams that defies "objective" reality, always just eluding literary capture. Each writer glimpses a different reflection in this hall of mirrors, each one discovering a subtly different city.

Patricia Brady
New Orleans

Preface

New Orleans has inspired great writers for centuries. The intent of this anthology is to capture the literary spirit of this unique city through a collection of diverse voices spanning its history. Faced with the monumental task of making selections from the vast canon of literature about New Orleans, I chose writings which, when pieced together, would provide a mosaic portrait of the Crescent City.

I have been careful to give voice to authors whose works are not among those generally anthologized and to select lesser known works by well-known authors. I have chosen pieces which illuminate the cross-fertilized culture of New Orleans by showing the city from male, female, black, white, and various class perspectives.

I have included in my definition of "literary," letters, journals, and travel accounts from Louisiana's colonial and early statehood periods. The first blossoming of a literary culture in New Orleans was between 1820 and 1860, with the majority of literature written in French. I have not included selections from these French works, but recommend Ruby Van Allen Caulfield's *The French Literature of Louisiana* (1929) and the poetry of Adrien and Dominique Rouquette.

Journalism has played a prominent role in the development of the literary community of the city. Since the mid-nineteenth century, local newspapers, including the *Daily Crescent*, the *Item*, and the *Times-Picayune*, have published some of the first works of many fine writers. For this reason I have selected newspaper articles by Hearn and Whitman. The *Double Dealer* (1921–1926) literary journal published some of the country's finest writers including Sherwood Anderson, William Faulkner, and Ernest Hemingway. I have included an essay by Anderson which appeared in the pages of the *Double Dealer* to pay homage to the importance of the little-magazine tradition in New Orleans.

Literature written in the English language flourished in New Orleans after 1873 when George Washington Cable's first published short story, "'Sieur George" (1873) appeared in *Scribner's* magazine. Rather than reprint one of Cable's often anthologized stories, I have selected a letter written by Cable in 1884 during the New Orleans renaissance of the 1870s to 1890s.

Due to the limitation of space, I have with great regret excluded authors whose work I deem important in chronicling the literary history of New Orleans. In no way does this imply a judgment on the quality of his or her work. Those authors include Hamilton Basso, Roark Bradford, Charles Gayarré, Francis Parkinson Keyes, Oliver La Farge, and Ruth McEnery Stuart.

Faced with the formidable task of excerpting from the numerous volumes of Shirley Ann Grau and Anne Rice, two of the most celebrated native New Orleans writers, I decided the wisest decision was to direct readers to the complete works of these authors. Grau, winner of the Pulitzer Prize in fiction, has written numerous works set in New Orleans, including the novel, *The Condor Passes* (1971). Best-selling author Anne Rice successfully captures "the dream landscape" of the city in her books, including *Interview with the Vampire* (1976).

I also recommend the works of the following fine writers who are beloved by New Orleanians: Poppy Z. Brite, James Gregory Brown, Quo Vadis Gex-Breaux, Julie Harris, Sybil Kein,Valerie Martin, Stan Rice, Kalamu ya Salaam, James Sallis, and Mona Lisa Saloy.

Students of the literature of New Orleans would be rewarded by reading the literary studies of Thomas and Judith Bonner, Violet Harrington Bryan, W. Kenneth Holditch, and Richard S. Kennedy, as well as any of the city's numerous journals, including the *Double Dealer Redux*, *New Orleans Review*, the *Xavier Review*, and the online *CyberCorpse*.

I would like to especially thank Patricia Brady and the staff of the Historic New Orleans Collection for their assistance, as well as Michael C. Terranova for permission to use his photograph on the cover of this book.

New Orleans is indeed a center of the literary arts, and *Literary New Orleans* is dedicated to all writers and readers in the city.

Letter to Comte de Pontchartrain

DE RÉMONVILLE (DATES UNKNOWN)

De Rémonville was born in France to an important family and traveled with Robert de la Salle on his exploratory voyage from Canada down the Mississippi River in 1682. Although de Rémonville did not accompany de la Salle further south than what is now known as the state of Illinois, he learned of the lower Mississippi Valley from de la Salle. De la Salle followed the Mississippi to its mouth and claimed possession of all territory watered by the Mississippi in the name of France. He called the territory Louisiana in honor of Louis XIV. De Rémonville addressed the following letter, urging the establishment of ports on the Gulf of Mexico and in Louisiana, to Louis de Phelypeaux, Comte de Pontchartrain, who served as the royal Minister of Marine, under Louis XIV.

Paris, December 10, 1697

Monseigneur:

The country wherein we propose to establish a colony is one of vast extent. It is watered by the Mississippi, and its tributaries, more than sixteen hundred leagues in extent. The Mississippi has its source in the northwestern part of North America, and its mouth in the southwest, where it empties into the Gulf of Mexico. There are many large and beautiful rivers which flow into the Mississippi, both on the eastern and western sides, which embrace a vast extent of territory that is now inhabited only by Indians.

The estuary of the Mississippi is in about the thirtieth degree of north latitude; and, although the climate is warm, it is very salubrious in most places. The country abounds in everything necessary for the conveniences of life. It produces two crops of maize, or Indian Corn, annually. It is an excellent article of food; when one becomes accustomed to it, the corn of Europe can be easily dispensed with. There are also a great variety of grapes, which make excellent wines, and we may reasonably hope that with proper culture, upon the most approved plan, a sufficient quantity of wine could be produced to supply the wants of all the inhabitants of that country.

A great abundance of wild cattle are also found there, which might be domesticated by rearing up the young calves, besides every variety of wild game. In the southwest, towards the Spanish settlements of New Mexico, the country abounds in wild horses, which the Indians readily exchange for articles of merchandise. The greater part of European fruits which grow there are of larger size and better quality. The country is covered with beautiful natural meadows, affording abundant pasturage, and the forests yield an abundance of building material in most places, which, on account of the navigable streams, could be cheaply transported, and the settlers comfortably housed in a short space of time.

The country is beautifully diversified with hill and dale; the air is pure and invigorating, and the winter is seldom felt there. From these causes the colonists could subsist there agreeably, easily, and abundantly. The trade in furs and peltry would be immensely valuable and exceedingly profitable. We could also draw from thence a great quantity of buffalo hides every year, as the plains and forests are filled with those animals.

The country abounds with white mulberry trees, and the climate being the same as that of Sicily and a part of India, silk worms could be easily raised, and the article of silk would, in time, become a source of infinite value to France. There are, besides, large districts of country where iron, lead, tin, and copper is found in rich deposits. There is also an abundance of cedar and other wood, of variegated colors, which are articles of prime necessity for the kingdom.

Hemp is indigenous and grows to the height of eight or ten feet without cultivation. In many places the country is covered with it. This article would be of great utility for ropes, cables, sails, and the coarsest linen fabrics. The oak forests are admirable for the ship-timber they produce, and masts may there be obtained equal to those of Norway, so that his Majesty could, in a short time, construct all his vessels by simply sending over the necessary workmen.

Such are some of the advantages which may be reasonably expected, without counting those resulting from daily endeavor. We might, for example, try the experiment of cultivating fine and long staple cotton, as well as tobacco, which can be produced of as good quality as any that comes from Cuba or Virginia.

It is almost certain that, with good pilots, two or three convenient ports on the Gulf of Mexico and in Louisiana might be established, which it would be the interest of the government to fortify; and, in this manner, his Majesty could, by force of arms, soon secure to himself legitimate possession of the whole of Mexico and Louisiana.

De Rémonville

from *Journal of a Voyage to North America*

PIERRE FRANÇOIS XAVIER DE CHARLEVOIX

(1682–1761)

Pierre François Xavier de Charlevoix was born in Saint Quentin, France and entered the Society of Jesus in 1698. He was assigned to the mission of New France and taught composition and literature in Quebec City, Canada from 1705-1709. He returned to Paris and was ordained as a priest in 1712. De Charlevoix was commissioned by the French Regency's Conseil de Marine to travel to Quebec and gather information for France's negotiations with England over the boundaries of Acadia, New France, and New England. In 1721 he set out on a journey which led him up the St. Lawrence and across the Great Lakes before heading South on the Mississippi River. De Charlevoix wrote that the confluence of the Mississippi and the Missouri Rivers was "the finest confluence of two rivers . . . to be met with in the whole world." His travels brought him to New Orleans in 1722 and he recorded his visit in *Journal of a Voyage to North America*, which was published in French in 1744 along with his *History and General Description of New France*, the first "historian's history" of Canada and Louisiana. De Charlevoix paid particular attention to topography and geography and during his lifetime these works were considered the definitive studies of New France. The Treaty of Paris of 1763 gave Quebec to England, as well as all of Louisiana east of the Mississippi, except New Orleans and its "island." In order to satisfy the English language public's curiosity about these new acquisitions, translators quickly issued three English editions of de Charlevoix's *Journal*. In the following entry from the *Journal*, de Charlevoix writes about the "Famous city of *Nouvelle Orleans*."

LETTER THIRTY-FIRST.

Voyage from the Natchez to New Orleans. Description of the Country and of several Indian Villages, with that of the Capital of Louisiana.

New Orleans, January 10, 1722

Madam,

I am now at last arrived at this famous city of *Nouvelle Orleans*, New Orleans. Those who have given it this name, must have imagined Orleans was of the feminine gender. But of what consequence is this? Custom, which is superior to all the laws of grammar, has fixed it so.

This is the first city, which one of the greatest rivers in the world has seen erected on its banks. If the eight hundred fine houses and the five parishes, which our Mercury bestowed upon it two years ago, are at present reduced to a hundred barracks, placed in no very good order; to a large ware-house built of timber; to two or three houses which would be no ornament to a village in France; to one half of a sorry ware-house, formerly set apart for divine service, and was scarce appropriated for that purpose, when it was removed to a tent: what pleasure, on the other hand, must it give to see this future capital of an immense and beautiful country increasing insensibly, and to be able, not with a sigh like Virgil's hero, when speaking of his native country consumed by the flames, *et campus ubi Trojae fuit*, but full of the best grounded hopes to say, that this wild and desart place, at present almost entirely covered over with canes and trees, shall one day, and perhaps that day is not very far off, become the capital of a large and rich colony.

Your Grace will, perhaps, ask me upon what these hopes are founded? They are founded on the situation of this city on the banks of a navigable river, at the distance of thirty-three leagues from the sea, from which a vessel may come up in twenty-four hours; on the fertility of its soil; on the mildness and wholesomeness of the climate, in thirty degrees north latitude; on the industry of the inhabitants; on its neighbourhood to Mexico, the Havanna, the finest islands of America, and lastly, to the English colonies. Can there be any thing more requisite to render a city flourishing? Rome and Paris had not such considerable beginnings, were not built under such happy auspices, and their founders met not with those advantages on the Seine and the Tiber, which we have found on the Mississippi, in comparison of which, these two rivers are no more than brooks.

But before I engage in the description of what is curious in this place, I shall, to preserve due order, resume my journal where I left off.

I stayed among the Natchez much longer than I expected, which was owing to the destitute condition in which I found the French with respect to spiritual assistance. The dew of heaven has not as yet fallen upon this fine country, which is more than any other enriched with the fat of the earth. The late M. d'Iberville had designed a Jesuit for this place, who accompanied him in his second voyage to Louisiana, in order to establish Christianity in a nation, the conversion of which he doubted not would draw after it, that of all the rest; but this missionary on passing through the village of the Bayagoulas, imagined he found more favourable dispositions towards religion there, and while he was thinking on fixing his residence amongst them, was recalled to France, by order of his superiors.

An ecclesiastic of Canada was in the sequel sent to the Natchez, where he resided a sufficient time, but made no proselites, though he so far gained the good graces of the woman-chief, that out of respect to him, she called one of her sons by his name. This missionary being obliged to make a voyage to the *Mobile*, was killed on his way thither by some Indians, who probably had no other motive for this cruel action, but to plunder his baggage, as had before happened to another priest, on the side of the Akansas. From this time forth all Louisiana, below the Illinois, has been without any ecclesiastic, excepting the *Tonicas*, who for several years have had a missionary whom they love and esteem, and would even have chosen for their chief, but who has not been able, notwithstanding all this, to persuade one single person to embrace Christianity.

But how can we imagine measures are to be taken to convert the infidels, when the children of the faith themselves are, almost all of them, without pastors? I have already had the honour to inform your Grace, that the canton of the Natchez is the most populous of this colony; yet it is five years since the French there have heard mass, or even seen a priest. I was indeed, sensible, that if the greatest number of the inhabitants had an indifference towards the exercises of religion, which is the common effect of the want of the sacraments; several of them, however, expressed much eagerness to lay hold of the opportunity my voyage afforded them, to put the affairs of their conscience in order, and I did not believe it my duty, to suffer myself to be much entreated on this occasion.

The first proposal made to me was to marry, in the face of the Church, those inhabitants, who by virtue of a civil contract, executed in presence of the commandant and principal clerk of the place, had cohabited together without any scruple, alledging, for excuse, along with those who had authorized this concubinage, the necessity there was of peopling the country, and the impossibility of procuring a priest. I represented to them, that there were priests at the Yasous and New Orleans, and that the affair was well worth the trouble of a voyage thither; it was answered, that the contracting parties were not in a condition to undertake so long a journey, nor of being at the expence of procuring a priest. In short, the evil being done, the question was only how to remedy it, which I did. After this, I confessed all those who offered themselves; but their number was not so great as I expected.

Nothing detaining me longer at the Natchez, I set out from thence on the 26th of December pretty late, in company with M. de Pauger, King's engineer, who was employed in visiting the colony, in order to examine the proper places for building forts. We advanced four leagues, and encamped on the banks of a small river on the left; next day we reimbarked two hours before it was light, with a pretty strong wind against us. The river in this place makes a circuit or winding of fourteen leagues, and according as we turned, the wind being reflected by the land, and the islands which are here in great number turned with us, so that we had it the whole day in our teeth. Notwithstanding we got ten leagues farther, and entered another small river on the same side. The whole night we heard a very great noise, which I imagined was the effect of the winds growing stronger; but I was told that the river had been very calm, and that the noise which kept us awake had been occasioned by the fishes beating the water with their tails.

On the 28th, after advancing two leagues farther, we arrived at the river of the *Tonicas*, which at first appears to be no more than a brook; but at the distance of a musket-shot from its mouth, forms a very pretty lake. If the river continues to carry its stream or course towards the other side, as it has done for some time past, all this place will become inaccessable. The river of the Tonicas rises in the country of the *Tchactas*, and its navigation is very much interrupted with falls or rapid currents. The village stands beyond the lake on a pretty eminence; yet its air is said to be unwholesome, which is attributed to the bad quality of the water of the river; but I am rather of the opinion, it is owing to the stagnation of the waters in the lake. This village is built round a very large square, and is indifferently populous.

The chief's cabbin is finely decorated for an Indian's, on the outside; on which there are figures in relief, not so badly executed as one would expect. It is very obscure within doors, and I could see nothing in it but chests, full, as I was told, of goods and money. The chief received us very politely, he was dressed after the French fashion, and seemed in no-ways incommoded with his cloaths. Our commandants repose greater confidence in this man, than in any other of the Indians of Louisiana: he loves our nation, and has no reason to repent the services he has done us. He carries on a trade with the French, supplying them with horses and poultry, and is very expert at business. He has learned from us the art of laying up money, and is accounted very rich. He has long left off wearing the Indian habit, and takes great pride in appearing always well-dressed.

The rest of the cabbins in this village are partly square, like that of the chief, and partly round, as at the Natchez; the square upon which they all stand is about a hundred paces in diameter, where though it was that day extremely hot, the young people were diverting themselves at a sort of truck, not unlike ours in Europe. There are two other villages belonging to this nation at no great distance from this, which are all that remains of a people heretofore very numerous. I have already observed, that they had a missionary whom they greatly esteemed, but have since learned they once expelled him, on account of his setting their temple on fire, which, however, they have not rebuilt or rekindled its fire, a certain proof of their indifference with respect to religion: soon after they even recalled the missionary, but he in his turn has now left them, on finding they listened to all he was able to say with an indolence which he was unable to get the better of.

From the bottom of the lake or bay of the Tonicas, were we to use canoes of bark, by a carrying place of two leagues, ten might be saved in the navigation of the river. Two leagues lower than the Tonicas, on the right-hand, is Red-river, or *Rio Colorado*, at the entrance of which the famous Ferdinand de Soto, the conqueror of Florida, ended his exploits and life together. This river runs east and west for some time, and then turns to the south. For the space of forty leagues it is navigable for pirogues, beyond which are nothing but impassable morasses. Its mouth seems to be about two hundred toises in breadth; ten leagues above, it receives on the right-hand Black-river, otherwise called the river of the Ouatchitas, which runs from the north, and for seven months in the year, has little or no water in it.

Notwithstanding, some grants have been obtained here, which, in all probability, never will be good for anything; the motive for these settlements is the neighbourhood of the Spaniards, which has ever been a fatal temptation to this colony, and through the hopes of trading with them, the best lands in the world have been left uncultivated. The *Natchitoches* settled on the banks of the Red-river, and we have thought proper to build a fort amongst them, in order to prevent the Spaniards from fixing themselves nearer us. We encamped on the 29th, a little below the mouth of the Red-river, in a very fine creek.

On the 30th, after advancing five leagues, we passed a second *pointe coupée*, or cut point; the river makes a very great turning in this place, and the Canadians, by means of digging the channel of a small brook, have carried the waters of the river into it, where such is the impetuosity of the stream, that the point has been entirely cut through, and thereby travellers save fourteen leagues of their voyage. The old bed is now actually dry, having never any water in it, but in the time of an inundation; an evident proof that the river inclines its channel towards the east, and a circumstance which cannot be too much attended to, by those who settle on either side. This new channel has been, since that time, sounded with a line of thirty fathoms, without finding any bottom.

Immediately below and on the same side, we saw the feeble beginnings of a grant, called *Sainte Reine*, belonging to Messrs. Coetlogon and Kolli. It is situated on a very fertile spot, and has nothing to fear from the over-flowing of the river; but from nothing, nothing can proceed, especially when people are not industrious, and in such a situation this settlement appeared to be. Advancing a league farther this day, we arrived at the grant of Madame de Mezieres, where the rain detained us all the following day. A few huts covered with the leaves of trees, and a large tent made of canvas, are what the whole of this settlement at present consists of. Planters and goods are expected from the Black-river, where the warehouses are, which they seem resolved not to abandon. But I am very much afraid, that by endeavouring to make two settlements at once, both will probably miscarry.

The soil where this last is begun is very good, but it must be built a quarter of a league from the river, behind a cypress wood, where the bottom is marshy, which may be employed in raising rice or garden-stuff. Two leagues farther within the woods is a lake two leagues in circuit, the banks of which are covered with game, and which perhaps would also furnish abundance of fish, were the alligators with which it swarms at present destroyed. At this place I learned some secrets which I shall communicate to your Grace at the price they cost me; for I have not had time to make trial of them.

The male cypress in this country bears a sort of husk, which, as they say, must be gathered green, and yields a balm which is sovereign to the cure of cuts or wounds. The tree from which the copalm distills, has, among other virtues, that of curing the dropsy. The roots of those large cotton trees, which I have already spoken of, and which are found all along the road from lake Ontario, are a certain remedy for all kinds of burns; the interior pellicle must be boiled in water, the wound fomented with this water, and afterwards the ashes of the pellicle itself laid upon it.

On the first day of the new year we said mass about three leagues from the habitation of Madam de Mezieres, in a grant belonging to M. Diron d'Artaguette inspector-general of the troops of Louisiana. We had here a monstrous large tortoise brought us; and we were told that these animals had just broke through a large bar of iron; if the fact is true, and to believe it I should have seen it, the spittle of these animals must be a strong dissolvent: I should not, indeed, chuse to trust my leg in their throat. What is certain is, that the creature I saw was large enough to satisfy ten men of the strongest appetites. We staid the whole day in this grant, which is no farther advanced than the rest, and is called *le Baton rouge*, or the Red-staff Plantation.

The next day, we advanced eleven leagues, and encamped a little below the Bayagoulas, which we left upon our right, after having visited the ruins of an ancient village, which I have already mentioned. This was very well peopled about twenty years ago; but the smallpox destroyed part of the inhabitants, and the rest have dispersed in such a manner, that no accounts have been heard of them for several years, and it is doubted if so much as one single family of them is now remaining. Its situation was very magnificent, and the Messrs. Paris have now a grant here, which they planted with white mulberries, and have already raised very fine silk. They have likewise begun to cultivate tobacco and indigo with success. If the proprietors of the grants were everywhere as industrious, they would soon be reimbursed their expences.

On the third of January, at ten in the morning, we arrived at the little village of the *Oumas*, which stands on the left, and has some French houses in it. A quarter of a league farther within the country stands the great village. This nation is very well affected towards us. Two leagues above this, the Mississippi divides into branches: on the right, to which side it has a constant propensity, it has hollowed out for itself a channel called the *fork of the Chetimachas* or *Sitimachas* which, before it carries its waters to the sea, forms a pretty large lake. The nation of the Chetimachas is almost entirely destroyed, the few that remain being slaves in the colony.

This day we advanced six leagues beyond the Oumas, and passed the night upon a very fine spot, where the Marquis d'Ancenis has a settlement, which the burning of the publick ware-house and several other accidents happening one after another, have reduced to ruin. The *Colapissas* had built a small village here, which subsisted no long time. On the fourth before noon, we arrived at the great village of the Colapissas. This is the finest in all Louisiana, though there are not above two hundred warriors in it, who, however, have the reputation of being very brave. Their cabbins are in the form of a pavilion, like those of the Sioux; and like them they light fires in them very seldom. They have a double covering, that within being a tissue of the leaves of Lataniers trees, and that without consists of matts.

The chief's cabbin is thirty-six feet in diameter: I have not hitherto seen any of a larger size, that of the chief of the Natchez being no more than thirty. As soon as we came in sight of the village, they saluted us with beat of drum, and we had no sooner landed than I was complimented on the part of the chief. I was surprized, on advancing towards the village, to see the drummer dressed in a long fantastical parti-coloured robe. I enquired into the origin of this custom, and was informed that it was not very ancient; that a governor of Louisiana had made a present of this drum to these Indians, who have always been our faithful allies; and that this sort of beadle's coat, was of their own invention. The women here are handsomer than those of Canada, and are, besides, extremely neat in their dress.

After dinner we made a progress of five leagues farther, and stopt at a place called *Cannes brulées*, or *Burnt- canes*, belonging to M. le Comte d'Artagnan, who has a settlement here, which is to serve him as an *entrepôt*, or staple, provided it do not share the same fate with most of the rest. This plantation stands on the left, and the first object that attracted my notice, was a large cross erected on the banks of the river, round which I found them singing vespers. This is the first place of the colony, after leaving the country of the Illinois, where I saw this ceremony of our religion. Two Musquetaires, Messrs. d'Artiguere and de Benac, are the managers of this grant, and it is M. de Benac who has the direction of the plantation of *Cannes brulées*, together with M. Chevalier, nephew to the mathematical master to the King's pages. They have no priest which is not their fault, there having been one sent them, whom they were obliged to send away for his drunkenness, wisely concluding, that more harm than good was to be expected from a bad priest, in a new settlement, where there was no superior to watch over his conduct. Between the Colapissas and the *Cannes brulées*, you leave on your right, a place where an Indian nation called the *Taensas* were formerly settled, and who, in the time of M. de la Salle, made a great figure in this colony, but have for some years past entirely disappeared. This has one of the most beautiful situations as well as one of the best soils in all Louisiana. M. de Meuse to whom it has been granted has as yet done nothing in it, notwithstanding he maintains a director who has neither goods nor work-men.

We stopped to dine, on the fifth, at a place called the *Chapitoulas*, which is distant only three leagues from New Orleans, at which place we arrived about five o'clock in the evening. The Chapitoulas and some of the neighbouring plantations are in a very good condition, the soil is very fertile and has fallen into the hands of expert and laborious people. They are M. de Breuil and three Canadian brothers, of the name of Chauvin, who having brought nothing with them to this country but their industry, have attained to a perfection in that through the necessity of working for their subsistence. They have lost no time, and have spared themselves in nothing, and their conduct affords an useful lesson to those lazy fellows, whose misery unjustly discredits a country, which is capable of producing an hundred fold, of whatever is sown in it.

I am, &c.

Letter to Her Father

SISTER HACHARD DE SAINT-STANISLAS

(DATE UNKNOWN–1760)

Sister Hachard de Saint-Stanislas was born Marie Madeleine Hachard in Normandy, the youngest daughter of a distinguished French Catholic family. At age eighteen, she asked to be sent with the Ursuline group of nuns to New Orleans. Hachard became Sister Hachard de Saint-Stanislas in January of 1727, when she received the religious habit at Hennebont, and her service with the Ursulines officially began. The Ursulines were dedicated to Christian education, but their primary assignment was caring for the military sick. Sister Hachard de Saint Stanislaus dedicated thirty-three years to the service of the Catholic Church in New Orleans. Her letters to her father are important records of the French Colonial Period in Louisiana. In the letter presented here, dated 1728, she describes the lay-out of the city of New Orleans and writes about the construction of the Ursuline Convent, which still stands today and is the oldest building in the Mississippi Valley.

New Orleans

Apr. 24, 1728

My dear Father:

I think I have told you that New Orleans, the capital of all Louisiana is on the banks of the Mississippi, on the east side. At this part it is larger than the Seine is at Rouen. On our side of the river there is a well-built levee to prevent the overflow of the river into the city, and along this levee, on the side of the city, is a large ditch to carry off the waters which do run over, with a wooden fence to close it in. On the other side of the river are wild woods in which are several small huts where slaves of the India Company live.

Our town is very beautiful, well laid out and evenly built, as well as I can tell. The streets are wide and straight. The main street is a league long. The houses are well-built of timber and mortar. The tops of the houses are covered with shingles, which are little planks, sharpened in the form of slates—one must see them to believe it—for this roofing has all the appearance and beauty of slate. There is a popular song sung here which says that this city is as beautiful as Paris. However, I find a difference between this city and Paris. Perhaps the song could convince people who have not seen the capital of France, but I have seen it, and the song does not persuade me to the contrary. It is true that New Orleans grows day by day, and could become in time as beautiful and large as the principal cities of France, if enough workmen and colonists come over.

The women are careless of their salvation, but not of their vanity. Everyone here has luxuries, all of an equal magnificence. The greater part of them live on hominy but are dressed in velvet or damask, trimmed with ribbons. The women use powder and rouge to hide the wrinkles of their faces, and wear beauty-spots. The devil has a vast empire here, but that only strengthens our hope of destroying it, God willing. The stronger the enemy, the more encouraged we are to fight. The children please us—one can turn them as one wills. The Negroes are also easy to teach, once they know French, but the women, under a modest air, hide the strongest of passions.

Since our arrival, we have lived in the most beautiful house in the town. It has two floors and an attic. We have all the rooms we need, six doors on the first floor, and large windows everywhere. Only we have no window panes in them. The frames are hung with fine, thin cloth which gives as much light as glass. We have a farm-yard and a garden, which adjoins a great woods of huge trees. From these woods come clouds of mosquitoes, gnats, and another kind of fly that I never met before and whose name— or surname—I do not know. At this moment several are sailing around me and wish to assassinate me. These wicked animals bite without mercy. We are assailed by them all night, but happily, they go back in the woods in the day.

Our convent is being built at the extreme other end of the town. It will be all of brick and will have all the rooms we could wish for, well built and airy with large windows, with panes. But it doesn't progress at all. M. Périer, our Governor, gave us reason to hope it would be ready the end of this year; but workmen are so scarce that we shall be lucky to take possession by Easter, 1729. We will then need more help.

M. Périer and Madame, his wife, who are amiable and very pious, come often to see us. The King's lieutenant is also a fine man and officer. He gave us two cows with their calves, a sow and her young, some chickens and ducks. All this started our farm-yard. We also have some turkeys and geese. The parents, since we do not accept money for teaching our day pupils, are so grateful that they give us all they can.

In Lent we fast three days a week, and outside of Lent fast only on Friday. We drink beer, and our most ordinary food is rice with milk, little wild beans, meat and fish. In summer we eat little meat. It is killed but twice a week and it is difficult to keep it in the heat. In winter there is hunting, beginning in October, and ten miles from the town many wild cattle are slaughtered and sold for three sols a pound—as is deer. Both are better than the beef and mutton we get in Rouen. Wild ducks are cheap and very common, but we buy scarcely any—we do not want to pamper ourselves. It is a charming country all winter and in summer there are the fish and oysters, fruits and sweet potatoes, which one cooks in the ashes, like chestnuts. Everything, dear Papa, is just as I report it, and I tell you of nothing which I have not experienced. From the plantation they send us such an abundance of fruit, especially peaches and figs, that we make preserves. Father Beaubois has a beautiful garden, full of orange trees, some of which bear sweet and beautiful oranges. He gave us 300 bitter ones for marmalade.

Our little community grows. We have twenty boarders now, eight of whom made their First Communion today. We also have three orphans, and seven slave boarders to instruct for Baptism and First Communion, along with a great number of day pupils and the Negro and Indian women who come two hours a day for instruction.

It was the custom, before our arrival, for girls to marry at the age of twelve or fourteen—many of whom did not even know how many Gods existed—judge the rest for yourself. But since we are here no one is allowed to marry who has not first come to us for instruction.

We are accustomed to black faces. We had two Negro boarders, one six and one seventeen, sent to us for religious instruction, and they stayed on to work for us. You can imagine, dear Father, the pleasure it gives us to instruct these young boarding-pupils of twelve to fifteen who have never been to Confession, nor even to Mass, raised on their plantations, five or six leagues from town, without any spiritual guidance, and who have never even heard God spoken of. We find them docile and anxious to be taught, and they all wish to become nuns. But this is not Father Beaubois' idea. He wishes them to become Christian mothers and establish their religion in the country by their good example.

I am very happy to be in this country and my joy redoubles as the time approaches for me to take my final vows in a foreign land where Christianity is almost unknown. There are many honest, good people here, but not the slightest sign of devotion, nor even of Christianity, and we shall be happy indeed if we can establish it with the aid of our Reverend Father Superior and several Capuchin monks, who are trying to do likewise.

I pray to the Lord for your perfect health and am from the bottom of my heart, dear Father, your very humble and very obedient daughter and servant,

Hachard de Saint-Stanislas

Letter to Robert Livingston

THOMAS JEFFERSON (1743–1826)

Thomas Jefferson was born in Shadwell, in the Virginia Piedmont, and in 1760 he entered the College of William and Mary. Jefferson studied law from 1762–1767, and in 1768 began building Monticello, which would be his lifelong passion. He published *A Summary Review of the Rights of British America* in 1774, and as a member of the Continental Congresses of 1775–76 was largely responsible for the drafting of the Declaration of Independence. He served as governor of Virginia (1779–1781), ambassador to Paris (1784–1789), secretary of state under Washington (1789–1793), vice-president under John Adams (1797–1801), and as the nation's third president (1801–1809). In retrospect the Louisiana Purchase (1803) is viewed as the major event of Jefferson's presidency and the defining moment of the young U.S. republic. Robert Livingston, then U.S. Ambassador to France, signed the treaty which transferred the vast territory known as Louisiana from France to the U.S. for the sum of fifteen million dollars. In the following letter to Livingston, written on April 18, 1802, Jefferson expresses his anxiety over the threat of losing access to the port of New Orleans.

"The cession of Louisiana and the Floridas to France works most sorely on the United States. It completely reverses all the political relations of the United States and will form a new epoch in our political course. Of all nations of any consideration, France is the one which hitherto has offered the fewest points on which we could have any conflict of right. From these causes we have ever looked to her as our natural friend. Her growth, therefore, we viewed as our own; her misfortunes, ours. There is on the globe one single spot, the possessor of which is our natural and habitual enemy. It is New Orleans, through which the produce of three-eighths of our territory must pass to market, and from its fertility it will ere long yield more than half of our whole produce and contain more than half of our inhabitants. France, placing herself in that door, assumes to us the attitude of defiance. Spain might have retained it quietly for years. Her pacific dispositions, her feeble state, would induce her to increase our facilities there. . . . The day that France takes possession of New Orleans fixes the sentence which is to restrain her forever within her low water mark. It seals the union of two nations who in conjunction can maintain exclusive possession of the ocean. From that moment we must marry ourselves to the British fleet and nation."

Thomas Jefferson

from *Sketches of America*

HENRY BRADSHAW FEARON

(1770–DATE UNKNOWN)

Henry Bradshaw Fearon was a British surgeon who was sent to the United States by thirty-nine English families in 1817 "to ascertain whether any, and what part of the United States would be suitable for their residence." Fearon wrote that, "Emmigration had, at the time of my appointment, assumed a totally new character: it was no longer merely the poor, the idle, the profligate, or the wildly speculative, who were proposing to quit their native country; but men also of capital, of industry, . . . of upright and conscientious minds, to whose happiness civil and religious liberty were essential. . . ." He brought back eight "Reports" which were published in *Sketches of America: A Narrative of a Journey of Five Thousand Miles through the Eastern and Western States of America* (1818). The following excerpt is Fearon's "Report" on his visit to New Orleans.

Approaching to New Orleans, a more civilized country than I had previously seen presented itself, though there were (according to the old story) no men hanging in chains. The banks were cultivated, settlements multiplied, good houses were not uncommon: while numerous extensive sugar plantations bespoke wealth and population. Upon my arrival at *New Orleans*, it is hardly possible to conceive the delight which I experienced; after a tedious and dreary journey, even the masts of ships afforded me pleasure, as recalling by association what I should now denominate the *comforts* of New York or Philadelphia. The increase of this city since it has become a part of the United States is truly extraordinary, affording another proof of the advantages possessed by a people who are unshackled. . . .

The French language is still predominant in New Orleans. The population is said to be 30,000; two-thirds of which do not speak English. I find that the general manners and habits are very relaxed. The first day of my residence here was Sunday, and I was not a little surprised to find in the United States the markets, shops, theatre, circus, and public ball-rooms open. Gambling houses *throng* the city: all coffee-houses, together with the exchange, are occupied from morning until night by gamesters. It is said that when the Kentuckians arrive at this place they are in their glory, finding neither limit to, nor punishment of their excesses. The general style of living is luxurious. Houses are elegantly furnished. The ball-room, at Davis's hotel, I have never seen exceeded in splendour. Private dwellings partake of the same character; and the ladies dress with expensive elegance. The sources of public amusement are numerous and varied; among them I remark the following:

Interesting Exhibition

On Sunday the 9th inst. will be represented in the place where Fire-works are generally exhibited, near the Circus, an extraordinary fight of *Furious Animals*. The place where the animals will fight is a rotunda of 160 feet in circumference, with a railing 17 feet in height, and a circular gallery well conditioned and strong, inspected by the Mayor and surveyors by him appointed.

1st *Fight*—A strong Attakapas Bull, attacked and subdued by six of the strongest dogs of the country.
2d Fight—Six Bull-dogs against a Canadian Bear.
3d *Fight*—A beautiful Tiger against a black Bear.
4th *Fight*—Twelve dogs against a strong and furious Opeloussas Bull.

If the Tiger is not vanquished in his fight with the Bear, he will be sent alone against the last Bull, and if the latter conquers all his enemies, several pieces of fire-works will be placed on his back, which will produce a very entertaining amusement.

In the Circus will be placed two Manakins, which, notwithstanding the efforts of the Bulls, to throw them down, will always rise again, whereby the animals will get furious.

The doors will be opened at three and the Exhibition begins at four o'clock precisely.

Admittance, one dollar for grown persons, and 50 cents for children.

A military band will perform during the Exhibition.

If Mr. Renault is so happy as to amuse the spectators by that new spectacle, he will use every exertion to diversify and augment it, in order to prove to a generous public, whose patronage has been hitherto so kindly bestowed upon him how anxious he is to please them.

A few nights ago I visited the theatre: it is an old building, about two-thirds the size of the little theatre in the Haymarket. The play was *John of Calais* well performed by a French company to a French audience. At a tavern opposite, I witnessed a personal conflict, in which I suppose one of the parties was *dirkd*. These things are of every-day occurrence; and it is not often that they are taken cognizance of by the police. . . .

Provisions are of very bad quality, and most enormously dear. Hams and cheese from England, potatoes, butter, and beef from Ireland, are common articles of import. Cabbages are now tenpence per head; turkeys, three to five dollars each. Rents are also very extravagant. Yet to all men whose desire only is to live a short life but a merry one, I have no hesitation in recommending New Orleans.

from *Journal of John James Audubon*

JOHN JAMES AUDUBON (1785–1851)

John James Audubon was born Jean Rabin, the son of Jean Audubon and a Creole woman, Jeanne Rabin, on Saint-Dominique, now the island of Haiti. After his mother was killed in a slave revolt, he moved to France where he was raised by his father's wife. He devoted much of his time to the study of painting until, at the age of eighteen, Audubon fled to the U.S. to avoid conscription into Napoleon's armies. After failing at various business ventures, Audubon turned to drawing instruction and portrait painting and began depicting the birds of Kentucky and other neighboring wild areas. He traveled widely in the U.S. and Canada searching for material for his study of birds which he drew in detail and tinted with watercolor. His ardent efforts evolved into Audubon's *The Birds of America* (1827–1838), a collection of color prints of over five hundred species of birds. In 1821 he came to New Orleans, where he lived in a cottage at 505 Dauphine Street in the French Quarter and worked on *The Birds of America* in his studio on Barracks Street. Audubon returned to the city in 1837 to paint and today both Audubon Park and Audubon Zoo bear his name as a lasting memorial from the city of New Orleans. In 1929 the *Journal of John James Audubon* was published in two volumes. The first journal was kept by Audubon during his trip to New Orleans "on that famous journey down the Ohio and Mississippi rivers in 1820–1821." The following selections are from his journal entries dated October and November 1821, in which Audubon describes his daily life in New Orleans, including watching "Green Back Swallows Gamboling over the City."

OCTR 20TH 1821

This Morning about 6 o'clock We left Mr *Perrie's* Plantation for New Orleans, Which Place we Reachd on Monday the 21st at 2 o'clock . . .

the Weather Cool and Rainy, I left the Boat and Walked to My good acquaintance R. Pamar—I had perceived that My Long flowing buckled hair was Looked on with astonishment by the Passengers on board and saw that the effect Was stronger in town—My Large Loose Dress of Whitened Yellow Nankeen and the unfortunate *Cut* of My features Made me decide to be dressed as soon as Possible Like other folks and I had My Chevelure parted from My head the Reception of Mr Pamar's familly was very gratefull to My Spirits. I Was Looked upon as of a Son returned from a Long Painfull Voyage, the Children, the Parents the servants all hung about Me; What Pleasures for the Whole of us—

I dined there, afterwards Visiting the famous hunter Lewis Adam—and the Dimitry familly who also Received Me very Kindly . . . Rented une Chamber garnie in Rue St Anne No 29 for 16$ per Month and removed our baggage thereto from the boat—

We Spent Tuesday Wednesday & Thursday, Looking over the City for a Suitable House for My Litle Familly—this appeared a very dificult task and I nearly Concluded to take one we visited in Dauphine Street—

My Clothes being extremely Shabby and forced against My Will to provide some New ones, I bought some clothes and Now Wait very impatiently on the Gentleman Taylor for them that I May go and Procure some Pupils with a better grace—

having renewed our early Morning Visits to the Market to Look at all there—We found it allmost as well suplied of Vegetables, fruits, fish, Meats, flowers, & C as in the Spring—delightfull radishes Letuce & C plenty—

OCTR 25TH 1821

Raining hard the Whole of the day spent the greater part of it at R. Pamar and his Relation *Lewis Adam the hunter*; Rented a House in Dauphine Street for 17$ Per Month—

OCTR 26TH 1821

. . . Walked a good Deal, Visited the familly Dimitry, Spend Much of the Day at Pamar's—in the evening Went some distance down the Levee, the Sky beautifull & serene—Miss Pamar Much Improved in Music and Manners—Many Men formerly *My Friend* passed *Me* without uttering a Word to me and *I* as *Willing* to Shun those Rascalls—

fatigued of being *Idle* so powerfull are habits of all Kinds that to spend a Month thus would render me sick of Life—

Hetchberger Visited us Much Pleased at My addition of Drawings since I Left Cincinnati Octr 12th 1820 I have finished 62 Drawings of *Birds & Plants*, 3 quadrupeds, 2 Snakes, 50 Portraits of all sorts and My Father *Don Antonio* have Made out to Live in humble Comfort with Only My Talents and Industry, Without *One Cent* to begin on at My Departure—

I have Now 42 Dollars, health, and as much anxiety to pursue My Plans of Accomplishing My Collection as Ever I had and Hope God Will Grant Me the same Powers to Proceed

My Present Prospects to Procure Birds this Winter are More Ample than ever being now Well Known by the Principal hunters on Lake Borgne, Barataria—Pontchartrain, and the Country of Terre a Boeuf—

OCTR 27TH SUNDAY

Dressed all new, Hair Cut, my appearance altered beyond My expectations, fully as much as a handsome Bird is when robbed of all its feathering, the Poor thing Looks, Bashfull dejected and is either entirely Neglected or Lookd upon With Contempt; such was my situation Last Week—but When the Bird is Well fed, taken care of; sufered to Enjoy Life and dress himself; he is cherished again, Nai admired—Such my situation this day—Good God that 40 Dollars should thus be *enough* to Make a *Gentleman*—ah My Beloved Country When will thy Sons value more Intrinsectly each Brother's Worth? Never!!

Exibited My Drawings at My good acquaintance Pamar's—received much valuable Intelligence coroborating With My own observations on these things that trully pleases My feelings—Dined there—*Payd* a Visit to Mrs Clay and the young Ladies there, with My Portfolio—unknown, Passed for a *German* until the latter part of My Stay—the Company Much Pleased With My Work—but no pupil as I expected to have—

took a Long Walk to the Canal, talked Much With My Hunter *Gilbert* Who Leaves for Barataria Tomorrow—Weather Beautifull and very warm, good Deal of Game in Market this Morning—

Green Back Swallows Gamboling over the City and the River the Whole day have great Hopes of ascertaining their Winter quarters Not far from this . . .

Octr 30th 1821 NEW ORLEANS

Returned to Wam Braud and Procured his Son for a Pupil at 2$ per Leson of one hour, and have some Hopes of having Mrs B. a pupil of *French* and Painting—

Visited another College. Politly Received by the Ladies Who examined My Port Folio with apparent satisfaction. No Pupils however, a Certain Mr *Torain* having antecedented Me every Where—Dined at Pamar and Drew My American Hare—to Exibit to the Public—

. . . the Market Well suplied With game & Vegetables have resumed our Habit of taking a Walk there as soon as the Day

Dawns—

The day Warm, Swallows Plenty and quite as gay in their flight as in June—

To find here those Birds in aboundance 3 Months after they have left the Midle States, and to Know that they Winter Within 40 Miles in Multitudes is one of the Gratifications the Most Exquisite I ever Wishd to feel in Ornithological Subjects and that Puts compleat *Dash* over *all* the Nonsense Wrote about their Torpidity during Cold Weather; No Man could ever have enjoyed the Study of Nature in her all Femine Bosomy Wild and errd so Wide—

OCTR 31ST 1821 NEW ORLEANS

Begun giving Lessons of Drawing to Mrs Braud and Young Master Wam Braud this Day at 3 Dollars per Lesson—

Spent some time at Work on Father Antoine and My Drawing of My American Hare—

Received a Visit of Mr Pamar, Mr Dimitry and Dumatras

Weather Warm in the Morning, Much fish Condemned in the Market—also some Game—Excellent regulations—the Wind Shifted to the Northwest and I premidited Cold Weather by the Swallows flying South about noon at Night quite Cool—What Knowledge these Litle Creatures possess and how true they are in their Movements—

NEW ORLEANS NOVEMBER, FRIDAY 9TH 1821

Weather quite Cool a diference in the atmosphere of 22 Degrees from that of yesterday and the Swallows that Were Numerous Last Evening are all gone for the Present—

—SATURDAY 10TH—

Weather Very beautifull but Cold Drew a female of the *Gadwall Duck a* remarkably fine Specimen—sent Me by My Hunter Gilbert—

Mr Basterop at My Lodgings—Wished that I should Join him in a Painting of a Panorama of this City—but My Birds My Beloved Birds of America feel all my time and nearly My thoughts I do not Wish to See any other *Perspective* than the Last Specimen of them Drawed—

"New Orleans in 1848"

WALT WHITMAN (1819–1892)

Walt Whitman was born on Long Island and raised and educated in Brooklyn. Whitman worked for ten newspapers and magazines in New York, serving as the editor of both the *Long Islander* (1838–1839) and the *Brooklyn Eagle* (1846–1847). After being fired from that position, Whitman was hired by one of the owners of the New Orleans *Daily Crescent* to be the editor of the new paper which was started in an attempt to take possession of the city's journalistic field from the *Picayune*. At that time New Orleans was one of the most important news centers in the U.S. because it was a point of embarkation for soldiers serving in Mexico during the Mexican War. In February 1848 Walt Whitman and his brother Jeff began a leisurely journey from New York to New Orleans, taking a steamer down the Ohio and the Mississippi Rivers. The inspiration for his best known work *Leaves of Grass* (1855) came from this exposure to the American landscape. Whitman edited the *Daily Crescent*, then located at 93 St. Charles Street, from March to May 1848. He also contributed a series of "sketches" to the paper in which he recorded his observations on the rich panorama of life in the city. Although Whitman reports that he was "quite happily fix'd," in New Orleans, his brother Jeff was not happy and for that reason he "made no very long stay in the South." Whitman lived the last nineteen years of his life in Camden, New Jersey, where he wrote the following piece about his New Orleans days for the fiftieth anniversary edition of the *Picayune*, published January 25, 1887.

Among the letters brought this morning (Camden, New Jersey, Jan. 15, 1887,) by my faithful post-office carrier, J. G., is one as follows:

> "New Orleans, Jan. 11, '87.—We have been informed that when you were younger and less famous than now, you were in New Orleans and perhaps have helped on the *Picayune*. If you have any remembrance of the *Picayune*'s young days, or of journalism in New Orleans of that era, and would put it in writing (verse or prose) for the *Picayune*'s fiftieth year edition, Jan. 25, we shall be pleased," etc.

In response to which: I went down to New Orleans early in 1848 to work on a daily newspaper, but it was not the *Picayune* though I saw quite a good deal of the editors of that paper, and knew its personnel and ways. But let me indulge my pen in some gossipy recollections of that time and place, with extracts from my journal up the Mississippi and across the great lakes to the Hudson.

Probably the influence most deeply pervading everything at that time through the United States, both in physical facts and in sentiment, was the Mexican War, then just ended. Following a brilliant campaign (in which our troops had march'd to the capital city, Mexico, and taken full possession,) we were returning after our victory. From the situation of the country, the city of New Orleans had been our channel and *entrepôt* for everything, going and returning. It had the best news and war correspondents; it had the most to say, through its leading papers, the *Picayune* and *Delta* especially, and its voice was readiest listen'd to; from it "Chapparal" had gone out and his army and battle letters were copied everywhere, not only in the United States, but in Europe. Then the social cast and results; no one who has never seen the society of a city under similar circumstances can understand what a strange vivacity and *rattle* were given throughout by such a situation. I remember the crowds of soldiers, the gay young officers, going or coming, the receipt of important news, the many discussions, the returning wounded, and so on.

I remember very well seeing Gen. Taylor with his staff and other officers at the St. Charles Theatre one evening (after talking with them during the day.) There was a short play on the stage, but the principal performance was of Dr. Colyer's troupe of "Model Artists," then in the full tide of their popularity. They gave many fine group and solo shows. The house was crowded with uniforms and shoulder-straps. Gen. T. himself, if I remember right, was almost the only officer in civilian clothes; he was a jovial, old, rather stout, plain man, with a wrinkled and dark-yellow face, and, in ways and manners, show'd the least of conventional ceremony or etiquette I ever saw; he laugh'd unrestrainedly at everything comical. (He had a great personal resemblance to Fenimore Cooper, the novelist, of New York.) I remember Gen. Pillow and quite a duster of other militaires also present.

One of my choice amusements during my stay in New Orleans was going down to the old French Market, especially of a Sunday morning. The show was a varied and curious one; among the rest, the Indian and negro hucksters with their wares. For there were always fine specimens of Indians, both men and women, young and old. I remember I nearly always on these occasions got a large cup of delicious coffee with a biscuit, for my breakfast, from the immense shining copper kettle of a great Creole mulatto woman (I believe she weigh'd 230 pounds.) I never have had such coffee since. About nice drinks, anyhow, my recollection of the "cobblers" (with strawberries and snow on top of the large tumblers,) and also the exquisite wines, and the perfect and mild French brandy, help the regretful reminiscence of my New Orleans experiences of those days. And what splendid and roomy and leisurely bar-rooms! particularly the grand ones of the St. Charles and St. Louis. Bargains, auctions, appointments, business conferences, &c., were generally held in the spaces or recesses of these bar-rooms.

I used to wander a midday hour or two now and then for amusement on the crowded and bustling levees, on the banks of the river. The diagonally wedg'd-in boats, the stevedores, the piles of cotton and other merchandise, the carts, mules, negroes, etc., afforded never-ending studies and sights to me. I made acquaintances among the captains, boatmen, or other characters, and often had long talks with them—sometimes finding a real rough diamond among my chance encounters. Sundays I sometimes went forenoons to the old Catholic Cathedral in the French quarter. I used to walk a good deal in this arrondissement; and I have deeply regretted since that I did not cultivate, while I had such a good opportunity, the chance of better knowledge of French and Spanish Creole New Orleans people. (I have an idea that there is much and of importance about the Latin race contributions to American nationality in the South and Southwest that will never be put with sympathetic understanding and tact on record.)

Let me say, for better detail, that through several months (1848) I work'd on a new daily paper, the *Crescent*; my situation rather a pleasant one. My young brother, Jeff, was with me; and he not only grew very homesick, but the climate of the place, and especially the water, seriously disagreed with him. From this and other reasons (although I was quite happily fix'd) I made no very long stay in the South.

from *Life on the Mississippi*

MARK TWAIN

(SAMUEL LANGHORNE CLEMENS)

(1835–1910)

Mark Twain was born Samuel Langhorne Clemens in Florida, Missouri, and at the age of four he moved to Hannibal, Missouri, on the Mississippi River. Growing up, Twain absorbed life in the river town, which proved to be the richest source of his literary material. When he was fourteen Twain was apprenticed to two Hannibal printers, and he worked as a journeyman printer from 1853 to 1857 in various cities, including New York. He returned to the Mississippi River where he served as a pilot's apprentice and later worked as a steamboat pilot, frequently visiting New Orleans until the Civil War brought an end to river travel in 1861. After serving briefly in the Confederate army, he moved to the Nevada territory. After his attempts at silver mining failed in this territory, he became a reporter and in 1863 first used the pseudonym "Mark Twain," a river boat pilot's phrase meaning two fathoms deep. Twain moved to San Francisco and continued to write, publishing his first book, *The Celebrated Jumping Frog of Calaveras County* in 1867. The book brought him national celebrity, and he launched a career as a lecturer and published numerous books that brought him great financial reward. The Mississippi River served as the setting for many of his fictional works, including *The Adventures of Tom Sawyer* (1876), and *The Adventures of Huckleberry Finn* (1885), as well as the nonfiction account, *Life on the Mississippi* (1883). The book includes the following selection, "City Sights," in which George Washington Cable, "the South's finest literary genius" according to Twain, serves as his guide through the French Quarter.

The old French part of New Orleans—anciently the Spanish part—bears no resemblance to the American end of the city: the

American end which lies beyond the intervening brick business-centre. The houses are massed in blocks; are austerely plain and dignified; uniform of pattern, with here and there a departure from it with pleasant effect; all are plastered on the outside, and nearly all have long, iron-railed verandas running along the several stories. Their chief beauty is the deep, warm, varicolored stain with which time and the weather have enriched the plaster. It harmonizes with all the surroundings, and has as natural a look of belonging there as has the flush upon sunset clouds. This charming decoration cannot be successfully imitated; neither is it to be found elsewhere in America.

The iron railings are a specialty, also. The pattern is often exceedingly light and dainty, and airy and graceful—with a large cipher or monogram in the centre, a delicate cobweb of baffling, intricate forms, wrought in steel. The ancient railings are hand-made, and are now comparatively rare and proportionately valuable. They are become bric-a-brac.

The party had the privilege of idling through this ancient quarter of New Orleans with the South's finest literary genius, the author of *The Grandissimes*. In him the South has found a masterly delineator of its interior life and its history. In truth, I find by experience, that the untrained eye and vacant mind can inspect it and learn of it and judge of it more clearly and profitably in his books than by personal contact with it.

With Mr. Cable along to see for you, and describe and explain and illuminate, a jog through that old quarter is a vivid pleasure. And you have a vivid *sense* as of unseen or dimly seen things—vivid, and yet fitful and darkling; you glimpse salient features, but lose the fine shades or catch them imperfectly through the vision of the imagination: a case, as it were, of ignorant near-sighted stranger traversing the rim of wide vague horizons of Alps with an inspired and enlightened long-sighted native.

We visited the old St Louis Hotel, now occupied by municipal offices. There is nothing strikingly remark-able about it; but one can say of it as of the Academy of Music in New York, that if a broom or a shovel has ever been used in it there is no circumstantial evidence to back up the fact. It is curious that cabbages and hay and things do not grow in the Academy of Music; but no doubt it is on account of the interruption of the light by the benches, and the impossibility of hoeing the crop except in the aisles. The fact that the ushers grow their buttonhole-bouquets on the premises shows what might be done if they had the right kind of an agricuitural head to the establishment.

We visited also the venerable Cathedral, and the pretty square in front of it; the one dim with religious light, the other brilliant with the worldly sort, and lovely with orange trees and blossomy shrubs; then we drove in the hot sun through the wilderness of houses and out on to the wide dead level beyond, where the villas are, and the water wheels to drain the town, and the commons populous with cows and children; passing by an old cemetery where we were told lie the ashes of an early pirate; but we took him on trust, and did not visit him. He was a pirate with a tremendous and sanguinary history; and as long as he preserved unspotted, in retirement, the dignity of his name and the grandeur of his ancient calling, homage and reverence were his from high and low; but when at last he descended into politics and became a paltry alderman, the public "shook" him, and turned aside and wept. When he died, they set up a monument over him; and little by little he has come into respect again; but it is respect for the pirate, not the alderman. To-day the loyal and generous remember only what he was, and charitably forget what he became.

Thence, we drove a few miles across a swamp, along a raised shell road, with a canal on one hand and a dense wood on the other; and here and there, in the distance, a ragged and angular-limbed and moss-bearded cypress, top standing out, clear cut against the sky, and as quaint of form as the apple-trees in Japanese pictures—such was our course and the surroundings of it. There was an occasional alligator swimming comfortably along in the canal, and an occasional picturesque colored person on the bank, flinging his statue-rigid reflection upon the still water and watching for a bite.

And by and by we reached the West End, a collection of hotels of the usual light summer-resort pattern, with broad verandas all around, and the waves of the wide and blue Lake Pontchartrain lapping the thresholds. We had dinner on a ground-veranda over the water—the chief dish the renowned fish called the pompano, delicious as the less criminal forms of sin.

Thousands of people come by rail and carriage to West End and to Spanish Fort every evening, and dine, listen to the bands, take strolls in the open air under the electric lights, go sailing on the lake, and entertain themselves in various and sundry other ways.

We had opportunities on other days and in other places to test the pompano. Notably, at an editorial dinner at one of the clubs in the city. He was in his last possible perfection there, and justified his fame. In his suite was a tall pyramid of scarlet cray-fish—large ones; as large as one's thumb; delicate, palatable, appetizing. Also devilled whitebait; also shrimps of choice quality; and a platter of small soft-shell crabs of a most superior breed. The other dishes were what one might get at Delmonico's, or Buckingham Palace; those I have spoken of can be had in similar perfection in New Orleans only, I suppose.

In the West and South they have a new institution,—the Broom Brigade. It is composed of young ladies who dress in a uniform costume, and go through the infantry drill, with broom in place of musket. It is a very pretty sight, on private view. When they perform on the stage of a theatre, in the blaze of colored fires, it must be a fine and fascinating spectacle. I saw them go through their complex manual with grace, spirit, and admirable precision. I saw them do everything which a human being can possibly do with a broom, except sweep. I did not see them sweep. But I know they could learn. What they have already learned proves that. And if they ever should learn, and should go on the war-path down Tchoupitoulas or some of those other streets around there, those thoroughfares would bear a greatly improved aspect in a very few minutes. But the girls themselves wouldn't; so nothing would be really gained, after all.

The drill was in the Washington Artillery building. In this building we saw many interesting relics of the war. Also a fine oil-painting representing Stonewall Jackson's last interview with General Lee. Both men are on horseback. Jackson has just ridden up, and is accosting Lee. The picture is very valuable, on account of the portraits, which are authentic. But, like many another historical picture, it means nothing without its label. And one label will fit it as well as another:—

First Interview between Lee and Jackson.
Last Interview between Lee and Jackson.
Jackson Introducing Himself to Lee.
Jackson Accepting Lee's Invitation to Dinner.
Jackson Declining Lee's Invitation to Dinner—with Thanks.
Jackson Apologizing for a Heavy Defeat.
Jackson Reporting a Great Victory.
Jackson Asking Lee for a Match.

It tells *one* story, and a sufficient one; for it says quite plainly and satisfactorily, "Here are Lee and Jackson together." The artist would have made it tell that this is Lee and Jackson's last interview if he could have done it. But he couldn't, for there wasn't any way to do it. A good legible label is usually worth, for information, a ton of significant attitude and expression in a historical picture. In Rome, people with fine sympathetic natures stand up and weep in front of the celebrated "Beatrice Cenci the Day before her Execution." It shows what a label can do. If they did not know the picture, they would inspect it unmoved, and say, "Young girl with hay fever; young girl with her head in a bag."

I found the half-forgotten Southern intonations and elisions as pleasing to my ear as they had formerly been. A Southerner talks music. At least it is music to me, but then I was born in the South. The educated Southerner has no use for an *r*, except at the beginning of a word. He says "honah," and "dinnah," and "Gove'nuh," and "befo' the waw," and so on. The words may lack charm to the eye, in print, but they have it to the ear. When did the *r* disappear from Southern speech, and how did it come to disappear? The custom of dropping it was not borrowed from the North, nor inherited *from* England. Many Southerners—most Southerners—put a *y* into occasional words that begin with the *k* sound. For instance, they say Mr. K'yahtah (Carter) and speak of playing k'yahds or of riding in the k'yahs. And they have the pleasant custom—long ago fallen into decay in the North—of frequently employing the respectful "Sir." Instead of the curt Yes, and the abrupt No, they say "Yes, Suh"; "No, Suh."

But there are some infelicities. Such as "like" for "as", and the addition of an "at" where it isn't needed. I heard an educated gentleman say, "Like the flag-officer did." His cook or his butler would have said, "Like the flag-officer done." You hear gentlemen say, "Where have you been at?" And here is the aggravated form—heard a ragged street Arab say it to a comrade: "I was ask'n' Tom whah you was a-sett'n' at." The very elect carelessly say "will" when they mean "shall"; and many of them say, "I didn't go to do it," meaning "I didn't mean to do it." The Northern word "guess"—imported from England, where it used to be common, and now regarded by satirical Englishmen as a Yankee original—is but little used among Southerners. They say "reckon." They haven't any "doesn't" in their language; they say "don't" instead. The unpolished often use "went" for "gone." It is nearly as bad as the Northern "had n't ought." This reminds me that a remark of a very peculiar nature was made here in my neighborhood (in the North) a few days ago: "He had n't ought to have went." How is that? Isn't that a good deal of a triumph? One knows the orders combined in this half-breed's architecture without inquiring: one parent Northern, the other Southern. To-day I heard a school-mistress ask, "Where is John gone?" This form is so common—so nearly universal, in fact—that if she had used "whither" instead of "where," I think it would have sounded like an affectation.

We picked up one excellent word—a word worth travelling to New Orleans to get; a nice limber, expressive, handy word—"Lagniappe." They pronounce it lanny-*yap*. It is Spanish—so they said. We discovered it at the head of a column of odds and ends in the *Picayune,* the first day; heard twenty people use it the second; inquired what it meant the third; adopted it and got facility in swinging it the fourth. It has a restricted meaning, but I think the people spread it out a little when they choose. It is the equivalent of the thirteenth roll in a "baker's dozen." It is something thrown in, gratis, for good measure. The custom originated in the Spanish quarter of the city. When a child or a servant buys something in a shop—or even the mayor or the governor, for aught I know—he finishes the operation by saying,—"Give me something for lagniappe."

The shopman always responds; gives the child a bit of liquorice-root, gives the servant a cheap cigar or a spool of thread, gives the governor—I don't know what he gives the governor; support, likely.

When you are invited to drink,—and this does occur now and then in New Orleans,—and you say, "What, again?—no, I've had enough;" the other party says, "But just this one time more,— this is for lagniappe." When the beau perceives that he is stacking his compliments a trifle too high, and sees by the young lady's countenance that the edifice would have been better with the top compliment left off, he puts his "I beg pardon,— no harm intended," into the briefer form of "Oh, that's for lagniappe." If the waiter in the restaurant stumbles and spills a gill of coffee down the back of your neck, he says, "For lagniappe, sah," and gets you another cup without extra charge.

Letter to Major Pond

GEORGE WASHINGTON CABLE

(1844–1925)

George Washington Cable was born in New Orleans and began work at a local customhouse at the age of fifteen. He enlisted as a Confederate soldier in the Civil War at the age of nineteen, and worked as a clerk in the New Orleans Cotton Exchange after the war. Cable was a newspaper reporter and columnist for the *Picayune* from 1870–1871. He began studying Louisiana's colonial history and wrote a series of short stories about Creole New Orleans because he said "it seemed a pity for the stuff to go so to waste." He was discovered by Edward King, a journalist for *Scribner's Monthly*, and Cable's first published short story, "'Sieur George," appeared in the October, 1873 issue of the magazine. The story was later collected in *Old Creole Days* (1879), a book which is now considered a milestone in American literature, but at the time of publication was as vehemently denounced in the South, as it was highly acclaimed in the North. Cable lived at 1313 Eighth Street and entertained many writers there, including Joel Chandler Harris, Lafcadio Hearn, Mark Twain, and Oscar Wilde. Many critics consider Cable's novel *The Grandissimes*(1880) to be the first modern Southern novel because it dealt with racial injustice. His writing continued to cause tremendous resentment throughout the South, particularly *Dr. Sevier* (1884), a novel about prison reform. Mark Twain invited Cable to join him on a reading tour for several months in 1884 and 1885. In preparation for the tour, Cable gave his first public reading in New Orleans on May 15, 1884. Cable writes of his "royal triumph" in the following letter to Major Pond, manager of the Cable and Twain tour.

---

229 8th Street
New Orleans, May 16, 1884

Dear Major:

Last night was a royal triumph. The hall was full, full, to the doors and to the ceiling, and the audience was absolutely brilliant. Never have I enjoyed quite such a superb reception. Men stood against the walls clear around from the stage to the stage again. Extra chairs did not half accommodate the overplus. A committee of leading citizens formed the reception corps. This was notwithstanding the fact that there were two of the great social events of the season on hand, the Metairie Jockey Club free open air concert, & "Miss Stewart's ball." I enclose programme & clippings from T-Dem & Picayune. They called me out after the reading. I never suffered so from the heat before, and how the audience endured it I don't know; but the way they clapped and pounded would have done your big heart good. The advance sale was 427 seats at $1.25 each & would have been more but there were no more reserved seats to sell. There was considerably over $1000 in the house. It makes me laugh to think of the beaming patience with which that audience sat and roasted for two hours and a half.

Good-bye. I charged $150.00. The ladies must have *cleared* close to $700. I shall not repeat. The town will keep and ripen beautifully for next winter.

I want to write Mr. Roswell Smith, must rush to a close. Photos rec'd. Everybody at home delighted with them. Yours is just what they had imagined you. Now, they want to see *you*.

Yours truly

G. W. Cable

Grunewald, the owner of the hall, says the audience was the largest ever gathered in the hall & it certainly was the finest.

"A Matter of Prejudice"

KATE CHOPIN (1851–1904)

Kate Chopin was born Kate O'Flaherty in St. Louis, Missouri, where she received a conventional Catholic education. She first visited New Orleans in April, 1869 and made the following entry in her journal: "New Orleans I liked immensely; it is so clean—so white and green. Although in April, we had profusions of flowers—strawberries and even blackberries." In 1870, she married Oscar Chopin, a Louisianan entrepreneur, and the couple moved to New Orleans. Chopin fulfilled the social expectations of the city's Creole society, and yet her behavior often drew attention from aristocratic neighbors. She smoked, dressed in odd clothing, and took rambling walks and horse rides through the streets of New Orleans and the surrounding countryside. Chopin met a diverse group of people and began recording her observations. After the failure of his business in 1880, Oscar Chopin moved his wife and children to Natchitoches Parish, where they lived until his death in 1883. Chopin then returned to St. Louis and began writing stories for popular magazines in order to support herself and her six children. Her first novel, *At Fault* (1890), was a treatment of the then taboo subject of divorce. Chopin gained national fame with the publication of two story collections, *Bayou Folk* (1894) and *A Night in Acadie* (1895), which dealt with the Creole and Cajun life she had left behind in Louisiana. Her last novel, *The Awakening* (1899), now considered a literary masterpiece, was critically denounced and banned from bookstores and library shelves. The short story presented here, "A Matter of Prejudice" appeared in *A Night in Acadie.*

Madame Carambeau wanted it strictly understood that she was not to be disturbed by Gustave's birthday party. They carried her big rocking-chair from the back gallery, that looked out upon the garden where the children were going to play, around to the front gallery, which closely faced the green levee bank and the Mississippi coursing almost flush with the top of it.

The house—an old Spanish one, broad, low and completely encircled by a wide gallery—was far down in the French quarter of New Orleans. It stood upon a square of ground that was covered thick with a semitropical growth of plants and flowers. An impenetrable board fence, edged with a formidable row of iron spikes, shielded the garden from the prying glances of the occasional passer-by.

Madame Carambeau's widowed daughter, Madame Cécile Lalonde, lived with her. This annual party, given to her little son, Gustave, was the one defiant act of Madame Lalonde's existence. She persisted in it, to her own astonishment and the wonder of those who knew her and her mother.

For old Madame Carambeau was a woman of many prejudices—so many, in fact, that it would be difficult to name them all. She detested dogs, cats, organ-grinders, white servants and children's noises. She despised Americans, Germans and all people of a different faith from her own. Anything not French had, in her opinion, little right to existence.

She had not spoken to her son Henri for ten years because he had married an American girl from Prytania street. She would not permit green tea to be introduced into her house, and those who could not or would not drink coffee might drink tisane of *fleur de Laurier* for all she cared.

Nevertheless, the children seemed to be having it all their own way that day, and the organ-grinders were let loose. Old madame, in her retired corner, could hear the screams, the laughter and the music far more distinctly than she liked. She rocked herself noisily, and hummed "Partant pour la Syrie."

She was straight and slender. Her hair was white, and she wore it in puffs on the temples. Her skin was fair and her eyes blue and cold.

Suddenly she became aware that footsteps were approaching, and threatening to invade her privacy—not only footsteps, but screams! Then two little children, one in hot pursuit of the other, darted wildly around the corner near which she sat.

The child in advance, a pretty little girl, sprang excitedly into Madame Carambeau's lap, and threw her arms convulsively around the old lady's neck. Her companion lightly struck her a "last tag," and ran laughing gleefully away.

The most natural thing for the child to do then would have been to wriggle down from madame's lap, without a "thank you" or a "by your leave," after the manner of small and thoughtless children. But she did not do this. She stayed there, panting and fluttering, like a frightened bird.

Madame was greatly annoyed. She moved as if to put the child away from her, and scolded her sharply for being boisterous and rude. The little one, who did not understand French, was not disturbed by the reprimand, and stayed on in madame's lap. She rested her plump little cheek, that was hot and flushed, against the soft white linen of the old lady's gown.

Her cheek was very hot and very flushed. It was dry, too, and so were her hands. The child's breathing was quick and irregular. Madame was not long in detecting these signs of disturbance.

Though she was a creature of prejudice, she was nevertheless a skillful and accomplished nurse, and a connoisseur in all matters pertaining to health. She prided herself upon this talent, and never lost an opportunity of exercising it. She would have treated an organ-grinder with tender consideration if one had presented himself in the character of an invalid.

Madame's manner toward the little one changed immediately. Her arms and her lap were at once adjusted so as to become the most comfortable of resting places. She rocked very gently to and fro. She fanned the child softly with her palm leaf fan, and sang "Partant pour la Syrie" in a low and agreeable tone.

The child was perfectly content to lie still and prattle a little in that language which madame thought hideous. But the brown eyes were soon swimming in drowsiness, and the little body grew heavy with sleep in madame's clasp.

When the little girl slept Madame Carambeau arose, and treading carefully and deliberately, entered her room, that opened near at hand upon the gallery. The room was large, airy and inviting, with its cool matting upon the floor, and its heavy, old, polished mahogany furniture. Madame, with the child still in her arms, pulled a bell-cord; then she stood waiting, swaying gently back and forth. Presently an old black woman answered the summons. She wore gold hoops in her ears, and a bright bandanna knotted fantastically on her head.

"Louise, turn down the bed," commanded madame. "Place that small, soft pillow below the bolster. Here is a poor little unfortunate creature whom Providence must have driven into my arms." She laid the child carefully down.

"Ah, those Americans! Do they deserve to have children? Understanding as little as they do how to take care of them!" said madame, while Louise was mumbling an accompanying assent that would have been unintelligible to any one unacquainted with the negro patois.

"There, you see, Louise, she is burning up," remarked madame; "she is consumed. Unfasten the little bodice while I lift her. Ah, talk to me of such parents! So stupid as not to perceive a fever like that coming on, but they must dress their child up like a monkey to go play and dance to the music of organ-grinders.

"Haven't you better sense, Louise, than to take off a child's shoe as if you were removing the boot from the leg of a cavalry officer?" Madame would have required fairy fingers to minister to the sick. "Now go to Mamzelle Cécile, and tell her to send me one of those old, soft, thin nightgowns that Gustave wore two summers ago."

When the woman retired, madame busied herself with concocting a cooling pitcher of orange-flower water, and mixing a fresh supply of *eau sédative* with which agreeably to sponge the little invalid.

Madame Lalonde came herself with the old, soft nightgown. She was a pretty, blonde, plump little woman, with the deprecatory air of one whose will has become flaccid from want of use. She was mildly distressed at what her mother had done.

"But, mamma! But, mamma, the child's parents will be sending the carriage for her in a little while. Really, there was no use. Oh dear! oh dear!"

If the bedpost had spoken to Madame Carambeau, she would have paid more attention, for speech from such a source would have been at least surprising if not convincing. Madame Lalonde did not possess the faculty of either surprising or convincing her mother.

"Yes, the little one will be quite comfortable in this," said the old lady, taking the garment from her daughter's irresolute hands.

"But, mamma! What shall I say, what shall I do when they send? Oh, dear; oh, dear!"

"That is your business," replied madame, with lofty, indifference. "My concern is solely with a sick child that happens to be under my roof. I think I know my duty at this time of life, Cécile."

As Madame Lalonde predicted, the carriage soon came, with a stiff English coachman driving it, and a red-cheeked Irish nurse-maid seated inside. Madame would not even permit the maid to see her little charge. She had an original theory that the Irish voice is distressing to the sick.

Madame Lalonde sent the girl away with a long letter of explanation that must have satisfied the parents; for the child was left undisturbed in Madame Carambeau's care. She was a sweet child, gentle and affectionate. And, though she cried and fretted a little throughout the night for her mother, she seemed, after all, to take kindly to madame's gentle nursing. It was not much of a fever that afflicted her, and after two days she was well enough to be sent back to her parents.

Madame, in all her varied experience with the sick, had never before nursed so objectionable a character as an American child. But the trouble was that after the little one went away, she could think of nothing really objectionable against her except the accident of her birth, which was, after all, her misfortune; and her ignorance of the French language, which was not her fault.

But the touch of the caressing baby arms; the pressure of the soft little body in the night; the tones of the voice, and the feeling of the hot lips when the child kissed her, believing herself to be with her mother, were impressions that had sunk through the crust of madame's prejudice and reached her heart.

She often walked the length of the gallery, looking out across the wide, majestic river. Sometimes she trod the mazes of her garden where the solitude was almost that of a tropical jungle. It was during such moments that the seed began to work in her soul—the seed planted by the innocent and undesigning hands of a little child.

The first shoot that it sent forth was Doubt. Madame plucked it away once or twice. But it sprouted again, and with it Mistrust and Dissatisfaction. Then from the heart of the seed, and amid the shoots of Doubt and Misgiving, came the flower of Truth. It was a very beautiful flower, and it bloomed on Christmas morning.

As Madame Carambeau and her daughter were about to enter her carriage on that Christmas morning, to be driven to church, the old lady stopped to give an order to her black coachman, François. François had been driving these ladies every Sunday morning to the French Cathedral for so many years—he had forgotten exactly how many, but ever since he had entered their service, when Madame Lalonde was a little girl. His astonishment may therefore be imagined when Madame Cararmbeau said to him:

"François, to-day you will drive us to one of the American churches."

"Plait-il, madame?" the negro stammered, doubting the evidence of his hearing.

"I say, you will drive us to one of the American churches. Any one of them," she added, with a sweep of her hand. "I suppose they are all alike," and she followed her daughter into the carriage.

Madame Lalonde's surprise and agitation were painful to see, and they deprived her of the ability to question, even if she had possessed the courage to do so.

François, left to his fancy, drove them to St. Patrick's Church on Camp street. Madame Lalonde looked and felt like the proverbial fish out of its element as they entered the edifice. Madame Carambeau, on the contrary, looked as if she had been attending St. Patrick's church all her life. She sat with unruffled calm through the long service and through a lengthy English sermon, of which she did not understand a word.

When the mass was ended and they were about to enter the carriage again, Madame Carambeau turned, as she had done before, to the coachman.

"François," she said, coolly, "you will now drive us to the residence of my son, M. Henri Carambeau. No doubt Mamzelle Cécile can inform you where it is," she added, with a sharply penetrating glance that caused Madame Lalonde to wince.

Yes, her daughter Cécile knew, and so did François, for that matter. They drove out St. Charles avenue—very far out. It was like a strange city to old madame, who had not been in the American quarter since the town had taken on this new and splendid growth.

The morning was a delicious one, soft and mild; and the roses were all in bloom. They were not hidden behind spiked fences. Madame appeared not to notice them, or the beautiful and striking residences that lined the avenue along which they drove. She held a bottle of smelling-salts to her nostrils, as though she were passing through the most unsavory instead of the most beautiful quarter of New Orleans.

Henri's house was a very modern and very handsome one, standing a little distance away from the street. A well-kept lawn, studded with rare and charming plants, surrounded it. The ladies, dismounting, rang the bell, and stood out upon the banquette, waiting for the iron gate to be opened.

A white maid-servant admitted them. Madame did not seem to mind. She handed her a card with all proper ceremony, and followed with her daughter to the house.

Not once did she show a sign of weakness; not even when her son, Henri, came and took her in his arms and sobbed and wept upon her neck as only a warm-hearted Creole could. He was a big, good-looking, honest-faced man, with tender brown eyes like his dead father's and a firm mouth like his mother's.

Young Mrs. Carambeau came, too, her sweet, fresh face transfigured with happiness. She led by the hand her little daughter, the "American child" whom madame had nursed so tenderly a month before, never suspecting the little one to be other than an alien to her.

"What a lucky chance was that fever! What a happy accident!" gurgled Madame Lalonde.

"Cécile, it was no accident, I tell you; it was Providence," spoke madame, reprovingly, and no one contradicted her.

They all drove back together to eat Christmas dinner in the old house by the river. Madame held her little granddaughter upon her lap; her son Henri sat facing her, and beside her was her daughter-in-law.

Henri sat back in the carriage and could not speak. His soul was posessed by a pathetic joy that would not admit of speech. He was going back again to the home where he was born, after a banishment of ten long years.

He would hear again the water beat against the green levee-bank with a sound that was not quite like any other that he could remember. He would sit within the sweet and solemn shadow of the deep and overhanging roof; and roam through the wild, rich solitude of the old garden, where be had played his pranks of boyhood and dreamed his dreams of youth. He would listen to his mother's voice calling him, "mon fils," as it had always done before that day he had had to choose between mother and wife. No; he could not speak.

But his wife chatted much and pleasantly in a French, however, that must have been trying to old madame to listen to.

"I am so sorry, mère," she said, "that our little one does not speak French. It is not my fault, I assure you," and she flushed and hesitated a little. "It—it was Henri who would not permit it."

"That is nothing," replied madame, amiably, drawing the child close to her. "Her grandmother will teach her French; and she will teach her grandmother English. You see, I have no prejudices. I am not like my son. Henri was always a stubborn boy. Heaven only knows how he came by such a character!"

"Odalie"

ALICE DUNBAR-NELSON (1875–1935)

Alice Dunbar-Nelson was born Alice Ruth Moore in New Orleans, where she spent the first twenty years of her life. Dunbar-Nelson graduated from an education program at Straight College in New Orleans in 1891. While attending Straight, she served as editor of the women's page of the *New Orleans Journal of the Lodge*. Her first book, *Violets and Other Tales* (1895), a collection of short stories, sketches, essays, reviews, and poetry, was published when she was twenty years old. Dunbar-Nelson began her teaching career in 1892 and it remained an important part of her life until 1931. She devoted an equal amount of time to her writing, working as a journalist, essayist, short story writer, and diarist. In 1895, the poet Paul Lawrence Dunbar fell in love with Dunbar-Nelson after seeing her photograph in an issue of the *Boston Monthly Review*. He initiated an epistolary courtship with her, but they did not meet until she moved to New York City in 1897 to teach public school in Brooklyn. They married secretly in 1898 and divorced in 1902. In her honest portrayal of blacks and Creoles, Dunbar-Nelson helped to educate a reading public conditioned to expect contrived dialect and racial stereotypes. Her second book, *The Goodness of St. Rocque and Other Stories* (1899), which includes "Odalie," was the first collection of short stories by a black woman to be published in America and focuses on the New Orleans Creole culture.

Now and then Carnival time comes at the time of the good Saint Valentine, and then sometimes it comes as late as the warm days in March, when spring is indeed upon us, and the greenness of the grass outvies the green in the royal standards.

Days and days before the Carnival proper, New Orleans begins to take on a festive appearance. Here and there the royal flags with their glowing greens and violets and yellows appear, and then, as if by magic, the streets and buildings flame and burst like poppies out of bud, into a glorious refulgence of colour that steeps the senses into a languorous acceptance of warmth and beauty.

On Mardi Gras day, as you know, it is a town gone mad with folly. A huge masked ball emptied into the streets at daylight; a meeting of all nations on common ground, a pot-pourri of every conceivable human ingredient, but faintly describes it all. There are music, and flowers, cries and laughter and song and joyousness, and never an aching heart to show its sorrow or dim the happiness of the streets. A wondrous thing, this Carnival!

But the old cronies down in French-town, who know everything, and can recite you many a story, tell of one sad heart on Mardi Gras years ago. It was a woman's, of course; for "Il est toujours les femmes qui sont malheureuses," says an old proverb, and perhaps it is right. This woman—a child, she would be called elsewhere, save in this land of tropical growth and precocity—lost her heart to one who never knew, a very common story, by the way, but one which would have been quite distasteful to the haughty judge, her father, had he known.

Odalie was beautiful. Odalie was haughty too, but gracious enough to those who pleased her dainty fancy. In the old French house on Royal Street, with its quaint windows and Spanish courtyard green and cool, and made musical by the splashing of the fountain and the trill of caged birds, lived Odalie in convent-like seclusion. Monsieur le Juge was determined no hawk should break through the cage and steal his dove; and so, though there was no mother, a stern duenna aunt kept faithful watch.

Alas for the precautions of la Tante! Bright eyes that search for other bright eyes in which lurks the spirit of youth and mischief are ever on the look-out, even in church. Dutifully was Odalie marched to the Cathedral every Sunday to mass, and Tante Louise, nodding devoutly over her beads, could not see the blushes and glances full of meaning, a whole code of signals as it were, that passed between Odalie and Pierre, the impecunious young clerk in the courtroom.

Odalie loved, perhaps, because there was not much else to do. When one is shut up in a great French house with a grim sleepy tante and no companions of one's own age, life becomes a dull thing, and one is ready for any new sensation, particularly if in the veins there bounds the tempestuous Spanish-French blood that Monsieur le Juge boasted of. So Odalie hugged the image of her Pierre during the week days, and played tremulous little love-songs to it in the twilight when la Tante dozed over her devotion book, and on Sundays at mass there were glances and blushes, and mayhap, at some especially remembered time, the touch of finger-tips at the holy-water font, while la Tante dropped her last genuflexion.

Then came the Carnival time, and one little heart beat faster, as the gray house on Royal Street hung out its many-hued flags, and draped its grim front with glowing colours. It was to be a time of joy and relaxation, when every one could go abroad, and in the crowds one could speak to whom one chose. Unconscious plans formulated, and the petite Odalie was quite happy as the time drew near.

"Only think, Tante Louise," she would cry, "what a happy time it is to be!"

But Tante Louise only grumbled, as was her wont.

It was Mardi Gras day at last, and early through her window Odalie could hear the jingle of folly bells on the maskers' costumes, the tinkle of music, and the echoing strains of songs. Up to her ears there floated the laughter of the older maskers, and the screams of the little children frightened at their own images under the mask and domino. What a hurry to be out and in the motley merry throng, to be pacing Royal Street to Canal Street, where was life and the world!

They were tired eyes with which Odalie looked at the gay pageant at last, tired with watching throng after throng of maskers, of the unmasked, of peering into the cartsful of singing minstrels, into carriages of revellers, hoping for a glimpse of Pierre the devout. The allegorical carts rumbling by with their important red-clothed horses were beginning to lose charm, the disguises showed tawdry, even the gay-hued flags fluttered sadly to Odalie. Mardi Gras was a tiresome day, after all, she sighed, and Tante Louise agreed with her for once.

Six o'clock had come, the hour when all masks must be removed. The long red rays of the setting sun glinted athwart the many-hued costumes of the revellers trooping unmasked homeward to rest for the night's last mad frolic.

Down Toulouse Street there came the merriest throng of all. Young men and women in dainty, fairy-like garb, dancers, and dresses of the picturesque Empire, a butterfly or two and a dame here and there with powdered hair and graces of olden time. Singing with unmasked faces, they danced toward Tante Louise and Odalie. She stood with eyes lustrous and tear-heavy, for there in the front was Pierre, Pierre the faithless, his arms about the slender waist of a butterfly, whose tinselled powdered hair floated across the lace ruffles of his Empire coat.

"Pierre!" cried Odalie, softly. No one heard, for it was a mere faint breath and fell unheeded. Instead the laughing throng pelted her with flowers and candy and went their way, and even Pierre did not see.

You see, when one is shut up in the grim walls of a Royal Street house, with no one but a Tante Louise and a grim judge, how is one to learn that in this world there are faithless ones who may glance tenderly into one's eyes at mass and pass the holy water on caressing fingers without being madly in love? There was no one to tell Odalie, so she sat at home in the dull first days of Lent, and nursed her dear dead love, and mourned as women have done from time immemorial over the faithlessness of man. And when one day she asked that she might go back to the Ursulines' convent where her childish days were spent, only to go this time as a nun, Monsieur le Juge and Tante Louise thought it quite the proper and convenient thing to do; for how were they to know the secret of that Mardi Gras day?

"Cherchez la Femme"

O. HENRY

(WILLIAM SYDNEY PORTER)

(1862–1910)

O. Henry was born William Sydney Porter in Greensboro, North Carolina, where he spent the first twenty years of his life. In 1882 he moved to Texas and worked at various jobs, including stints as a bookkeeper and bank teller. O. Henry published a humor paper, the *Rolling Stone* (1894-1895), where his own skits and short sketches appeared. His efforts to keep the weekly afloat led to his "borrowing" of funds from the bank where he was employed. O. Henry claimed he intended to replace the money, but he was indicted for embezzlement in 1896 and fled to New Orleans. During his brief stay in the city he lived on Bienville Street and wrote for local papers, including the *Picayune*. He fled to Honduras to escape imprisonment, but returned to the United States when he learned of his wife's terminal illness. In 1898 O. Henry was convicted and sentenced to five years in the Ohio State Penitentiary. There have been many stories about the origin of his famous pseudonym, but O. Henry said that he "found the name in the society column of a New Orleans newspaper." He was recognized as a master of short fiction during his lifetime, and today the annual O. Henry Memorial Award is the most prestigious American prize awarded in the field of short-story writing. He wrote several stories with a New Orleans setting, including "Cherchez la Femme," (1903) in which two reporters indulge in an activity which O. Henry enjoyed, sipping on "concoctions of absinthe" at a favorite café.

Robbins, reporter for the *Picayune*, and Dumars, of *L'Abellie*—the old French newspaper that has buzzed for nearly a century—

were good friends, well proven by years of ups and downs together. They were seated where they had a habit of meeting—in the little, Creole-haunted café of Madame Tibault, in Dumaine Street. If you know the place, you will experience a thrill of pleasure in recalling it to mind. It is small and dark, with six little polished tables, at which you may sit and drink the best coffee in New Orleans, and concoctions of absinthe equal to Sazerac's best. Madame Tibault, fat and indulgent, presides at the desk, and takes your money. Nicolette and Mémé, madame's nieces, in charming bib aprons, bring the desirable beverages.

Dumars, with true Creole luxury, was sipping his absinthe, with half-closed eyes, in a swirl of cigarette smoke. Robbins was looking over the morning *Pic*, detecting, as young reporters will, the gross blunders in the make-up, and the envious blue-penciling his own stuff had received. This item, in the advertising columns, caught his eye, and with an exclamation of sudden interest he read it aloud to his friend:

> PUBLIC AUCTION—At three o'clock this afternoon there will be sold to the highest bidder all the common property of the Little Sisters of Samaria, at the home of the Sisterhood, in Bonhomme Street. The sale will dispose of the building, ground, and the complete furnishings of the house and chapel, without reserve.

This notice stirred the two friends to a reminiscent talk concerning an episode in their journalistic career that had occurred about two years before. They recalled the incidents, went over the old theories, and discussed it anew, from the different perspective time had brought.

There were no other customers in the café. Madame's fine ear had caught the line of their talk, and she came over to their table—for had it not been her lost money—her vanished twenty thousand dollars—that had set the whole matter going?

The three took up the long-abandoned mystery, threshing over the old, dry chaff of it. It was in the chapel of this house of the Little Sisters of Samaria that Robbins and Dumars had stood during that eager, fruitless news search of theirs, and looked upon the gilded statue of the Virgin.

"Thass so, boys," said madame, summing up. "Thass ver' wicked man, M'sieur Morin. Everybody shall be cert' he steal those money I plaze in his hand for keep safe. Yes. He's boun' spend that money, somehow." Madame turned a broad and comprehensive smile upon Dumars. "I ond'stand you, M'sieur Dumars, those day you come ask me fo' tell ev'ything I know 'bout M'sieur Morin. Ah! yes, I know most time when those men lose money you say, '*Cherchez la femme*'—there is somewhere the woman. But not for M'sieur Morin. No, boys. Before he shall die, he is like one saint. You might's well, M'sieur Dumars, go try find those money in those statue of Virgin Mary that M'sieur Morin present at those *p'tite soeurs*, as try find one *femme*."

At Madame Tibault's last words, Robbins started slightly and cast a keen, sidelong glance at Dumars. The Creole sat, unmoved, dreamily watching the spirals of his cigarette smoke.

It was then nine o'clock in the morning, and, a few minutes later, the two friends separated, going different ways to their day's duties. And now follows the brief story of Madame Tibault's vanished thousands:

New Orleans will readily recall to mind the circumstances attendant upon the death of Mr. Gaspard Morin, in that city. Mr. Morin was an artistic goldsmith and jeweler, in the old French Quarter, and a man held in the highest esteem. He belonged to one of the oldest French families and was of some distinction as an antiquary and historian. He was a bachelor, about fifty years of age. He lived in quiet comfort, at one of those rare old hostelries in Royal Street. He was found in his rooms one morning, dead from unknown causes.

When his affairs came to be looked into, it was found that he was practically insolvent, his stock of goods and personal property barely—but nearly enough to free him from censure—covering his liabilities. Following, came the disclosure that he had been intrusted with the sum of twenty thousand dollars by a former upper servant in the Morin family, one Madame Tibault, which she had received as a legacy from relatives in France.

The most searching scrutiny by friends and the legal authorities failed to reveal the disposition of the money. It had vanished, and left no trace. Some weeks before his death, Mr. Morin had drawn the entire amount, in gold coin, from the bank where it had been placed while he looked about (he told Madame Tibault) for a safe investment. Therefore, Mr. Morin's memory seemed doomed to bear the cloud of dishonesty, while madame was, of course, disconsolate.

Then it was that Robbins and Dumars, representing their respective journals, began one of those pertinacious private investigations which, of late years, the press has adopted as a means to glory and the satisfaction of public curiosity.

"*Cherchez la femme*," said Dumars.

"That's the ticket!" agreed Robbins. "All roads lead to the eternal feminine. We will find the woman."

They exhausted the knowledge of the staff of Mr. Morin's hotel, from the bell-boy down to the proprietor. They gently, but inflexibly, pumped the family of the deceased as far as his cousins twice removed. They artfully sounded the employees of the late jeweler, and dogged his customers for information concerning his habits. Like bloodhounds, they traced every step of the supposed defaulter, as nearly as might be, for years along the limited and monotonous paths he had trodden.

At the end of their labors, Mr. Morin stood, an immaculate man. Not one weakness that might be served up as a criminal tendency, not one deviation from the path of rectitude, not even a hint of a predilection for the opposite sex, was found to be placed to his debit. His life had been as regular and austere as a monk's; his habits, simple and unconcealed. Generous, charitable, and a model in propriety, was the verdict of all who knew him.

"What, now?" asked Robbins, fingering his empty notebook.

"*Cherchez la femme*," said Dumars, lighting a cigarette. "Try Lady Bellairs."

This piece of femininity was the race-track favorite of the season. Being feminine, she was erratic in her gaits, and there were a few heavy losers about town who had believed she could be true. The reporters applied for information.

Mr. Morin? Certainly not. He was never even a spectator at the races. Not that kind of a man. Surprised the gentlemen should ask.

"Shall we throw it up?" suggested Robbins, "and let the puzzle department have a try?"

"*Cherchez la femme,*" hummed Dumars, reaching for a match. "Try the Little Sisters of What-d'you-call-'em."

It had developed, during the investigation, that Mr. Morin had held this benevolent order in particular favor. He had contributed liberally toward its support, and had chosen its chapel as his favorite place of private worship. It was said that he went there daily to make his devotions at the altar. Indeed, toward the last of his life his whole mind seemed to have fixed itself upon religious matters, perhaps to the detriment of his worldly affairs.

Thither went Robbins and Dumars, and were admitted through the narrow doorway in the blank stone wall that frowned upon Bonhomme Street. An old woman was sweeping the chapel. She told them that Sister Félicité, the head of the order, was then at prayer at the altar in the alcove. In a few moments she would emerge. Heavy, black curtains screened the alcove. They waited.

Soon the curtains were disturbed, and Sister Félicité came forth. She was tall, tragic, bony and plain-featured, dressed in the black gown and severe bonnet of the sisterhood.

Robbins, a good rough-and-tumble reporter, but lacking the delicate touch, began to speak.

They represented the press. The lady had, no doubt, heard of the Morin affair. It was necessary, injustice to that gentleman's memory, to probe the mystery of the lost money. It was known that he had come often to this chapel. Any information, now, concerning Mr. Morin's habits, tastes, the friends he had, and so on, would be of value in doing him posthumous justice.

Sister Félicité had heard. Whatever she knew would be willingly told, but it was very little. Monsieur Morin had been a good friend to the order, sometimes contributing as much as a hundred dollars. The sisterhood was an independent one, depending entirely upon private contributions for the means to carry on its charitable work. Mr. Morin had presented the chapel with silver candlesticks and an altar cloth. He came every day to worship in the chapel, sometimes remaining for an hour. He was a devout Catholic, consecrated to holiness. Yes, and also in the alcove was a statue of the Virgin that he had, himself, modeled, cast, and presented to the order. Oh, it was cruel to cast a doubt upon so good a man!

Robbins was also profoundly grieved at the imputation. But, until it was found what Mr. Morin had done with Madame Tibault's money, he feared the tongue of slander would not be stilled. Sometimes—in fact, very often—in affairs of the kind there was—er—as the saying goes—er—a lady in the case. In absolute confidence, now—if—perhaps—

Sister Félicité's large eyes regarded him solemnly.

"There was one woman," she said, slowly, "to whom he bowed—to whom he gave his heart."

"Behold the woman!" said Sister Félicité, suddenly, in deep tones.

She reached a long arm and swept aside the curtain of the alcove. In there was a shrine, lit to a glow of soft color by the light pouring through a stained glass window. Within a deep niche in the bare stone wall stood an image of the Virgin Mary, the color of pure gold.

Dumars, a conventional Catholic, succumbed to the dramatic in the act. He knelt for an instant upon the stone flags, and made the sign of the cross. The somewhat abashed Robbins, murmuring an indistinct apology, backed awkwardly away. Sister Félicité drew back the curtain, and the reporters departed.

On the narrow stone sidewalk of Bonhomme Street, Robbins turned to Dumars, with unworthy sarcasm.

"Well, what next? Churchy law fem?"

"Absinthe," said Dumars.

With the history of the missing money thus partially related, some conjecture may be formed of the sudden idea that Madame Tibault's words seemed to have suggested to Robbins' brain.

Was it so wild a surmise—that the religious fanatic had offered up his wealth—or, rather, Madame Tibault's—in the shape of a material symbol of his consuming devotion? Stranger things have been done in the name of worship. Was it not possible that the lost thousands were molded into that lustrous image? That the goldsmith had formed it of the pure and precious metal, and set it there, through some hope of a perhaps disordered brain, to propitiate the saints, and pave the way to his own selfish glory?

That afternoon, at five minutes to three, Robbins entered the chapel door of the Little Sisters of Samaria. He saw, in the dim light, a crowd of perhaps a hundred people gathered to attend the sale. Most of them were members of various religious orders, priests and churchmen, come to purchase the paraphernalia of the chapel, lest they fall into desecrating hands. Others were business men and agents come to bid upon the realty. A clerical-looking brother had volunteered to wield the hammer, bringing to the office of auctioneer the anomaly of choice diction and dignity of manner.

A few of the minor articles were sold, and then two assistants brought forward the image of the Virgin.

Robbins started the bidding at ten dollars. A stout man, in an ecclesiastical garb, went to fifteen. A voice from another part of the crowd raised to twenty. The three bid alternately, raising by bids of five, until the offer was fifty dollars. Then the stout man dropped out, and Robbins, as a sort of *coup demain*, went to a hundred.

"One hundred and fifty," said the other voice.

"Two hundred," bid Robbins, boldly.

"Two-fifty," called his competitor, promptly.

The reporter hesitated for the space of a lightning flash, estimating how much he could borrow from the boys in the office, and screw from the business manager from his next month's salary.

"Three hundred," he offered.

"Three-fifty," spoke up the other, in a louder voice—a voice that sent Robbins diving suddenly through the crowd in its direction, to catch Dumars, its owner, ferociously by the collar.

"You unconverted idiot!" hissed Robbins, close to his ear—"pool!"

"Agreed!" said Dumars, coolly. "I couldn't raise three hundred and fifty dollars with a search warrant, but I can stand half. What you come bidding against me for?"

"I thought I was the only fool in the crowd," explained Robbins.

No one else bidding, the statue was knocked down to the syndicate at their last offer. Dumars remained with the prize, while Robbins hurried forth to wring from the resources and credit of both the price. He soon returned with the money and the two musketeers loaded their precious package into a carriage and drove with it to Dumar's room, in old Chartres Street, nearby. They lugged it, covered with a cloth, up the stairs, and deposited it on a table. A hundred pounds it weighed, if an ounce, and at that estimate, according to their calculation, if their daring theory were correct, it stood there, worth twenty thousand golden dollars.

Robbins removed the covering, and opened his pocketknife.

"*Sacré*" muttered Dumars, shuddering. "It is the Mother of Christ. What would you do?"

"Shut up, Judas!" said Robbins, coldly. "It's too late for you to be saved now."

With a firm hand, he chipped a slice from the shoulder of the image. The cut showed a dull, grayish metal, with a thin coating of gold leaf.

"Lead!" announced Robbins, hurling his knife to the floor—"gilded!"

"To the devil with it!" said Dumars, forgetting his scruples. "I must have a drink." Together they walked moodily to the café of Madame Tibault, two squares away. It seemed that madame's mind had been stirred that day to fresh recollections of the past services of the two young men in her behalf.

"You musn' sit by those table," she interposed, as they were about to drop into their accustomed seats. "Thass so, boys. But, no. I mek you come at this room, like my *très bons amis*. Yes, I goin' mek for you myself one *anisette* and one *cafe royale* ver' fine. Ah! I lak treat my fren' nize. Yes. Plis come in this way."

Madame led them into the little back room, into which she sometimes invited the especially favored of her customers. In two comfortable armchairs, by a big window that opened upon the courtyard, she placed them, with a low table between. Bustling hospitably about, she began to prepare the promised refreshments.

It was the first time the reporters had been honored with admission to the sacred precincts. The room was in dusky twilight, flecked with gleams of the polished, fine woods and burnished glass and metal that the Creoles love.

From the little courtyard a tiny fountain sent in an insinuating sound of trickling waters, to which a banana plant by the window kept time with its tremulous leaves.

Robbins, an investigator by nature, sent a curious glance roving about the room. From some barbaric ancestor, madame had inherited a *penchant* for the crude in decoration.

The walls were adorned with cheap lithographs-florid libels upon nature, addressed to the taste of the *bourgeoise*—birthday cards, garish newspaper supplements and specimens of art—advertising calculated to reduce the optic nerve to stunned submission. A patch of something unintelligible in the midst of the more candid display puzzled Robbins, and he rose and took a step nearer, to interrogate it at closer range. Then he leaned weakly against the wall, and called out;

"Madame Tibault! Oh, madame! Since when—oh! since when-have you been in the habit of papering your walls with five thousand dollar United States four per cent gold bonds? Tell me—is this a Grimm's fairy tale, or should I consult an oculist?"

At his words, Madame Tibault and Dumars approached.

"H'what you say?" said madame, cheerily. "H'what you say, M'sieur Robbin'? *Bon*? Ah! thoze nize li'l peezes papier! One tam I think those w'at you call calendair, wiz ze li'l day of mont' below But, no. Those wall is broke in those plaze, M'sieur Robbin', and I plaze those li'l peezes papier to conceal ze crack. I did think the couleur harm'nize so well with the wall papier. Where I get them from? Ah, yes, I remem' ver' well. One day M'sieur Morin, he come at my houze—thass 'bout one mont' before he shall die—thass 'long 'bout tam he promise fo' inves' those money fo' me. M'sieur Morin, he leave thoze li'l peezes papier in those table, and say ver' much 'bout money thass hard for me to ond'stan. *Mais* I never see those money again. Thass ver' wicked man, M'sieur Morin. H'what you call those peezes papier, M'sieur Robbin'—*bon*?"

Robbins explained.

"There's your twenty thousand dollars, with coupons attached," he said, running his thumb around the edge of the four bonds. "Better get an expert to peel them off for you. Mister Morin was all right. I'm going out to get my ears trimmed."

He dragged Dumars by the arm into the outer room. Madame was screaming for Nicolette and Mémé to come observe the fortune returned to her by M'sieur Morin, that best of men, that saint in glory.

"Marsy," said Robbins, "I'm going on a jamboree. For three days the esteemed *Pic.* will have to get along without my valuable services. I advise you to join me. Now, that green stuff you drink is no good. It stimulates thought. What we want to do is to forget to remember. I'll introduce you to the only lady in this case that was guaranteed to produce the desired results. Her name is Belle of Kentucky, twelve-year-old Bourbon. In quarts. How does the idea strike you?"

"*Allons*!" said Dumars. "*Cherchez la femme*."

"The Battle of the Handkerchiefs"

ADELAIDE STUART DIMITRY

(DATES UNKNOWN)

Adelaide Stuart Dimitry was born Adelaide Stuart in Mississippi, a member of the Stuart family of Virginia, which included her cousin, Confederate general, J. E. B. Stuart. The events of her life are sketchy before her marriage to John Dimitry, one of many educators in the prominent New Orleans Dimitry family. He provided his wife with a life of culture in the city. As Historian of the Stonewall Jackson Chapter of the United Daughters of the Confederacy (1909–1911), Dimitry sought to preserve the historic events of the Civil War by gathering tales from "those who were participants in that memorable struggle." The war-time reminiscences of women in the Chapter reflect "the high courage and quick wit of the women in the Southland." Dimitry meshed these oral accounts with written history in *War-Time Sketches: Historical and Otherwise* (1911), and the following selection from the book recounts a celebrated "battle" fought by the Confederate women of New Orleans on February 20, 1863.

In the early forenoon of February 20th, 1863, a whisper ran through New Orleans that the Confederate soldiers in the city were to be taken that day aboard the *Empire Parish*, Capt. Caldwell commanding, and transported to Baton Rouge for an exchange of Union prisoners.

The whisper grew in volume until it reached the ears of the Confederate women of the city. At once, gentle and simple, old and young, matron and maid hurried to the levee to give the boys in gray a warm, "God bless you and good-bye." One o'clock was the hour fixed for the departure of the prisoners, but long before the stroke of the hammer on its bell, the levee for many blocks was densely crowded with people—a number estimated by some at 20,000. No New Orleans woman who had a brother, husband, or son on that prison boat could have kept away. These loving and patriotic women—many of them wearing knots of red-white-and-red-ribbon or rosettes of palmetto, or carrying magnificent bouquets of roses, camellias and violets—like the flow of an ocean tide, steadily poured through Canal Street on their way to the river front. They debouched, a living torrent, upon the levee in front of the *Empire Parish*—a boat around which guerilla guns had recently been quite busy. What a waving of handkerchiefs was there and glad cries, and wafting of kisses as the sight of a loved face was caught in the prisoner crowd on deck! In the throng on the levee, redeeming it from the epithet *mob* could be noted many ladies prominent in culture and social position. Among these were the poet Xariffa, dear to all Louisiana hearts; Miss Kate Walker, the courageous young heroine of Confederate flag episode, and Mrs. D. R. Graham, then a young wife and mother.

At first, the crowd was orderly though emotional, as was to be expected. Soon, between the soldiers on the boat and some of the Federals on shore began a banter of wits as to what each might expect the next time they met. Some ladies also, who were adept in the use of the deaf and dumb language, were using this form of wireless telegraphy in talking to their prisoner friends. Through the dumb spelling tossed off upon their fingers under the eye of the unwitting sentinel, they learned that the baskets and boxes of delicacies sent to the Confederate prisoners in the Foundry prison had fed the thievish Federal guards instead of the dear ones for whom intended. This unwelcome news made more pronounced the attitude of defiance gradually assumed by the crowd. A wave of restlessness was sweeping over it. Some one cheered for Jeff Davis. A dozen resonant voices joined in the cheer, and quickly followed with a "Hurrah for the Confederacy," or as a Northern writer puts it,"shouted other diabolical monstrosities." The feeling growing more tense every minute was too strained for safety, and sure to snap in twain. Listen to the narrative of a participator in much that occurred on this eventful occasion:

> "I do not know who conceived the idea of going (in order to be nearer the prisoners), on the *Laurel Hill*, the large river steamer lying beside the *Empire Parish*. My companions and myself saw the move and followed the crowd on board. As the day advanced, the numbers grew so great that their demonstrations of love and respect nettled the Federals. It was an ovation to treason, as they were pleased to term it, and they peremptorily ordered us to leave the boat, go off the levee, disperse. The women could see no treason in what they were doing—merely looking at their friends and waving a farewell to them—so they made no move to obey. And *this* was what started the trouble. An officer, presumably under the orders from Captain Thomas, then in charge, gave the order to withdraw the plank and cut the *Laurel Hill* loose from its moorings. Jammed from stem to stern with brave and dauntless women, little children and nurses with babes in their arms, the boat, with stars and stripes flying from the jack staff, drifted slowly far down the river to the Algiers side. We held our breath as we went off, for we were much startled to find ourselves running away from the *Empire Parish*, but we waved a brave good-bye with our handkerchiefs to those on shore and they could not be kept from waving to us.
>
> After passing beyond the city, we wondered if they were taking us to Fort Jackson to shut us up as prisoners of war. Many a good Confederate has groaned within its stony walls, 'why should we escape?'—we whispered to each other drearily—'but at least it will be better than Ship Island.'
>
> During our enforced excursion down the river, we learned afterward the Federals had certain streets guarded and permitted no one to pass. Relatives of the unwilling passengers on the *Laurel Hill* were wild with fear for their loved ones, and tried to get to the levee, but the guards brutally turned them back."

While the *Laurel Hill* was drifting out of sight, on the levee the crisis had been reached. The Federal guards grew tired of the noisy but harmless demonstrations and arbitrarily ordered the women to "fall back, fall back, and stop waving their handkerchiefs." They talked to the winds. Above the rasping order of the guards was heard a laughing retort: "Can't do it. General Jackson is in the rear, and stands like a *Stonewall*." Again was the order repeated and still above the din of voices and confusion of the multitude came the same jeering response that was caught up by the crowd like the echo from a burglar's blast. In the bright sunshine and friendly river breeze, more briskly, than ever, fluttered and waved the exasperating and much anathemized handkerchiefs. Finally, Gen. Banks being informed of the state of affairs, sent down the 26th Massachusetts Regiment to clear the levee.

With the hope of quelling the rising tumult, augmented by the arrival of the regiment, a cannon was brought out and trained upon the multitude, the soldiers not caring who were terrified or hurt. In the meantime, imagine the feelings of those Confederate prisoners on the boat, forced to witness the cruel act of cutting loose the *Laurel Hill* with its freight of five hundred women and children, and the cannons turned on the helpless crowd on the levee.

But Gen. Banks met more than he reckoned upon. His cannon neither killed nor drove the women away, for, according to a Union writer, they presented "an impenetrable wall of silks, flounces, and graceless impudence." The excitement was at fever heat. The women now wrought to frenzy with heartache and nerves, would not budge an inch, would not drop a single handkerchief even though faced by the murderous cannon. The soldiers first threatened them with the bayonet, and afterwards actually charged upon them, driving every woman and child two squares from the levee. But *Defiant*, both of blow and threat, their handkerchiefs still waved, and the onset of the soldiers was unflinchingly met with the parasols and handkerchiefs of the women. Only one casualty was reported—that of a lady wounded in the hand by the thrust of a bayonet. After the fray the ground was covered with handkerchiefs and broken parasols. At last, the belligerent women, tired but not subdued, went home to sleep on their beds. So much for the battle on the levee. Our narrator on the *Laurel Hill* resumes:

> "I do not know how far down the river we were taken, but I do know we had nothing to eat. In the late afternoon the boat hands were marched into the cabin to eat their supper and, when they had finished and marched out again, we were told we could have the hard-tack and black coffee that was left. Some of us were too hungry to resist eating, but the majority took no notice of the invitation. Not one of the ladies showed fear or anxiety. If they felt either, they would not gratify the Federals that much. The bright and witty girls made things very amusing with their repartee, when a good humored officer came among us, but some there were that were surly, and the guards at the head of the gangway heard many a caustic aside expressive of contempt for Yankees and devotion to the Confederates. There was no white feather among them.
>
> Slowly we drifted on, and no one would tell us where the Captain was taking us. After we were prisoners for a few hours, the ladies in passing would ring the bell to let our captors know we were hungry, but none took the gentle hint and soon the bell disappeared.
>
> That night about nine o'clock we were brought back to the city, and when we were near landing and saw that it was indeed home, dear old New Orleans, we felt so happy that we broke out into singing "The Marseillaise," "The Bonnie Blue Flag," and all the Confederate songs we could think of—our own dear poet Xariffa leading the singing. This deeply angered our Federal captors. To punish us, they said we should not land, and proceeded to back out into midstream, where they anchored for the night. The next morning, after sunrise, we were brought to the levee again—a starving crowd and cold from the night air. They set us free, I suppose because they did not know what else to do with so many obstinate rebel women."

So ends the celebrated "Battle of the Handkerchiefs" courageously fought on the levee, February 20th, 1863, by the Confederate women of New Orleans.

from *The Pleasant Ways of St. Médard*

GRACE KING (1852–1932)

Grace King was born in New Orleans to a prominent family who escaped the city during the Civil War and crossed enemy lines to live on their sugar plantation in Southern Louisiana. After the war, her family returned to New Orleans in 1865 to find that their town house had been appropriated, and the Kings were forced to find lodging in a working-class district. King was educated in French schools and developed a life-long loyalty to the Creole culture. Her displeasure with George Washington Cable's depiction of the Creoles motivated King to write her first short story, "Monsieur Motte" (1885), in defense of the Creoles. She expanded the story into the book, *Monsieur Motte*, which was published in 1888. King fostered literary thought in the city and ran an informal "salon" at her home at 1749 Coliseum Street, inviting local and visiting authors for Friday afternoon teas. King is the author of thirteen books, including *Balcony Stories* (1893), *New Orleans, the Place and the People* (1895), and *Creole Families of New Orleans* (1921). King based her episodic novel, *The Pleasant Ways of St. Médard* (1916), on the King family's experiences following their return to New Orleans after the war. King said, "I wrote *St. Médard* at the request of a Northern publisher—who wanted to know about Reconstruction. I told him the problem was one of meat and bread." The following excerpt from the novel, "It was a Famous Victory," follows the Talbot family on an outing to the field of the Battle of New Orleans.

As usual, the father strode on ahead, the captain. His wife followed next, now walking: fast to keep up with him, now slow so as not to leave the children behind; her head ever-turning to look ahead, and then to look behind her; her feet tripping and stumbling in her uneven path and attention. The little path made a subservient détour around a plateau shaded with trees, where the officers of the barracks lounging on benches, were smoking and playing with their dogs. Behind them, facing the road, stood the heavy-looking red brick Spanish buildings of the barracks, with its towers, from whose loopholes protruded the grim muzzles of cannon. Sentries paced in front, squads of soldiers were marching around inside, booted and spurred cavalrymen were galloping up and away from the gateway—at whose posts horses bridled and saddled were hitched in readiness for an alarm. The river, itself, was not more fate-fully portentous in its aspect. But out of sight, it quickly went out of mind and the "nature," as Madame Joachim called the country, that succeeded, was in no wise akin to it in mood. In truth, it seemed as merry and convivial to the eye as the spirits of the holiday-makers, in the dusty road: the bands of boys returning from hunting or fishing frolics; negro men and women, in their gaudy Sunday finery and gaudy Sunday boisterousness; noisy Gascons with their noisy families packed in little rattling milk or vegetable carts; antique buggies and chaises, with their shabby-looking horses or mules, filled with voluble French chatterers; and every now and then, shining new traps behind spanking teams driven by gay young officers who looked neither to the right nor left—greeting no one, greeted by no one. Sprawling on the river-side of the levee and hidden from view, parties of white and negro soldiers were playing cards or throwing dice, or lying outstretched on the grass asleep or drunk.

Built so as to face the river and dominate it by their elegance, as the barracks did by its fierceness, stately mansions of the *ancien régime* succeeded—memorials of a day when the city's suburb of the *élite* was expected to grow down stream; and specimens of the elegant architecture that is based on the future stability of wealth—massive brick and stucco structures surrounded with balconies, upheld by pillars sturdy enough to support the roof of a church; with ceremonious avenues shaded by magnolias or cedars leading up to great gardens whose flower beds were disposed around fountains or white statuettes. And after these, unrolling in the bright sunlight like a panorama to the promenaders on the levee, came the plantations, the old and famous plantations as they used to be reckoned, whose musical French and Spanish names bespoke the colonial prestige of their owners. Hedges of wild orange, yucca or banana screened the fences, but every now and then the thick foliage was pierced by little belvideres; from whence the soft voices of women and the laughter of children—sitting within, to enjoy the view and breezes of the river,—would fall like songs of birds from cages upon the road below. Or out on the levee, itself, the families would be gathered in little pavilions, sitting in pleasant sociability, as the families of these plantations had been doing for generations, looking at the river and at the pleasant view also of their own possessions: mansion, quarters, sugar house, brick kiln, fields of sugar or corn, pastures studded with pecans, cherry trees, or oaks, smithies, warehouses,—some of the buildings and appurtenances as aged-looking and out-of-date as the great-grandmothers in their loose gowns, reclining in their rocking-chairs in the pavilions gazing with the pensiveness of old age at the swift and sure current of the river.

At one place the stream had undermined its bank and swallowed up a huge horseshoe of land, taking levee and road with it. A new levee, whose fresh earth crumbled under the feet, had been thrown up around the breach; and a new road run, curving boldly into the privacy of a garden, or the symmetrical furrows of a field. A half-mile beyond, the river seemed to drop its booty of soil seized above, and was forming a new bank; the *batture*, as it is called, could be seen shoaling up bare and glistening wet, far outside the levee.

"There!" the father stopped suddenly, and turning his back to the river, pointed with fine dramatic effect in the opposite direction, his face beaming with pleasure at the culmination of his carefully guarded surprise. "There it is! The field of the Battle of New Orleans! That is the monument!"

As he glanced down to see the effect, he could behold the glow from his face reflected in each little face looking up to him, as the glow of the sunset had been reflected in the surface of the river. And yet what could be more commonplace to these children than a battlefield? What else had they heard of for years but of winning and losing battles? Each one of the little band was surely qualified to say "Whatever my ignorance about other things, I at least know war." But now, it was as if they knew it not. Their eyes were gleaming and their little hearts beating as at the sight and sound of martial glory too great for earth to beat—the martial glory of poetry and history, not of plain every-day life! Breathless, they ran down the levee after their father, looking, as he looked, nowhere but in front, where rose the tall shaft that commemorated the famous victory. Faster and faster he strode, and they after him, until they reached the steps of the monument and climbing up, could look over the land roundabout; seeing only a bush here, a tree there, a house in the distance and still farther away the line of the forest. A bare, ugly, desolate scene enough, but not so to the little band—

"There were the British headquarters! There Jackson's! Along there ran the ramparts! In that swamp were the Kentuckians! There, next the river, the Barratarians! Away over there, hidden by the woods, the little bayou through which the British army came from the lake to the river! Across that field advanced Pakenham! Over there he fell! Up the levee came Lambert! Out there on the river was the Carolina firing hot shot and shell! Down the road we have been walking ran the reinforcements from New Orleans!" The fine old story sped on and on. . . . As he talked the little boys stretched themselves, taller and taller, and looked before them with the swaggering insolence of Barratarians looking at the English, and the little girls' heads rose higher and stiffer and they curled their lips disdainfully at the foe, as ladies do in triumph.

On the other side of the monument, stood Polly's friend of the car, the old gentleman who looked like General Lee, listening rather wistfully. . . . "The British marched up to the line of death as if they were on dress parade," the father continued his historical lesson, "and they died in their ranks as they marched. When the smoke lifted, and when the Americans saw them lying in regular lines on the field,—the brave red uniforms, and the dashing Tartans of the Highlanders,—a great sigh went down the line, a sigh of regret and admiration. . . ."

Polly's sharp eyes, roving around, had detected the old gentleman. Running to him, she caught his hand and drew him forward. The movement was so frank and hearty, that neither he nor the parents could resist it and at once they entered into cordial acquaintanceship with one another.

He was so tall and erect of figure, so noble of face, so soldierly in his bearing, that the civilian clothes he wore were a poor disguise. One knew at once, rather than guessed, that he had been an officer and had worn the gray, and that in short, he was one of the ruined and defeated Southerners.

"My father," he said, as he came forward, "was one of the Kentuckians."

"Was he?" exclaimed the mother enthusiastically. "'A hunter of Kentucky.'" And with a smile and a toss of the head, she gave the refrain "'Oh, the hunters of Kentucky.' My grandfather sang the song at dessert on every anniversary of the battle. And my grandmother used to say that they were the handsomest men she ever saw," glancing involuntarily at the stranger, who in this regard was every inch a Kentuckian, "as they came marching down Royal Street, in their hunting shirts and coonskin caps with the tails hanging down behind."

"Sharpshooters every man of them," interjected her husband, "hitting a squirrel in the eye, on the top of the tallest tree."

"She said," continued the wife, "that there were no men in the city to compare with them and all the young ladies fell in love with them and used to dream of them at night; rifles, hunting shirts and all. Oh, the women looked upon them as deliverers. You remember the motto of the British?" . . . She paused, and as no one answered went on: "My grandmother said the ladies all carried daggers in their belts, and as they sat together in each other's houses, scraping lint and making bandages, they would talk of what they would do in case of the British victory. And one day they became so excited that they sent a messenger to General Jackson, and he answered like the hero he was, 'The British will never enter the city except over my dead body.'" . . . And still no one took up the conversation, so she carried it a step farther: "My grandfather never approved of General Jackson's course after the battle, but she, my grandmother always defended him. She could never forgive my grandfather for not casting his vote for him for president, she vowed if she had had a hundred votes she would cast them all for him."

The stranger laughed heartily.

"After the battle, you know, the ladies; all drove down to the field in their carriages carrying their lint and bandages, and refreshments for the wounded, . . . and they brought back the wounded British officers with them and took them in their homes and nursed them. My grandmother had one, a young boy not over eighteen, and so fair that he looked like an angel, she said. He was a gentleman of good family. But all the British officers were gentlemen, of course; and the young ladies lost their hearts to them, as they had done before to the Kentuckians. For years afterwards, Grandmama's prisoner used to write to her."

"Would you have liked them as well, if they had whipped you?" the stranger asked with a twinkle in his eye

"Whipped us! They never could have done that! We would have burned the city! We would have fought from house to house! We would have retired to our swamps! No! We never would have surrendered the city." And then as the absurdity of these old hereditary boastings came to her in the light of the present, she stopped short and laughed merrily, "that is the way we used to talk."

They walked back slowly to the levee and mounted to the path on top just as a large vessel slowly steamed upstream. The children read out the name on the stern. It was from Liverpool.

The sun was sinking on the opposite side of the river amid clouds of gorgeous splendor. The vague green bank came now into clear vision with its plantation buildings, its groves, and its people walking like ants upon its levee. The rippling current and every eddy along the bank shone in unison with the sky or, indeed, as if another sun were burning under its depths. The great steamship passed into the circle of illumination and out of it, as the little group watched it from the levee.

"I should be ashamed to come here, if I was them, wouldn't you?" Polly's clear voice broke the solemn silence as she twitched the hand of the old gentleman, with free *camaraderie*.

"Ashamed? Why?"

"Because we whipped them so."

"Whipped them! Oh! You mean the British in the battle."

"Yes, we whipped them right here, where they have to pass by. I wouldn't like that, would you?"

"Perhaps they don't know it on the ship."

"Don't know it! I reckon everybody knows when they are whipped. I would hate to be whipped, wouldn't you?"

"I used to hate it when I was whipped."

"Oh! I don't mean that! I mean in battle. If I were a man I would never be whipped."

"What would you do if the other army were stronger."

"I don't care if it were stronger, I would whip it." The path on top of the levee following the bending and curving banks produced the effect of a meandering sunset. Now it shone full opposite, now it glowed obliquely behind a distant forest, now the burning disk touched the ripples of the current straight ahead, and the British vessel seemed to be steering into it. Another turn and it had sunken halfway down behind the distant city, whose roofs, steeples, chimneys, and the masts of vessels, were transfigured into the semblance of a heavenly vision for a brief, a flitting moment. Further on the bank turned them out of sight of it all,—and shadows began to creep over the water,—and when next they saw the West, the sun had disappeared, and all its brilliant splendor with it. In the faint rose flush of twilight beamed the evening star . . . far away from the little church of St. Médard came the tinkling bell of the Angelus . . . the evening gun fired at the barracks.

"New Orleans, the *Double Dealer* and the Modern Movement in America"

SHERWOOD ANDERSON (1876–1941)

Sherwood Anderson was born and raised in Ohio and began working at the age of fourteen, drifting from job to job until he found work writing advertising copy in Chicago. The city was a center of literary activity from 1912 to 1925, and after meeting many of the authors who comprised the Chicago Group, including Theodore Dreiser and Carl Sandburg, Anderson decided to pursue the vocation of writing. He published his first novel *Windy McPherson's Son* in 1916, but it was not until the publication of *Winesburg, Ohio* (1919) that he gained wide recognition. Anderson lived in New Orleans from 1922 to 1925 in an apartment in the Pontalba building and ran an informal literary salon frequented by many writers, including William Faulkner and Edna St. Vincent Millay. He had considerable influence on Faulkner, the budding writer, who ranked Anderson's "I'm a Fool" as one of the best stories he had ever read. Anderson's short story, "A Meeting South" (1925), in which a young poet is taken by an older writer to visit an elderly madame in the French quarter, is partially based on his first meeting with Faulkner. Both writers were published in the *Double Dealer* (1921–1926), the New Orleans avant-garde literary magazine. Faulkner wrote to his mother in 1925 that, "I sold a thing to the *Double Dealer* for cash, money you can buy things with, you know. There is only one other person in history to whom the *Double Dealer* has paid real actual money and that man is Sherwood Anderson." Anderson wrote of his belief that the Vieux Carré was a haven for a new generation of artists and writers in the following article for the March 1922 issue of the *Double Dealer*.

When I came from New York to New Orleans, a few weeks ago, there was an oyster shucking contest going on in Lafayette Square, in the heart of the city. It was for the oyster opening championship of the world. Mike Algero, a handsome Italian, won it. I took that in and then went for a long walk on the docks, extending for miles along the Mississippi river front, looking at Negro laborers at work. They are the only laborers I have ever seen in America who know how to laugh, sing and play in the act of doing hard physical labor. And the man who thinks that, man for man, they do not achieve more work in a day than a white laborer of the North is simply mistaken.

That was a day for me.

By that time and by the time I had taken a ride through the "Vieux Carré," the old French Creole town, and had gone, in the evening, to see a bang-up Negro prize fight out under the stars in an open air arena—

Well, you see, I went back to my room and wrote a letter to a friend declaring New Orleans the most cultural city I had yet found in America.

"Blessed be this people. They know how to play. They are truly a people of culture."

That was the substance of what I wrote to my friend.

Really, you see, we Americans have always been such a serious, long-faced people. Some one must have told us long ago that we had to make ourselves world-saviours or something like that. And it got under our skin. Every long-jawed, loose-mouthed politician in the country began to talk about our saving the human race. We got unnecessarily chesty. The grand manner got to be the vogue. It sticks to us.

What is the matter with us anyway? What are we bluffing ourselves about?

Does not a real culture in any people consist first of all in the acceptance of life, life of the flesh, mind and spirit? That, and a realization of the inter-dependence of all these things in making a full and a flowering life.

What I think is that the Modern Spirit in America really means something like a return to common sense. I am sure that even such serious representatives of the Anglo-Saxon race as H. G. Wells or Oswald Garrison Villard aren't after all so much fussed about the destinies of the English and American peoples. I am sure any man is at bottom more concerned with what he is to have for dinner, how he is to spend his evening, explain himself to his friends, or perhaps even with the anticipation of the woman he hopes to hold in his arms, than he is with the destiny of any nation.

"Where can a man get six bottles of good wine? I have some friends coming to my house to dinner."

"I am a working man and my wife is going to have another kid. What kind of tobacco is that you are smoking? The bird I got this stuff from stuck me with something that bites my tongue like the devil."

I proclaim myself an American and one of the Moderns. At the present moment I am living in New Orleans, I have a room in the "Vieux Carré" with long French windows, through which one can step out upon a gallery, as wide as the sidewalk below. It is charming to walk there, above the street and to look down at others hustling off to work. I do not love work too much. Often I want to loaf and I want others to loaf with me, talk with me of themselves and their lives.

It happens that I have a passion for writing stories about people and there is a kind of shrewdness in me too. If I can understand people a little better perhaps they in turn will understand me. I like life and haven't too much of it to live. Perhaps if I take things in a more leisurely way I shall find more friends and lovers.

I sit in my room writing until the world of my imagination fades. Then I go out to walk on my gallery or take my stick and go walk in the streets.

There are two girls walking in Saint Peter Street. A man has stopped at a street crossing to light a pipe. A quiet, suggestive life stirs my imagination.

There is an old city here, on the lip of America, as it were, and all about it has been built a new and more modern city. In the old city a people once lived who loved to play, who made love in the moonlight, who walked under trees, gambled with death in the dueling field.

These people are pretty much gone now, but their old city is still left. Men here call it the "Vieux Carré."

And that I think charming too. They might have called it uptown or downtown.

And to me it is altogether charming that almost all of the old city still stands. From my window, as I sit writing, I see the tangled mass of the roofs of the old buildings. There are old galleries with beautiful hand-wrought railings, on which the people of the houses can walk above the street, or over which the housewife can lean in the morning to call to the vegetable man pushing his cart along the roadway below.

What colors in the old walls and doors of these buildings. Yellows fade into soft greens. There is a continual shifting interplay of many colors as the sunlight washes over them.

I go to walk. It is the dusk of evening and men are coming home from work. There are mysterious passageways leading back into old patios.

> My beloved put in his hand by the hole in the door,
> And my bowels were moved for him.
> I rose up to open to my beloved;
> And my hand dropped with myrrh,
> And my fingers with liquid myrrh,
> Upon the handle of the bolt.
> I opened to my beloved;
> But my beloved had withdrawn himself and was gone.

I am in New Orleans and I am trying to proclaim something I have found here and that I think America wants and needs.

There is something left in this people here that makes them like one another, that leads to constant outbursts of the spirit of play, that keeps them from being too confoundedly serious about death and the ballot and reform and other less important things in life.

The newer New Orleans has no doubt been caught up by the passions of our other American cities. Outside the "Vieux Carré" there is no doubt a good deal of the usual pushing and shoving so characteristic of American civilization. The newer New Orleans begs factories to come here from other cities. I remember to have seen page advertisements, pleading with factory owners of the North to bring their dirt and their noise down here, in the pages of the *Saturday Evening Post*, if I remember correctly.

However, I am sure these people do not really mean it. There are too many elements here pulling in another direction, and an older and I believe more cultural and sensible direction.

At any rate there is the fact of the "Vieux Carré" —the physical fact. The beautiful old town still exists. Just why it isn't the winter home of every sensitive artist in America, who can raise money enough to get here, I do not know. Because its charms aren't known, I suppose. The criers-out of the beauty of the place may have been excursion boomers.

And so I proclaim New Orleans from my own angle, from the angle of the Modern. Perhaps the city will not thank me, but anyway it is a truly beautiful city. Perhaps if I can bring more artists here they will turn out a ragtag enough crew. Lafcadio Hearn wasn't such a desirable citizen while he lived in the "Vieux Carré."

However, I address these fellows. I want to tell them of long quiet walks to be taken on the levee in back-of-town, where old ships, retired from service, thrust their masts up into the evening sky. On the streets here the crowds have a more leisurely stride, the Negro life issues a perpetual challenge to the artists, sailors from many lands come up from the water's edge and idle on the street corners, in the evening soft voices, speaking strange tongues, come drifting up to you out of the street.

I have undertaken to write an article on the Modern Spirit and because I am in New Orleans and have been so completely charmed by life in the "Vieux Carré" I may have seemed to get off the track.

I haven't really. I stick to my pronouncement that culture means first of all the enjoyment of life, leisure and a sense of leisure. It means time for a play of the imagination over the facts of life, it means time and vitality to be serious about really serious things and a background of joy in life in which to refresh the tired spirits.

In a civilization where the fact becomes dominant, submerging the imaginative life, you will have what is dominant in the cities of Pittsburgh and Chicago today.

When the fact is made secondary to the desire to live, to love, and to understand life, it may be that we will have in more American cities a charm of place such as one finds in the older parts of New Orleans now.

There has been a good deal of talk about the solid wall of preferred prejudices and the sentimentalities of the South and there may be a good deal of truth in the charge of southern intellectual backwardness.

Perhaps the South has only been waiting for the Modern Spirit, to assert itself to come into its own. It is, I believe, coming into its own a little through such efforts as the publication of the *Double Dealer*, a magazine devoted to the Arts, in New Orleans.

And, as I am supposed to be proclaiming the Modern Spirit, I repeat again that it means nothing to me if it does not mean putting the joy of living above the much less subtle and I think altogether more stupid joy of growth and achievement.

"The Glamour of New Orleans"

LAFCADIO HEARN (1850-1904)

Lafcadio Hearn was born on the Isle of Santa Maura off the western coast of Greece, and was educated in England, France, and Ireland. He immigrated to the United States at the age of nineteen and worked as a journalist in Cincinnati. After reading George Washington Cable's "Jean-ah Poquelin" in the May 1875 issue of *Scribner's Magazine*, Hearn was inspired to visit Louisiana so he could learn more about the Creole culture. In 1877 he moved to New Orleans and began writing "Creole Sketches," a series of vignettes depicting local scenes for the New Orleans *Item*. Hearn lived for a time at 516 Bourbon Street and was befriended by Cable, who shared his interest in collecting Creole stories and songs. Hearn saw a market for books on the Creole culture and published *La Cuisine Créole* (1885) and *Gombo Zhèbes: A Little Dictionary of Créole Proverbs* (1885). He later joined the staff of the New Orleans *Times-Democrat*, where his translations of the works of Flaubert, Gautier, and Zola appeared. His impressionistic novel *Chita: A Memory of an Island* (1889), grew out of a stay on Grand Isle and is a classic of Louisiana literature. Hearn longed for the exotic and left New Orleans in 1887, first for Martinique and then for New York, where he received a commission from Harper and Brothers to write *Glimpses of Unfamiliar Japan* (1894). Hearn moved to Japan in 1890 to work on the book and lived there until his death in 1904. A selection of Hearn's vignettes written for the New Orleans *Item*, including "The Glamour of New Orleans," were published in *Creole Sketches* (1924).

The season has come at last when strangers may visit us without fear, and experience with unalloyed pleasure the first picturesque old city in North America. For in this season is the glamour of

New Orleans strongest upon those whom she attracts to her from less hospitable climates, and fascinates by her nights of magical moonlight, and her days of dreamy languors and perfumes. There are few who can visit her for the first time without delight; and few who can ever leave her without regret; and none who can forget her strange charm when they have once felt its influence. To a native of the bleaker Northern clime—if he have any poetical sense of the beautiful in nature, any love of bright verdure and luxuriance of landscape—the approach to the city by river must be in itself something indescribably pleasant. The white steamer gliding through an unfamiliar world of blue and green—blue above and blue below, with a long strip of low green land alone to break the ethereal azure; the waving cane; the ever-green fringe of groves weird with moss; the tepid breezes and golden sunlight—all deepening in their charm as the city is neared, make the voyage seem beautiful as though one were sailing to some far-off glimmering Eden, into the garden of Paradise itself. And then, the first impression of the old Creole city slumbering under the glorious sun; of its quaint houses; its shaded streets; its suggestions of a hundred years ago; its contrasts of agreeable color; its streets reechoing the tongues of many nations; its general look of somnolent contentment; its verdant antiquity; its venerable memorials and monuments; its eccentricities of architecture; its tropical gardens; its picturesque surprises; its warm atmosphere, drowsy perhaps with the perfume of orange flowers, and thrilled with the fantastic music of mocking-birds—cannot ever be wholly forgotten. For a hundred years and more has New Orleans been drawing hither wandering souls from all the ends of the earth. The natives of India and of Japan have walked upon her pavements; Chinese and swarthy natives of Manila; children of the Antilles and of South America; subjects of the Sultan and sailors of the Ionian Sea have sought homes here. All civilized nations have sent wandering children hither. All cities of the North, East, and West have yielded up some restless souls to the far-off Southern city, whose spell is so mystic, so sweet, so universal. And to these wondering and wandering ones, this sleepy, beautiful, quaint old city murmurs:

> Rest with me. I am old; but thou hast never met with a younger more beautiful than I. I dwell in eternal summer; I dream in perennial sunshine; I sleep in magical moonlight. My streets are flecked with strange sharp shadows; and sometimes also the Shadow of Death falleth upon them; but if thou wilt not fear, thou art safe. My charms are not the charms of much gold and great riches; but thou mayst feel with me such hope and content as thou hast never felt before. I offer thee eternal summer, and a sky divinely blue; sweet breezes and sweet perfumes, bright fruits, and flowers fairer than the rainbow. Rest with me. For if thou leavest me, thou must forever remember me with regret.

And assuredly those who wander from her may never cease to behold her in their dreams—quaint, beautiful, and sunny as of old—and to feel at long intervals the return of the first charm—the first delicious fascination of the fairest city of the South.

from *Mosquitoes*

WILLIAM FAULKNER (1897–1962)

William Cuthbert Faulkner was born in New Albany, Mississippi and grew up in nearby Oxford, where he would reside for most of his life. Faulkner became the foremost Southern writer of the twentieth century and one of America's greatest literary talents, winning the Nobel Prize for Literature in 1950. His major works include *The Sound and the Fury* (1929), *As I Lay Dying* (1930), and *Absalom, Absalom!* (1936). Faulkner published his first book, *The Marble Faun*, a volume of poetry, in 1924. From early 1925 to the end of 1926, with the exception of a brief stay in Europe, Faulkner lived in New Orleans. The city played an important role in his development as a writer, for it was in New Orleans that Faulkner, who thought of himself primarily as a poet, began to publish fiction. He contributed a group of short sketches, titled "New Orleans" to the *Double Dealer*, and short fiction to the *Times-Picayune*. He met Sherwood Anderson, who encouraged him to write his first novel, *Soldier's Pay* (1926). Faulkner loved the French Quarter, which was known as "Greenwich Village South," and lived for several months at 624 Pirate's Alley, now the location of Faulkner House Books. Faulkner and William Spratling published *Sherwood Anderson and Other Famous Creoles* (1926), with text by Faulkner and caricatures of the "artful and crafty ones of the French Quarter" by Spratling. In the 1930s Faulkner gave this account of his life, "Met man named Sherwood Anderson. Said, 'Why not write novels? Maybe won't have to work.' Did. *Soldier's Pay*. Did. *Mosquitoes* . . . Own and operate own typewriter." Faulkner gave a party at Galatoire's to celebrate signing a contract for the publication of his second novel, *Mosquitoes* (1927), a satiric account of the lives of the artists and writers living in the French Quarter. In the following excerpt from the book, Ernest Talliaferro wends his way through the French Quarter and winds up at the dinner table of novelist Dawson Fairchild, whose character is based on Sherwood Anderson.

He opened the street door. Twilight ran in like a quiet violet dog and nursing his bottle he peered out across an undimensional feathered square, across stencilled palms and Andrew Jackson in childish effigy bestriding the terrific arrested plunge of his curly balanced horse, toward the long unemphasis of the Pontalba building and three spires of the cathedral graduated by perspective, pure and slumbrous beneath the decadent languor of August and evening. Mr Talliaferro thrust his head modestly forth, looking both ways along the street. Then he withdrew his head and closed the door again.

He employed his immaculate linen handkerchief reluctantly before thrusting the bottle beneath his coat. It bulged distressingly under his exploring hand, and he removed the bottle in mounting desperation. He struck another match, setting the bottle down at his feet to do so, but there was nothing in which he might wrap the thing. His impulse was to grasp it and hurl it against the wall: already he pleasured in its anticipated glassy crash. But Mr Talliaferro was quite honourable: he had passed his word. Or he might return to his friend's room and get a bit of paper. He stood in hot indecision until feet on the stairs descending decided for him. He bent and fumbled for the bottle, struck it and heard its disconsolate empty flight, captured it at last and opening the street door anew he rushed hurriedly forth.

The violet dusk held in soft suspension lights slow as bell-strokes, Jackson Square was now a green and quiet lake in which abode lights round as jellyfish, feathering with silver mimosa and pomegranate and hibiscus beneath which lantana and cannas bled and bled. Pontalba and cathedral were cut from black paper and pasted flat on a green sky; above them taller palms were fixed in black and soundless explosions. The street was empty, but from Royal Street there came the hum of a trolley that rose to a staggering clatter, passed on and away leaving an interval filled with the gracious sound of inflated rubber on asphalt, like a tearing of endless silk. Clasping his accursed bottle, feeling like a criminal, Mr Talliaferro hurried on.

He walked swiftly beside a dark wall, passing small indiscriminate shops dimly lighted with gas and smelling of food of all kinds, fulsome, slightly overripe. The proprietors and their families sat before the doors in tilted chairs, women nursing babies into slumber spoke in soft south European syllables one to another. Children scurried before him and about him, ignoring him or becoming aware of him and crouching in shadow like animals, defensive, passive and motionless.

He turned the corner. Royal Street sprang in two directions and he darted into a grocery store on the corner, passing the proprietor sitting in the door with his legs spread for comfort, nursing the Italian balloon of his belly on his lap. The proprietor removed his short terrific pipe and belched, rising to follow the customer. Mr Talliaferro set the bottle down hastily.

The grocer belched again, frankly. "Good afternoon," he said in a broad West End accent much nearer the real thing than Mr Talliaferro's. "Meelk, hay?"

Mr Talliaferro extended the coin, murmuring, watching the man's thick reluctant thighs as he picked up the bottle without repugnance and slid it into a pigeon-holed box and opening a refrigerator beside it, took therefrom a fresh one. Mr Talliaferro recoiled.

"Haven't you a bit of paper to wrap it in?" he asked diffidently. "Why, sure," the other agreed affably. "Make her in a parcel, hay?" He complied with exasperating deliberation, and breathing freer but still oppressed, Mr Talliaferro took his purchase and glancing hurriedly about, stepped into the street. And paused, stricken.

She was under full sail and accompanied by a slimmer one when she saw him, but she tacked at once and came about in a hushed swishing of silk and an expensive clashing of impediments—handbag and chains and beads. Her hand bloomed fatly through bracelets, ringed and manicured, and her hot-house face wore an expression of infantile trusting astonishment.

"Mister Talliaferro! What a surprise," she exclaimed, accenting the first word of each phrase, as was her manner. And she really was surprised. Mrs Maurier went through the world continually amazed at chance, whether or not she had instigated it. Mr Talliaferro shifted his parcel quickly behind him, to its imminent destruction, being forced to accept her hand without removing his hat. He rectified this as soon as possible. "I would never have expected to see you in this part of town at this hour," she continued. "But you have been calling on some of your artist friends, I suppose?"

The slim one had stopped also, and stood examining Mr Talliaferro with cool uninterest. The older woman turned to her. "Mr Talliaferro knows all the interesting people in the Quarter, darling. All the people who are—who are creating—creating things. Beautiful things. Beauty, you know." Mrs Maurier waved her glittering hand vaguely toward the sky in which stars had begun to flower like pale and tarnished gardenias. "Oh, do excuse me, Mr Talliaferro—This is my niece, Miss Robyn, of whom you have heard me speak. She and her brother have come to comfort a lonely old woman—" her glance held a decayed coquetry, and taking his cue Mr Talliaferro said:

"Nonsense, dear lady. It is we, your unhappy admirers, who need comforting. Perhaps Miss Robyn will take pity on us, also?" He bowed toward the niece with calculated formality. The niece was not enthusiastic.

"Now, darling," Mrs Maurier turned to her niece with rapture. "Here is an example of the chivalry of our southern men. Can you imagine a man in Chicago saying that?"

"Not hardly," the niece agreed. Her aunt rushed on:

"That is why I have been so anxious for Patricia to visit me, so she can meet men who are—who are—My niece is named for me, you see, Mr Talliaferro. Isn't that nice?" She pressed Mr Talliaferro with recurrent happy astonishment.

Mr Talliaferro bowed again, came within an ace of dropping the bottle, darted the hand which held his hat and stick behind him to steady it. "Charming, charming," he agreed, perspiring under his hair.

"But, really, I am surprised to find you here at this hour. And I suppose you are as surprised to find us here, aren't you? But I have just found the most won-derful thing! Do look at it, Mr Talliaferro: I do so want your opinion." She extended to him a dull lead plaque from which in dim bas-relief of faded red and blue simpered a Madonna with an expression of infantile astonishment identical with that of Mrs Maurier, and a Child somehow smug and complacent looking as an old man. Mr Talliaferro, feeling the poised precariousness of the bottle, dared not release his hand. He bent over the extended object. "Do take it, so you can examine it under the light," its owner insisted. Mr Talliaferro perspired again mildly. The niece spoke suddenly:

"I'll hold your package."

She moved with young swiftness and before he could demur she had taken the bottle from his hand. "Ow," she exclaimed, almost dropping it herself, and her aunt gushed:

"Oh, you have discovered something also, haven't you? Now I've gone and shown you my treasure, and all the while you were concealing something much, much nicer." She waggled her hands to indicate dejection. "You will consider mine trash, I know you will," she went on with heavy assumed displeasure. "Oh, to be a man, so I could poke around in shops all day and really discover things! Do show us what you have, Mr Talliaferro."

"It's a bottle of milk," remarked the niece, examining Mr Talliaferro with interest.

Her aunt shrieked. Her breast heaved with repression, glinting her pins and beads. "A bottle of milk? Have you turned artist, too?"

For the first and last time in his life Mr Talliaferro wished a lady dead. But he was a gentleman: he only seethed inwardly. He laughed with abortive heartiness.

"An artist? You flatter me, dear lady. I'm afraid my soul does not aspire so high. I am content to be merely a—"

"Milkman," suggested the young female devil.

"—Maecenas alone. If I might so style myself."

Mrs Maurier sighed with disappointment and surprise. "Ah, Mr Talliaferro, I am dreadfully disappointed. I had hoped for a moment that some of your artist friends had at last prevailed on you to give something to the world of Art. No, no; don't say you cannot: I am sure you are capable of it, what with your—your delicacy of soul, your—" she waved her hand again vaguely toward the sky above Rampart Street. "Ah, to be a man, with no ties save those of the soul! To create, to create." She returned easily to Royal Street. "But, really, a bottle of milk, Mr Talliaferro?"

"Merely for my friend Gordon. I looked in on him this afternoon and found him quite busy. So I ran out to fetch him milk for his supper. These artists!" Mr Talliaferro shrugged. "You know how they live."

"Yes, indeed. Genius. A hard taskmaster, isn't it? Perhaps you are wise in not giving your life to it. It is a long lonely road. But how is Mr Gordon? I am so continually occupied with things—unavoidable duties, which my conscience will not permit me to evade (I am very conscientious, you know)—that I simply haven't the time to see as much of the Quarter as I should like. I had promised Mr Gordon faithfully to call, and to have him to dinner soon. I am sure he thinks I have forgotten him. Please make my peace with him, won't you? Assure him that I have not forgotten him."

"I am sure he realises how many calls you have on your time," Mr Talliaferro assured her gallantly. "Don't let that distress you at all."

"Yes, I really don't know how I get anything done: I am always surprised when I find I have a spare moment for my own pleasure." She turned her expression of happy astonishment on him again. The niece spun slowly and slimly on one high heel: the sweet young curve of her shanks straight and brittle as the legs of a bird and ending in the twin inky splashes of her slippers, entranced him. Her hat was a small brilliant bell about her face, and she wore her clothing with a casual rakishness, as though she had opened her wardrobe and said, Let's go downtown. Her aunt was saying:

"But what about our yachting party? You gave Mr Gordon my invitation?"

Mr Talliaferro was troubled. "Well—You see, he is quite busy now. He—He has a commission that will admit of no delay," he concluded with inspiration.

"Ah, Mr Talliaferro! You haven't told him he is invited. Shame on you! Then I must tell him myself, since you have failed me."

"No, really—"

She interrupted him. "Forgive me, dear Mr Talliaferro. I didn't mean to be unjust. I am glad you didn't invite him. It will be better for me to do it, so I can overcome any scruples he might have. He is quite shy, you know. Oh, quite, I assure you. Artistic temperament, you understand: so spiritual. . . ."

"Yes," agreed Mr Talliaferro, covertly watching the niece who had ceased her spinning and got her seemingly boneless body into an undimensional angular flatness pure as an Egyptian carving.

"So I shall attend to it myself. I shall call him to-night: we sail at noon to-morrow, you know. That will allow him sufficient time, don't you think? He's one of these artists who never have much, lucky people." Mrs Maurier looked at her watch. "Heavens above! seven-thirty. We must fly. Come, darling. Can't we drop you somewhere, Mr Talliaferro?"

"Thank you, no. I must take Gordon's milk to him, and then I am engaged for the evening."

"Ah, Mr Talliaferro! It's a woman, I know." She rolled her eyes roguishly. "What a terrible man you are." She lowered her voice and tapped him on the sleeve. "Do be careful what you say before this child. My instincts are all bohemian, but she . . . unsophisticated . . ." Her voice bathed him warmly and Mr Talliaferro bridled: had he had a moustache he would have stroked it. Mrs Maurier jangled and glittered again: her expression became one of pure delight. "But, of course! We will drive you to Mr Gordon's and then I can run in and invite him for the party. The very thing! How fortunate to have thought of it. Come, darling."

Without stooping the niece angled her leg upward and outward from the knee, scratching her ankle. Mr Talliaferro recalled the milk bottle and assented gratefully, falling in on the curbside with meticulous thoughtfulness. A short distance up the street Mrs Maurier's car squatted expensively. The negro driver descended and opened the door and Mr Talliaferro sank into gracious upholstery, nursing his milk bottle, smelling flowers cut and delicately vased, promising himself a car next year.

They rolled smoothly, passing between spaced lights and around narrow corners, while Mrs Maurier talked steadily of hers and Mr Talliaferro's and Gordon's souls. The niece sat quietly. Mr Talliaferro was conscious of the clean young odour of her, like that of young trees; and when they passed beneath lights he could see her slim shape and the impersonal revelation of her legs and her bare sexless knees. Mr Talliaferro luxuriated, clutching his bottle of milk, wishing the ride need not end. But the car drew up to the curb again, and he must get out, no matter with what reluctance.

"I'll run up and bring him down to you," he suggested with premonitory tact.

"No, no: let's all go up," Mrs Mauner objected. "I want Patricia to see how genius looks at home."

"Gee, Aunty, I've seen these dives before," the niece said. "They're everywhere. I'll wait for you." She jackknifed her body effortlessly, scratching her ankles with her brown hands.

"It's so interesting to see how they live, darling. You'll simply love it." Mr Talliaferro demurred again, but Mrs Maurier overrode him with sheer words. So against his better judgment he struck matches for them, leading the way up the dark tortuous stairs while their three shadows aped them, rising and falling monstrously upon the ancient wall. Long before they reached the final stage Mrs Maurier was puffing and panting, and Mr Talliaferro found a puerile vengeful glee in hearing her laboured breath. But he was a gentleman; he put this from him, rebuking himself. He knocked on a door, was bidden, opened it:

"Back, are you?" Gordon sat in his single chair, munching a thick sandwich, clutching a book. The unshaded light glared savagely upon his undershirt.

"You have callers," Mr Talliaferro offered his belated warning, but the other looking up had already seen beyond his shoulder Mrs Maurier's interested face. He rose and cursed Mr Talliaferro, who had begun immediately his unhappy explanation.

"Mrs Maurier insisted on dropping in—"

Mrs Maurier vanquished him anew. "Mister Gordon!" She sailed into the room, bearing her expression of happy astonishment like a round platter stood on edge. "How *do* you do? Can you ever, ever forgive us for intruding like this?" she went on in her gushing italics. "We just met Mr Talliaferro on the street with your milk, and we decided to brave the lion in his den. How do you do?" She forced her effusive hand upon him, staring about in happy curiosity. "So this is where genius labours. How charming: so—so original. And that"—she indicated a corner screened off by a draggled length of green rep—"is your bedroom, isn't it? How delightful! Ah, Mr Gordon, how I envy you this freedom. And a view—you have a view also, haven't you?" She held his hand and stared entranced at a high useless window framing two tired looking stars of the fourth magnitude.

"I would have if I were eight feet tall," he corrected. She looked at him quickly, happily. Mr Talliaferro laughed nervously.

"That would be delightful," she agreed readily. "I was so anxious to have my niece see a real studio, Mr Gordon, where a real artist works. Darling"—she glanced over her shoulder fatly, still holding his hand—"darling, let me present you to a real sculptor, one from whom we expect great things. . . . Darling," she repeated in a louder tone.

The niece, untroubled by the stairs, had drifted in after them and she now stood before the single marble. "Come and speak to Mr Gordon, darling." Beneath her aunt's saccharine modulation was a faint trace of something not so sweet after all. The niece turned her head and nodded slightly without looking at him. Gordon released his hand.

"Mr Talliaferro tells me you have a commission." Mrs Maurier's voice was again a happy astonished honey. "May we see it? I know artists don't like to exhibit an incomplete work, but just among friends, you see. . . . You both know how sensitive to beauty I am, though I have been denied the creative impulse myself."

"Yes," agreed Gordon, watching the niece.

"I have long intended visiting your studio, as I promised, you remember. So I shall take this opportunity of looking about—Do you mind?"

"Help yourself. Talliaferro can show you things. Pardon me." He lurched characteristically between them and Mrs Maurier chanted:

"Yes, indeed. Mr Talliaferro, like myself, is sensitive to the beautiful in Art. Ah, Mr Talliaferro, why were you and I given a love for the beautiful, yet denied the ability to create it from stone and wood and clay. . . ."

Her body in its brief simple dress was motionless when he came over to her. After a time he said:

"Like it?"

Her jaw in profile was heavy: there was something masculine about it. But in full face it was not heavy, only quiet. Her mouth was full and colourless, unpainted, and her eyes were opaque as smoke. She met his gaze, remarking the icy blueness of his eyes (like a surgeon's she thought) and looked at the marble again. "I don't know," she answered slowly. Then: "It's like me."

"How like you?" he asked gravely.

She didn't answer. Then she said: "Can I touch it?"

"If you like," he replied, examining the line of her jaw, her firm brief nose. She made no move and he added: "Aren't you going to touch it?"

"I've changed my mind," she told him calmly. Gordon glanced over his shoulder to where Mrs Maurier pored volubly over something. Mr Talliaferro yea'd her with restrained passion.

"Why is it like you?" he repeated.

She said irrelevantly: "Why hasn't she anything here?" Her brown hand flashed slimly across the high unemphasis of the marble's breast, and withdrew.

"You haven't much there yourself." She met his steady gaze steadily. "Why should it have anything there?" he asked.

"You're right," she agreed with the judicial complaisance of an equal. "I see now. Of course she shouldn't. I didn't quite—quite get it for a moment."

Gordon examined with growing interest her flat breast and belly, her boy's body which the poise of it and the thinness of her arms belied. Sexless, yet somehow vaguely troubling. Perhaps just young, like a calf or a colt. "How old are you?" he asked abruptly.

"Eighteen, if it's any of your business," she replied without rancour, staring at the marble. Suddenly she looked up at him again. "I wish I could have it," she said with sudden sincerity and longing, quite like a four-year-old.

"Thanks," he said. "That was quite sincere, too, wasn't it? Of course you can't have it, though. You see that, don't you?"

She was silent. He knew she could see no reason why she shouldn't have it.

"I guess so," she agreed at last. "I just thought I'd see, though."

"Not to overlook any bets?"

"Oh, well, by to-morrow I probably won't want it, anyway. . . . And if I still do, I can get something just as good."

"You mean," he amended, "that if you still want it to-morrow, you can get it. Don't you?"

Her hand, as if it were a separate organism, reached out slowly, stroking the marble. "Why are you so black?" she asked.

"Black?"

"Not your hair and beard. I like your red hair and beard. But you. You are black. I mean . . ." her voice fell and he suggested Soul? "I don't know what that is," she stated quietly.

"Neither do I. You might ask your aunt, though. She seems familiar with souls."

She glanced over her shoulder, showing him her other unequal profile. "Ask her yourself. Here she comes."

Mrs Maurier surged her scented upholstered bulk between them. "Wonderful, wonderful," she was exclaiming in sincere astonishment. "And this . . ." her voice died away and she gazed at the marble, dazed. Mr Talliaferro echoed her immaculately, taking to himself the showman's credit.

"Do you see what he has caught?" he bugled melodiously. "Do you see? The spirit of youth, of something fine and hard and clean in the world; something we all desire until our mouths are stopped with dust." Desire with Mr Talliaferro had long since become an unfulfilled habit requiring no longer any particular object at all.

"Yes," agreed Mrs Maurier. "How beautiful. What—what does it signify, Mr Gordon?"

"Nothing, Aunt Pat," the niece snapped. "It doesn't have to."

"But, really—"

"What do you want it to, signify? Suppose it signified a—a dog, or an ice cream soda, what difference would it make? Isn't it all right like it is?"

"Yes, indeed, Mrs Maurier," Mr Talliaferro agreed with soothing haste, "it is not necessary that it have objective significance. We must accept it for what it is: pure form untrammelled by any relation to a familiar or utilitarian object."

"Oh, yes: untrammelled." Here was a word Mrs. Maurier knew. "The untrammelled spirit, freedom like the eagle's."

"Shut up, Aunty," the niece told her. "Don't be a fool."

"But it has what Talliaferro calls objective significance," Gordon interrupted brutally. "This is my feminine ideal: a virgin with no legs to leave me, no arms to hold me, no head to talk to me."

"Mister Gordon!" Mrs Maurier stared at him over her compressed breast. Then she thought of something that did possess objective significance. "I had almost forgotten our reason for calling so late. Not," she added quickly, "that we needed any other reason to—to—Mr Talliaferro, how was it those old people used to put it, about pausing on Life's busy highroad to kneel for a moment at the Master's feet? . . ." Mrs Maurier's voice faded and her face assumed an expression of mild concern. "Or is it the Bible of which I am thinking? Well, no matter: we dropped in to invite you for a yachting party, a few days on the lake—"

"Yes. Talliaferro told me about it. Sorry, but I shall be unable to come."

Mrs Maurier's eyes became quite round. She turned to Mr. Talliaferro. "Mister Talliaferro! You told me you hadn't mentioned it to him!"

Mr Talliaferro writhed acutely. "Do forgive me, if I left you under that impression. It was quite unintentional. I only desired that you speak to him yourself and make him reconsider. The party will not be complete without him, will it?"

"Not at all. Really, Mr Gordon, won't you reconsider? Surely you won't disappoint us." She stooped creaking, and slapped at her ankle. "Pardon me."

"No. Sorry. I have work to do."

Mrs Maurier transferred her expression of astonishment and dejection to Mr Talliaferro. "It can't be that he doesn't want to come. There must be some other reason. Do say something to him, Mr Talliaferro. We simply must have him. Mr Fairchild is going, and Eva and Dorothy: we simply must have a sculptor. Do convince him, Mr Talliaferro."

"I'm sure his decision is not final: I am sure he will not deprive us of his company. A few days on the water will do him no end of good; freshen him up like a tonic. Eh, Gordon?"

Gordon's hawk's face brooded above them, remote and insufferable with arrogance. The niece had turned away, drifting slowly about the room, grave and quiet and curious, straight as a poplar. Mrs Maurier implored him with her eyes doglike, temporarily silent. Suddenly she had inspiration.

"Come, people, let's all go to my house for dinner. Then we can discuss it at our ease."

Mr Talliaferro demurred. "I am engaged this evening, you know," he reminded her.

"Oh, Mr Talliaferro." She put her hand on his sleeve. "Don't you fail me, too. I always depend on you when people fail me. Can't you defer your engagement?"

"Really, I am afraid not. Not in this case," Mr Talliaferro replied smugly. "Though I am distressed . . ."

Mrs Maurier sighed. "These women! Mr Talliaferro is perfectly terrible with women," she informed Gordon. "But you will come, won't you?"

The niece had drifted up to them and stood rubbing the calf of one leg against the other shin. Gordon turned to her. "Will you be there?"

Damn their little souls, she whispered on a sucked breath. She yawned. "Oh, yes. I eat, but I'm going to bed darn soon." She yawned again, patting the broad pale oval of her mouth with brown fingers.

"Patricia!" her aunt exclaimed in shocked amazement. "Of course you will do nothing of the kind. The very idea! Come, Mr Gordon."

"No, thanks. I am engaged myself," he answered stiffly. "Some other time, perhaps."

"I simply won't take No for an answer. Do help me, Mr Talliaferro. He simply must come."

"Do you want him to come as he is?" the niece asked.

Her aunt glanced briefly at the undershirt, and shuddered. But she said bravely: "Of course, if he wishes. What are clothes, compared with this?" she described an arc with her hand; diamonds glittered on its orbit. "So you cannot evade it, Mr Gordon. You must come."

Her hand poised above his arm, pouncing. He eluded it brusquely. "Excuse me." Mr Talliaferro avoided his sudden movement just in time, and the niece said wickedly:

"There's a shirt behind the door, if that's what you are looking for. You won't need a tie, with that beard."

He picked her up by the elbows, as you would a high narrow table, and set her aside. Then his tall controlled body filled and emptied the door and disappeared in the darkness of the hallway. The niece gazed after him. Mrs Maurier stared at the door, then to Mr Talliaferro in quiet amazement. "What in the world—" Her hands clashed vainly among her various festooned belongings. "Where is he going?" she said at last.

The niece said suddenly: "I like him." She too gazed at the door through which, passing, he seemed to have emptied the room. "I bet he doesn't come back," she remarked.

Her aunt shrieked. "Doesn't come back?"

"Well, I wouldn't if I were him." She returned to the marble, stroking it with slow desire. Mrs Maurier gazed helplessly at Mr Talliaferro.

"Where—" she began.

"I'll go see," he offered, breaking his own trance. The two women regarded his vanishing neat back.

"Never in my life—Patricia, what did you mean by being so rude to him? Of course he is offended. Don't you know how sensitive artists are? After I have worked so hard to cultivate him, too!"

"Nonsense. It'll do him good. He thinks just a little too well of himself as it is."

"But to insult the man in his own house. I can't understand you young people at all. Why, if I'd said a thing like that to a gentleman, and a stranger . . . I can't imagine what your father can mean, letting you grow up like this. He certainly knows better than this—"

"I'm not to blame for the way he acted. You are the one, yourself. Suppose you'd been sitting in your room in your shimmy, and a couple of men you hardly knew had walked in on you and tried to persuade you to go somewhere you didn't want to go, what would you have done?"

"These people are different," her aunt told her coldly. "You don't understand them. Artists don't require privacy as we do: it means nothing whatever to them. But anyone, artist or no, would object—"

"Oh, haul in your sheet," the niece interrupted coarsely. "You're jibbing."

Mr Talliaferro reappeared panting with delicate repression. "Gordon was called hurriedly away. He asked me to make his excuses and to express his disappointment over having to leave so unceremoniously."

"Then he's not coming to dinner." Mrs Maurier sighed, feeling her age, the imminence of dark and death. She seemed not only unable to get new men any more, but to hold to the old ones, even . . . Mr Talliaferro, too . . . age, age. . . . She sighed again. "Come, darling," she said in a strangely chastened tone, quieter, pitiable in a way. The niece put both her firm tanned hands on the marble, hard, hard. O beautiful, she whispered in salutation and farewell, turning quickly away.

"Let's go," she said, "I'm starving."

Mr Talliaferro had lost his box of matches: he was desolated. So they were forced to feel their way down the stairs, disturbing years and years of dust upon the rail. The stone corridor was cool and dank and filled with a suppressed minor humming. They hurried on.

Night was fully come and the car squatted at the curb in patient silhouette; the negro driver sat within with all the windows closed. Within its friendly familiarity Mrs Maurier's spirits rose again. She gave Mr Talliaferro her hand, sugaring her voice again with a decayed coquetry.

"You will call me, then? But don't promise: I know how completely your time is taken up"—she leaned forward, tapping him on the cheek—"Don Juan!"

He laughed deprecatingly, with pleasure. The niece from her corner said:

"Good evening, Mr Tarver."

Mr Talliaferro stood slightly inclined from the hips, frozen. He closed his eyes like a dog awaiting the fall of the stick, while time passed and passed . . . he opened his eyes again, after how long he knew not. But Mrs Maurier's fingers were but leaving his cheek and the niece was invisible in her corner: a bodiless evil. Then he straightened up, feeling his cold entrails resume their proper place.

The car drew away and he watched it, thinking of the girl's youngness, her hard clean youngness, with fear and a troubling unhappy desire like an old sorrow. Were children really like dogs? Could they penetrate one's concealment, know one instinctively?

Mrs Maurier settled back comfortably. "Mr Talliaferro is perfectly terrible with women," she informed her niece.

"I bet he is," the niece agreed, "perfectly terrible."

. . .

Handling his stick smartly he turned into Broussard's. As he had hoped, here was Dawson Fairchild, the novelist, resembling a benevolent walrus too recently out of bed to have made a toilet, dining in company with three men. Mr Talliaferro paused diffidently in the doorway and a rosy-cheeked waiter resembling a studious Harvard undergraduate in an actor's dinner coat, assailed him courteously. At last he caught Fairchild's eye and the other greeted him across the small room, then said something to his three companions that caused them to turn half about in their chairs to watch his approach. Mr Talliaferro, to whom entering a restaurant alone and securing a table was an excruciating process, joined them with relief. The cherubic waiter spun a chair from an adjoining table deftly against Mr Talliaferro's knees as he shook Fairchild's hand.

"You're just in time," Fairchild told him, propping his fist and a clutched fork on the table. "This is Mr Hooper. You know these other folks, I think."

Mr Talliaferro ducked his head to a man with iron gray hair and an orotund humourless face like that of a thwarted Sunday school superintendent, who insisted on shaking his hand, then his glance took in the other two members of the party—a tall, ghostly young man with a thin evaporation of fair hair and a pale prehensile mouth, and a bald Semitic man with a pasty loose jowled face and sad quizzical eyes.

"We were discussing—" began Fairchild when the stranger interrupted with a bland and utterly unselfconscious rudeness.

"What did you say the name was?" he asked, fixing Mr Talliaferro with his eye. Mr Talliaferro met the eye and knew immediately a faint unease. He answered the question, but the other brushed the reply aside. "I mean your given name. I didn't catch it to-day."

"Why, Ernest," Mr Talliaferro told him with alarm.

"Ah, yes: Ernest. You must pardon me, but travelling, meeting new faces each Tuesday, as I do—" he interrupted himself with the same bland unconsciousness. "What are your impressions of the get-together to-day?" Ere Mr Talliaferro could have replied, he interrupted himself again. "You have a splendid organisation here," he informed them generally, compelling them with his glance, "and a city that is worthy of it. Except for this southern laziness of yours. You folks need more northern blood, to bring out all your possibilities. Still, I won't criticise: you boys have treated me pretty well." He put some food into his mouth and chewed it down hurriedly, forestalling any one who might have hoped to speak.

"I was glad that my itinerary brought me here, to see the city and be with the boys to-day, and that one of your reporters gave me the chance to see something of your bohemian life by directing me to Mr Fairchild here, who, I understand, is an author." He met Mr Talliaferro's expression of courteous amazement again. "I am glad to see how you boys are carrying on the good work; I might say, the Master's work, for it is only by taking the Lord into our daily lives—" He stared at Mr Talliaferro once more. "What did you say the name was?"

"Ernest," suggested Fairchild mildly.

"—Ernest. People, the man in the street, the breadwinner, he on whom the heavy burden of life rests, does he know what we stand for, what we can give him in spite of himself—forgetfulness of the trials of day by day? He knows nothing of our ideals of service, of the benefits to ourselves, to each other, to you"—he met Fairchild's burly quizzical gaze—"to himself. And, by the way," he added coming to earth again, "there are a few points on this subject I am going to take up with your secretary to-morrow." He transfixed Mr Talliaferro again. "What were your impressions of my remarks to-day?"

"I beg pardon?"

"What did you think of my idea for getting a hundred percent church attendance by keeping them afraid they'd miss something good by staying away?"

Mr Talliaferro turned his stricken face to the others, one by one. After a while his interrogator said in a tone of cold displeasure: "You don't mean to say you do not recall me?"

Mr Talliaferro cringed. "Really, sir—I am distressed—" The other interrupted heavily.

"You were not at lunch to-day?"

"No," Mr Talliaferro replied with effusive gratitude, "I take only a glass of buttermilk at noon. I breakfast late, you see." The other man stared at him with chill displeasure, and Mr Talliaferro added with inspiration: "You have mistaken me for someone else, I fear."

The stranger regarded Mr Talliaferro for a cold moment. The waiter placed a dish before Mr Talliaferro and he fell upon it in a flurry of acute discomfort.

"Do you mean—" began the stranger. Then he put his fork down and turned his disapproval coldly upon Fairchild. "Didn't I understand you to say that this—gentleman was a member of Rotary?"

Mr Talliaferro suspended his fork and he too looked at Fairchild in shocked unbelief. "I a member of Rotary?" he repeated.

"Why, I kind of got the impression he was," Fairchild admitted. "Hadn't you heard that Talliaferro was a Rotarian?" he appealed to the others. They were noncommittal and he continued: "I seem to recall somebody telling me you were a Rotarian. But then, you know how rumours get around. Maybe it is because of your prominence in the business life of our city. Talliaferro is a member of one of our largest ladies' clothing houses," he explained. "He is just the man to help you figure out some way to get God into the mercantile business. Teach Him the meaning of service, hey, Talliaferro?"

"No: really, I—" Mr Talliaferro objected with alarm. The stranger interrupted again.

"Well, there's nothing better on God's green earth than Rotary. Mr Fairchild had given me to understand that you were a member," he accused with a recurrence of cold suspicion. Mr Talliaferro squirmed with unhappy negation. The other stared him down, then he took out his watch. "Well, well. I must run along. I run my day to schedule. You'd be astonished to learn how much time can be saved by cutting off a minute here and a minute there," he informed them. "And—"

"I beg pardon?"

"What do you do with them?" Fairchild asked.

"When you've cut off enough minutes here and there to make up a sizable mess, what do you do with them?"

"—Setting a time limit to everything you do makes a man get more punch into it; makes him take the hills on high, you might say." A drop of nicotine on the end of the tongue will kill a dog, Fairchild thought, chuckling to himself. He said aloud:

"Our forefathers reduced the process of gaining money to proverbs. But we have beaten them; we have reduced the whole of existence to fetiches."

"To words of one syllable that look well in large red type," the Semitic man corrected.

The stranger ignored them. He half turned in his chair. He gestured at the waiter's back, then he snapped his fingers until he had attracted the waiter's attention. "Trouble with these small second-rate places," he told them. "No pep, no efficiency, in handling trade. Check, please," he directed briskly. The cherubic waiter bent over them.

"You found the dinner nice?" he suggested.

"Sure, sure, all right. Bring the bill, will you, George?" The waiter looked at the others, hesitating.

"Never mind, Mr Broussard," Fairchild said quickly. "We won't go right now. Mr Hooper here has got to catch a train. You are my guest," he explained to the stranger. The other protested conventionally: he offered to match coins for it, but Fairchild repeated: "You are my guest to-night. Too bad you must hurry away."

"I haven't got the leisure you New Orleans fellows have," the other explained. "Got to keep on the jump, myself." He arose and shook hands all around. "Glad to've met you boys," he said to each in turn. He clasped Mr Talliaferro's elbow with his left hand while their rights were engaged. The waiter fetched his hat and he gave the man a half dollar with a flourish. "If you're ever in the little city"—he paused to reassure Fairchild.

"Sure, sure," Fairchild agreed heartily, and they sat down again. The late guest paused at the street door a moment, then he darted forth shouting, "Taxi! Taxi!" The cab took him to the Monteleone hotel, three blocks away, where he purchased two to-morrow's papers and sat in the lobby for an hour, dozing over them. Then he went to his room and lay in bed staring at them until he had harried his mind into unconsciousness by the sheer idiocy of print.

from *Fabulous New Orleans*

LYLE SAXON (1891–1946)

Lyle Saxon was born in Baton Rouge, Louisiana, where he attended Louisiana State University. He worked as a reporter in Chicago and in 1918 moved to New Orleans, where he was a feature writer for the *Item* and later for the *Times-Picayune*. He contributed stories and articles to several magazines, winning the O. Henry Award Prize in 1926. Within a three year period, Saxon wrote four books, *Father Mississippi* (1927), *Fabulous New Orleans* (1928), *Old Louisiana* (1929) and *Lafitte the Pirate* (1930), which Cecil B. DeMille made into a movie titled *The Buccaneer* (1938). He became known as "Mr. French Quarter" for his work restoring houses at 536 and 612 Royal Street, where he entertained writers including William Faulkner, Sherwood Anderson, and Edmund Wilson. Saxon is portrayed lying against a pillow and reading Strachly's *Emminent Victorians* by his neighbor William Spratling in *Sherwood Anderson and Other Famous Creoles*. For a time he resided at Melrose Plantation in Natchitoches and his only novel, *Children of Strangers* (1937), is set on a Cane River country plantation similar to Melrose. Saxon took an apartment at the St. Charles hotel during the 1930s and ran an informal literary salon there until 1944. As director of the Federal Writers' Projects in Louisiana, he edited *A Collection of Folk Tales: Gumbo Ya-Ya* (1945) with Edward Dreyer and Robert Tallant. In the following selection, "An Afternoon Walk," from *Fabulous New Orleans*, a series of descriptive impressions and stories, Saxon takes the reader on an afternoon stroll through the Vieux Carré, "because at that time the soft colors of evening will fall across the battered facades of the old houses and will treat them kindly."

Would you like to visit the old section of New Orleans unchaperoned by the usual guide? Do you care to wander at will along the quaint old streets of the Vieux Carré? If you do, you may get your hat and come along with me. We will start in the late afternoon, because at that time the soft colors of evening will fall across the battered facades of the old houses and will treat them kindly. They are like wrinkled faces, these old houses, and one must look upon them with the deference that youth should show to age. Some of the houses have outlived their usefulness, like so many of the old, and while you may look upon them as much as you please, you must look with friendly eyes. If you do not, you may come away with only the idea of dirt and squalor—and you may miss altogether that lingering charm which clings to these old mansions even in the last stages of their decay.

How shall we make this trip? Walk, of course. The Quarter is small, only ten squares from end to end and less than that distance from the river to Rampart Street. Why do they call it Vieux Carré? It means literally "old square," that is all, the old square which constituted the walled city of *Nouvelle Orléans*, when Americans such as you and I did not profane the streets. Are you ready? Very well, then we will start at once.

We will leave Canal Street at Royal, and turn from our present-day world into the past. Royal Street is the same as St. Charles, but the name changes when you have crossed Canal Street. Notice how narrow the street is. Notice how the balconies overhang the sidewalk. And by the way, we call the sidewalks *banquettes*—that's a Creole word. No, not French, just plain Creole. No, you won't find it in the French dictionary. It is a word that is particularly our own.

Modern needs are pushing the Quarter further and further from Canal Street. We will walk hastily along the street until we have passed the Monteleone Hotel, this large and gleaming hostelry on our right at the first corner. Oh, wait! Don't forget to look at the old Union Bank at Iberville and Royal streets. That is one of the oldest buildings here. If you will look up at the cornice, you can still see the raised lettering with the bank's name, but the lower portion of the structure has been changed beyond recognition. I remember the old columns which supported the roof. Only a few years ago they were taken away. There is a legend in New Orleans, and perhaps it is true, that the word "Dixie" came from this very spot. Before that building was occupied by the Union Bank it was occupied by an institution known as the Citizens Bank, which still exists to-day. There was a Louisiana bank-note, a "dix," issued by the old Citizens Bank. Money was plentiful in New Orleans then. Ten-dollar bills were easier to obtain than they are now. Strangers in New Orleans referred to the city as the "land of dixies." That was the American way of saying that money was plentiful in New Orleans. I have heard other explanations offered, but this one seems logical to me.

Well, let's be going. You can stop if you will and look into the windows of the antique shops. There are many beautiful things to be found here. It has always seemed to me that these shops are the most interesting and the most tragic things in the city. How tragic? Well, they contain the wreckage of old families—people who once had everything that their hearts desired. Where are these old families now? Lord, I don't know. Here are their most cherished possessions; you can buy them if you like. Can't you be satisfied with that?

What does "Creole" mean? No, of course not. I don't know why tourists always say that. The Creole is not of colored blood. Locally, the word means of French or Spanish descent, or of a mixed descent, French and Spanish. The Creole was the child of European parents born in a French or Spanish colony. The New Orleans Creole is our finest product. The women are lovely, and the men are brave. They have charming manners. They are exclusive; they are clannish; they keep to themselves. Can any one blame them? They have their own language, their own society, and their own customs. What language do they speak? They spoke, and they still speak, a pure French. The reason the word "Creole" has been so often misunderstood is because their slaves spoke a Creole dialect bearing about the same relation to pure French as our Southern negro talk bears to English purely spoken. Then, of course, there was the Acadian French—or the "Cajan" French— which is the language spoken in the outlying districts of Louisiana. Then, too, there is the "gumbo" French—that means simply French incorrectly spoken-a sort of patois.

Well here we are at Royal and Conti streets, three squares from Canal. Let us stop here for a moment in front of the Court House and I will point out the interesting houses from here. The Court House is new, of course, it was built in 1910 when a whole square of delightful old houses was destroyed in order to make room for it. But on the corner of Royal and Conti, the corner toward the river, is the old Hall of Mortgages. It was the Bank of Louisiana, built in 1812. Notice how interesting it is architecturally. Do you see its irregularities? The pilasters which support the cornice are not the same distance apart, and the pedestals at the top of the cornice are not placed above the pilasters, and even the urns on the pedestals are not placed in the center of the pedestals. Odd? Of course. But following the law of symmetry nevertheless. That's what gives these old houses their intense personality. Do you see what I mean? Look closely.

Now notice the iron scrollwork on the balconies of that antique shop on the opposite corner, the southwest corner. All hand-hammered wrought iron. It is very beautiful. They tell us it was all made in the workshops here, the old forges, hammered out by negro slaves. It is priceless to-day, and to duplicate it is a process so expensive that few are willing to undertake it.

Now look at the old mansion opposite on the southwest corner. It is always called "The Dome" on account of the vaulted ceiling inside. This was another bank building. Notice the monogram in the ironwork upon the balcony. The building is peculiarly typical of the residences of its day. Did "first families" live above shops? Yes, they did; some of them still do. The rooms upstairs are tremendous. They have most magnificent marble mantlepieces and crystal chandeliers. In the old days it was the custom for the banker's family to live above the bank, just as the lawyer's family lived above his law offices. There was a reason for this, of course. The city was so congested, so small, that space was at a premium. Of course, this was not always true. There were many houses which were only residences. But on the principal streets of the Vieux Carré you will find throughout this combination of business and dwelling houses.

From where we are standing we can see the Paul Morphy house at 417 Royal Street. Notice the round windows on the third floor. The Creole was fond of window decoration. This building was also a bank once and the banker's family lived above. Later the Morphy family lived there. They were prominent Creoles. Paul Morphy was the world's greatest chess player, he died in that house. They tell us that he used to play chess in the courtyard. And behind one of those round windows under the roof is a tiny room reached by a secret staircase. It was his study. Of course, it is not secret any longer; everybody knows about it now. Yes, you can go into the courtyard if you like. The court is one of the loveliest in the city. Look, do you see the magnolia trees growing there? In the spring they are filled with large white flowers heavy with perfume. One can lean from the balcony and pick them. A lovely place. Now it is known as the "Patio Royal." You may lunch there if you like.

Come, let's be going. We must continue down Royal Street. Just beyond the court house at the corner of Royal and St. Louis streets on this empty stretch of ground there once stood the old St. Louis Hotel, sometimes called the Hotel Royal. In its day it was the most fashionable hotel in the South. It was torn down in 1917, and a great pity it was, too. It should have been preserved, for it was a beautiful building. I remember so well how a group of us tried to save it from destruction and how we were laughed at for our pains. It was a fascinating old building with its winding stair, its magnificent dome, its frescoes; it was all so ornate, and such a complete outgrowth of its period. It was to the old St. Louis Hotel that the rich planters came when they shipped their cotton to New Orleans in the fall. It was here that magnificent balls were given, and in the great hall downstairs, that hall paved with black and white marble, stood the slave block where the negroes were sold at auction. It was the center of society once, but in time it was outmoded. The hotel lost money. For years it stood deserted. When John Galsworthy, the English writer, was in New Orleans, he wandered through the old building and met a white horse ambling through one of its corridors. This surprised him so that he wrote an essay about it. It is called "That Old Time Place."

At the corner of Chartres and St. Louis streets, just opposite the site of the St. Louis Hotel, stands the Napoleon house. It has a cupola. This was once the residence of Governor Girod. They tell us that the house was built for Napoleon, built and furnished for him. It is interesting to think what it might have meant to New Orleans had Napoleon been rescued from St. Helena and had come to spend his declining years here. The plot to rescue Napoleon was fostered by the young Creole bloods of the old New Orleans. They planned to send a light sailing vessel for him as he languished on St. Helena. Dominique You, one of Lafitte the Pirate's lieutenants, had been engaged to head the expedition, but on the eve of the sailing of the vessel, the news reached New Orleans that Napoleon was dead. It is a pretty story. One wonders how much truth there is in it. Governor Girod afterward occupied the house. All in all, it has had a peculiar history. It has been sold over and over again. For many years it was a tenement, filled with Italians and negroes. When Lord Dunsany visited New Orleans a few years ago, he stood looking up at the façade of the Napoleon house, watching the negro children who played in and out of the old doors, looking upon the lines of drying clothes which stretched from the windows, and he said to the man who was walking with him, "What a strange, wonderful doom." The whole French Quarter, he said, was as fantastic as though he had invented it himself.

As we continue down Royal Street, we find just next door to the site of the St. Louis Hotel a very beautiful old house. It is now known as "The Arts and Crafts Club," and its courtyard is as charming as any in New Orleans. You may go in if you like, the courtyard gate is always open. If you are interested in exhibitions of paintings, there will be something for you to see in the studio beyond the court. Once this was the house of Brulatour, the richest wine merchant in New Orleans. His shop was on the ground floor. His family lived at the top of the house, and in the *entresol*, that half story between the main floors of the house; he kept his casks of wine. On damp days, if you climb to the *entresol* you can still smell the faint vinegary odor left behind. You will notice that this house is more Spanish than French. It was built by Spanish architects shortly after the fire of 1788. Notice the large slave quarters at the rear of the building. And notice on the south side the open terrace of the roof. There is much charming detail in the old Brulatour house. The winding wooden staircase ascending under archways of masonry, the overhanging balconies, the batten shutters, all this is very typical of the houses of the old régime.

As you proceed down Royal Street, you will find that you have reached the heart of the Vieux Carré. Here you find overhanging balconies across the second floors of the houses and small individual balconies before the windows on the third floor. It is quite easy to imagine the Creole beauties leaning out looking down, waving a scarf to a suitor, perhaps. The old house at the southwest corner of Royal and Toulouse streets is particularly interesting. It has an Egyptian design on the pilasters supporting the roof. That was the influence of Napoleon's visit to Egypt. Egyptian fashions were popular in all of Europe then. It seems odd, doesn't it, that because Napoleon went to Egypt there should be Egyptian designs in the French Quarter of New Orleans? That is the reason, nevertheless. The entrance to this old mansion is on Toulouse Street, just around the corner. Two stone lions guard the gateway. It is a rooming-house now, and a second-hand furniture shop occupies the ground floor, but once this was the very center of fashion in the old New Orleans.

Toulouse Street was the street of banks and cotton brokers. It was the Wall Street of the old New Orleans. At 628 Toulouse, in the square between Royal and Chartres, is the house occupied by Claiborne, the first American governor. It is filled with artists' studios now.

The house at 612 Royal Street, sometimes called the Court of the Palm, is typical of the fine old residences. The courtyard is particularly lovely, with a gigantic palm-tree rising in the center, a palm-tree which shades the entire court with its wide leaves. Opposite, at 613 Royal Street, is one of the most famous courtyards. Yes, this is the one you see on post-cards. It is quite typical. Once there was a formal garden here with an old iron fountain and conventional flower beds. If you will go far back into the court and look at the house you will notice its beautiful irregularities. Heavy fan-shaped windows which swing some in and some out, a large slave wing, once said to house thirty-seven servants. This is called the "Court of the Two Sisters." The house has no particular history, but it was on this spot that de Vaudreuil's house stood—he was the Grand Marquis of the early settlers. The house that he occupied was destroyed in the fire of 1788. This house dates from about 1800.

Some of the old New Orleans families still live in the square of Royal Street between Toulouse and St. Peter streets. One family has occupied the same house for more than ninety years. The fine old residence at 624 Royal Street was built by Dr. Isidore Labatut in 1831. His descendants still live there. The lower floor was formerly occupied by the office of Justice Bermudez, a distinguished jurist, and it was here that Edward Douglas White received his early law training.

Just opposite the quaint two-story dwelling at 629 Royal Street was the home of Adelina Patti, the opera singer, on the year of her memorable début at the French Opera. The young Creoles of that day used to promenade before her window to try to catch a glimpse of her or to hear her practise for her nightly performance.

At the end of the next square you will find a small garden just back of the Cathedral. This is called St. Anthony's Close, where duels were fought in the old days. Orleans Street begins here, and standing at the corner of Royal and Orleans Street you can see the old Orleans Theater and Ball Room, the scene of the notorious quadroon balls. It is a convent of negro nuns now, called the Convent of the Holy Family. You may go in if you like. The colored nuns will show you through if they are not too busy and if you will leave a small offering for the negro children. Be sure and notice the old houses which flank St. Anthony's Garden. They are most interesting. Walk through the alley beside the Cathedral and you will emerge at Jackson Square, the Place d'Armes. This is the very center of social life in old New Orleans. From the center of the square. you can see the Cabildo, the Cathedral, the Presbytery, and the two Pontalba buildings.

The Cabildo now is the state museum, and it is open to the public. If you are interested in the old New Orleans, take an hour and wander through. In there are enough relics to enable you to reconstruct the whole life of the Creoles. The paintings of the types existing in wartimes and before are particularly interesting. Notice the beauty of the women; notice the poetic expression of the young men. You do not see faces like these nowadays; our commercial spirit has killed the poetry in young men's faces. There are many other things to be seen here. Relics of the Indian days, old furniture, old jewelry, glass, and even the death mask of Napoleon. The Cabildo was erected in 1795 and was the scene of the transfer of Louisiana from France to the United States in 1803. Later it was the city hall. Here Lafayette was housed when he visited New Orleans in 1825.

The St. Louis Cathedral stands where the first church of New Orleans stood. The present building was erected by Don Almonaster y Roxas and presented to his fellow Catholics in 1794. The building flanking the Cathedral on the other side is the Presbytery. It is almost identically like the Cabildo. Once a Capuchin monastery, later the Civil District Court, it is now a museum.

Now a word about the Square itself. This is the Place d'Armes laid out, by Bienville, founder of New Orleans, in 1718. The French and the Spanish flag flew here, and the American flag was unfurled in 1803 to mark the possession of the United States after the transfer of Louisiana from France. It was in this square that the executions took place in the old days. It was here that the celebrations were held. It was here that General Jackson was acclaimed after his victory at the Battle of New Orleans. A statue of General Jackson, designed by Clark Mills, stands in the center of the square—General Jackson on his rearing horse, his hat raised in salute.

To the north and south of the square you will see the Pontalba buildings which occupy the entire block on St. Peter and St. Ann streets. They were built by Micaela, the daughter of Don Almonaster. Micaela was the Baroness Pontalba. You can see the Almonaster-Pontalba monogram in hundreds of places, interwoven in the ironwork. At one time these houses were filled with the most aristocratic families of the old city. Many famous guests have been entertained here. Jenny Lind, the Swedish Nightingale, and her manager P. T. Barnum; Adelina Patti, the opera singer, Fannie Kemble, the dancer, and Lola Montez, "The Uncrowned Queen of Bavaria," who flashed like a comet through Creole New Orleans, leaving a string of duels in her wake.

The old New Orleans is a city of intense personality. Time and decay have not killed its pristine charm. The old houses to-day are as full of beauty as they were in their prime. Architecturally they are tremendously interesting. My advice to you is to stay for a while in the old section of the city, sit for a time in Jackson Square and let the old world charm you. Give the atmosphere a chance to lull you. Take your time and wander slowly; look twice at the old houses, they are worth it. Talk to the beggars in the street; talk to any one you chance to meet. The natives of the Quarter are pleasant people and they will gladly tell you anything they happen to know. Those who live in the Quarter live there because they like it. They are proud of the old houses; they like your admiration and your interest. Go where you will; do what you please, you will not be molested nor will you be annoyed. Take your time and wander through, and then if you have a heart in you, you will want to return, for in the Vieux Carré of New Orleans, and in the Vieux Carré alone, you will find that lingering charm of the Old World, that remnant of a bygone culture which is unique in America.

from *Mules and Men*

ZORA NEALE HURSTON (1891–1960)

Zora Neale Hurston was born in Notasulga, Alabama and grew up in Eatonville, Florida, the nations' first all-black incorporated township. She left home soon after her mother's death in 1904 and little is known of her vagabond existence until her entry into a Baltimore, Maryland high school in 1917. Graduating in 1918, she then enrolled in Howard University, where she studied intermittently for the next four years. In 1921 her first short story was published in *Stylus*, the campus literary magazine. After winning second place in a short story contest sponsored by *Opportunity* in 1925, Hurston moved to New York. She established herself as a dominant personality in the Harlem Renaissance, making friends with fellow writers including Langston Hughes and Arna Bontemps. From 1925 to 1927 she studied anthropology with noted scholar Franz Boas at Barnard College. Boas encouraged her to collect folklore on African American culture, and with the financial backing of a patron, Hurston conducted fieldwork throughout the South from 1928 to 1932. After a query from publisher J. B. Lippincott, she wrote her first novel, *Jonah's Gourd Vine* (1934), and that led to the publication of her folklore field notes as *Mules and Men* (1935), the first such study by an African American. Hurston's other works include an autobiography, *Dust Tracks on a Road* (1942), the novel, *Their Eyes Were Watching God* (1937), and numerous essays, plays, and stories. She died in poverty and obscurity, but today is considered one of the seminal writers of the twentieth century. In the following selection from the "Hoodoo" section of *Mules and Men*, Hurston describes her study of hoodoo in 1928 under the tutelage of Luke Turner, the purported nephew of Marie Laveau,"the queen of conjure" in New Orleans, which Hurston viewed as the "hoodoo capital of America."

Now I was in New Orleans and I asked. They told me Algiers, the part of New Orleans that is across the river to the west. I went there and lived for four months and asked. I found women reading cards and doing mail order business in names and insinuations of well known factors in conjure. Nothing worth putting on paper. But they all claimed some knowledge and link with Marie Leveau. From so much of hearing the name I asked everywhere for this Leveau and everybody told me differently. But from what they said I was eager to know to the end of the talk. It carried me back across the river into the Vieux Carré. All agreed that she had lived and died in the French quarter of New Orleans. So I went there to ask.

I found an oil painting of the queen of conjure on the walls of the Cabildo, and mention of her in the guide books of New Orleans, but I did a lot of stumbling and asking before I heard of Luke Turner, himself a hoodoo doctor, who says that he is her nephew.

When I found out about Turner, I had already studied under five two-headed doctors and had gone thru an initiation ceremony with each. So I asked Turner to take me as a pupil. He was very cold. In fact he showed no eagerness even to talk with me. He feels sure of his powers and seeks no one. He refused to take me as a pupil and in addition to his habitual indifference I could see he had no faith in my sincerity. I could see him searching my face for whatever was behind what I said. The City of New Orleans has a law against fortune tellers, hoodoo doctors and the like, and Turner did not know me. He asked me to excuse him as he was waiting upon someone in the inner room. I let him go but I sat right there and waited. When he returned, he tried to shoo me away by being rude. I stayed on. Finally he named an impossible price for tuition. I stayed and dickered. He all but threw me out, but I stayed and urged him.

I made three more trips before he would talk to me in any way that I could feel encouraged. He talked about Marie Leveau because I asked. I wanted to know if she was really as great as they told me. So he enlightened my ignorance and taught me. We sat before the soft coal fire in his grate.

"Time went around pointing out what God had already made. Moses had seen the Burning Bush. Solomon by magic knowed all wisdom. And Marie Leveau was a woman in New Orleans.

"She was born February 2, 1827. Anybody don't believe I tell the truth can go look at the book in St. Louis Cathedral. Her mama and her papa, they wasn't married and his name was Christophe Glapion.

"She was very pretty, one of the Creole Quadroons and many people said she would never be a hoodoo doctor like her mama and her grandma before her. She liked to go to the balls very much where all the young men fell in love with her. But Alexander, the great two-headed doctor felt the power in her and so he tell her she must come to study with him. Marie, she rather dance and make love, but one day a rattlesnake come to her in her bedroom and spoke to her. So she went to Alexander and studied. But soon she could teach her teacher and the snake stayed with her always.

"She has her house on St. Anne Street and people come from the ends of America to get help from her. Even Queen Victona ask her help and send her a cashmere shawl with money also.

"Now, some white people say she hold hoodoo dance on Congo Square every week. But Marie Leveau never hold no hoodoo dance. That was a pleasure dance. They beat the drum with the shin bone of a donkey and everybody dance like they do in Hayti. Hoodoo is private. She give the dance the first Friday night in each month and they have crab gumbo and rice to eat and the people dance. The white people come look on, and think they see all, when they only see a dance.

"The police hear so much about Marie Leveau that they come to her house in St. Anne Street to put her in jail. First one come, she stretch out her left hand and he turn round and round and never stop until some one come lead him away. Then two come together—she put them to running and barking like dogs. Four come and she put them to beating each other with night sticks. The whole station force come. They knock at her door. She know who they are before she ever look. She did work at her altar and they all went to sleep on her steps.

"Out on Lake Pontchartrain at Bayou St. John she hold a great feast every year on the Eve of St. John's, June 24th. It is

Midsummer Eve, and the Sun give special benefits then and need great honor. The special drum be played then. It is a cowhide stretched over a half-barrel. Beat with a jaw-bone. Some say a man but I think they do not know. I think the jawbone of an ass or a cow. She hold the feast of St. John's partly because she is a Catholic and partly because of hoodoo.

"The ones around her altar fix everything for the feast. Nobody see Marie Leveau for nine days before the feast. But when the great crowd of people at the feast call upon her, she would rise out of the waters of the lake with a great communion candle burning upon her head and another in each one of her hands. She walked upon the waters to the shore. As a little boy I saw her myself when the feast was over, she went back into the lake, and nobody saw her for nine days again.

"On the feast that I saw her open the waters, she looked hard at me and nodded her head so that her tignon shook. Then I knew I was called to take up her work. She was very old and I was a lad of seventeen. Soon I went to wait upon her Altar, both on St. Anne Street and her house on Bayou St. John's.

"The rattlesnake that had come to her a little one when she was also young was very huge. He piled great upon his altar and took nothing from the food set before him. One night he sang and Marie Leveau called me from my sleep to look at him and see. 'Look well, Turner,' she told me. 'No one shall hear and see such as this for many centuries.'

"She went to her Great Altar and made great ceremony. The snake finished his song and seemed to sleep. She drove me back to my bed and went again to her Altar.

"The next morning, the great snake was not at his altar. His hide was before the Great Altar stuffed with spices and things of power. Never did I know what become of his flesh. It is said that the snake went off to the woods alone after the death of Marie Leveau, but they don't know. This is his skin that I wear about mv shoulders whenever I reach for power.

"Three days Marie, she set at the Altar with the great sun candle burning and shining in her face. She set the water upon the

Altar and turned to the window, and looked upon the lake. The sky grew dark. The lightning raced to the seventeen quarters of the heavens and the lake heaved like a mighty herd of cattle rolling in a pasture. The house shook with the earth.

"She told me, 'You are afraid. That is right, you should fear. Go to your own house and build an altar. Power will come.' So I hurried to my mother's house and told them.

"Some who loved her hurried out to Bayou St. John and tried to enter the house but she try hard to send them off. They beat upon the door, but she will not open. The terrible strong wind at last tore the house away and set it in the lake. The thunder and lightning grow greater. Then the loving ones find a boat and went out to where her house floats on one side and break a window to bring her out, but she begs, 'NO! Please, no,' she tell them. 'I want to die here in the lake,' but they would not permit her. She did not wish their destruction, so she let herself be drawn away from her altar in the lake. And the wind, the thunder and lightning, and the water all ceased the moment she set foot on dry land.

"That night she also sing a song and is dead, yes. So I have the snake skin and do works with the power she leave me."

. . .

I studied under Turner five months and learned all of the Leveau routines; but in this book all of the works of any doctor cannot be given. However, we performed several of Turner's own routines.

Once a woman, an excited, angry woman wanted something done to keep her husband true. So she came and paid Turner gladly for his services.

Turner took a piece of string that had been "treated" at the altar and gave it to the woman.

"Measure the man where I tell you. But he must never know. Measure him in his sleep then fetch back the string to me."

The next day the woman came at ten o'clock instead of nine as Turner had told her, so he made her wait until twelve o'clock, that being a good hour. Twelve is one of the benign hours of the day while ten is a malignant hour. Then Turner took the string and tied nine knots in it and tied it to a larger piece of string which he tied about her waist. She was completely undressed for the ceremony and Turner cut some hair from under her left armpit and some from the right side of the groin and put it together. Then he cut some from the right armpit and a tuft from the left groin and it was all placed on the altar, and burned in a votive light with the wish for her husband to love her and forget all others. She went away quite happy. She was so satisfied with the work that she returned with a friend a few days later.

Turner, with this toothless mouth, his Berber-looking face, said to the new caller:

"I can see you got trouble." He shivered. "It is all in the room. I feel the pain of it; Anger, Malice. Tell me who is this man you so fight with?"

"My husband's brother. He hate me and make all the trouble he can," the woman said in a tone so even and dull that it was hard to believe she meant what she said. "He must leave this town or die. Yes, it is much better if he is dead." Then she burst out, "Yeah, he should be dead long time ago. Long before he spy upon me, before he tell lies, lies, lies. I should be very happy for his funeral."

"Oh I can feel the great hate around you," Turner said. "It follow you everywhere, but I kill nobody, I send him away if you want so he never come back. I put guards along the road in the spirit world, and these he cannot pass, no. When he go, never will he come back to New Orleans. You see him no more. He will be forgotten and all his works."

"Then I am satisfied, yes," the woman said. When will vou send him off?"

"I ask the spirit, you will know."

She paid him and he sent her off and Turner went to his snake altar and sat in silence for a long time. When he arose, he sent me out to buy nine black chickens, and some Four Thieves Vinegar. He himself went out and got nine small sticks upon which he had me write the troublesome brother-in-law's name—one time on each stick. At ten that night we went out into the small interior court so prevalent in New Orleans and drove nine stakes into the ground. The left leg of a chicken was tied to each stake. Then a fire was built with the nine sticks on which the name had been written. The ground was sprinkled all over with the Four Thieves Vinegar and Turner began his dance. From the fire to the circle of fluttering chickens and back again to the fire. The feathers were picked from the heads of the chickens in the frenzy of the dance and scattered to the four winds. He called the victim's name each time as he whirled three times with the chicken's head-feathers in his hand, then he flung them far.

The terrified chickens flopped and fluttered frantically in the dim firelight. I had been told to keep up the chant of the victim's name in rhythm and to beat the ground with a stick. This I did with fervor and Turner danced on. One by one the chickens were seized and killed by having their heads pulled off. But Turner was in such a condition with his whirling and dancing that he seemed in a hypnotic state. When the last fowl was dead, Turner drank a great draught of wine and sank before the altar. When he arose, we gathered some ashes from the fire and sprinkled the bodies of the dead chickens and I was told to get out the car. We drove out one of the main highways for a mile and threw one of the chickens away. Then another mile and another chicken until the nine dead chickens had been disposed of. The spirits of the dead chickens had been instructed never to let the trouble-maker pass inward to New Orleans again after he had passed them going out.

One day Turner told me that he had taught me all that he could and he was quite satisfied with me. He wanted me to stay and work with him as a partner. He said that soon I would be in possession of the entire business, for the spirit had spoken to him and told him that I was the last doctor that he would make; that one year and seventy-nine days from then he would die. He wanted me to stay with him to the end. It has been a great sorrow to me that I could not say yes.

"New Orleans (1946)"

TRUMAN CAPOTE (1924–1984)

Truman Capote was born Truman Strekfus Persons in the Touro Infirmary in New Orleans, where his parents were living in a suite in the Monteleone Hotel. He was one of the most famous Southern authors of the twentieth century and achieved celebrity status after the film adaptations of several of his books, including *A Christmas Memory* (1956), *Breakfast at Tiffany's* (1958), and *In Cold Blood* (1966). His father, Archibald Persons, named his son Strekfus after the New Orleans family that employed him for their Streckfus company's fleet of Mississippi excursion boats. His parents divorced when he was four, and left him in the care of elderly cousins in Monroeville, Alabama. By the age of ten, he had decided to become a professional writer, and after his mother's marriage to Joseph Capote, he joined her in New York and took the name of his step-father. In 1945 Capote rented a room, "noisy as a steel mill," at 711 Royal Street where he wrote and painted quick studies which he tried to sell to tourists in Jackson Square. Capote looked back on his months in the French Quarter as "the freest time of my life." He was invited to the writers' colony, Yaddo, in 1946 and worked on his first novel, *Other Voices, Other Rooms* (1948). Upon completion of his time at Yaddo, he returned to New Orleans to write a travel article about the city for *Harper's Bazaar*. Capote reported that he and Henri Cartier Bresson, photographer for *Bazaar*, marched "miles every day in the New Orleans tropical heat." The result of that visit is the impressionistic "New Orleans (1946)," which later appeared in Capote's essay collection, *Local Color* (1950).

In the courtyard there was an angel of black stone, and its angel head rose above giant elephant leaves; the stark glass angel eyes, bright as the bleached blue of sailor eyes, stared upward. One observed the angel from an intricate green balcony—mine, this balcony, for I lived beyond in three old white rooms, rooms with elaborate wedding-cake ceilings, wide sliding doors, tall French windows. On warm evenings, with these windows open, conversation was pleasant there, tuneful, for wind rustled the interior like fan-breeze made by ancient ladies. And on such warm evenings the town is quiet. Only voices: family talk weaving on an ivy-curtained porch; a barefoot woman humming as she rocks a sidewalk chair, lulling to sleep a baby she nurses quite publicly; the complaining foreign tongue of an irritated lady who, sitting on her balcony, plucks a fryer, the loosened feathers floating from her hands, slipping into air, sliding lazily downward.

One morning—it was December, I think, a cold Sunday with a sad gray sun—I went up through the Quarter to the old market, where at that time of year there are exquisite winter fruits, sweet satsumas, twenty cents a dozen, and winter flowers, Christmas poinsettia and snow japonica. New Orleans streets have long, lonesome perspectives; in empty hours their atmosphere is like Chirico, and things innocent, ordinarily (a face behind the slanted light of shutters, nuns moving in the distance, a fat dark arm lolling lopsidedly out some window, a lonely black boy squatting in an alley, blowing soap bubbles and watching sadly as they rise to burst), acquire qualities of violence. Now, on that morning, I stopped still in the middle of a block, for I'd caught out of the corner of my eye a tunnel-passage, an overgrown courtyard. A crazy-looking white hound stood stiffly in the green fern light shining at the tunnel's end, and compulsively I went toward it. Inside there was a fountain; water spilled delicately from a monkey-statue's bronze mouth and made on pool pebbles desolate bell-like sounds. He was hanging from a willow, a bandit-faced man with kinky platinum hair; he hung so limply, like the willow itself. There was terror in that silent suffocated garden. Closed windows looked on blindly; snail tracks glittered silver on elephant ears, nothing moved except his shadow. It swung a little, back and forth, yet there was no wind. A rhinestone ring he wore winked in the sun, and on his arm was tattooed a name, "Francy." The hound lowered its head to drink in the fountain, and I ran. Francy—was it for her he'd killed himself? I do not know. N.O. is a secret place.

My rock angel's glass eyes were like sundials, for they told, by the amount of light focused on them, time: white at noon, they grew gradually dimmer, dark at dusk, black—nightfall eyes in a nightfall head.

The torn lips of golden-haired girls leer luridly on faded leaning house fronts: Drink Dr. Nutt, Dr. Pepper, NEHI, Grapeade, 7-Up, Koke, Coca-Cola. N.O., like every Southern town, is a city of soft-drink signs; the streets of forlorn neighborhoods are paved with Coca-Cola caps, and after rain, they glint in the dust like lost dimes. Posters peel away, lie mangled until storm wind blows them along the street, like desert sage—and there are those who think them beautiful; there are those who paper their walls with Dr. Nutt and Dr. Pepper, with Coca-Cola beauties who, smiling above tenement beds, are night guardians and saints of the morning. Signs everywhere, chalked, printed, painted: Madame Ortega-Readings, Love-potions, Magic Literature, C Me; If You Haven't Anything To Do . . . Don't Do It Here; Are You Ready To Meet Your Maker?; B Ware, Bad Dog; Pity The Poor Little Orphans; I Am A Deaf & Dumb Widow With 2 Mouths To Feed; Attention; Blue Wing Singers At Our Church Tonight (signed) The Reverend.

There was once this notice on a door in the Irish Channel district, "Come In And See Where Jesus Stood."

"And so?" said a woman who answered when I rang the bell. "I'd like to see where Jesus stood," I told her, and for a moment she looked blank; her face, cut in razorlike lines, was marshmallow-white; she had no eyebrows, no lashes, and she wore a calico kimono. "You too little, honey," she said, a jerky laugh bouncing her breasts, "you too damn little for to see where Jesus stood."

In my neighborhood there was a certain café no fun whatever, for it was the emptiest café around N.O., a regular funeral place. The proprietress, Mrs. Morris Otto Kunze, did not, however, seem to mind; she sat all day behind her bar, cooling herself with a palmetto fan, and seldom stirred except to swat flies. Now glued over an old cracked mirror backing the bar were seven little signs all alike: Don't Worry About Life ... You'll Never Get Out Of It Alive.

July 3. An "at home" card last week from Miss Y., so I made a call this afternoon. She is delightful in her archaic way, amusing, too, though not by intent. The first time we met, I thought: Edna May Oliver; and there is a resemblance most certainly. Miss Y. speaks in premediated tones but what she says is haphazard, and her sherry-colored eyes are forever searching the surroundings. Her posture is military, and she carries a man's Malacca cane, one of her legs being shorter than the other, a condition which gives her walk a penguinlike lilt. "It made me unhappy when I was your age; yes, I must say it did, for Papa had to squire me to all the balls, and there we sat on such pretty little gold chairs, and there we sat. None of the gentlemen ever asked Miss Y. to dance, indeed no, though a young man from Baltimore, a Mr. Jones, came here one winter, and gracious!-poor Mr. Jones—fell off a ladder, you know—broke his neck—died instantly."

My interest in Miss Y. is rather clinical, and I am not, I embarrassedly confess, quite the friend she believes, for one cannot feel close to Miss Y.: she is too much a fairy tale, someone real—and improbable. She is like the piano in her parlor—elegant, but a little out of tune. Her house, old even for N.O., is guarded by a black broken iron fence; it is a poor neighborhood she lives in, one sprayed with room-for-rent signs, gasoline stations, jukebox cafes. And yet, in the days when her family first lived here—that, of course, was long ago—there was in all N.O. no finer place. The house, smothered by slanting trees, has a graying exterior; but inside, the fantasy of Miss Y.'s heritage is everywhere visible: the tapping of her cane as she descends birdwing stairs trembles crystal; her face, a heart of wrinkled silk, reflects fumelike on ceiling-high mirrors; she lowers herself (notice, as this happens, how carefully she preserves the comfort of her bones) into father's father's father's chair, a wickedly severe receptacle with lion-head hand-rests. She is beautiful here in the cool dark of her house, and safe. These are the walls, the fence, the furniture of her childhood. "Some people are born to be old; I, for instance, was an atrocious child lacking any quality whatever. But I like being old. It makes me feel somehow more"—she paused, indicated with a gesture the dim parlor—"more suitable."

Miss Y. does not believe in the world beyond N.O.; at times her insularity results, as it did today, in rather chilling remarks. I had mentioned a recent trip to New York, whereupon she, arching an eyebrow, replied gently, "Oh? And how *are* things in the country?"

1. Why is it, I wonder, that all N.O. cab drivers sound as though they were imported from Brooklyn?

2. One hears so much about food here, and it is probably true that such restaurants as Arnaud's and Kolb's are the best in America. There is an attractive, lazy atmosphere about these restaurants: the slow-wheeling fans, the enormous tables and lack of crowding, the silence, the casual but expert waiters who all look as though they were sons of the management. A friend of mine, discussing N.O. and New York, once pointed out that comparable meals in the East, aside from being considerably more expensive, would arrive elaborate with some chef's mannerisms, with all kinds of froufrou and false accessories. Like most good things, the quality of N.O. cookery derived, he thought, from its essential simplicity.

3. I am more or less disgusted by that persistent phrase "old charm." You will find it, I suppose, in the architecture here, and in the antique shops (where it rightly belongs), or in the minglings of dialect one hears around the French Market. But N.O. is no more charming than any other Southern city—less so, in fact, for it is the largest. The main portion of this city is made up of spiritual bottomland, streets and sections rather outside the tourist belt.

(From a letter to R. R.) There are new people in the apartment below, the third tenants in the last year; a transient place, this

Quarter, hello and good-bye. A real bona-fide scoundrel lived there when I first came. He was unscrupulous, unclean and crooked—a kind of dissipated satyr. Mr. Buddy, the one-man band. More than likely you have seen him—not here of course, but in some other city, for he keeps on the move, he and his old banjo, drum, harmonica. I used to come across him banging away on various street corners, a gang of loafers gathered round. Realizing he was my neighbor, these meetings always gave me rather a turn. Now, to tell the truth, he was not a bad musician—an extraordinary one, in fact, when, late of an afternoon, and for his own pleasure, he sang to his guitar, sang ghostly ballads in a grieving whiskey voice: how terrible it was for those in love.

"Hey, boy, you! You up there..." I was *you*, for he never knew my name, and never showed much interest in finding it out. "Come on down and help me kill a couple."

His balcony, smaller than mine, was screened with sweet-smelling wisteria; as there was no furniture to speak of, we would sit on the floor in the green shade, drinking a brand of gin close kin to rubbing alcohol, and he would finger his guitar, its steady plaintive whine emphasizing the deep roll of his voice. "Been all over, been in and out, all around; sixty-five, and any woman takes up with me ain't got no use for nobody else; yessir, had myself a lota wives and a lota kids, but christamighty if I know what come of any of 'em—and don't give a hoot in hell—'cept maybe about Rhonda Kay. There was a woman, man, sweet as swamp honey, and was she hot on me! On fire all the time, and her married to a Baptist preacher, too, and her got four kids—five, countin' mine. Always kinda wondered what it was—boy or girl—boy, I spec. I always give 'em boys... Now that's all a long time ago, and it happened in Memphis, Tennessee. Yessir, been everywhere, been to the penitentiary, been in big fine houses like the Rockefellers' houses, been in and out, been all around."

And he could carry on this way until moonrise, his voice growing froggy, his words locking together to make a chant.

His face, stained and wrinkled, had a certain deceptive kindness, a childish twinkle, but his eyes slanted in an Oriental manner, and he kept his fingernails long, knife-sharp and polished as a Chinaman's. "Good for scratching, and handy in a fight, too."

He always wore a kind of costume: black trousers, engine-red socks, tennis shoes with the toes slit for comfort, a morning coat, a gray velvet waistcoat which, he said, had belonged to his ancestor Benjamin Franklin, and a beret studded with Vote for Roosevelt buttons. And there is no getting around it—he *did* have a good many lady friends—a different one each week, to be sure, but there was hardly ever a time when some woman wasn't cooking his meals; and on those occasions when I came to visit he would invariably, and in a most courtly fashion, say, "Meet Mrs. Buddy."

Late one night I woke with the feeling I was not alone; sure enough, there was someone in the room, and I could see him in the moonlight on my mirror. It was he, Mr. Buddy, furtively opening, closing bureau drawers, and suddenly my box of pennies splattered on the floor, rolled riotously in all directions. There was no use pretending then, so I turned on a lamp, and Mr. Buddy looked at me squarely, scarcely fazed, and grinned. "Listen," he said, and he was the most sober I'd ever seen him. "Listen, I've got to get out of here in a hurry."

I did not know what to say, and he looked down at the floor, his face turning slightly red. "Come on, be a good guy, have you got any money?"

I could only point to the spilt pennies; without another word he got down on his knees, gathered them and, walking very erectly, went out the door.

He was gone the next morning. Three women have come around asking for him, but I do not know his whereabouts. Maybe he is in Mobile. If you see him around there, R., won't you drop me a card, please? *I want a big fat mama, yes yes*! Shotgun's fingers, long as bananas, thick as dill pickles, pound the keys, and his foot, pounding the floor, shakes the café. Shotgun! The biggest show in town! Can't sing worth a damn, but man, can he rattle that piano—listen: *She's cool in the summer and warm in the fall, she's a four-season mama and that ain't all. . .* There he goes, his fat mouth yawning like a crocodile's, his wicked red tongue tasting the tune, loving it, making love to it; jelly, Shotgun, jelly-jelly-jelly. Look at him laugh, that black, crazy face all scarred with bullet-shot, all glistening with sweat. Is there any human vice he doesn't know about? A shame, though . . . Hardly any white folks ever see Shotgun, for this is a Negro café. Last year's dusty Christmas decorations color the peeling arsenic walls; orange-green-purple strips of fluted paper, dangling from naked light bulbs, flutter in the wind of a tired fan; the proprietor, a handsome quadroon with hooded milk-blue eyes, leans over the bar, squalling, "Look here, what you think this is, some kinda charity? Get up that two-bits, nigger, and mighty quick."

And tonight is Saturday. The room floats in cigarette smoke and Saturday-night perfume. All the little greasy wood tables have double rings of chairs, and everyone knows everyone, and for a moment the world is this room, this dark, jazzy, terrible room; our heartbeat is Shotgun's stamping foot, every joyous element of our lives is focused in the shine of his malicious eyes. *I want a big fat mama, yes yes!* He rocks forward on his stool, and as he lifts his face to look straight at us, a great riding holler goes up in the night: *I want a big fat mama with the meat shakin' on her, yes!*

from *Satchmo: My Life in New Orleans*

LOUIS ARMSTRONG (1901–1971)

Louis "Satchmo" Armstrong was born Daniel Louis Armstrong in New Orleans, where he began his musical career at the age of twelve when he was sent to live at the Colored Waif's Home for Boys. The home's bandmaster taught Armstrong how to play the coronet and read music, and after his release he began perfecting his music by playing on the streets of New Orleans. Armstrong took coronet lessons from Joseph "King" Oliver and listened to the jazz of Charles "Buddy" Bolden and William "Bunk" Johnson. At the age of fifteen, he performed his first nightclub gig in his hometown, and in 1918 became a professional musician, joining Edward "Kid" Ory's band. Armstrong led his own jazz bands, the Hot Five and the Hot Seven, in the 1920s, and began recording with them in 1925. In the 1930s his band toured Europe, and it was while playing the London Palladium that Armstrong acquired the nickname "Satchmo," given to him by the editor of a British music magazine. His recordings made him an international celebrity by the early 1940s, and he made frequent appearances at major jazz festivals, and on radio and television. Armstrong appeared in over sixty movies during his career, including *Cabin in the Sky* (1943), *New Orleans* (1947), and *Hello, Dolly* (1969). Although Armstrong became a "jazz emissary to the world," he never forgot his New Orleans roots. In the following selection from *Satchmo: My Life in New Orleans* (1954), Armstrong recounts those early days of playing for "Kid" Ory's band in the Crescent City.

Along about the middle of the summer of 1918 Joe Oliver got an offer from Chicago to go there to play for Mrs. Major, who owned the Lincoln Gardens. He took Jimmie Noone with him to play the clarinet.

I was back on my job driving a coal cart, but I took time off to go to the train with them. Kid Ory was at the station, and so were the rest of the Ory-Oliver jazz band. It was a rather sad parting. They really didn't want to leave New Orleans, and I felt the old gang was breaking up. But in show business you always keep thinking something better's coming along.

The minute the train started to pull out I was on my way out of the Illinois Central Station to my cart—I had a big load of coal to deliver—when Kid Ory called to me.

"You still blowin' that cornet?" he hollered.

I ran back. He said he'd heard a lot of talk about Little Louis. (That's what most folks called me when I was in my teens, I was so little and so cute.)

"Hmmm. . ." I pricked up my ears.

He said that when the boys in the band found out for sure that Joe Oliver was leaving, they told him to go get Little Louis to take Joe's place. He was a little in doubt at first, but after he'd looked around the town he decided I was the right one to have a try at taking that great man's place. So he told me to go wash up and then come play a gig with them that very same night.

What a thrill that was! To think I was considered up to taking Joe Oliver's place in the best band in town! I couldn't hardly wait to get to Mayann's to tell her the good news. I'd been having so many bad breaks, I just had to make a beeline to Mayann's.

Mayann was the one who'd always encouraged me to carry on with my cornet blowing because I loved it so much.

I couldn't phone her because we didn't have phones in our homes in those days—only the filthy rich could afford phones, and we were far from being in that class.

I wasn't particular about telling Mama Lucy just yet about my success, because she would always give me a dirty dig of some kind. Like the night I played my first job. That was more of a hustle than anything else; in fact, I didn't make but fifteen cents.

I sure was proud to bring that money home to my mother. Mama Lucy heard me tell my mother:

"Mama, here's what we made last night. Saturday night, too. We worked for tips, and fifteen cents was all we made, each of us."

My sister raised up out of a sound sleep and said: "Hmmm! Blow your brains out for fifteen cents!"

I wanted to kill her. Mama had to separate us to keep us from fighting that morning.

So when I got my first big break from Kid Ory, I looked up my mother first, instead of my sister. I just let Lucy find it out for herself. And then when Lucy praised me with enthusiasm, I just casually said:

"Thanks, sis."

Cute, huh? But inwardly I was glad they were happy for me. The first night I played with Kid Ory's band, the boys were so surprised they could hardly play their instruments for listening to me blow up a storm. But I wasn't frightened one bit. I was doing everything just exactly the way I'd heard Joe Oliver do it. At least I tried to. I even put a big towel around my neck when the band played a ball down at Economy Hall. That was the first thing Joe always did—he'd put a bath towel around his neck and open up his collar underneath so's he could blow free and easy.

And because I'd listened to Joe all the time he was with Kid Ory I knew almost everything that band played, by ear anyway. I was pretty fast on my horn at that time, and I had a good ear. I could catch on real fast.

Kid Ory was so nice and kind, and he had so much patience, that first night with them was a pleasure instead of a drag. There just wasn't a thing for me to do except blow my head off. Mellow moments, I assure you.

After that first gig with the Kid I was in. I began to get real popular with the dance fans as well as the musicians. All the musicians came to hear us and they'd hire me to play in their bands on the nights I wasn't engaged by Kid Ory.

I was doing great, till the night I got the biggest scare of my life. I was taking the cornet player's place in the Silver Leaf

Band, a very good band too. All the musicians in that band read the music of their parts. The clarinet player was Sam Dutrey, the brother of Honore Dutrey, the trombonist. Sam was one of the best clarinetists in town. (He also cut hair on the side.) He had an airy way about him that'd make one think he was stuck up, but he was really just a jolly, goodnatured fellow and liked to joke a lot. But I didn't know that!

The night I was to fill in for the clarinet player, I went early to sort of compose myself, because since I was playing with a strange band I didn't want anything to go wrong if I could help it. Most of the band began straggling in one by one about fifteen minutes before hitting time. Sam Dutrey was the last to arrive. I had never seen him before in my life. So while we were warming up and getting in tune, Sam came up on the bandstand. He said good evening to the fellows in the band and then he looked directly at me.

"What the hell is this?" he roared. "Get offa here, boy!" He had a real voice.

I was real scared. "Yassuh," I said. I started to pack up my cornet.

Then one of the men said: "Leave the boy alone, Sam. He's working in Willie's place tonight." Then he introduced me to Sam.

Sam laughed and said: "I was only kidding, son."

"Yassuh," I still said.

The whole night went down with us, swinging up a mess. But still I had that funny feeling. Sometimes now I run into Sam Dutrey, and we almost laugh ourselves sick over that incident.

Sam and Honore both were tops on their instruments. Honore Dutrey had one of the finest tones there could be had out of a trombone. But he messed up his life while he was in the Navy. One day aboard ship he fell asleep in a powder magazine and gassed himself so badly he suffered from asthma for years afterward. It always bothered him something terrible blowing his trombone.

When I had the band in Chicago in 1926, playing for Joe Glaser, who's now my personal manager, Dutrey was the trombone player. He would do real fine on all the tunes except the *Irish Medley*, in which the brass had to stay in the upper register at the ending. That's when Dutrey would have to go behind the curtains and gush his atomizer into his nostrils. Then he would say, "Take 'em on down." Well, you never heard such fine strong trombone in all your life. I'll come back to Honore later.

There's lots of musicians I'll be mentioning, especially the ones I played with and had dealings with from time to time. All in all, I had a wonderful life playing with them. Lots of them were characters, and when I say "characters" I mean *characters*! I've played with some of the finest musicians in the world, jazz and classic. God bless them, all of them!

While I was playing just gigs with Kid Ory's band we all had jobs during the day. The war was still going full blast and the orders were: "Work or Fight." And since I was too young to fight, I kept on driving my coal cart. Outside the cornet, it seemed like the coal cart was the only job I enjoyed working. Maybe it was because of all those fine old-timers.

Kid Ory had some of the finest gigs, especially for the rich white folks. Whenever we'd play a swell place, such as the Country Club, we would get more money, and during the intermissions the people giving the dance would see that the band had a big delicious meal, the same as they ate. And by and by the drummer and I would get in with the colored waiters and have enough food to take home to Mayann and Mama Lucy.

The music-reading musicians like those in Robechaux's band thought that we in Kid Ory's band were good, but only good together. One day those big shots had a funeral to play, but most of them were working during the day and couldn't make it. So they engaged most of Ory's boys, including me. The day of the funeral the musicians were congregating at the hall where the Lodge started their march, to go up to the dead brother's house. Kid Ory and I noticed all those stuck-up guys giving us lots of ice. They didn't feel we were good enough to play their marches.

I nudged Ory, as if to say, "You dig what I'm diggin'?"

Ory gave me a nod, as if to say yes, he digged.

We went up to the house playing a medium fast march. All the music they gave us we played, and a lot easier than they did. They still didn't say anything to us one way or the other.

Then they brought the body out of the house and we went on to the cemetery. We were playing those real slow funeral marches. After we reached the cemetery, and they lowered the body down six feet in the ground, and the drummer man rolled on the drums, they struck a ragtime march which required swinging from the band. And those old fossils just couldn't cut it. That's when we Ory boys took over and came in with flying colors.

We were having that good old experience, swinging that whole band! It sounded so good!

The second line—the raggedy guys who follow parades and funerals to hear the music—they enjoyed what we played so much they made us take an encore. And that don't happen so much in street parades.

We went into the hall swinging the last number, *Panama*. I remembered how Joe Oliver used to swing that last chorus in the upper register, and I went on up there and got those notes, and the crowd went wild.

After that incident those stuck-up guys wouldn't let us alone. They patted us on the back and just wouldn't let us alone. They hired us several times afterward. After all, we'd proved to them that any learned musician can read music, but they can't all swing. It was a good lesson for them.

Several times later they asked us to join their band, but I had already given Celestin (another fine cornet player, and the leader of the Tuxedo Brass Band) my consent to join him and replace Sidney Desvigne, another real good and fancy cornet man. Personally I thought Celestin's Tuxedo Band was the hottest in town since the days of the Onward Brass Band with Emmanuel Perez and Joe Oliver holding down the cornet section. My, my, what a band! So after Joe Oliver went to Chicago, the Tuxedo Brass Band got all the funerals and parades.

More about Papa Celestin later.

The last time I saw Lady, the mule I used to drive, was November 11, 1918, the day the Armistice was signed, the day the United States and the rest of the Allies cut the German Kaiser and his army a brand 'noo one. At eleven o'clock that morning I was unloading coal at Fabacher's restaurant on St. Charles Street, one of the finest restaurants in town. I was carrying the coal inside and sweating like mad when I heard several automobiles going down St. Charles Street with great big tin cans tied to them, dragging on the ground and making all kinds of noise. After quite a few cars had passed I got kind of curious and asked somebody standing nearby, "What's all the fuss about?"

"They're celebratin' 'cause the war is over," he said to me.

When he said that, it seemed as though a bolt of lightning struck me all over.

I must have put about three more shovels of coal into the wheelbarrow to take inside, when all of a sudden a thought came to me. "The war is over. And here I am monkeyin' around with this mule. Huh!"

I immediately dropped that shovel, slowly put on my jacket, looked at Lady and said: "So long, my dear. I don't think I'll ever see you again." And I cut out, leaving mule cart, load of coal and everything connected with it. I haven't seen them since.

I ran straight home. Mayann, noticing I was home much earlier than usual, asked me what was the matter, trouble?

"No, mother," I said. "The war is over, and I quit the coal yard job for the last time. Now I can play my music the way I want to. And when I want to."

The very next day all the lights went on again. And all the places commenced opening up in droves. Oh, the city sure did look good again, with all those beautiful lights along Canal Street, and all the rest. Matranga called me to come back to play in his honky-tonk, but he was too late. I was looking forward to bigger things, especially since Kid Ory had given me the chance to play the music I really wanted to play. And that was all kinds of music, from jazz to waltzes.

Then Kid Ory really did get a log of gigs. He even started giving his own dances, Monday nights downtown at the Economy Hall. Monday night was a slow night in New Orleans at that time, and we didn't get much work other places. But Kid Ory did so well at the Economy Hall that he kept it up for months and made a lot of dough for himself. He paid us well too.

A lot of Saturday nights we didn't work either, so on those nights I would play over in Gretna, across the river, at the Brick House, another honky-tonk. This was a little town near Algiers, Red Allen's home, which paid pretty well, including the tips from the drunken customers, the whores, the pimps and the gamblers.

There also were some real bad characters who hung around the joint, and you could get your head cut off, or blown off, if you weren't careful.

We had a three-piece band, and we had to play a lot of blues to satisfy those hustling women who made quite a bit of money selling themselves very cheap.

The Brick House was located right by the levee and the Jackson Avenue ferry. Going back home to New Orleans on the Jackson Avenue streetcar after we finished work at the Brick House used to frighten me a lot because there weren't many people out that time of the morning. Just a few drunks, white and colored. Lots of times the two races looked as if they were going to get into a scrap over just nothing at all. And down there, with something like that happening and only a few Spades (colored folks) around, it wasn't so good. Even if we colored ones were right, when the cops arrived they'd whip our heads first and ask questions later.

One night when just a few colored people, including me, were coming back from Gretna in the wee hours of the morning, a middle-aged colored woman was sitting on a bench by the railing of the boat, lushed to the gills. The deckhands were washing the floor and it was very slippery. Just before the boat pulled off an elderly white lady came running up the gangplank and just managed to make the ferry. Not knowing the floor was wet, she slipped and almost fell. Immediately the colored woman raised up and looked at the white one and said: "Thank God!"

Talk about your tense moments!

My, my, the Lord was with us colored people that night, because nothing happened. I'm still wondering why. I have seen trouble start down there from less than that.

Louis Armstrong met his first wife at the Brick House. But before I tell you how I got to know Daisy Parker, I want to take one last look again at the good old days of Storyville.

For instance, I haven't said anything yet about Lulu White. Poor Lulu White! What a woman!

I admired her even when I was a kid, not because of the great business she was in, but because of the great business she made of her Mahogany Hall. That was the name of the house she ran at Storyville. It was a pleasure house, where those rich ofay (white) business men and planters would come from all over the South and spend some awful large amounts of loot.

Lulu had some of the biggest diamonds anyone would want to look at. Some of the finest furs. . . . And some of the finest yellow gals working for her. . . .

Champagne would flow like water at Lulu's. If anyone walked in and ordered a bottle of beer, why, they'd look at him twice and then—maybe—they'd serve it. And if they did, you'd be plenty sorry you didn't order champagne.

Jelly Roll Morton made a lot of money playing the piano for Lulu White, playing in one of her rooms.

Of course when the drop came and the Navy and the law started clamping down on Storyville, Lulu had to close down too. She had enough salted away to retire for life and forget all about the business. But no, she was like a lot of sporting house landladies I've known through life—they were never satisfied and would not let well enough alone, and would try to make that big fast money regardless of the law showering down on them.

Mayor Martin Behrman made them cut out from Storyville within days. Lulu White moved from 325 North Basin Street to 1200 Bienville Street, and tried her luck at another house. That's where she did the wrong thing, to try to continue running her house with the law on her like white on rice, taking all the loot she'd made over the years along with her diamonds and jewelry and all.

I remember Detective Harry Gregson gave her a real tough time. He was a tough man, and he's still living. All the dicks in Storyville—Hessel, Fast Mail, Gregson, the others—I got to know when as a kid I delivered hard coal to all of those cribs where the girls used to stand in their doorways and work as the men went by.

There were all kinds of thrills for me in Storyville. On every corner I could hear music. And such good music! The music I wanted to hear. It was worth my salary—the little I did get—just to go into Storyville. It seemed as though all the bands were shooting at each other with those hot riffs. And that man Joe Oliver! My, my, that man kept me spellbound with that horn of his. . . .

Storyville! With all those glorious trumpets—Joe Oliver, Bunk Johnson—he was in his prime then—Emmanuel Perez, Buddy Petit, Joe Johnson—who was real great, and it's too bad he didn't make some records. . . .

It struck me that Joe Johnson and Buddy Petit had the same identical styles. Which was great! In fact all the trumpet and cornet players who were playing in my young days in New Orleans were hellions—that's the biggest word I can say for them. They could play those horns for hours on end.

But Joe Oliver, a fat man, was the strongest and the most creative. And Bunk Johnson was the sweetest. Bunk cut everybody for tone, though they all had good tones. That was the first thing Mr. Peter Davis taught me—out in the Colored Waifs' Home for Boys. "Tone," he said. "A musician with a tone can play any kind of music, whether it's classical or ragtime."

It seemed like everyone was pulling for Lulu White to give up and lead a decent life. But she just wouldn't. She held on to her horses and her carriage and her Negro driver as long as she could. But the law she defied dragged her down like a dog until they broke her completely. It was a shame the way they snatched her mansion—furniture, diamonds galore, things worth a fortune.

Oh well, although Lulu's gone, the name of Mahogany Hall on Basin Street will live forever. And so will Basin Street.

"Mornings on Bourbon Street"

TENNESSEE WILLIAMS (1911–1983)

Tennessee Williams was born Thomas Lanier Williams in Columbus, Mississippi, where his family lived with his maternal grandparents in the Episcopal rectory. His father moved the family to St. Louis around 1919, and this move away from the South to the meaner living conditions of the city proved traumatic for Williams and his sister Rose and is reflected in much of his work, especially *The Glass Menagerie* (1944). The play was his first successful stage production and won the Critics' Circle Award. Williams became the South's greatest playwright and was one of the most original forces in the American theatre during the post World War II era. Williams experienced wanderlust throughout his life and divided his time mostly between Key West, Italy, New Orleans, and New York. When Williams came to New Orleans as an aspiring writer at the end of the 1930s, he found there a freedom he had never experienced elsewhere. In a 1945 letter to Donald Windham, Williams wrote about New Orleans: "And tonight I am being taken to a place called 'The Goat House' where everything goes on including 'Ether parties,' which is something I haven't seen yet. Town is *wide* open." From 1946 to 1947, Williams lived at 632 Peter Street and wrote one of his best known plays, *A Streetcar Named Desire* (1947), which won the Pulitzer Prize. His other works include *Summer and Smoke* (1948), *Cat on a Hot Tin Roof* (1955), *Suddenly Last Summer*, poetry, short stories, a novel, and *Memoirs* (1975). The Tennessee Williams/New Orleans Literary Festival, an annual spring celebration of the written word, is a living memorial to Williams. "Mornings on Bourbon Street" appeared in the poetry volume, *In the Winter of Cities* (1956).

He knew he would say it. But could he believe it again?

He thought of the innocent mornings on Bourbon Street,
of the sunny courtyard and the iron
lion's head on the door.

He thought of the quality light could not be expected
to have again after rain,

the pigeons and drunkards coming together from under
the same stone arches, to move again in the sun's
faint mumble of benediction with faint surprise.

He thought of the tall iron horseman before the Cabildo,
tipping his hat so gallantly toward old wharves,
the mist of the river beginning to climb about him.

He thought of the rotten-sweet odor the Old Quarter had,
so much like a warning of what he would have to learn.

He thought of belief and the gradual loss of belief
and the piercing together of something like it again.

But, oh, how his blood had almost turned in color
when once, in response to a sudden call from a window,
he stopped on a curbstone and first thought,

Love. Love. Love.

He knew he would say it. But could he believe it again?

He thought of Irene whose body was offered at night
behind the cathedral, whose outspoken pictures were hung
outdoors, in the public square,
as brutal as knuckles smashed into grinning faces.

He thought of the merchant sailor who wrote of the sea,
haltingly, with a huge power locked in a halting tongue—

lost in a tanker off the Florida coast,
the locked and virginal power burned in oil.

He thought of the opulent antique dealers on Royal
whose tables of rosewood gleamed as blood under lamps.

He thought of his friends.

He thought of his lost companions,
of all he had touched and all whose touch he had known.

He wept for remembrance.

But when he had finished weeping, he washed his face,

he smiled at his face in the mirror, preparing to say
to you, whom he was expecting,

Love. Love. Love.

But could he believe it again?

from *Half of Paradise*

JAMES LEE BURKE (1936–)

James Lee Burke was born in Houston, Texas, and grew up on the Texas and Louisiana Gulf coast. He attended the University of Southwest Louisiana, where he began writing short stories. Burke says, "I have a real embarrassing employment record." He has worked on an oil rig, as a newspaper reporter, and as an English instructor at the University of Southwestern Louisiana and the University of Montana. His first novel, *Half of Paradise*, (1965) was published to much critical acclaim, but was followed by two novels which brought him less than enthusiastic reviews. He "fell onto bad days" and went for twelve years before publishing his fourth novel, *Two for Texas* (1983). However, it was the publication of *The Lost Get-Back Boogie* by Louisiana State Press in 1986 which resurrected his career and earned him a Pulitzer Prize nomination. In his next book, *Neon Rain* (1987), Burke introduced Dave Robicheaux, a Cajun Louisiana detective, recovering alcoholic, and ex-New Orleans police officer. That book launched the highly successful series of "Dave Robicheaux" crime novels, which included *Black Cherry Blues* (1989), winner of the Edgar Award, *In the Electric Mist with the Confederate Dead* (1993), *Dixie City Jam* (1994), and *Cadillac Jukebox* (1996). In these books Burke writes eloquently about crime and punishment in Southern Louisiana, depicting both the best and the worst sides of the city of New Orleans. The following selection from *Half of Paradise* focuses on Avery Broussard, the last survivor of a once prosperous Louisiana family. Upon his release from prison, Broussard hitches a ride "all the way to New Orleans" where he meets up with another "agrarian romanticist."

He took the pint bottle out of his pocket and cut the seal off. He unscrewed the cap and drank; he felt the whiskey hot in his stomach. It tasted good after so long. He took another swallow and put the cap back on and replaced the bottle in his pocket. He wrapped the rest of his groceries in the paper sack and got up and stood by the shoulder of the highway to hitch another ride. Three cars passed him by, and then he caught a lift with a salesman who was going all the way to New Orleans.

He got into the city late that night. The salesman gave him directions to an inexpensive rooming house and dropped him off on the lower end of Magazine. Avery walked through the dark streets of a Negro area until he found St. Charles. He caught the streetcar and rode downtown to Canal. He stood on the corner and looked at the white sweep of the boulevard with its grass esplanade and palm trees and streetcar tracks, and the glitter like hard candy of the lighted storefronts. The sidewalks were still crowded, and he could hear the tinny music from the bars and strip places. He walked down to Liberty Street and found the rooming house the salesman had told him of. It was an old wood building that had a big front porch with a swing. It was one block off Canal and three blocks from Bourbon, and the Frenchwoman who owned it kept it very clean and she served coffee and rolls to her tenants every morning.

He took a room for the night, and in the morning the woman brought in his coffee on a tray. She poured the coffee and hot milk into his cup from two copper pots with long tapered spouts. She wore a housecoat, and her hair was loose and uncombed.

"Will you keep the room for another night?" she said.

"I'm looking for a job. I'll stay if I find one," Avery said.

"Your name is French. *Tu parles français*?"

"I understand it."

"*D'où tu viens*?"

"Martinique parish."

"What kind of work do you do?"

"Anything. I'm going down to the docks today," he said.

"My husband is a welder on the pipeline. He can get you work."

"I've never worked on a pipeline."

"You can learn. He will teach you."

"Where is he?" Avery said.

"He is eating breakfast. Finish the coffee and you can talk with him."

Avery met her husband and drove to work with him. He got a job as a welder's helper on a twelve-inch natural gas line that had just kicked off and was to run from an oil refinery to the other end of the parish. He worked with the tack crew, cleaning wells, driving the truck, and regulating the welding machine. He liked the job. Each morning they went out on the right-of-way that was cut through the woods and marsh, and the joints of pipe would be laid along the wooden skids by the ditch; he followed behind the truck with the electric ground that he clamped on the pipe to give the welder a circuit and with the wire brushes and the icepick in his back pocket that he used to clean the joints; the welder would bend over the pipe with his dark goggles on and his bill-hat turned around backwards and his khaki shirt buttoned at the collar and sleeves, and the electric arc would move in an orange flame around the pipe, and there was the acrid smell of tar and hot metal and the exhaust from the heavy machinery.

He stayed on at the rooming house, and sometimes in the evening he went down into the Quarter and ate dinner in an Italian place off Bourbon Street, then he would walk through the narrow cobble lanes and look at the old red and pink stucco buildings and the iron grillwork along the balconies and those fine flagstone courtyards with the willow trees and palms that hung over the walls. At night he could see the back of Saint Louis Cathedral with the ivy growing up its walls under the moon, and there was the park in the square across from the French Market where the bums and the drunks slept under the statue of Andrew Jackson.

One night he found a small bar on Rampart where the band was good and there were no tourists. He had been drinking since he had gotten off work. He sat at the bar and drank whiskey sours and listened to the band knock out the end of "Yellow Dog Blues." The drummer twirled the sticks in his hands and played on the nickel-plated rim of his snare. The man on the next stool to Avery was having an argument with the bartender. He was dressed in sports clothes, and was quite handsome and quite drunk. He had thin red hair and blue eyes and a pale classic face like Lord Byron's. He didn't have enough money to pay for his drink. He turned to Avery.

"I say, have you a dime?" he said.

Avery pushed a coin towards him.

He gave the dime to the bartender with some other change.

"The fellow was going to take my drink away," he said.

"You're spilling it," Avery said.

"Spilling?"

"On your coat. You're spilling your drink."

"Don't want to do that." He wiped his sleeve with his hand. "My name is Wally."

"I'm Avery Broussard."

"You look like a good chap. Do you want to go to a party?"

"Where?"

"On Royal. A friend of mine is giving a debauch."

"I wouldn't know anyone."

"Of no importance. The literary and artistic group. We'll tell them you're an agrarian romanticist. Do you have a bottle?"

"No."

"We'll have to get one. The artistic group asks that you bring your own booze."

They left the bar and went to a package store down the street.

"Do you mind making it Scotch?" Wally said.

Avery went in and bought a half pint.

"Good man," Wally said.

"Are you English?" Avery took a drink and passed the bottle.

"Who would want to be English when they can belong to the American middle class?"

"You sound English."

"Went to school in England. Drank my way through four years of Tulane, then tried graduate work at Cambridge and was sent down. Acquired nothing but a taste for Scotch and a bad accent. Now make my home in the Quarter writing."

"Pass the bottle," Avery said.

"What do you do?"

"Pipeline."

"I say, we're emptying the bottle rather fast."

"Have to buy more.

"I'm stony broke. Hate to use your money like this." Avery took a long drink.

"Mind if I have a bit?" Wally said.

Avery gave him the bottle. He leaned against the side of a building and drank.

"I think I'm tight," he said.

"Where is the party?"

"Royal Street."

"We're going the wrong way," Avery said.

They turned the corner towards Royal. The half pint was almost finished.

"You have the last drink," Wally said.

"Go ahead."

"Your bottle."

Avery drank it off and dropped the bottle in an alley.

"Puts us in an embarrassing way. Can't go to a party without liquor," Wally said.

"Dago red."

"Never drink it."

"It's cheap."

"Unconventional to go to party with dago red," Wally said.

"There's an Italian place with good wine."

"A little restaurant off Bourbon?"

"Yes."

"Have to wait outside. Can't go in," Wally said.

"Why not?"

"Broke some glasses they say. Don't remember it. Was inebriated at the time."

"They have good wine," Avery said.

"I'll wait for you. It's always awkward to have scenes with Italian restaurant owners.

Avery walked down two blocks and bought a large two-liter bottle of red wine in a straw basket.

He met Wally at the corner.

"I forgot to get a corkscrew," he said.

He cut out the top part of the cork with his pocketknife and pushed the rest through the neck into the wine.

"Good man," Wally said.

They each had a drink. They could taste the cork when it floated up inside the neck. They walked along, Avery holding the bottle by the straw loops of the basket. They came to an apartment building with a Spanish type courtyard that had an iron gate and an arched brick entrance. The courtyard was strung with paper lanterns, and there was a stone well with a banana tree beside it in the center. The walls were grown with ivy, and there were potted ferns in earthenware jars on the flagging. People moved up and down the staircase, and laughing girls called down from the balcony to young men in the court.

"Hello!" Wally said.

"It's Wally," someone said.

"I say, is there a party here?"

"Come in. You look shaky on your feet," another said.

"Does anyone know if there's a party here?" he said.

"Someone help Wally in," a girl said.

"We're agrarian romanticists. This is Freneau Crèvecoeur Broussard."

"Avery."

"That's not agrarian enough. You'll have to change your name," Wally said.

Everyone turned and looked at Wally.

"Do you remember my party last Saturday?" a girl said.

"I was helping out at the mission last Saturday. We're starting a campaign to make New Orleans dry."

"He said he was somebody out of *War and Peace*," she told

the others. "He stood backwards on the edge of my balcony and tried to drink a fifth of Scotch without falling."

"Couldn't have been me. I've never read Chekhov."

"You would have broken your neck if you hadn't fallen in the flower bed," she said.

"Don't like those Russian chaps, anyway. A bunch of bloody moralists," Wally said.

"Sit down, fellow. You're listing," someone said.

"Won't be able to get up."

"Tell Freneau Crèvecoeur to sit down. He doesn't look well," the girl said.

"Avery."

"Beg your pardon?" she said.

"My name is Avery."

"Excuse me, Mr. Avery."

"We're agrarian romanticists," Wally said.

"Avery is my first name."

"Who wants to read a bunch of bloody Russians when they can have the agrarian romanticists?"

"What does your friend have in his bottle?" the girl said.

"The best Italian import that a pair of unwashed feet could mash down in a bathtub. I say, let's have a drink."

He took the bottle from Avery and turned it up.

"Your turn, old pal."

Avery sat down on the well and drank.

"Damn good man. Wonderful capacity," Wally said. "Everyone take a swallow. Pass it around. I insist. Each of you must take a swallow. I never drink alone. It's a sign of alcoholism."

"You're impossible, Wally," the girl said.

"I cannot stand people who do not drink."

A man took the bottle and held it for his girl to drink. She laughed and a few drops went down her chin. The bottle was passed from one couple to another.

"I refuse to go to parties where everyone is not smashed," Wally said.

"Do you live in the Quarter, Mr. Crèvecoeur?" another girl said.

"No writer would live in the Quarter," Wally said.

"Are you a writer?"

"Work on the pipeline," Avery said.

"What did he say?"

"He's a disillusioned agrarian," Wally said.

"Have you really written anything?"

"We've made an agreement with a publisher to write dialogue for comic books," Wally said.

"Be serious."

"He did his thesis on Wordsworth's sonnets to the dark lady."

"I'm interested in writing myself," she said to Avery.

"She's a copy reader for the *Picayune*."

"Where is the wine?" Avery said.

"All gone."

"Have to get more."

"I've written a few poems and sent them off," the girl said.

"We had a full bottle when we came in," Avery said.

"It's a lovely trick. You let everyone have a sip of yours, and then you drink out of theirs for the rest of the night."

"Do you publish often?" she said.

"I'm a welder's helper."

"You said you were a writer."

"He is."

"I almost failed high school English," Avery said.

"Why did you say you were a writer?"

"I tell you he is," Wally said.

"We need another bottle."

"Let's go upstairs.

"I wouldn't have told you about my poems," the girl said.

"Crèvecoeur will be happy to read your poetry and give you a criticism."

"You take things too far," the girl said.

"Oh I say."

"It's true."

"Apologize to her, Crèvecoeur."

"I'm going down to the package store."

"These other chaps owe us a round. Let's toggle upstairs."

They went up the staircase and entered the living room of an apartment. It was crowded and they had to push their way through to the kitchen where the liquor was kept. Wally took a bottle of Scotch off the sideboard and two glasses from the cabinet. There was a sack of crushed ice in the sink. He fixed the drinks and handed one to Avery. They went back into the living room. There was a combo playing in one corner. The guitar player was a Negro. It was very loud in the room. Someone dropped a glass on the coffee table. Someone was saying that a girl had passed out in the bathroom. Avery tripped across a man and a girl sitting on the floor. The glass doors to the outside balcony were open to let in the night air. He started to go out on the balcony but he heard a girl whisper and laugh in the darkness. The piano player in the combo was singing an obscene song in Spanish. Avery couldn't find Wally in the crowd. Two men who looked like homosexuals were talking in the corner by the bookcase. One of them waved girlishly at someone across the room. The girl who had passed out in the bath was brought out to the balcony for some air.

Avery moved through the groups of people. He finished his drink and put his glass on a table. He could feel the blood in his face. The noise in the room seemed louder. He wanted to get outside. He remembered that he had to be out on the job at seven in the morning. He looked up and saw a girl watching him from the other side of the room. She smiled at him and excused herself from the people she was with. It was Suzanne. She wore a wine-colored dress, and there was a gold cross and chain around her throat. She looked even better than when he had seen her last.

"I couldn't tell if it was you or not," she said.

"Hello, Suzanne."

"You kept walking through the crowd. I wanted to call out, but I was afraid it wasn't you."

"I thought you were in Spain or someplace."

"I was. What are you doing here?"

"I'm not sure. I was leaving when I saw you," he said.

"Don't leave."

"I'm not."

"Let's go outside. It's too loud in here."

"I've tried. Couldn't make the door."

"We can go out through the kitchen," she said.

They went out through a back door that opened onto the balcony over the courtyard. The air was cool, and the moonlight fell on the tile roofing of the buildings.

"I didn't believe it was you. You look changed," she said.

"You look good," he said. She really did. She had never looked so good.

"It's been awfully long since we've seen each other."

"Did You like Spain?"

"I loved it."

"Are you living here now?"

"Over on Dauphine. Another girl and I rented a studio. You have to see it. It's like something out of nineteenth-century Paris."

They sat on the stone steps leading down to the court.

"I'm one of those sidewalk artists you see in Pirates Alley," she said. "Daddy was furious when he found out. He said he would stop my allowance.

"He won't."

"I know. He always threatens to do it, and then he sends another check to apologize."

He looked at her profile in the darkness. She kept her face turned slightly away from him when she talked. The light from the paper lanterns caught in her hair. He wished he had not drunk as much as he had. He was trying very hard to act sober.

"I came with some fellow named Wally. He put a drink in my hand and I never saw him again."

"How in the world did you meet Wally?"

"He was broke. I lent him a dime."

"One night he went down Bourbon asking donations for the Salvation Army."

"What happened?"

"He used the money to buy two winos a drink in The Famous Door."

A couple brushed past them down the steps. Others followed them. Part of the party was moving outside. Wally came out on the balcony and called down.

"Who in the hell would read a bunch of Russian moralists?"

"Let's go to the Café du Monde," Suzanne said. "They have wonderful pastry and coffee, and we can sit outside at the tables."

"What about the people you're with?"

"I've been trying to get away from them all evening. They come down from L.S.U. to see the bohemians."

They left the party and walked towards the French Market through the brick and cobbled streets. They passed the rows of stucco buildings that had once been the homes of the French and Spanish aristocracy, and which were now gutted and remodeled into bars, whorehouses, tattoo parlors, burlesque theaters, upper-class restaurants, and nightclubs that catered to homosexuals. They could hear the loud music from Bourbon and the noise of the people on the sidewalk and the spielers in front of the bars calling in the tourists, who did not know or care who had built the Quarter.

"I didn't find out what happened to you until I came back from Spain," she said. "I'm very sorry."

"It's over now."

"I couldn't believe it when Daddy told me. It seems so unfair."

"I did a year. They might have kept me for three."

"Was it very bad?" she said.

"Yes."

"I wish I had known. I was enjoying myself, and you were in one of those camps."

"I'm finished with it now."

"It makes me feel awful to think of you in there."

"You're a good girl."

"It must have been terrible."

"It was worse for some of the others," he said.

"I couldn't bear thinking about you in a prison."

They walked across Jackson Square through the park and crossed the street to the Café du Monde. They sat outside at one of the tables. There was a breeze from the river. The waiter in a white jacket brought them coffee and a dish of pastry.

"We never wrote to each other after my first year in college,"she said. "I wanted to write but anything I could say seemed inadequate."

"I wasn't sure you wanted to hear from me."

"You know I did. It all went to nothing over such small things."

"I passed out on the beach in Biloxi."

"I wasn't angry. It just hurt me to see you do it to yourself."

"I felt like hell when I saw the way you looked the next morning,"he said.

"I didn't sleep all night. I was so worried over you."

"You were always a good girl."

"Stop it."

"You were always damn good-looking too."

"Oh for heaven's sake, Avery."

"Did you see those men turn and look at you in the park?"

"You're being unfair."

"Why are you so damn good-looking?" he said.

"I want to show you my apartment. Can you come over tomorrow evening for supper?"

"You're changing the subject."

"Can you come?"

"All right."

"I cook beautifully. My roommate refuses to eat with me."

"Good. Tell her to leave."

"What were you drinking tonight?" she said.

"I thought I fooled you."

"Your face was white. I was afraid to light a cigarette near you."

"Tell your roommate to leave, anyway."
"You're still tight."
"Dago red leaves me like this for a couple of days."
"It's good to be with you again, Avery."
"Let's walk home," he said.

from *An Unfinished Woman: A Memoir*

LILLIAN HELLMAN (1905–1984)

Lillian Hellman, the only child of Max and Julia Newhouse Hellman, was born in New Orleans in the boardinghouse run by her aunts, Hannah and Jenny Hellman. Hellman grew up spending half of each year in New Orleans and half in New York because her father's job as a shoe merchant required that he divide his time between the two cities. She attended New York University for three years and in 1925 took a job with Boni & Liveright, where she was a manuscript reader for William Faulkner's *Mosquitoes*. In 1930 she moved to Hollywood with her husband, dramatist Arthur Kober, and found work as a scenario reader for Metro-Goldwyn-Mayer. She soon met Dashiell Hammett, who would become her lifelong companion. Taking critical advice from Hammett, Hellman wrote her first successful play, *The Children's Hour* (1934), which was notable for its frank treatment of homosexuality. Hellman became one of the most important dramatists to come from the South. The Newhouses, her mother's family in Alabama, were the prototypes of the scheming Hubbard family in Hellman's most famous play *The Little Foxes* (1939), and her two Hellman aunts became the prototypes of the sisters in *Toys in the Attic* (1960). Hellman worked as a writer in Hollywood until she was blacklisted after being called to testify before the House Un-American Activities Committee in 1952. She wrote four highly acclaimed memoirs, including *An Unfinished Woman* (1969), winner of the National Book Award, and *Pentimento* (1973). In the following excerpt from *An Unfinished Woman*, Hellman writes of her childhood days spent daydreaming and reading in her aunts' boardinghouse at 1718 Prytania Street, her "first and most beloved home."

There was a heavy fig tree on the lawn where the house turned the corner into the side street, and to the front and sides of the fig tree were three live oaks that hid the fig from my aunts' boardinghouse. I suppose I was eight or nine before I discovered the pleasures of the fig tree, and although I have lived in many houses since then, including a few I made for myself, I still think of it as my first and most beloved home.

I learned early, in our strange life of living half in New York and half in New Orleans, that I made my New Orleans teachers uncomfortable because I was too far ahead of my schoolmates, and my New York teachers irritable because I was too far behind. But in New Orleans, I found a solution: I skipped school at least once a week and often twice, knowing that nobody cared or would report my absence. On those days I would set out for school done up in polished strapped shoes and a prim hat against what was known as "the climate," carrying my books and a little basket filled with delicious stuff my Aunt Jenny and Carrie, the cook, had made for my school lunch. I would round the corner of the side street, move on toward St. Charles Avenue, and sit on a bench as if I were waiting for a streetcar until the boarders and the neighbors had gone to work or settled down for the post-breakfast rest that all Southern ladies thought necessary. Then I would run back to the fig tree, dodging in and out of bushes to make sure the house had no dangers for me. The fig tree was heavy, solid, comfortable, and I had, through time, convinced myself that it wanted me, missed me when I was absent, and approved all the rigging I had done for the happy days I spent in its arms: I had made a sling to hold the school books, a pulley rope for my lunch basket, a hole for the bottle of afternoon cream-soda pop, a fishing pole and a smelly little bag of elderly bait, a pillow embroidered with a picture of Henry Clay on a horse that I had stolen from Mrs. Stillman, one of my aunts' boarders, and a proper nail to hold my dress and shoes to keep them neat for the return to the house.

It was in that tree that I learned to read, filled with the passions that can only come to the bookish, grasping, very young, bewildered by almost all of what I read, sweating in the attempt to understand a world of adults I fled from in real life but desperately wanted to join in books. (I did not connect the grown men and women in literature with the grown men and women I saw around me. They were, to me, another species.)

It was in the fig tree that I learned that anything alive in water was of enormous excitement to me. True, the water was gutter water and the fishing could hardly be called that: sometimes the things that swam in New Orleans gutters were not pretty, but I didn't know what was pretty and I liked them all. After lunch—the men boarders returned for a large lunch and a siesta—the street would be safe again, with only the noise from Carrie and her helpers in the kitchen, and they could be counted on never to move past the back porch, or the chicken coop. Then I would come down from my tree to sit on the side street gutter with my pole and bait. Often I would catch a crab that had wandered in from the Gulf, more often I would catch my favorite, the crayfish, and sometimes I would, in that safe hour, have at least six of them for my basket. Then, about 2:30, when house and street would stir again, I would go back to my tree for another few hours of reading or dozing or having what I called the ill hour. It is too long ago for me to know why I thought the hour "ill," but certainly I did not mean sick. I think I meant an intimation of sadness, a first recognition that there was so much to understand that one might never find one's way and the first signs, perhaps, that for a nature like mine, the way would not be easy. I cannot be sure that I felt all that then, although I can be sure that it was in the fig tree, a few years later, that I was first puzzled by the conflict which would haunt me, harm me, and benefit me the rest of my life: simply, the stubborn, relentless, driving desire to be alone as it came into conflict with the desire not to be alone when I wanted not to be. I already guessed that other people wouldn't allow that, although, as an only child, I pretended for the rest of my life that they would and must allow it to me.

I liked my time in New Orleans much better than I liked our six months apartment life in New York. The life in my aunts' boardinghouse seemed remarkably rich. And what a strange lot my own family was. My aunts Jenny and Hannah were both tall, large women, funny and generous, who coming from a German, cultivated, genteel tradition had found they had to earn a living and earned it without complaint, although Jenny, the prettier and more complex, had frequent outbursts of interesting temper. It was strange, I thought then, that my mother, who so often irritated me, was treated by my aunts as if she were a precious Chinese clay piece from a world they didn't know. And in a sense, that was true: her family was rich, she was small, delicately made and charming—she was a sturdy, brave woman, really, but it took years to teach me that—and because my aunts loved my father very much, they were good to my mother, and protected her from the less wellborn boarders. I don't think they understood—I did, by some kind of child's malice—that my mother enjoyed the boarders and listened to them with the sympathy Jenny couldn't afford. I suppose none of the boarders were of great interest, but I was crazy about what I thought went on behind their doors.

I was conscious that Mr. Stillman, a large, loose, goodlooking man, flirted with my mother and sang off key. I knew that a boarder called Collie, a too thin, unhappy looking, no-age man, worked in his uncle's bank and was drunk every night. He was the favorite of the lady boarders, who didn't think he'd live very long. (They were wrong: over twenty years later, on a visit to my retired aunts, I met him in Galatoire's restaurant looking just the same.) And there were two faded, sexy, giggly sisters called Fizzy and Sarah, who pretended to love children and all trees. I once overheard a fight between my mother and father in which she accused him of liking Sarah. I thought that was undignified of my mother and was pleased when my father laughed it off as untrue. He was telling the truth about Sarah: he liked Fizzy, and the day I saw them meet and get into a taxi in front of a restaurant on Jackson Avenue was to stay with me for many years. I was in a black rage, filled with fears I couldn't explain, with pity and contempt for my mother, with an intense desire to follow my father and Fizzy to see whatever it was they might be doing, and to kill them for it. An hour later, I threw myself from the top of the fig tree and broke my nose, although I did not know I had broken a bone and was concerned only with the hideous pain.

I went immediately to Sophronia, who had been my nurse when I was a small child before we moved, or half moved, to New York. She worked now for people who lived in a large house a streetcar ride from ours, and she took care of two little red-haired boys whom I hated with pleasure in my wicked jealousy. Sophronia was the first and most certain love of my life. (Years later, when I was a dangerously rebellious young girl, my father would say that if he had been able to afford Sophronia through the years, I would have been under the only control I ever recognized.) She was a tall, handsome, light tan woman—I still have many pictures of the brooding face—who was for me, as for so many other white Southern children, the one and certain anchor so needed for the young years, so forgotten after that. (It wasn't that way for us: we wrote and met as often as possible until she died when I was in my twenties, and the first salary check I ever earned she returned to me in the form of a gold chain.) The mother of the two red-haired boys didn't like my visits to Sophronia and so I always arrived by the back door.

But Sophronia was not at home on the day of my fall. I sat on her kitchen steps crying and holding my face until the cook sent the upstairs maid to Audubon Park on a search for Sophronia. She came, running, I think for the first time in the majestic movements of her life, waving away the two redheads. She took me to her room and washed my face and prodded my nose and put her hand over my mouth when I screamed. She said we must go immediately to Dr. Fenner, but when I told her that I had thrown myself from the tree, she stopped talking about the doctor, bandaged my face, gave me a pill, put me on her bed and lay down beside me. I told her about my father and Fizzy and fell asleep. When I woke up she said that she'd walk me home. On the way she told me that I must say nothing about Fizzy to anybody ever, and that if my nose still hurt in a few days I was only to say that I had fallen on the street and refuse to answer any questions about how I fell. A block away from my aunts' house we sat down on the steps of the Baptist church. She looked sad and I knew that I had displeased her. I touched her face, which had always been between us a way of saying that I was sorry.

She said, "Don't go through life making trouble for people."

I said, "If I tell you I won't tell about Fizzy, then I won't tell."

She said, "Run home now. Goodbye."

And it was to be goodbye for another year, because I had forgotten that we were to leave for New York two days later, and when I telephoned to tell that to Sophronia the woman she worked for said I wasn't to telephone again. In any case, I soon forgot about Fizzy, and when the bandage came off my nose—it looked different but not different enough—our New York doctor said that it would heal by itself, or whatever was the nonsense they believed in those days about broken bones.

We went back to New Orleans the next year and the years after that until I was sixteen, and they were always the best times of my life. It was Aunt Hannah who took me each Saturday to the movies and then to the French Quarter, where we bought smelly old leather books and she told me how it all had been when she was a girl: about my grandmother—I remembered her—who had been a very tall woman with a lined, severe face and a gentle nature; about my grandfather, dead before I was born, who, in his portrait over the fireplace, looked too serious and distinguished. They had, in a middle-class world, evidently been a strange couple, going their own way with little interest in money or position, loved and respected by their children. "Your grandfather used to say" was a common way to begin a sentence, and although whatever he said had been law, he had allowed my father and aunts their many eccentricities in a time and place that didn't like eccentrics, and to such a degree that not one of his children ever knew they weren't like other people. Hannah, for example, once grew angry—the only time I ever saw her show any temper—when my mother insisted I finish my dinner: she rose and hit the table, and told my mother and the startled boarders that when she was twelve years old she had decided she didn't ever want to eat with people again and so she had taken to sitting on the steps of the front porch and my grandmother, with no comment, had for two years brought her dinner on a tray, and so what was wrong with one dinner I didn't feel like sitting through?

I think both Hannah and Jenny were virgins, but if they were, there were no signs of spinsterhood. They were nice about married people, they were generous to children, and sex was something to have fun about. Jenny had been the consultant to many neighborhood young ladies before their marriage night, or the night of their first lover. One of these girls, a rich ninny, Jenny found irritating and unpleasant. When I was sixteen I came across the two of them in earnest conference on the lawn, and later Jenny told me that the girl had come to consult her about how to avoid pregnancy.

"What did you tell her?"

"I told her to have a glass of ice water right before the sacred act and three sips during it."

When we had finished laughing, I said, "But she'll get pregnant."

"He's marrying her for money, he'll leave her when he gets it. This way at least maybe she'll have a few babies for herself."

And four years later, when I wrote my aunts that I was going to be married, I had back a telegram: FORGET ABOUT THE GLASS OF ICE WATER TIMES HAVE CHANGED.

I think I learned to laugh in that house and to knit and embroider and sew a straight seam and to cook. Each Sunday it was my job to clean the crayfish for the wonderful bisque, and it was Jenny and Carrie, the cook, who taught me to make turtle soup, and how to kill a chicken without ladylike complaints about the horror of dealing death, and how to pluck and cook the wild ducks that were hawked on our street every Sunday morning. I was taught, also, that if you gave, you did it without piety and didn't boast about it. It had been one of my grandfather's laws, in the days when my father and aunts were children, that no poor person who asked for anything was ever to be refused, and his children fulfilled the injunction. New Orleans was a city of many poor people, particularly black people, and the boardinghouse kitchen after the house dinner was, on most nights, a mighty pleasant place: there would often be as many as eight or ten people, black and white, almost always very old or very young, who sat at the table on the kitchen porch while Carrie ordered the kitchen maids and me to bring the steaming platters and the coffeepots.

It was on such a night that I first saw Leah, a light tan girl of about fifteen with red hair and freckles, a flat, ugly face, and a big stomach. I suppose I was about fourteen years old that night, but I remember her very well because she stared at me through her hungry eating. She came again about a week later, and this time Carrie herself took the girl aside and whispered to her, but I don't think the girl answered her because Carrie shrugged and moved away. The next morning, Hannah, who always rose at six to help Jenny before she went to her own office job, screamed outside my bedroom window. Leaning out, I saw Hannah pointing underneath the house and saying softly, "Come out of there."

Slowly the tan-red girl crawled out. Hannah said, "You must not stay under there. It's very wet. Come inside, child, and dry yourself out. From that day on Leah lived somewhere in the house, and a few months later had her baby in the City Hospital. The baby was put out for adoption on Sophronia's advice with a little purse of money from my mother. I never knew what Leah did in the house, because when she helped with the dishes Carrie lost her temper, and when she tried making beds Jenny asked her not to, and once when she was raking leaves for the gardener he yelled, "You ain't in your proper head," so in the end, she took to following me around.

I was, they told me, turning into a handful. Mrs. Stillman said I was wild, Mr. Stillman said that I would, of course, bring pain to my mother and father, and Fizzy said I was just plain disgusting mean. It had been a bad month for me. I had, one night, fallen asleep in the fig tree and, coming down in the morning, refused to tell my mother where I had been. James Denery the Third had hit me very hard in a tug-of-war and I had waited until the next day to hit him over the head with a porcelain coffeepot and then his mother complained to my mother. I had also refused to go back to dancing class.

And I was now spending most of my time with a group from an orphanage down the block. I guess the orphan group was no more attractive than any other, but to be an orphan seemed to me desirable and a self-made piece of independence. In any case, the orphans were more interesting to me than my schoolmates, and if they played rougher they complained less. Frances, a dark beauty of my age, queened it over the others because her father had been killed by the Mafia. Miriam, small and wiry, regularly stole my allowance from the red purse my aunt had given me, and the one time I protested she beat me up. Louis Calda was religious and spoke to me about it. Pancho was dark, sad, and, to me, a poet, because once he said, "*Yo te amo*." I could not sleep a full night after this declaration, and it set up in me forever after both sympathy and irritability with the first sexual stirrings of little girls, so masked, so complex, so foolish as compared with the sex of little boys. It was Louis Calda who took Pancho and me to a Catholic Mass that could have made me a fourteen-year-old convert. But Louis explained that he did not think me worthy, and Pancho, to stop my tears, cut off a piece of his hair with a knife, gave it to me as a gift from royalty, and then shoved me into the gutter. I don't know why I thought this an act of affection, but I did, and went home to open the back of a new wristwatch my father had given me for my birthday and to put the lock of hair in the back. A day later when the watch stopped, my father insisted I give it to him immediately, declaring that the jeweler was unreliable.

It was that night that I disappeared, and that night that Fizzy said I was disgusting mean, and Mr. Stillman said I would forever pain my mother and father, and my father turned on both of them and said he would handle his family affairs himself without comments from strangers. But he said it too late. He had come home very angry with me: the jeweler, after my father's complaints about his unreliability, had found the lock of hair in the back of the watch. What started out to be a mild reproof on my father's part soon turned angry when I wouldn't explain about the hair. (My father was often angry when I was most like him.) He was so angry that he forgot that he was attacking me in front of the Stillmans, my old rival Fizzy, and the delighted Mrs. Dreyfus, a new, rich boarder who only that afternoon had complained about my bad manners. My mother left the room when my father grew angry with me. Hannah, passing through, put up her hand as if to stop my father and then, frightened of the look he gave her, went out to the porch. I sat on the couch, astonished at the pain in my head. I tried to get up from the couch, but one ankle turned and I sat down again, knowing for the first time the rampage that could be caused in me by anger. The room began to have other forms, the people were no longer men and women, my head was not my own. I told myself that my head had gone somewhere and I have little memory of anything after my Aunt Jenny came into the room and said to my father, "Don't you remember?" I have never known what she meant, but I knew that soon after I was moving up the staircase, that I slipped and fell a few steps, that when I woke up hours later in my bed, I found a piece of angel cake—an old love, an old custom—left by my mother on my pillow. The headache was worse and I vomited out of the window. Then I dressed, took my red purse, and walked a long way down St. Charles Avenue. A St. Charles Avenue mansion had on its back lawn a famous doll's-house, an elaborate copy of the mansion itself, built years before for the small daughter of the house. As I passed this showpiece, I saw a policeman and moved swiftly back to the doll palace and crawled inside. If I had known about the fantasies of the frightened, that ridiculous small house would not have been so terrible for me. I was surrounded by ornate, carved reproductions of the mansion furniture, scaled for children, bisque figurines in miniature, a working toilet seat of gold leaf in suitable size, small draperies of damask with a sign that said "From the damask of Marie Antoinette," a miniature samovar with small bronze cups, and a tiny Madame Récamier couch on which I spent the night, my legs on the floor. I must have slept, because I woke from a nightmare and knocked over a bisque figurine. The noise frightened me, and since it was now almost light, in one of those lovely mist mornings of late spring when every flower in New Orleans seems to melt and mix with the air, I crawled out. Most of that day I spent walking, although I had a long session in the ladies' room of the railroad station. I had four dollars and two bits, but that wasn't much when you meant it to last forever and when you knew it would not be easy for a fourteen-year-old girl to find work in a city where too many people knew her. Three times I stood in line at the railroad ticket windows to ask where I could go for four dollars, but each time the question seemed too dangerous and I knew no other way of asking it.

Toward evening, I moved to the French Quarter, feeling sad and envious as people went home to dinner. I bought a few Tootsie Rolls and a half loaf of bread and went to the St. Louis Cathedral in Jackson Square. (It was that night that I composed the prayer that was to become, in the next five years, an obsession, mumbled over and over through the days and nights: "God forgive me, Papa forgive me, Mama forgive me, Sophronia, Jenny, Hannah, and all others, through this time and that time, in life and in death." When I was nineteen, my father, who had made several attempts through the years to find out what my lip movements meant as I repeated the prayer, said, "How much would you take to stop that? Name it and you've got it." I suppose I was sick of the nonsense by that time because I said, "A leather coat and a feather fan," and the next day he bought them for me.) After my loaf of bread, I went looking for a bottle of soda pop and discovered, for the first time, the whorehouse section around Bourbon Street. The women were ranged in the doorways of the cribs, making the first early evening offers to sailors, who were the only men in the streets. I wanted to stick around and see how things like that worked, but the second or third time I circled the block, one of the girls called out to me. I couldn't understand the words, but the voice was angry enough to make me run toward the French Market.

The Market was empty except for two old men. One of them called to me as I went past, and I turned to see that he had opened his pants and was shaking what my circle called "his thing." I flew across the street into the coffee stand, forgetting that the owner had known me since I was a small child when my Aunt Jenny would rest from her marketing tour with a cup of fine, strong coffee.

He said, in the patois, "*Que faites, ma 'fant? Je suis fermé.*"

I said, "*Rien. My tante attend*—Could I have a doughnut?"

He brought me two doughnuts, saying one was *lagniappe*, but I took my doughnuts outside when he said, "*Mais où est vo' tante à c' heure?*"

I fell asleep with my doughnuts behind a shrub in Jackson Square. The night was damp and hot and through the sleep there were many voices and, much later, there was music from somewhere near the river. When all sounds had ended, I woke, turned my head, and knew I was being watched. Two rats were sitting a few feet from me. I urinated on my dress, crawled backwards to stand up, screamed as I ran up the steps of St. Louis Cathedral and pounded on the doors. I don't know when I stopped screaming or how I got to the railroad station, but I stood against the wall trying to tear off my dress and only knew I was doing it when two women stopped to stare at me. I began to have cramps in my stomach of a kind I had never known before. I went into the ladies' room and sat bent in a chair, whimpering with pain. Afer a while the cramps stopped, but I had an intimation, when I looked into the mirror, of something happening to me: my face was blotched, and there seemed to be circles and twirls I had never seen before, the straight blonde hair was damp with sweat, and a paste of green from the shrub had made lines on my jaw. I had gotten older.

Sometime during that early morning I half washed my dress, threw away my pants, put cold water on my hair. Later in the morning a cleaning woman appeared, and after a while began to ask questions that frightened me. When she put down her mop and went out of the room, I ran out of the station. I walked, I guess, for many hours, but when I saw a man on Canal Street who worked in Hannah's office, I realized that the sections of New Orleans that were known to me were dangerous for me.

Years before, when I was a small child, Sophronia and I would go to pick up, or try on, pretty embroidered dresses that were made for me by a colored dressmaker called Bibettera. A block up from Bibettera's there had been a large ruin of a house with a sign, ROOMS—CLEAN—CHEAP, and cheerful people seemed always to be moving in and out of the house. The door of the house was painted a bright pink. I liked that and would discuss with Sophronia why we didn't live in a house with a pink door.

Bibettera was long since dead, so I knew I was safe in this Negro neighborhood. I went up and down the block several times, praying that things would work and I could take my cramps to bed. I knocked on the pink door. It was answered immediately by a small young man.

I said, "Hello." He said nothing.

I said, "I would like to rent a room, please."

He closed the door but I waited, thinking he had gone to get the lady of the house. After a long time, a middle-aged woman put her head out of a second-floor window and said, "What you at?"

I said, "I would like to rent a room, please. My mama is a widow and has gone to work across the river. She gave me money and said to come here until she called for me."

"Who your mama?"

"Er. My mama."

"What you at? Speak out."

"I told you. I have money . . ." But as I tried to open my purse, the voice grew angry.

"This is a nigger house. Get you off. *Vite*."

I said, in a whisper, "I know. I'm part nigger."

The small young man opened the front door. He was laughing. "You part mischief. Get the hell out of here."

I said, "Please"—and then, "I'm related to Sophronia Mason. She told me to come. Ask her."

Sophronia and her family were respected figures in New Orleans Negro circles, and because I had some vague memory of her stately bow to somebody as she passed this house, I believed they knew her. If they told her about me I would be in trouble, but phones were not usual then in poor neighborhoods, and I had no other place to go.

The woman opened the door. Slowly I went into the hall.

I said, "I won't stay long. I have four dollars and Sophronia will give more if . . ."

The woman pointed up the stairs. She opened the door of a small room. "Washbasin place down the hall. Toilet place behind the kitchen. Two-fifty and no fuss, no bother."

I said, "Yes ma'am, yes ma'am," but as she started to close the door, the young man appeared.

"Where your bag?"

"Bag?"

"Nobody put up here without no bag."

"Oh. You mean the bag with my clothes? It's at the station. I'll go and get it later . . ." I stopped because I knew I was about to say I'm sick, I'm in pain, I'm frightened.

He said, "I say you lie. I say you trouble. I say you get out."

I said, "And I say you shut up."

Years later, I was to understand why the command worked, and to be sorry that it did, but that day I was very happy when he turned and closed the door. I was asleep within minutes.

Toward evening, I went down the stairs, saw nobody, walked a few blocks and bought myself an oyster loaf. But the first bite made me feel sick, so I took my loaf back to the house. This time, as I climbed the steps, there were three women in the parlor, and they stopped talking when they saw me. I went back to sleep immediately, dizzy and nauseated.

I woke to a high, hot sun and my father standing at the foot of the bed staring at the oyster loaf.

He said, "Get up now and get dressed."

I was crying as I said, "Thank you, Papa, but I can't."

From the hall, Sophronia said, "Get along up now. *Vite*. The morning is late."

My father left the room. I dressed and came into the hall carrying my oyster loaf. Sophronia was standing at the head of the stairs. She pointed out, meaning my father was on the street.

I said, "He humiliated me. He did. I won't. . . . "

She said, "Get you going or I will never see you whenever again."

I ran past her to the street. I stood with my father until Sophronia joined us, and then we walked slowly, without speaking, to the streetcar line. Sophronia bowed to us, but she refused my father's hand when he attempted to help her into the car. I ran to the car meaning to ask her to take me with her, but the car moved and she raised her hand as if to stop me. My father and I walked again for a long time.

He pointed to a trash can sitting in front of a house. "Please put that oyster loaf in the can."

At Vanalli's restaurant, he took my arm. "Hungry?"

I said, "No, thank you, Papa."

But we went through the door. It was, in those days, a New Orleans custom to have an early black coffee, go to the office, and after a few hours have a large breakfast at a restaurant. Vanalli's was crowded, the headwaiter was so sorry, but after my father took him aside, a very small table was put up for us—too small for my large father, who was accommodating himself to it in a manner most unlike him.

He said, "Jack, my rumpled daughter would like cold crayfish, a nice piece of pompano, a separate bowl of Bearnaise sauce, don't ask me why, French fried potatoes . . ."

I said, "Thank you, Papa, but I am not hungry. I don't want to be here."

My father waved the waiter away and we sat in silence until the crayfish came. My hand reached out instinctively and then drew back.

My father said, "Your mother and I have had an awful time."

I said, "I'm sorry about that. But I don't want to go home, Papa."

He said, angrily, "Yes, you do. But you want me to apologize first. I do apologize but you should not have made me say it."

After a while I mumbled, "God forgive me, Papa forgive me, Mama forgive me, Sophronia, Jenny, Hannah . . ."

"Eat your crayfish."

I ate everything he had ordered and then a small steak. I suppose I had been mumbling throughout my breakfast.

My father said, "You're talking to yourself. I can't hear you. What are you saying?"

"God forgive me, Papa forgive me, Mama forgive me, Sophronia, Jenny . . ."

My father said, "Where do we start your training as the first Jewish nun on Prytania Street?"

When I finished laughing, I liked him again. I said, "Papa, I'll tell you a secret. I've had very bad cramps and I am beginning to bleed. I'm changing life."

He stared at me for a while. Then he said, "Well, it's not the way it's usually described, but it's accurate, I guess. Let's go home now to your mother."

We were never, as long as my mother and father lived, to mention that time again. But it was of great importance to them and I've thought about it all my life. From that day on I knew my power over my parents. That was not to be too important: I was ashamed of it and did not abuse it too much. But I found out something more useful and more dangerous: if you are willing to take the punishment, you are halfway through the battle. That the issue may be trivial, the battle ugly, is another point.

"Talk To The Music"

ARNA BONTEMPS (1902–1973)

Arna Bontemps was born Arnaud Bontemps in Alexandria, Louisiana of French Creole ancestry, but grew up in Los Angeles, California, after his family left the South to escape racial oppression. He was educated in a predominantly white school where he found that black history was relegated to "two short paragraphs: a statement about jungle people in Africa and an equally brief account of the slavery issue in American history." Bontemps dedicated his life to correcting those omissions and to embracing the traditions of his folk heritage. After his graduation from Pacific Union College in 1923, he moved to New York where he taught in private schools and began publishing poems in *The Crisis* and *Opportunity*, winning prizes from both magazines. Bontemps became a key figure in the Harlem Renaissance and published his first novel, *God Sends Us Sunday* in 1931. It was followed by his most acclaimed novel, *Black Thunder* (1936), the story of a slave rebellion in Virginia, and *Drums at Dusk* (1939). Bontemps also wrote numerous prize-winning children's books and was the editor of numerous anthologies, including *The Harlem Renaissance Remembered* (1972). He co-edited *The Poetry of the Negro* (1949) and *The Book of American Negro Folklore* (1958) with Langston Hughes. Bontemps was university librarian at Fisk University in Nashville (1943–1965), and later served as the curator of the James Weldon Johnson Memorial Collection at Yale University. Bontemps was among the group of writers solicited by Marcus Christian of Dillard University to "collect material for a history of the Negro in Louisiana" (1936–1943) for the Negro Writers' Project, a unit of the WPA's Louisiana Writers' Project. Bontemps returned to his Louisiana roots for the setting of the following short story, "Talk to the Music" (1971).

You tells it to the music and
the music tells it to you.
—Sidney Bechet

My father used to say that when you heard one blues song, you've heard them all. He did not mean that all are the same, of course, or that one is enough to satisfy whatever it is in you that craves blues, but after you have listened to one blues, you can always recognize another. In the same way, when you've met one blues singer, you know the species. Ma Rainey, Mayme Smith, Bessie Smith—I could be talking about any one of them and you wouldn't be able to tell by the story which one I had in mind. But right now I'm thinking about the other Mayme—Mayme Dupree.

She never made records, and she never got to Broadway, and nobody ever called her Empress of the Blues, or Lady Day, or anything equivalent, but don't let that fool you. Mayme Dupree had what the others had and then some more. She could play the piano as well as sing and she made up her own songs. You've heard the Jelly-Roll Morton recording of the Mayme Dupree Blues. Well, that's what I'm talking about.

Chances are all this was before your time. What you know about women blues singers probably does not go back any further than Ethel Waters or Pearl Bailey or Billie Holiday, but ask Ethel or Pearl. They'll tell you about Mayme Dupree. Ask Kid Ory or Sidney Bechet. Mayme was singing blues before some of these were born.

There were still other things Mayme had that couldn't be matched by the three more celebrated women who brought the blues out of the South. She was a New Orleans woman with just enough Creole hauteur to make her interesting, and she was good looking. I'm still a bug about old New Orleans—though my own hometown was up the river a piece—and I can't remember a time when I had any objection to good looking women. Naturally I wanted to see and hear this Mayme Dupree people talked about.

But that wasn't easy. Mayme worked as an entertainer, but she worked in Storyville, and that was the legendary red-light district of the fabulous old city at the mouth of the Mississippi. I may have looked young, but age wasn't the obstacle. While there was a good bit of democracy in Storyville, believe me, there was not enough to open the doors of the place where Mayme sang to a black boy who was obviously not one of the employees.

As you know, Jelly-Roll Morton got around this by rushing the can; he made himself available for certain errands. He stood by to run around the corner with the beer can and get it refilled whenever this service was demanded. The wage was negligible, but the job gave the long-legged kid an excuse for being on the premises and provided excellent opportunities for him to hear the aching, heartsick songs of Mayme Dupree.

I, on the other hand, was never any good at masquerades of any kind. They still annoy me. The difference may have been that old Jelly was bent on learning Mayme's songs and nothing else, while I was curious about the singer herself and couldn't stop wondering what it was that troubled her and made her sing the way she did. In any case, I found out where she lived, and the time came when I went there to see her.

I put on my Sunday clothes, which was the only change I had at the time anyhow, fastened my two-toned shoes with a button hook, adjusted the stickpin in my tie, and gave an extra touch to my curly and rather flamboyantly parted hair. I was pleased with the raven sideburns, but my feathers fell when I looked at the mustache. Well, the devil with that, I sighed, but I remained confused as to the kind impression I wanted to make. As an afterthought, when I had put on my hat and started for the door, I picked up my mandolin case and the leather-covered roll of sheet music beside it.

It was pointless to carry these things everywhere I went, but I had formed the habit, and in almost any new situation I felt more comfortable with them than without. This was especially true in the late afternoon or early evening, and that was the time of day I had chosen to look up Mayme. I felt fine as I strolled on the wooden banquette that still served as a sidewalk in that part of town, but presently my feelings changed to dismay.

Neither the appearance nor the smell of the neighborhood was improving, and the quarters in which I asked for Mayme were over a pool hall. The steps were on the outside and the entrance was dirty; the hall beyond, dark. Here and there a shadow stirred. Something ponderous twisted and turned on a chair and finally spoke.

"You looking for somebody, ha'?"

It was the voice of an old woman, and the odd inflection with which she ended her question was pronounced as if she had started to say *hant* and cut it off in the middle.

"Mayme Dupree," I said.

"Mayme's apt to be sleep. She works at night."

"It's nearly dark now."

"Did you ever try to talk to Mayme when she's just waking up?"

"I don't know her yet, I just want to meet her," I explained.

"Well, you sure picked yourself a time." The old woman got out of the chair with more twisting and straining and started down the hall. "Mayme!" she blasted suddenly. "Mayme, somebody's asking for you here." She pounded the door in passing but continued on, finally disappearing down the hall.

Mayme came out soon afterwards, her lower lip hanging, her eyes almost closed, her hair in a tangle, a dingy garment thrown around her. "Do I know you?" she asked vaguely.

"I expect I've done wrong," I said, stuttering. "You don't know me; I'm from Rapides Parish. I just wanted to talk to you. I aimed to catch you when you were sitting around doing nothing."

"You never catch me sitting around doing nothing," Mayme muttered. "What's your name?"

"Norman Taylor."

Actually she didn't care what my name was. Before I could get the words out, she added, "If I was sitting around, I'd be drinking, I wouldn't be doing nothing."

I mean I want to hear the blues," I ventured. "I want to hear the blues like you sing them."

Her mind seemed to wander but presently she blurted, "What in the name of God you doing with that thing?"

"Would you like to hear me play something on my mandolin?" I asked.

She shook her head. "Not this early in the evening. I got to get myself together now. I'm not too much on mandolin playing when I'm wide awake."

"I didn't mean to break in on you," I apologized again. "I'll move on now, but can't you tell me when I could hear the blues?"

She yawned, scratching her head with all ten of her fingers. "Come back," she nodded. "Come back again sometime."

I did—about an hour later. She had left her room, but I found her down the block sitting alone in the "family" section of a saloon. There was a bottle of gin on the table, beside it a tiny glass and nothing else. I waited at the door till she noticed me. She gave me a shrug which I took to mean 'suit yourself,' so I took the seat across the table, and she didn't seem to mind. In fact, she scarcely noticed me again after I sat down.

"Don't you ever talk to anybody?" I asked eventually.

She ignored the question. "I got a hack that picks me up here every evening. It takes me to—to where I go. I'm waiting for it now."

Suddenly Mayme emptied her glass and put the bottle in her handbag, and I looked up and saw the hack driver standing in the door. He was wearing a frayed Prince Albert and a battered top hat. His shoes were rough, his pants and shirt grimy.

"Well, good-bye," I called.

She turned and smiled rather pleasantly, but she kept on walking, and she didn't actually answer.

A saloon was not a place in which I could feel at ease in those days, but somehow I hesitated to leave. After a few moments I went to the bar in the adjoining section and asked for a glass of beer. I stood there a long time nibbling on the "free lunch" as I drank, and gradually became aware of the activity around me.

The telephone rang frequently. Each time it was by the bartender whose name, it seemed, was Benny, and each time the message had to do with someone's need for a musician or a singer or a group to entertain at a party, a dance, a boatride, or some other merry occasion. The men at the bar and those lolling about the premises would prick their ears as soon as Benny took the receiver off the hook, and as quickly as he indicated what kind of performer was sought, one who could fill the bill would step forward. Sometimes the request was for a specific individual or combination, and sometimes those requested were unavailable due to previous engagement. Some were in the pool hall around the corner and had left instructions as to how they might be fetched. A few were independent enough to ask a few questions about the hours, the distance, the pay, and other details before accepting a gig, as they called the engagements, but in the end no job went unfilled, and I was almost tempted to indicate to Benny my own availability.

But I had not come to New Orleans to seek employment as a musician, so I promptly dismissed the idea from my mind. Even though I had already let myself be drawn into several activities which I did not plan to write home about, the temptation to capitalize on my modest musical skills was not strong enough to lure me into another. I had left my parents with the understanding that I would enroll at New Orleans University, and I had every intention of doing so—eventually. My determination to hear the blues first was an irregularity which I considered amply justified. It was not based on mere whim or a casual desire. I had heard strains of the music, and I was haunted. With me the blues had become a strange necessity. I knew that before I could undertake anything else in New Orleans, I had to hear Mayme Dupree sing.

Before leaving that evening, I gained a general impression of the business end of the music game as the boys around New Orleans knew it. While Benny's saloon and Buddy's barber shop, which was mentioned several times during the half hour I stood at the bar, were not employment agencies, they did serve as clearing houses of a sort. There was no competition between the places, and neither expected cuts or payoffs of any kind from the musicians or the employers. Benny was satisfied to have the fellows hang around his place and do their drinking there, and apparently Buddy Bolden's shop was content to shave the musicians and cut their hair. Buddy, of course, was a powerful cornet player and bandman himself, and this made things a little different in his case.

Other women came in after Mayme Dupree left. Some were accompanied by escorts. Others were joined in the "family" section by men who spotted them as they arrived. I did not get the impression that any of these women had come into Benny's to pick up musical gigs. On the contrary, I concluded that most of them were there to be picked up themselves. Like the musicians, they appeared to have slept all day. Getting their eye-openers at Benny's, they looked fresh and sassy, and their perfume filled the saloon. When I turned around and discovered a particularly giddy-looking one trying to trap me with her eyes, I decided it was time for me to look at my watch and go through the motions of hurrying to an appointment.

What Mayme said about the hack picking her up at Benny's every evening was true. She never missed, and the hackman was always on time. I could have set my watch by him. But I did no more than speak and pass the time of day the next few times with her. Mayme did not encourage conversation. Absorbed in her own thoughts, she would come into Benny's saloon just as twilight was falling and go to the most isolated table in the family room. Benny would give her the usual pleasantry as he filled her tiny glass and left the flask of gin beside it, but Mayme's eyes were shadowed by her bird of Paradise hat, and I could see nothing on her face to indicate she even heard him. But I did not give up hope, and the time came when she invited me to come over and have some sit-down.

"You come here pretty regular," she chided.

"You told me to come back sometime," I reminded her.

Mayme smiled. "You're too young a boy to hurrah a woman old as me."

"I couldn't smart-aleck anybody if I wanted to, Mayme," I confessed. "Besides, I've got too much on my mind."

"You still hankering for the blues?"

"I'd give my eye teeth to hear them."

"You look like a boy that's had good raising. You keeps your shoes shined and your hair combed. You ain't got no cause to be hanging around saloons, much less trying to hear boogie house music. If you're a stranger in New Orleans, why don't you try to meet some nice quadroon girls? There's lots of parties going on all the time. Go rowing on Lake Ponchartrain and play your mandolin. That's something you could write home and tell your people about."

"I aim to do all that sometime maybe," I admitted. "But don't feel like it now. I had a girl at home, pretty as you please, but she couldn't wait. She said I was too slow. I don't want to think about courting or sweet music again for a long, long time. I'd like to hear something lowdown, Mayme."

"I don't sing the blues just to be singing them," she said. "Not anymore, I don't. If you want to hear my blues, you got to go where I go, Norman, and I don't rightly think they'd let you in."

"Where's that?"

She put the cork in her bottle. "Storyville," she answered. "Do I have to say more?"

"The red-light district?"

"That's where I work. That's where this hack is waiting to take me."

The driver was standing in the doorway. She emptied her glass.

"You don't look like a fancy woman, Mayme, and you don't sound much like one."

"Along about nine or ten o'clock I sit down at the piano, and I sets my bottle of gin where I can reach it. I don't stop playing and singing till that bottle's empty. Then I get up and put on my hat. They pay me my money and I go home." She had started toward the door, but since she continued to talk, I followed her out to the hack. Seeing me standing there after she had climbed in, a sudden impulse seemed to strike her. "Get in if you want to," she said. "The hackman will bring you back this way. I don't keep him waiting around down there. He comes back for me in the morning."

Riding beside her in the rented carriage gave me a funny feeling. I had never considered myself a man of the world, but all at once I felt like one. "You ride in style," I told her.

"It takes a big cut out of what I make to pay for it, but it's the only way I can be sure of getting there." She fished in her handbag for cigarets, lit one in the darkness, and settled back for the slow drive. After a long pause she said, half-mischievously, I thought, "If you was out riding with a sure 'nough fancy gal, Norman, it wouldn't be like courting somebody you aimed to marry. You wouldn't study about age or color—things like that—so long as she smelled sweet and was soft to touch."

"If you're not careful, you'll be giving me ideas in a minute," I laughed.

She laughed too, but she added quickly, "Don't pay me no mind, boy. It ain't like me to carry on a lot of foolishness. I don't know what's come over me tonight."

"You're not as unfriendly as you try to make out," I encouraged.

Her answer was something between a sigh and a grunt. "Don't count on it," she added after a pause. "I'm a blue-gummed woman, and I know it. I'm poison, too."

"Aw, hush, Mayme."

"Don't hush me. I know what I'm saying. I bit a man once. It was just a love bite, but his arm swelled up like he'd been bit by a black widow spider or a copperhead snake."

"I don't pay any attention to the foolishness I hear people talk about blue-gummed women, women with crooked eyes, right black women. I'd go out with a girl that was black as a new buggy if I liked her, and I think blue gums are kind of interesting."

"Just go on thinking that," she scoffed, "and one of these days you'll find yourself all swoll up like a man with the dropsy."

The lights were coming on in Storyville as we reached the district, and there was a good bit of going and coming in the streets. Saloons were hitting it up, and in some the tinkle of glasses dissolved into a background of ragtime piano thumping. But the over-all mood, as I sensed it, was grim, and furtive shadows moved along the street. Can desire be anything but sad? I wondered as the carriage pulled up beside an ornate hitching post. I jumped out and waited for Mayme to put her foot on a large square-cut steppingstone.

"Is this as far as I can go?" I asked, looking up at the elegant doorway at the top of the steps.

"Here is where you turn back," she said.

"If there's any way you can fix it for me to hear you sing sometime," I reminded her, "I'll sure appreciate it, Mayme."

She didn't promise, but her voice still sounded indulgent as she let the hackman go, instructing him to drop me at a convenient point in the vicinity of Benny's.

I had enough mother wit to realize that Mayme was not the kind of woman you could persuade to do anything before she was good and ready. Having made it clear to her what I wanted, I settled back to another long wait, taking pains to let her see me occasionally and making sure she got a good chance to say anything that happened to be on her mind. Meanwhile, Benny's saloon hummed nightly. The telephone rang. Musicians were in and out, whistling for hacks, catching quick drinks before hurrying off to their gigs. Fancy women bright as flamingos fluttered in and settled down languidly at the family tables. And the giddy-looking one who had taken a shine to me kept making eyes.

Mayme's hack driver had appeared in the saloon and she had followed him out one evening when the place was more crowded than usual, but a few moments later he returned and tapped me on the shoulder.

"She wants to speak to you," he said.

I didn't wait to finish my sweeten' water (gin and rock candy), and when I reached the carriage, Mayme was leaning out with something to tell me. "They need a boy tonight—out at the place. Did you ever work in a white coat?"

"Does it matter?" I asked, climbing in beside her. "I'll wear one tonight and like it."

"Well, just mind your p's and q's. Keep a duster or a broom or a towel in your hand all the time and don't sit down. Somebody might ask you to do something every now and then, but if you don't pay them no mind, they won't pay you none. Anybody looks at you right hard, just kind of ease around and go to dusting the woodwork or picking up empty glasses."

That was as much I needed, and when Mayme presented me to the Madame as a boy who could take the place of some vague Leroy whom they did not expect to show up, we both nodded without speaking. She was a large woman, heavily jewelled, with glossy black hair piled on her head in great rolls. Her accent was French, but I couldn't be sure whether she was a Louisiana quadroon or a woman from southern Europe. It didn't matter. She led me out to the back and pointed to Leroy's closet. The equipment was in line with Mayme's description of the job: freshly starched white coat, a hanger for the one I was wearing, towels, lamp rags, dust cloths, mops, brushes, and the rest.

I put on the white coat and crept obsequiously into the big living room. When Mayme began playing the piano, I retreated into a corner where there were several pieces of erotic sculpture which I suddenly decided needed dusting. I think I succeeded in fading into the furniture and the fixtures, because neither the men who came through the front door nor the girls who glided down the stairs gave me a second glance. Presently Mayme took their minds completely away.

Good morning, blues,
Heard you when you opened my door.
I said, good morning, blues.
I heard you when you opened my door.

The sadness of the blues stabbed me with her first line, and immediately I wanted to ask Mayme Dupree who had hurt her and how and what made her take it so hard. Remembering how long she had kept me waiting to hear this first song and the price I'd had to pay—putting off my enrollment in college, hanging around Benny's, and now coming to this place with a dust cloth in my hand—I doubted that I could ever expect to learn what it was that made her sing as she did.

Men were calling for drinks and gals before she finished "Good-morning, Blues." The heavy beat of Mayme's song started things moving. When it was over, she reached for her bottle with one hand while the other hand kept up the rhythm. Then for a long spell the piano carried it alone, but more than once I was sure I saw Mayme press her lips together tightly as she played, like somebody deeply troubled in mind. Eventually she blurted another song as if she could hold it back no longer.

If I could holler like the mountain jack,
If I could holler like the mountain jack,
I'd go up on the mountain and call my lover back.

This was heady stuff, even for the hard-bitten habitués of Storyville, and the way Mayme sang it promptly went to the heads of some. One of the men responded with a sort of hog-calling yell that was not intended as a joke and did not provoke laughter. A girl closed her eyes and fluttered her hands high in the air. A few couples stood together as if to dance but did not move. I began wondering when Mayme would sing the song for which she was becoming known and which I had heard about all the way up in Rapides Parish.

Finally she got around to it—the blues that she had made up herself and that had started a sort of craze among the few people who had been fortunate enough to hear her sing it.

Two-nineteen done took my baby away
Two-nineteen done took my baby away
Two-seventeen bring him back someday.

Everyone seemed to expect her to repeat it several times, adding new verses as she sang, and she kept on until she could somehow get the folks to take their eyes off her and think about themselves again. But all I could think as I listened to Mayme Dupree sing her blues that night was that the blues are sad, terribly sad, and desire is sad too. The bottle of gin on the piano, the erotic sculpture, the motionless dancers, the girls with the flutters, the hog-calling man—all seemed to go very well with Mayme's blues. But I wondered if she thought so.

When I asked her, after I had been back several times, she did not show much interest. The blues she sang were just blues to her. There was nothing special about them. They were neither good nor bad. She could understand how some people might like them but not how anyone would want to talk about them. But I thought I would be ungrateful if I didn't make some effort to tell her how I felt about her songs.

I was convinced that there was power of some kind in the blues, their rhythms, and their themes. Fallen angels could never have wailed like this, no matter how they grieved over paradise. Adam and Eve might have perhaps, crying over their lost innocence, but somehow song was not given to them.

She pondered this conceit as the hack jogged homeward in the early dawn, and I thought it was making a good impression until she suddenly said, "You're crazy."

"secret messages"

(for Danny Barker)

TOM DENT (1932–1998)

Thomas Covington Dent was born in New Orleans, the son of Jessie Covington Dent, the first black musician honored with a Juilliard scholarship, and Albert Dent, president of Dillard University from 1941 to 1969. Growing up, Dent was influenced by the New Orleans poet Marcus Christian and his work in preserving and recording black culture in Louisiana. In 1952, he earned a bachelor's degree in political science from Morehouse College, and in 1959 he moved to New York City, where he worked as a reporter. In 1962, Dent co-founded the Umbra Workshop, which explored the interface of politics, art, and social reality with black identity. He moved back to New Orleans in 1965, and became chairman of the board of directors of the Free Southern Theater, an organization of theater professionals and political activists which challenged racism and segregation in the South. Dent's work includes two volumes of poetry, *Magnolia Street* (1976) and *Blue Lights and River Songs* (1982), and *Southern Journey: A Return to the Civil Rights Movement* (1997). His acclaimed play *Ritual Murder* was produced in 1976 by the Ethiopian Theater in New Orleans and in 1978 was published in *Callaloo*, a literary journal which Dent co-founded. He also directed the Congo Square Writers' Workshop in New Orleans. His poem "secret messages" from *Magnolia Street* is dedicated to the memory of Danny Barker, one of the great New Orleans jazz-entertainers.

---

rain
rain drenches the city
as we move past
stuffed black mammies
chained to Royal St. praline shops
check it out

past Bourbon St. beer cans
shadowed moorish cottages
ships slipping down the riversnake past
images of the bullet-riddled bodies of
Mark Essex & Bras Coupe
buried in the beckoning of the blk
shoeshine boy
when it rains it pours
check it out

past blk tap-dancers of the shit-eating grin
the nickel & dime shake-a-leg
shades of weaving flambeau carriers
of the dripping oil & grease-head
"we *are* mardi gras" one said
check it out

past that to where you play yr banjo
"it's plantation time agin" you say to us
& we laugh . . .
outside a blk cabdriver helps crippled
Sweet Emma into the front seat
she done boogied the piano another night
for maybe the 250th year
she laughs loudly to herself as tourists
watch
there is Ashanti saying
when one hears something but does not understand, they say:
"like singing to the white man"
check it out

tripping past raindrops with the ancient slick-haired
Jelly Roll piano player
to listen to some "modern musicians"
at Lu & Charlie's
& the old piano player saying

"they can play a little bit can't they"
teasing our god of fallen masks
check it out . . .

& maybe someday when nobody is
checking it out the drummers will come to life in
St. Louis No. 1 at midnight
beating out the secret messages
& all the masks will drop.
jest like we said they would.
secret messages
secret messages of the gods.

rain
rain drenches the city
as we move past grinning stuffed black mammies
the god of fallen masks offstage
waiting, waiting . . .

from "Shrovetide in Old New Orleans"

ISHMAEL REED (1938–)

Ishmael Reed was born in Chattanooga, Tennessee, where he spent the first four years of his life. He then moved with his mother to Buffalo, New York, where he lived for the next twenty years. Reed attended the University of Buffalo where he demonstrated his talent for writing. He said the "wide gap between social classes bothered him," and withdrew from the university, taking up residence in a Buffalo housing project as an act of solidarity against class and social distinctions. The next period of Reed's life was one of political activism in both the civil rights and black power movements. In 1962 Reed moved to New York City, where he founded the *East Village Other*, a radical newspaper, and participated in the Umbra Workshop, the influential black writer's group. Reed believes that the group, which included Tom Dent, "began the inflourescence of 'Black Poetry.'" His first novel, *The Free-Lance Pallbearers* was published in 1967, the same year he moved to California to teach at the University of California, Berkeley. Since that time Reed has received considerable critical attention for his experimental fiction and poetry and for his satirical treatment of American culture and literary forms. New Orleans and its importance as the American center of *vodoun*, known as voodoo or hoodoo in popular culture, figures prominently in several of Reed's works, including the novels, *Mumbo Jumbo* (1972) and *The Last Days of Louisiana Red* (1974), and in *Shrovetide in Old New Orleans* (1978), a collection of his articles and essays. In the following selection from the title essay, "Shrovetide in Old New Orleans," Reed relates the history of Mardi Gras, which he calls, "a bright moment on America's death calendar."

On March 3, 1699, a few Frenchmen, with bread and fish, celebrated Mardi Gras at a place called "Pointe du Mardi Gras," or "Bayou du Mardi Gras." Over a century and a half later, in 1857, six young men, from Mobile, Alabama (the only other American town where Mardi Gras is observed), of the Cowbellion de Rakin Society, organized the Mystick Krewe of Comus, which presented, on February 24, 1857, a New Orleans street parade. Its theme was "The Demon Actors in Milton's Paradise Lost," a Vodoun pageant if there ever was one, since Milton consigns African gods to hell.

Later came Rex, the carnival's elite krewe, which was hurriedly put together for the occasion of the visit to New Orleans of his Imperial Highness Alexis Romanoff Alexandrovitch, heir apparent to the Russian throne. A militant womanizer, the Prince, who had just hunted bison with Buffalo Bill, apparently followed an actress, Miss Lydia Thompson, to New Orleans. She was the star of the musical comedy called *Bluebeard*; according to contemporary accounts the Prince was a little too formal, and "stiff" in the land of hospitality and the Colgate smile. He is remembered as being rude to his hosts and refusing to shake people's hands. The Rex song that year, dedicated to his Royalvitch, contained the lines: "If ever I cease to love, If ever I cease to love, May the Grand Duke ride a buffalo in a Texas rodeo." Some historians claim that this song contributed to the Prince's irritable mood. The song, however, has endured.

Since those days, in the middle 1850s, many other krewes have been added, some formal and some outlaw, as this year's Krewe of Constipation, whose maskers dressed in boxes of Ex-Lax.

The history is interesting, but all but ignored by many of the Mardi Gras revelers. Vodoun interpretations vary from town to town, from family to family, and from individual to individual. Although the forms are similar, no two humfos (temples?) are alike.

"You get together with your friends to eat and drink," is the way San Francisco novelist Ernest Gaines defines Mardi Gras.

. . .

The important parades on Fat Tuesday were Comus, Rex, and Zulu. This year's Rex is Frank Garden Strachan, a businessman. He looks like the couple on the Delta, a shipper who looks as though he probably has no problems with regularity. His consort is Miss Alma Marie Atkinson. Mr. Strachan wore royal golden robes. His sacrificial maiden is surrounded by maids and jonquils, ribbons of purple and gold and green. Mardi Gras ladies wear laurel crowns. She wore a candy wool crepe suit. There's a "giant" ox. The Boeuf Gras, surrounded by huge berries and cocks. In the old days the oxen would have been slaughtered, a rite known as "burying the carnival." Interesting, when you realize carnival, loosely translated, means "farewell to meat." Other things, right out of pages of the *Golden Bough*: wild men are all over town, carrying clubs, acting savage, black and white. I took a photo of one in a leopard skin outfit and club.

Mr. Strachan's favorite lines in the Rex poem, written by Ashley Phelps, were, "He dresses with care, never tatterdemalion/As becomes every proper Episcopalian." Anglicism, the church of the Confederacy. The theme was "Jazz—New Orleans' Heritage." The HooDoo shrines and the jazz shrines are in the same neighborhood, suggesting a possible connection. The "HooDoo" guidebook says that "jazz" is based upon VooDoo ritual music. I'm thinking of all the musicians called "Papa." It was the one ritual in which the "Papa" or the "King" told people when to stop playing. There are Ragtime floats and Muskrat Ramble floats and an "Oriental" "Chinatown My Chinatown" float. The bakery equivalent of this aesthetic is blueberry cheesecake. But if you think that's rich, in 1838 the Mardi Gras procession contained ". . . several carriages superbly ornamented—bands of music, horses richly caparisoned—personations of Knights, cavaliers, horses, demigods, chanticleers, punchinellos, &c, all mounted. Many of them were dressed in female attire, and acted the lady with no small degree of grace." They knew how to put on the dog in those days. There seemed to have been more work put into the masks. Contemporary photos show the women of 1880, dressed in hoops, putting the masks together by hand.

Now, old-timers say that the Zulu Parade began as a response to Rex. Whereas Rex was white, mythical aristocratic, a Confederate pageant which once honored the daughter of Robert E. Lee, who was "took out" by Comus at the ball that 1870s night, the Zulu Parade involves an ancient Afro-American survival form. Adopting the oppressor's parody of themselves and evolving, from this, an art form with its own laws. I call this process loa-making.

If the whites had their King, Rex; we have our King, Zulu, a savage from the jungle like you say he is. While you're laughing at us we're laughing with you but the joke's on you. In the first Zulu Parade there was a jubilee quartet at each end of the parade. It was a proletariat parade of porters and laborers, who were put down by the Afro-American middle class, the colored six companies. What you put down you often join, someone once said, and so this year's Zulu King was Reverend Lawler P. Daniels of the great southern Negro industry death: preachers, insurance men, and undertakers, the millionaires of the race. His court included BigShot Soulful Warrior, and Witchdoctor. The social mobility of the Zulu Parade can be measured by comparing the style of this parade to that of earlier Zulu parades. King Peter Williams, the first Zulu King, wore a starched white suit, and for a scepter he carried a loaf of Italian bread. By 1914 the King could afford a buggy, and by 1922, the Zulus owned a yacht. This year's King wore turquoise vestments, and jeweled crown. He waved a feathered spear. His wife wore a trailing turquoise gown. The reminders of former times were those wearing animal skins, grass skirts, and Afro wigs. Coconuts are Zulu's doubloons.

Rudy Lombard is a handsome bearded architect who was dressed in SNNC denims! Chic. I told him that Lombard was the name of a family which appears in Dante's *Inferno*. I'm always saying dumb shit like that. So when he said, "Yeah, I met him," after Toni Morrison introduced us, in that tone which sounded like a dismissal, I could understand where he was coming from. Well, he kind of made out that the Black Indians were a hermetic krewe, so secret that those who revealed them were not looked upon favorably. Jules Cahn, a film maker, has done a film on the Mardi Gras Indians, which was being shown at the Historic New Orleans Collection. Unkind remarks were made about his activities as we saw him walking down the street, during the Black Indian ceremonies. People have made so many billions of dollars from "The Black Experience," it ain't funny. And some wish to protect the last remaining secrets. I don't think the Black Indians are going to be so secret for long, if they ever were. I've seen them cited in a number of books concerning New Orleans and the carnival. Even Dick Cavett cited one book entitled *Gumbo-Ya-Ya* on nationwide television while touring the city in the company of Tennessee Williams.

I was told that they never cross Canal Street—"white zones"—but I followed them to Canal Street and beyond. But nobody had to tell me what to mention and what not to mention. In fact, some of the middle-class blacks with whom I visited somehow feel that New Orleans belongs to them and anyone interested in the city is an interloper into the New Orleans Nation. In her remarkable book *Black Dance*, Lynne Fauley Emery claims that none of the original HooDoo ceremonies has ever been witnessed. But the Black Indian ceremony was quite visible to blacks and whites.

The first thing I noticed at the black intersection, one of the stops for Black Indians, was an old beat-up jalopy full of guedes. Guedes are statesmen, clowns, artists, known to "show each man his devil." In *Canapé-Vert*, by the Marcelin brothers, they are depicted as "Gay, rowdy, and a scandalous jester[s]." They are often proletariat gods who satirize government officials on their behalf, and are not afraid to mock the Houngan. Here they are on this New Orleans street, pouring beer into the water tank of the car. Six hours later, I saw them in the same car, making that car run on beer. There's a whole ritual of greeting, mock competition, Chief-saluting, and unintelligible, for me, lingo the

Black Indians go through. There was a little boy named Flyboy who was into some heavy discourse with Wildman, crowned with a bull's horn.

The most extraordinary feature was the costumes, richly decorated, and fantastic. People work on them throughout the year. They carried on with this procession, wending their way through the neighborhoods, then heading uptown on St. Claiborne Street. This krewe had no police escorts and traffic, at some points, became jammed. Some of the inconvenienced were good natured, like the fellow in Confederate battle dress with the Stars and Bars wrapped around his head. Others menaced the blacks with their auto bumpers and the blacks yelping and whooping menaced back, waving their flowered axes about their heads. It was a "mock" race war. I was trying to identify the costumes. Though whites consider the Black Indians to be odd some claim that cohabitation between Blacks and Indians has produced a new race in America. One theory has it that the geometric designs (vé-vés) made by cornmeal, on the ground, used by Houngans to order "down" loas were a technique Haitians learned from the indigenous Indians of Haiti. They made the African gods meaner, they hated the Spanish so. Now, Bob Callahan, President of the Turtle Island Foundation, publisher of *Apalache* by Paul Metcalf, Melville's great-grandson, has a keen eye. We were sitting at the Golden Gate racetrack and from his seat he identified the golden grass—the original Spanish grass, behind the University of California's football stadium. I showed him the photos I made of the Black Indians, and he said the costumes were Caribbean. I left the Indians, they were invading "white" territory like some kind of prophecy was taking place before my eyes.

Since the major American holidays seem to induce anxiety and depression Mardi Gras is a bright moment on the American Death calender. During Christmas, for example, everybody goes about with those airplane stewardess smiles in the winter when it's cold. The plot of Christmas was deliberately scripted to cause guilt, and the only Mardi Gras figure is Santa Claus, who is for kids. Mardi Gras is one of the few art forms in which the whole community can become immersed, just as in HooDoo, which not only Negroes but the Irish practiced in New Orleans.

It's a day of joy when people can act the fool and wild instead of acting that way for the whole year around. They ought to have a Mardi Gras in South Boston. There could be a San Francisco, Chicago, Detroit, and New York Mardi Gras as well as Mardi Gras in Atlanta, Denver, and Philadelphia. Cults all over the community could organize their floats and participate in parades. This could become a land of a million krewes. A non-political holiday could continue through July, where the only thing we have is the Fourth, a day set aside to commemorate feudal slave owners whom tennis court historians would have us believe spent most of their time talking like Alistair Cooke and sitting, hands clasped, in a winged Chippendale, saying profound things. How many people do you know who live in places like Monticello and Mount Vernon? I'd like to see each town work together to put its local histories, legends, and gossip on wheel and foot. Why not a sexy day during the month when the whole earth is doing sexy things, getting swollen to stand erect like the Legba symbol you find both here and in Africa? Legba is a loa who would appreciate Mardi Gras.

Mardi Gras is the one American art I have witnessed in which the audience doesn't sit intimidated or wait for the critics to tell them what to see. The Mardi Gras audience talks back to the performers instead of sitting there like dummies, and can even participate in the action. Oscar Wilde said, "Why shouldn't the Fourth of July pageant in Atlanta be as fine as the Mardi Gras carnival in New Orleans? Indeed, the pageant is the most perfect school of art for the people." Wilde, an admirer of the Confederacy, said he "engaged in voodoo rites with Negroes."

Just think of what artists could do with Mardi Gras. There could be Romare Bearden floats, and Marisol floats, and Ruth Asawa could do a float for the San Francisco Mardi Gras. I'd like to see a Mardi Gras band performing Donald Byrd's music. Amiri Baraka could design a whole parade.

I'd also like to see Karin Bacon, who staged those multi-media spectaculars during the last golden days of New York, co-ordinate a coast-to-coast Mardi Gras by video hookup.

I for one had been over-floated with this Mardi Gras. I headed away from the Black Indians and took one last photo of an interracial motorcycle gang all leathered up and giving the carnival some existentialist stares. I saw the last Black Indian chief, who was wearing those robes I imagined Quetzalcoatl of African and South American lore would be dressed in.

Sitting next to me on the plane was a brother man, dressed in an outfit and with the features of what could only be described as Barry White Cavalier. He stirred when the stewardess shook him.

"Did you go to Mardi Gras?" I asked.

"Yeah," he said.

"What did you think of it? An obscene Confederate pageant?"

"I don't know nothin' about that," he said. "Mardi Gras, to me, is gettin' together with your friends and eatin', and drinkin'."

He dozed off leaving me to watch the Mardi Gras southwest sky, and sipping a burgundy. Robert Tallant wrote in his book *Mardi Gras*, "Mardi Gras is a spirit." HooDoo, too. Watch out Christmas!

from *A Confederacy of Dunces*

JOHN KENNEDY TOOLE (1937–1969)

John Kennedy Toole was born in New Orleans, the only child of John and Thelma Ducoing Toole. Toole was an exceptional student, and at the age of sixteen wrote a short novel, *The Neon Bible* (1989), for a literary contest which he lost. He attended Tulane University and received a master's degree in English from Columbia University in 1959. Toole accepted a teaching position at Hunter College and began work on a novel, set in New Orleans, which would become *A Confederacy of Dunces* (1980). In 1959 he returned to Louisiana, where he taught at Southwestern Louisiana State University and then Dominican College. Toole completed *A Confederacy of Dunces* in 1964, and though the novel is now hailed as a comic masterpiece, it was rejected by several New York publishers. Toole was devastated and in 1969 committed suicide. His mother vowed to find a publisher for the book and persuaded Walker Percy to read the manuscript. His initial reluctance was replaced with astonishment and Percy convinced Louisiana State University Press to publish the book in 1980. In 1981 the novel won the Pulitzer Prize in fiction and both the hardback and paperback editions of the book were bestsellers. *A Confederacy of Dunces* is the story of Ignatius J. Reilly, a gargantuan malcontent, who maneuvers through the streets of New Orleans dispensing unsolicited advice. The following excerpt from the book is one of Reilly's diary entries describing a day spent suffering numerous indignities while peddling Paradise Vendor's hot dogs to tourists in the French Quarter. Reilly signs the entry using the name of his alter ego, Lance, the besieged working boy.

Dear Reader,

A good book is the precious life-blood of a master-spirit, embalmed and treasured up on purpose for a life beyond.

—Milton

The perverted (and I suspect quite dangerous) mind of Clyde has devised still another means of belittling my rather invincible being. At first I thought that I might have found a surrogate father in the czar of sausage, the mogul of meat. But his resentment and jealousy of me are increasing daily; no doubt they will ultimately overwhelm him and destroy his mind. The grandeur of my physique, the complexity of my worldview, the decency and taste implicit in my carriage, the grace with which I function in the mire of today's world—all of these at once confuse and astound Clyde. Now he has relegated me to working in the French Quarter, an area which houses every vice that man has ever conceived in his wildest aberrations, including, I would imagine, several modern variants made possible through the wonders of science. The Quarter is not unlike, I would imagine, Soho and certain sections of North Africa. However, the residents of the French Quarter, blessed with American "Stick-to-itiveness" and "Know-how," are probably straining themselves at this moment to equal and surpass in variety and imagination the diversions enjoyed by the residents of those other world areas of human degradation.

Clearly an area like the French Quarter is not the proper environment for a clean-living, chaste, prudent, and impressionable young Working Boy. Did Edison, Ford, and Rockefeller have to struggle against such odds?

Clyde's fiendish mind has not stopped at so simple an abasement, however. Because I am allegedly handling what Clyde calls "the tourist trade," I have been caparisoned in a costume of sorts.

(Judging from the customers I have had on this first day with the new route, the "tourists" seem to be the same old vagrants I was selling to in the business district. In a stupor induced by Sterno, they have doubtlessly stumbled down into the Quarter and thus, to Clyde's senile mind, qualify as "tourists." I wonder whether Clyde has even had an opportunity to see the degenerates and wrecks and drifters who buy and apparently subsist on Paradise products. Between the other vendors—totally beaten and ailing itinerants whose names are something like Buddy, Pal, Sport, Top, Buck, and Ace—and my customers, I am apparently trapped in a limbo of lost souls. However, the simple fact that they have been resounding failures in our century does give them a certain spiritual quality. For all we know, they may be—these crushed wretches—the saints of our age: beautifully broken old Negroes with tan eyes; downtrodden drifters from wastelands in Texas and Oklahoma; ruined sharecroppers seeking a haven in rodent-infested urban rooming houses.) . . .

But back to the matter at hand: Clyde's vengeance. The vendor who formerly had the Quarter route wore an improbable pirate's outfit, a Paradise Vendor's nod to New Orleans folklore and history, a Clydian attempt to link the hot dog with Creole legend. Clyde forced me to try it on in the garage. The costume, of course, had been made to fit the tubercular and underdeveloped frame of the former vendor, and no amount of pulling and pushing and inhaling and squeezing would get it onto my muscular body. Therefore, a compromise of sorts was made. About my cap I tied the red sateen pirate's scarf. I screwed the one golden earring, a large novelty store hoop of an earring, onto my left earlobe. I affixed the black plastic cutlass to the side of my white vendor's smock with a safety pin. Hardly an impressive pirate, you will say. However, when I studied myself in the mirror, I was forced to admit that I appeared rather fetching in a dramatic way. Brandishing the plastic cutlass at Clyde, I cried, "Walk the plank, Admiral!" This, I should have known, was too much for his literal and sausage-like mind. He grew most alarmed and proceeded to attack me with his spear-like fork. We lunged about in the garage like two swashbucklers in an especially inept historical film for several moments, fork and cutlass clicking against each other madly. Realizing that my plastic weapon was hardly a match for a long fork wielded by a maddened Methuselah, realizing that I was seeing Clyde at his *worst*, I tried to end our little duel. I called out pacifying words; I entreated; I finally surrendered. Still Clyde came, my pirate costume so great a success that it had apparently convinced him that we were back in the golden days of romantic old New Orleans when gentlemen decided matters of hot dog honor at twenty paces. It was then that a light dawned in my intricate mind. I know that Clyde was really trying to kill me. He would have the perfect excuse: self defense. I had played right into his hands. Fortunately for me, I fell to the floor. I had backed into one of the carts, lost my always precarious balance, and had fallen down. Although I struck my head rather painfully against the cart, I cried pleasantly from the floor, "You win, sir." Then I silently paid homage to dear old Fortuna for snatching me from the jaws of death by rusty fork.

I quickly rolled my cart out of the garage and set out for the Quarter. Along the way, many pedestrians gave my semi-costume favorable notice. My cutlass slapping against my side, my earring dangling from my lobe, my red scarf shining in the sun brightly enough to attract a bull, I strode resolutely across town, thankful that I was still alive, armoring myself against the horrors that awaited me in the Quarter. Many a loud prayer rose from my chaste pink lips, some of thanks, some of supplication. I prayed to St. Mathurin, who is invoked for epilepsy and madness, to aid Mr. Clyde (Mathurin is, incidentally, also the patron saint of clowns). For myself, I sent a humble greeting to St. Medericus, the Hermit, who is invoked against intestinal disorders. Meditating upon the call from the grave which I had almost received, I began to think about my mother, for I have always wondered what her reaction would be were I to die in the cause of paying for her misdeeds. I can see her at the funeral, a shoddy, low-cost affair held in the basement of some dubious funeral parlor. Insane with grief, tears boiling from her reddened eyes, she would probably tear my corpse from the coffin, screaming drunkenly, "Don't take him! Why do the sweetest flowers wither and fall from the stem?" The funeral would probably degenerate into a circus, my mother constantly poking her fingers into the two holes dug in my neck by Mr. Clyde's rusty fork, crying an illiterate Grecian cry of curses and vengeance. There would be a certain amount of spectacle involved in the proceedings, I imagine. However, with my mother acting as director, the inherent tragedy would soon become melodrama. Snatching the white lily from my lifeless hands, she would break it in half and wail to the throng of mourners, well-wishers, celebrants, and sightseers, "As this lily was, so was Ignatius. Now they are both snatched and broken." As she threw the lily back into the coffin, her feeble aim would send it flying directly into my whitened face.

For my mother I sent a prayer flying to St. Zita of Lucca, who spent her life as a house servant and practiced many austerities, in the hope that she would aid my mother in fighting her alcoholism and nighttime roistering.

Strengthened by my interlude of worship, I listened to the cutlass slapping against my side. It seemed, like some weapon of morality, to be spurring me toward the Quarter, each plastic slap saying, "Take heart, Ignatius. Thou hast a terrible swift sword." I was beginning to feel rather like a Crusader.

At last I crossed Canal Street pretending to ignore the attention paid me by all whom I passed. The narrow streets of the Quarter awaited me. A vagrant petitioned for a hot dog. I waved him away and strode forth. Unfortunately, my feet could not keep pace with my soul. Below my ankles, the tissues were crying for rest and comfort, so I placed the wagon at the curb and seated myself. The balconies of the old buildings hung over my head like dark branches in an allegorical forest of evil. Symbolically, a Desire bus hurtled past me, its diesel exhaust almost strangling me. Closing my eyes for a moment to meditate and thereby draw strength, I must have fallen asleep, for I remember being rudely awakened by a policeman standing next to me prodding me in the ribs with the toe of his shoe. Some musk which my system generates must be especially appealing to the authorities of the government. Who else would be accosted by a policeman while innocently awaiting his mother before a department store? Who else would be spied upon and reported for picking a helpless stray of a kitten from a gutter? Like a bitch in heat, I seem to attract a coterie of policemen and sanitation officials. The world will someday get me on some ludicrous pretext; I simply await the day that they drag me to some air-conditioned dungeon and leave me there beneath the florescent lights and sound-proofed ceiling to pay the price for scorning all that they hold dear within their little latex hearts.

Rising to my full height—a spectacle in itself—I looked down upon the offending policeman and crushed him with a comment which, fortunately, he failed to understand. Then I wheeled the wagon farther into the Quarter. Because it was early afternoon, there were few people stirring on the streets. I guessed that the residents of the area were still in bed recovering from whatever indecent acts they had been performing the night before. Many no doubt required medical attention: a stitch or two here and there in a torn orifice or a broken genital. I could only imagine how many haggard and depraved eyes were regarding me hungrily from behind the closed shutters. I tried not to think about it. Already I was beginning to feel like an especially toothsome steak in a meat market. However, no one called enticingly from the shutters, those devious mentalities throbbing away in their dark apartments were apparently more subtle seducers. I thought that a note, at least, might flutter down. A frozen orange juice can came flying out of one of the windows and barely missed me. I stooped over and picked it up in order to inspect the empty tin cylinder for a communication of some sort, but only a viscous residue of concentrated juice trickled out on my hand. Was this some obscene message? While I was pondering the matter and staring up at the window from which the can had been hurled, an old vagrant approached the wagon and pleaded for a frankfurter. Grudgingly I sold him one, ruefully concluding that, as always, work was interfering at a crucial moment.

By now, of course, the window from which the can had been sent flying was closed. I rolled farther down the street, staring at the closed shutters for a sign of some sort. Wild laughter issued from more than one building as I passed. Apparently the deluded occupants therein were indulging in some obscene diversion which amused them. I tried to close my virgin ears to their horrid cackling.

A group of tourists wandered along the streets, their cameras poised, their glittering eyeglasses shining like sparklers. Noticing me, they paused and, in sharp Midwestern accents which assailed my delicate eardrums like the sounds of a wheat thresher (however unimaginably horrible that must sound), begged me to pose for a photograph. Pleased by their gracious attentions, I acquiesced. For minutes they snapped away as I obliged them with several artful poses. Standing before the wagon as if it were a pirate's vessel, I brandished my cutlass menacingly for one especially memorable pose, my other hand holding the prow of the tin hot dog. As a climax, I attempted to climb atop the wagon, but the solidity of my physique proved too taxing for that rather flimsy vehicle. It began to roll from beneath me, but the gentlemen in the group were kind enough to grab it and assist me down. At last this affable group bade me farewell. As they wandered down the street madly photographing everything in sight, I heard one kindly lady say, "Wasn't that sad? We should have given her something." Unfortunately, none of the others (doubtless right-wing conservatives all) responded to her plea for charity very favorably, thinking, no doubt, that a few cents cast my way would be a vote of confidence for the welfare state. "He would only go out and spend it on more liquor," one of the other women, a shriveled crone whose face bespoke WCTU affiliation, advised her friends with nasal wisdom and an abundance of harsh *r*'s. Apparently the others sided with the WCTU drab, for the group continued down the street.

I must admit that I would not have turned down an offering of some sort. A Working Boy can use every penny that he can get his ambitious and striving hands on. In addition, those photographs could earn those corn-belt clods a fortune in some photographic contest. For a moment, I considered running behind these tourists, but just then an improbable satire on a tourist, a wan little figure in Bermuda shorts panting under the weight of a monstrous apparatus with lenses that certainly must have been a CinemaScope camera, called out a greeting to me. Upon closer inspection, I noted that it was, of all people, Patrolman Mancuso. I, of course, ignored the Machiavel's faint mongoloid grin by pretending to tighten my earring. Apparently he has been released from his imprisonment in the rest room. "How you doing?" he persisted illiterately. "Where is my book?" I demanded terrifyingly. "I'm still reading it. It's very good," he answered in terror. "Profit by its lesson," I cautioned. "When you have completed it, I shall ask you to submit to me a written critique and analysis of its message to humanity!" With that order still ringing magnificently in the air, I strode proudly off down the street. Then, realizing that I had forgotten the wagon, I returned grandly to retrieve it. (That wagon is a terrible liability. I feel as if I am stuck with a retarded child who deserves constant attention. I feel like a hen sitting on one particularly large tin egg.)

Well, here it was almost two o'clock, and I had sold exactly one hot dog. Your Working Boy would have to bustle if success was to be his goal. The occupants of the French Quarter obviously did not place frankfurters high on their list of delicacies, and the tourists were not apparently coming to colorful and picturesque old N. O. to gorge themselves upon Paradise products. Clearly I am going to have what is known in our commercial terminology as a merchandising problem. The evil Clyde has in vengeance given me a route that is a "White Elephant," a term which he once applied to me during the course of one of our business conferences. Resentment and jealousy have again struck me down.

In addition, I must devise some means of handling M. Minkoff's latest effronteries. Perhaps the Quarter will provide me with some material: a crusade for taste and decency, for theology and geometry, perhaps.

Social note: A new film featuring my favorite female star, whose recent circus musical excess stunned and overwhelmed me, is opening shortly at one of the downtown movie palaces. I must somehow get to see it. Only my wagon stands in the way. Her new film is billed as a "sophisticated" comedy in which she must certainly reach new heights of perversion and blasphemy.

Health note: Astonishing weight increase, due no doubt to the anxiety which my dear mother's increasing unpleasantness is causing me. It is a truism of human nature, that people learn to hate those who help them. Thus, my mother has turned on me.

Suspendedly,
Lance, Your Besieged Working Boy

from *The Annunciation*

ELLEN GILCHRIST (1935–)

Ellen Gilchrist was born in Vicksburg, Mississippi, and spent her early childhood there, living on the Hopedale Plantation in the turn of the century home where her mother had grown up. The roots of her writing lie in the Mississippi Delta, and she says, "I live there still and always in my heart." When she was twenty-seven she studied creative writing with Eudora Welty for one year at Millsaps College in Jackson, Mississippi, and later moved to New Orleans where she was a contributing editor for the *Vieux Carré Courier*. In 1976 Gilchrist continued her study of writing at the University of Arkansas in Fayetteville where she lives today. She published her first book, *The Land Surveyor's Daughter*, a volume of poems, in 1979. Her first collection of short stories, *In the Land of Dreamy Dreams* (1981), spans four decades among the rich in New Orleans and launched her career as a fiction writer. *Victory Over Japan* (1984), her second collection of stories, won the American Book Award for fiction. In her acceptance speech Gilchrist said, "The hard thing to do is to tell the truth, and that's what I always try to do." Her fiction focuses on spirited and rebellious female characters who are frustrated in their quests for love and often suffer disastrous marriages. Her other works include *Drunk with Love* (1986), *The Anna Papers* (1988), *I Cannot Get You Close Enough* (1990), *Net of Jewels* (1992), *Anabasis* (1994), *Rhoda* (1995), and *Flights of Angels*(1998). In the following selection from Gilchrist's first novel, *The Annunciation* (1983), her protagonist, Amanda McCarney, discovers that "life isn't supposed to be a holding action."

Amanda had an ally during the years she was married to Malcolm, a black woman named Lavertis, a beautiful Creole who had come with her husband to New Orleans to escape the sugar mills of South Louisiana. By the time Amanda knew her,

Lavertis was alone with small children to support and could only do work that allowed her to be home early in the afternoon. In New Orleans that meant housework, wearing a white uniform, washing a white lady's underwear, standing all morning ironing linen sheets and Brooks Brothers shirts and white tablecloths.

The day Amanda moved into the house on Henry Clay Avenue Malcolm's mother sent Lavertis around to help with the unpacking. "I'll give her to you if you like," she said. "She's too clever to be a laundress. She has nice manners and she's honest, but uppity. Too uppity for me, but she might work out for you. Well, see what you think. If you like her you can keep her."

Amanda kept her. Or the other way around. Amanda and Lavertis loved each other from the start. They liked the way each other looked. Lavertis *was* beautiful. She had lovely erect posture and a wonderful face. Everything she did in the world was done with courtesy and with love. If she opened a box she opened it with ceremony, one flap at a time, as if it might contain a surprise. If she ironed a lace-trimmed sheet, it was not as a servant irons, with resentment or impatience, but as a person in the business of augmenting and admiring the lace-maker's art. "Look a here," she was always saying to Amanda. "Look at this pretty thing. Imagine making something like that. I bet that come from Paris, France."

Lavertis thought Amanda looked like a movie star, flying all around the house unpacking everything at once, drinking orange juice out of a wineglass, her hair falling all over her face, unpacking and redecorating. Unpacking and talking and complaining about her hangover, pushing furniture around and asking Lavertis a million questions about herself.

All day that first day they pushed and shoved furniture around and opened windows and unpacked boxes and sorted sheets and towels and pillowcases.

Around four in the afternoon they sat down in the sun room to survey their work. "Well," Amanda said. "What do you think?"

"It looks a lot better," Lavertis said. "It doesn't look so much like a museum."

"Wait till I paint it. Wait till I get rid of those gray walls."

"They likes that color," she said. "His momma and his auntie got everything painted that color."

"Do they keep the drapes closed all the time?"

"Most of the time, unless we're dusting. I guess they don't want the sun coming in and fading things. Of course, they're old people. They got old ways."

"Well, we're new people," Amanda said. "We're going to have all the sunlight we can get."

Later, when Lavertis was ready to go home, Amanda insisted on driving her. "So I can see where you live," she said. "In case I need to get you for something."

They walked out to the car and Lavertis opened the back door. Amanda sighed and put her hands on her hips. She looked down at the ground, trying to decide what to do. "Look," she said at last. Lavertis wasn't looking. "Look here, Lavertis, we've got to get some things straight between us. I can't have you sitting in the back seat. I used to be a civil rights worker. Well, not much of one, but at least I helped. Anyway..."

"I knew all about that," Lavertis said. They were standing by the car beneath the live oak trees with the evening traffic going by down Henry Clay. The rich men were coming home to dinner. "I was right down there in Abbeville praying to the Lord every night that you all wouldn't get me killed."

"Oh, my," Amanda said. "I never thought of that. How old were you?"

"I was in high school when it was all in the papers. I was scared to go to school. I thought somebody was going to come and shoot me."

"Oh, my," Amanda said. "I'm sorry. I never thought of it that way."

"Well, it was for a good cause," Lavertis said. "Now I'm glad it happened."

"Well, come on," Amanda said. "Get in the car. Look, let me put it this way. Where do you want to sit?"

"I'll sit up there," she said. She very formally got into the front seat and put her pocketbook in her lap, and the two women drove off down Saint Charles Avenue looking straight ahead, getting used to being new people in the old museum of New Orleans, Louisiana.

Lavertis ran the house on Henry Clay Avenue to perfection, hiring other servants when she needed them, telling the gardener what to plant and when to trim the hedges, taking care of small repairs, making grocery lists.

It left Amanda plenty of time to drink.

Lavertis took care of her when she had hangovers, pretending they were colds or sinus headaches or flu. She would come into Amanda's bedroom bringing glasses of chocolate milk or iced tea, and sit on the bed listening to Amanda's morning-after remorse. By noon they would be together in the library watching *As the World Turns*. Lavertis would be ironing, Amanda lying on the couch beginning to feel better, comforted by the sound of the steam rising from Lavertis's tireless iron.

The hangovers might have gone on forever. Amanda might be lying on that Henredon sofa watching *As the World Turns* right this minute except for a series of accidents that even Amanda's ability to rationalize couldn't overlook.

Of course, even before the accidents Amanda hated being drunk. She hated never knowing where she left her car or her pocketbook or her evening wrap. She hated calling people up and apologizing for things. Dozens of times she swore off alcohol. A week or so would go by. She would start lecturing her friends on the evils of alcohol. Then there would be a party. Then she would decide to have a glass of wine. Then she would be drunk again.

When the accidents began they happened one right after the other. First she fell down a flight of stairs. She quit for two months after that. Then she turned the car around three times on a rain-soaked road and plowed into a power line pole. Then she got drunk at a bar called The Saints and went upstairs and started interviewing the hookers. She had been writing articles for a local paper and had the idea that a press card would take her anywhere. The first hooker liked being interviewed. The second hooker hit her in the face and knocked her down.

But the worst thing of all, the thing that caused Amanda to quit drinking forever, was the night Coretta Scott King came to New Orleans and the Ashes were invited to meet her.

The party was held in a famous French Quarter restaurant. The owner of the restaurant had given Mrs. King $200,000 to start a scholarship fund in her husband's name.

She was in town to accept the gift at a ceremony at Dillard College.

Amanda started getting drunk before she even left the house. They had been invited to the party because Malcolm was the restaurant owner's labor lawyer. He would never have told her about the invitation if he had dreamed she was going to accept it.

"Why are you going downtown to see that woman strut her black ass all around Knoll's Restaurant acting like the great martyr's wife when everybody knows her husband screwed half the women in the South. She probably wanted to shoot him herself. Hell, she might have done it. Why are you going down there, Amanda? Will you just tell me that?"

"You don't have to go if you don't want to" she said. "I happen to admire her very much. I don't want you to go with me anyway. I wouldn't be able to talk to her with you around."

"How much have you had to drink?"

"None of your goddamn business." She was putting on her shoes, getting up and starting to leave. "I wouldn't let you go with me if you wanted to. I wouldn't want Mrs. King to know I was with someone who does what you do for a living."

"As opposed to what you do for a living?" he said.

Amanda slammed out of the house, got into the car, and drove on down to the Quarter. She stopped on the way and bought a bottle of wine and drank most of it out of the bottle. By the time she got to Knoll's she was good and drunk. She sat down at the bar and started talking to the black bartenders in a conspiratorial tone. "Do you guys really think Mr. Knoll likes black people? Do you think he gave Mrs. King that money because he's such a good guy? He should have used that money to raise your salaries. Let me tell you something. I'm married to the man Mr. Knoll loves, the man who fixes it so you guys never get a union. I'm married to the man who oversees the hiring and firing of every single man and woman who works in this place. And if you think Jodie Knoll gives a damn about Dillard University or any goddamn thing in the world but his own profits you're just as crazy as he hopes you are. And the minute Mrs. King gets here I'm telling her so. I know Jodie Knoll. I know all about him. I know his humanitarian ideals and his fascist heart and his racist jokes."

Amanda was surrounded by black bartenders. They didn't know what to think. They knew this crazy white woman was fixing to get them fired. Beyond the circle of bartenders a group of well-dressed people were giving each other horrified looks and trying to decide what to do. Mr. Knoll knew what to do. He came charging across the room through a sea of black and white faces and took hold of Amanda's arm.

"Let go of me, you son-of-a-bitch," she said. She thought he was a bouncer. "I'm Mrs. Malcolm Ashe. I'm married to Mr. Knoll's labor lawyer and I'm here to organize your goddamn kitchen help."

"Get this woman out of here," Mr. Knoll said. "Somebody get this woman out of here. Willy, get over here and help me out with this."

"Where's Mrs. King?" Amanda was yelling. "I want to talk to Mrs. King."

Mrs. King was being escorted into the restaurant by an entourage of Dillard professors. She turned her head and looked Amanda's way.

"Coretta," Amanda called out. "Come here. Come over here. I've got to talk to you. I've got to tell you where you are. I have to tell you who these people are who have you. Coretta! I've got to talk to you!"

But the real bouncers were there now and three Secret Service men. "Take your hands off me, you sons-of-bitches," she was yelling. "Don't you dare touch me, you goddamn fascist pigs. Coretta, come help! Coretta, come let me tell you where you are!"

The men took Amanda out a side door and put her into a car. They drove off through the crowded streets of the French Quarter. Halfway home she passed out in the lap of a Secret Service man. When the car got to Henry Clay the driver helped Malcolm carry her into the house.

"That's it," she said when she woke. "That was the last straw. That was really the last goddamn straw." As soon as she could get out of the bed she pulled on a robe and went wandering around the house looking for Lavertis. She found her in the sun room watering plants.

"I've got to quit drinking," she said. "Lavertis, you wouldn't believe what I did last night. I can't even stand to tell you what I did."

Lavertis put the watering can down and took Amanda into her arms. "Oh, Mrs. Ashe," she said. "I been waiting so long to hear you say that. I've been praying and praying for that. Every Sunday I go down to the prayer circle and pray you'll stop doing yourself that way."

"What will I do?" Amanda said. "How will I do it? I don't know how to do it."

"First you got to find something else you like to do," Lavertis said. "You got to get you a baby or a job or something so you hadn't got so much time on your hands."

"It has to stop," Amanda said. "I'm going to end up like my mother if I don't stop. I'll end up spending my life in a back room where the sun can't even get in."

"You'll do it," Lavertis said. "I know you'll do it. You can do anything you want to do. A lady as smart and all as you are."

It was not easy to stop drinking. *I am a pocket of habits in a burning universe* Amanda read somewhere and stuck up on her mirror. The hardest part was going to parties. The hardest part was not actually being there. The hardest part was thinking about it beforehand.

"You're mindfucking, Amanda," the behaviorist she went to said. "You're spending more time dreading the party than you are being there. The party's only going to last two hours. Just suffer those two hours instead of thinking about it for days beforehand. Or don't go. You're a rich lady. You don't have to go anywhere you don't want to go. Are you listening, Amanda? Listen to me. Please listen to me."

"Do you want to fuck me?" she said.

"No, I want to make you well. Do you want a tranquilizer to take before you go to parties? To use for a month or two?"

"I don't think so. I don't like to take drugs."

"Alcohol is a drug."

"No it isn't, Walter. Alcohol is a way of life."

"All right. It's a way of life."

"It's a religion. It's Dionysius."

"I'm going to tell you something, Amanda. You can serve that god sober. You can do anything sober you can do drunk, including ecstasy. You were capable of ecstasy when you were a child weren't you?"

"Oh, God, yes. When I was little I lived in the water. I am deliriously happy in water. I go crazy in water."

"Do you want some Antabuse for the parties?"

"No, I wouldn't be caught dead taking that stuff. Let me see how much longer I can do it this way."

Needless to say Amanda's friends were horrified that she quit drinking. What did it mean, they whispered among themselves. Did it mean she would be wandering around their parties listening to every word they said?

"Oh, come on, Amanda," Dr. Lovett said. He was the Ashes' family doctor. "You can have a glass of wine."

"Leave me alone," she said. "I don't want a goddamn glass of wine. I quit drinking. I told you I quit drinking. Don't talk about it."

"What's that you've got in the glass? Is that water? In a wine-glass?"

"I'm made out of water, Drusy," she said. "I'm ninety-eight percent water and the rest is a finely balanced highly sensitive delicately tuned chemical mix and I'm tired of pouring alcohol into it so I'll be as dumb as all the rest of you."

"Jesus Christ, Amanda, you ought to hear yourself. You sound like some kind of evangelist. Well, there's nothing worse than a reformed whore, they always say."

"I'm trying to save my life, Drusy. I'm sick of having hang-overs all the time."

"People have been getting drunk since the dawn of time, Amanda. The first thing men did with the first grain they stored was find a way to make alcohol out of it."

"So it's time to find something better to do," she said. "Time to climb down out of the trees."

"Are you still drinking water?" Monroe Frazier said, coming up to them, trailing his mannerisms. "Dear heart, that's getting to be rather a bore."

"Excuse me," she said. "I have to be somewhere else. I have to collect Malcolm and get out of here."

"Now don't go off mad, Pussy Faye," Monroe said. "Don't go off in a huff."

"Fuck you, Monroe," Amanda said. "You'd give anything in the world if you could quit being a drunk. You're just mad because I'm doing something you can't do."

She pushed him out of the way. She put her hand on his pin-striped Christian Dior suit and shoved him out of her way and made for the door, leaving her coat and purse and Malcolm behind. She headed down the stone stairs to the sidewalk. I'm leaving this behind me if it's the last thing I ever do in my life, she told herself, moving on down Philip Street like a tank, head down, hands in the pockets of her three-hundred-dollar skirt, scuffing up her leather boots on the bricks. I'm leaving it. I hate them. I hate every goddamn one of them. I hate those goddamn little drunk Frenchmen and drunk Jews and drunk white Anglo-Saxon Protestant princes and princesses. I know there's something better to do in the world than hang around doing numbers on each other in this fucking dead old anachronistic world. Goddamn it, I know there's something to do in the world besides get drunk. . . .

"Did you really shove Monroe into a mirror?" Malcolm said. "Did you really insult him in his own house? I don't know about you, Amanda. I don't know . . .

"Don't you dare talk to me about that," she said. They were fighting it out in their bedroom. "You goddamn self-righteous bastard. Don't you dare say a word to me about anything. I hate this goddamn place. I hate this life. I hate it, Malcolm, do you hear me? And I'm getting out. I'm getting out of here if it's the last thing I ever do in my life."

"I hate their guts," she screamed at her behaviorist. "You don't know what it's like. You can't imagine what it's like at those parties."

"Then don't go," he said. "Don't go to the parties."

"How could I not go? You have to go. I hate Drusy. He's the worst one. Every time he sees me at a party he starts in on me about it."

"Are you getting plenty of exercise, Amanda?"

"God, yes. I'm doing ballet and yoga and swimming an hour a day. All I do is exercise. Goddammit, Walter, what am I going to do about those parties?"

"You're going to quit going. Now get in the chair. I'm going to hypnotize you and put some good ideas in your head. Then I'm going to take you to lunch."

"Are you sure you don't want to fuck me?"

"I never said I didn't want to, Amanda. I said I wasn't going to. And that's another thing. I want you to find somebody to fuck. It's unhealthy not to fuck anyone."

"I can't fuck anybody. I'm married. Malcolm would kill me."

"Then stop being married to him. Come on, get in that chair."

"Shrinks don't talk like that, Walter. They're going to kick you out of the club for saying things like that."

"They already did," he said. "Come on. Get in the chair. And I'm serious about you finding someone to fuck. If you keep putting it off, when it finally happens it's going to hit you like a ton of bricks."

"What a nice idea," she said, settling down into his chair, imagining a love affair falling down on top of her like a disintegrating skyscraper. "I've been waiting all my life for that to happen."

"Everything happens," he said. "Anything we can think of happens."

"I've stopped going to parties," she told Malcolm. "I mean it. Not a single one."

"Are you going to the firm dinner with me on Saturday night?"

"Nope. Those people bore the shit out of me. When they're all in a room together it's like some vast superego sucking the juice out of my brain. Or when we're all sitting down at the tables like good little lawyers and wifelets. I always think maybe Jesus will come and nail us all to the chairs to punish us...."

"Well, you're going with me to that dinner, Amanda. I don't care whether it bores you or not. It's something we have to do."

"I don't have to do a goddamn thing but get myself well. Besides, the Ballet of the Americas is in town. It's the first time it's toured in years. I'm going to see Maurice Béjart dance. He's going to dance *The Firebird*."

"I don't know who you are anymore, Amanda," Malcolm said. "I look at you and I can't find the girl I married. I don't know what you're talking about half the time."

But she had left the room.

"All I ever wanted from the stuff to begin with was the sugar," Amanda told Lavertis one morning. "I think now I was in it all along for the sugar. So anytime I want a drink I'm going to eat all the candy and ice cream and cake I want. I guess I can work my way up to protein later."

That afternoon Lavertis walked down to the store and bought all the ingredients and made a yellow cake and left it sitting on the counter in the kitchen. It had real caramel icing an inch thick that was made from scratch in an iron skillet. There was a note in Lavertis's careful handwriting propped up on the cake cover.

> I am so proud of you. Lisa's husband came back. I think he's planning on taking her child away. Grandpa got out the flower boxes for spring. Bob is back on the staff but he's still mad at David. He and Lisa are going to get together for lunch. More next week.

It was something Lavertis had started doing to keep Amanda up with the events of *As the World Turns*. Amanda never had time to watch *As the World Turns* anymore. She had taken Lavertis' advice and found something to do to fill up all the time she used to spend having hangovers. She had walked across the street to Tulane and signed up for five classes in the foreign languages and English departments. She was getting up at dawn to begin her work, sitting at the dining room table covering pages of paper with her huge illegible scrawl, relearning two languages and the craft of translation all at once, learning fast.

"I think I have enough left," she said to herself, meaning her brain cells. "I think I have plenty."

Soon she was the golden girl around the Tulane foreign languages department. Small magazines were accepting her translations almost by return mail.

Lavertis was as excited about Amanda's new career as Amanda was herself. It was Lavertis who thought up turning a spare bedroom into an office.

"You can't move those papers on and off the dining room table every time you want to have a meal," she said. "Make Mr. Malcolm send you out a desk from the office. They got a hundred desks down there."

"I think that old table in the basement will be fine," Amanda said. "Go call Clarence and tell him to get over here and help us move it."

Lavertis began to change her role in Amanda's life. She brought endless cups of coffee into the room on trays as she had seen secretaries do on television. She answered the door and the phone and told everyone Mrs. Ashe was working and couldn't be disturbed. She noticed if Amanda's spirits got low.

"I haven't heard that typewriter going lately," she would say over her shoulder as she dusted the piano. "I read about some big translator coming to talk at UNO," she would mention as she got out the vacuum. "Guess you'll be going out there to hear him. Guess you'll be traveling around giving speeches before we know it."

Amanda began signing her maiden name to her translations. *Amanda McCamey*, it said. *Translation by Amanda McCamey*. The first time she saw her name in print it excited her so much she took the magazine home and hid it.

After a few days, she got it out and showed it to Malcolm.

"Oh, my God," he said. Malcolm knew what he was seeing was more than a twelve-line poem in *The New England Review*. "Now you're going to start that. Why don't you go on and stop wearing my rings, while you're at it. Go all the way. Stop spending my money." This was an uncharacteristic thing for Malcolm to say. He never mentioned money to Amanda. He and Amanda just pretended money didn't exist.

"I would if I knew some other way to get some." She started out of the room. Then she came back and took his face in her hands. He was sitting in a high-backed Queen Anne chair looking so tired, looking so forlorn.

"Start thinking about a life without me," she said, relieved to be saying it at last. "I was the Wasp princess and it didn't work out. You don't have to stay here forever with an idea that didn't work. Get out of here and find a woman with black hair and have yourself some babies."

"Don't say that," he said. "It's like telling me my mother just died."

"I'm not your mother," Amanda said. "Your mother's right over there on State Street waiting to welcome you home."

"I'm sorry I said that about the money," he said. "I didn't mean that. You can have all the money you want as long as you want it. You know that."

"It doesn't have anything to do with money," Amanda said. "It has to do with us not having anything in common, not a single dream or idea. It has to do with the future. I want there to be one for me. As long as we stay in this dead marriage the future can't happen for either of us. Pretty soon I'm going to have to leave here, Malcolm. I feel it coming like a storm across the delta."

"Where are you planning on going, Miss Weather Barometer?"

"I don't know. I just know life isn't supposed to be a holding action."

The next month Amanda's grandmother died and left her half of Esperanza, seven hundred acres of delta land under cultivation.

Now, she said, driving home from the funeral. Now there is not a single thing to keep me from being free.

from *Almost Innocent*

SHEILA BOSWORTH (1950–   )

Sheila Bosworth was born and raised in a steadfast Catholic family in New Orleans, which she labels "a very, very Catholic city." She attended convent schools and graduated from Tulane University in 1971. In her novels, *Almost Innocent* (1984) and *Slow Poison* (1992), she writes about what it is like to be Southern, female, and Catholic in today's society. About New Orleans, Bosworth says, "Everything is so intense. Everything is *too* much. You know, it's *too* hot, it's *too* rainy, and the food is *too* good." She now lives in Covington, Louisiana, where she and Walker Percy were neighbors. Bosworth belonged to Percy's lunch group, the Sons and Daughters of the Apocalypse, which met at Bechac's restaurant in Mandeville and remembers that "we used to argue all the time because I was a cradle Catholic and he was a convert." He was very supportive of Bosworth's writing and called *Almost Innocent*, "a stunning achievement, a superior one." In the following excerpt from *Almost Innocent*, Percy serves as the model for the "famous writer who lived in Covington," a "noncrazy" who is dining at Galatoire's while the narrator, Clay-Lee Calvert, enjoys a Ramos gin fizz and her father, Rand Calvert, sips on Jack Daniel's.

He who is penitent is almost innocent.—Seneca

I saw my father yesterday. He was downtown in a short-sleeved shirt and khaki pants, coming from a new dentist probably. My father dresses down for the dentist, to keep his bill at a poor man's level. It usually works for two or three appointments, then he slips and says something like "I wrecked that back filling on a deep-fried ball bearing the Louisiana Club was passing off as an oyster." And the next bill he gets, sure enough, that particular dentist has upped his fee considerably. The funny part is, my father probably makes less a year than the waiters at the

Louisiana Club. All he can really count on is the closetful of expensive, wrong-size suits my Great-Uncle Baby Brother left to him, along with a lifetime, dues-and-fees-paid membership to that club, which is an old-line Mardi Gras organization. He also has his meager dividends from some La Dolce Vita sugar stock. Uncle Baby Brother—who was his mother's change-of-life child and bad luck from the word go—willed everything else, his entire self-made sugar fortune, to the Home for the Incurables on Henry Clay Avenue, where his wife Ida Marie had died in the 1950s of a progressive genetic disease. The rumor was, she was strapped into an indoor hammock at the time, watching *The Big Payoff* on Channel 6, just as happy as if she'd had her right senses.

My father shouted "Clay-Lee!" and caught up with me on the Canal Street neutral ground, after nearly sacrificing his life, he said, sidestepping a turning St. Charles streetcar. My mind was elsewhere, I told him. "I've just been over to that real-estate office, that Latter and Blum, for the hundred and tenth time. Another buyer for the Bogue Falaya property fell through. Nobody's got the money for a summer house right now."

"Rosehue could be a year-round house," said Daddy, looking hurt, although he knows as well as I do the place is ready to fall in on itself. I only said "summer house" instead of "wreck" to spare his feelings. He was proud of Rosehue; he painted the inside of it almost single-handedly, one summer many years ago. The house is in the town of Covington, on the Bogue Falaya River, just across Lake Pontchartrain from New Orleans. Once it was my favorite place to be, but my father never set foot in it again after he moved his clothes and things out, several months after my mother died.

"This house belongs to you, Clay-Lee. It's entirely yours," he told me then, dragging a loaded clothes tree across the porch. He was crying at the time, and had apparently forgotten I was only eleven years old.

"Mama would have wanted us to stay!" I begged him, not so sure of that; I'd never known exactly what my mother wanted, but what was the alternative? Spending all year round in our alleyway-shrouded, half-a-double house on Camp Street in New Orleans, where most of the sunlight shone through the windows on the rented-out side? It wasn't until after I finished Sophie Newcomb College of Tulane University, B.A., scholarship, in English literature, that I moved to Covington again by myself. That was years ago, and the daily drive across the lake to teach an eight o'clock class and then back home, seems, at times, to be too much for me. I put the house on the market again, late last spring.

Standing on the darkening neutral ground, my father asked me to have dinner with him; I knew by that it must be dividend day.

"I'm driving back to Covington tonight," I said. "So why don't we just go around the corner to Felix's and eat some oysters?" A pneumonia-weather wind was coming up and when I looked at my father's thin, half-covered arms, my knees shook.

"I can do better than that!" said Daddy. "We'll stop by St. Peter Street for my coat and tie, and then walk up for an early dinner at Galatoire's."

So we went down Bourbon Street together, past Galatoire's near the dust-blowing comer of Iberville Street, all the way to St. Peter and back again to Galatoire's. By then I wasn't even hungry. My father's little wooden house always saddens me, with its river damp, and unfinished canvases, and all the unopened mail. The unopened mail frightens me. I wish I had some good news to write to him.

At Galatoire's we were taken right away—it was still early for the dinner crowd—to a table near the little bar where the waiters mix the patrons' drinks. "Mr. Rand, Miss Clay-Lee," said Vallon, his thin face smiling at us atop the black tie of his waiter's tuxedo. "What can I bring you?" Vallon is old now, almost eighty. He used to give my father's father red beans and rice in one of the upstairs rooms, generations ago.

As I leaned back in my chair I saw several women looking at Daddy and at me, wondering, I guess, what our connection was. Because our coloring's so different, strangers never take us for parent and child. I have brown hair, like my mother had, but none of her beauty, and my father has the kind of blond good looks that don't betray his age unless the room is lit from overhead. I'd have settled for looking like either of them. Sis Honorine, who still cooks for me in Covington, told me I had the promise of becoming a beauty till about the time my mother passed away. I remember feeling beautiful just once, when I was about ten years old. My father was angry with my mother, a rare state for him, over a little sailboat, a Rainbow, that she had committed herself to buy and that he couldn't pay for. Uncle Baby Brother had to bail him out, of course, and then my uncle made my mother a present of the boat. I was delighted, and kept running my hands over the glossy colored photograph of it that Mama had placed on her little oak lady's desk. Daddy took the photograph away from me and put it on the top shelf of the bookcase. "Clay-Lee," he said, his gentle hand on my head, "on the night you graduate from Sacred Heart, I'm going to buy you a white convertible to match your dress, and we'll drive up St. Charles Avenue, the two of us. We'll leave your mother standing at the curb." To my knowledge, she didn't hear him tell me that. It didn't matter, as things turned out, if she had heard. My father spent my graduation night "not himself" in a bar on Napoleon Avenue, a block from the ceremony, and my mother had by then been dead a long time, past caring who left whom at the curb.

At our corner table with its good white cloth and heavy silver, I had a Ramos gin fizz and my father a Jack Daniel's. While I drank, I looked into the mirrored wall opposite my chair and picked out familiar faces in the early dinner crowd. Just behind us was the only son, middle-aged now, of a prominent coffee-importing family. He's in the process of dying from anorexia nervosa, that self-starvation ailment supposedly restricted to affluent young girls, but I guess nobody's passed the word along to Roger Addison, Jr., that he doesn't qualify for the disease. There he sat, enjoying his entrée, a double portion of cracked ice. At another table I saw the sad, olive-toned face of a woman who is the second wife of a third-generation heart surgeon. She met her future husband one night five years ago, while handing out menus at Brennan's, and as of two years ago she holds the current title of first woman to survive a leap from the Huey P. Long Bridge. ("Not crazy enough, you see, to leap with her coat on," Sis Honorine told me when it happened. Sis's brother Orville was a member of the bridge police. "Folded it up on the front seat of the car. Sealskin. Wouldn't wrap herself up in nothin' less, that one." Sis had been baby nurse to the first Mrs. Heart Surgeon's infants, and remained bitterly loyal.)

At a table for four with his elegantly dressed sister-in-law was a noncrazy, a famous writer who lived in Covington. I suddenly remembered that when we were twelve years old the writer's older daughter and I had planned to petition the pope for early entrance to the Carmelites, a religious order famous for its romantic iron grilles and nervous breakdowns among the novices. I caught myself smiling at nobody in the mirrored wall, and stopped.

"You can smile. I'll let you," said my father. "How do matters stand among the nontenured at Sophie Newcomb College?" He was already on his second Jack Daniel's and was saying a few words just to be polite. Daddy is a painter, a good one, and has always faded away during dinners; I like to think he retreats to some intricate new canvas in his mind. When I was a child and there was a noisy group at the table, my Uncle Baby Brother and my mother's cousins and aunts, all talking at once, he never had any idea what the conversation was about. If my mother tried to pull him in with a "What do you think about that, Rand?" he was likely to look up and answer, "Well, yes and no."

I looked at him now and saw the yellowness in the whites of his eyes. The sight of it gave me a sick, startling rush, like being retold without warning bad news I had managed to forget. I thought of Uncle Baby Brother on his deathbed, many years past, his face yellow as an old squash. Daddy had coerced me into visiting him, no doubt in the expectation I'd be remembered in Uncle Baby's will. I could've set him straight on that score, all right, and spared him one more terrible surprise. I didn't, though. The setting straight would've cost us both too much. . . .

Uncle Baby's bedroom. The perpetual gloom, ceiling fan noises, and the mahagony four-poster with a sunburst canopy in eggshell damask, the tucked and swirling design that made me sick to look at the time I broke my ankle skating on the hilly sidewalk in front of Uncle Baby's house. It made me sick to look at Uncle Baby, too.

"Your father's getting to be a drunk, same as me," he was saying. Tremendous revelation. "Lucky for you. In a few years he won't be able to find his way home to his turpentine-stinking hole in the Quarter, much less haul himself across the lake to bother you."

"What do I have in Covington to be bothered, Uncle Baby? Easy-crying infants and a husband who needs his peace?" Shutters banging someplace, and a smell of boiled brisket and vegetable soup.

"Don't try to stop him drinking," continued Uncle Baby. Who are you to warn me? I was thinking. "If you stop and consider, he's entitled. Then again, I don't have to tell you not to interfere. You've always known how to let nature take its course." I pretended not to hear, not to hear, not to hear.

"I declare, but Rand's impossible, at that," came Aunt Mathilde's unconcerned drawl from some gloomy corner of the bedroom. She apparently felt compelled to sit there all the time, as if it had been she instead of my mother who was related to my uncle by marriage. "Was he drinking last New Year's Open House when he referred to your poor little step-cousin as the whore of Mount Holyoke?"

Uncle Baby gave a rattling gasp intended to be a laugh.

"Couldn't forgive Cousin Megan, goddamn him, for wearing that gold ankle-bracelet and going on so proud about her Yankee women's college. Goddamn it, she is a Yankee woman! What was she supposed to've done, gone and pledged Kappa Delta at Ole Miss?"

Another terrible gasp-laugh; this one brought Leatrice, the Negro factotum, in from the kitchen with a forbidden cigarette still in her lips and brisket grease on her apron. He laughed a lot, my Uncle Baby. Laughed the whole time he was writing out his will that made life sweet for the Incurables. You don't have to be strapped into a hammock to be an Incurable, was Sis Honorine's remark. Bitterly loyal. . . .

"Gousin Courtenay was in town; she telephoned me yesterday," I said to Daddy. "She told me she looked in on you at St. Peter Street last Sunday afternoon, but you were sleeping like a little log." "Passed out" floated overhead, unspoken, on the scents of Trout Marguery and a more distant rum sauce. He looked up, back for a moment from the invisible canvas. "Don't hold it against me," he said, and smiled. He's got no right anymore to a smile like that. It's the smile of a young man, a man with his life ahead of him still, full of pleasure and expectation. The way he was when he first knew my mother, Constance, when the beginning of their life together must have seemed to him unmatched for reckless sentiment, and for love.

She was Constance Blaise Alexander, Queen of Comus, the most magnificent of the Carnival balls, on the night they fell in love. Just eighteen years old, her debut pushed ahead one year so that her father, Louisiana State Supreme Court Justice Thomas Alexander, whose health was failing (and whose wife had failed altogether and was buried in St. Louis Cemetery No. One), could be there to see his baby on her night. The photographs show a fine-boned beauty, her brown hair shoulder-length, dark against the silver collar of her robe. James Rand Calvert was a Comus duke that night, one of the privileged horsemen, masked and velvet-cloaked, who rode in the flambeaux-lit street parade before the ball. The floats stopped as always in front of the draped and purple-billowing balcony of the Pickwick Club, so that Comus could toast his Queen where she awaited him. As Constance leaned forward to greet her consort, Rand Calvert, far below, defied tradition by throwing aside his mask to see her face more clearly.

Unfortunately, it was apparent almost from the start that Judge Alexander didn't think much of the match.

"What's his future?" he shouted repeatedly to Constance.

Daddy says he can see him yet, propped up stiff as a corpse in an old leather wing chair in his study, clenching his fists and flinging off the restraining arm of Skinner, his manservant. "What's his future, I asked you? The whole goddamned bunch of 'em's either an artist or a cellist! A cellist, for Christ's sake!" (The Calverts, with the exception of Uncle Baby, were long on name but short on money, a condition common among certain New Orleanians since General "Beast" Butler came to town and confiscated the household silver of the Confederate aristocracy. Worse yet, to the Judge's way of thinking, the Calverts were politically liberal, and they were "artistic.") And so Mama's daddy continued to cry out and go on till his face darkened, and Skinner had to half-carry him to bed. The Judge was worried, as Mama told it, that no one could take care of her like he had. She was small, delicate, her lungs unsuited to the Louisiana dampness. Why, her father had taken one look at her, when she was just three hours old, and called her "Lamb."

When she married Rand Calvert, Constance brought with her to her new husband's house only a few of the Alexander treasures. The old, elaborately carved cypress four-poster that had belonged to her mother, Solange Mallard, a bed so high on its legs you needed a footstool to climb onto it, its headboard scarred with hairpin scratches where generations of Mallard ladies had rested against it. The circa 1780 rosewood secretary with the scent of an exotic, persistent perfume in its secret drawer. The Woodward oil portrait of Constance's father, its canvas cracked from decades of exposure to New Orleans heat and damp.

Tommy Alexander's last birthday present to his daughter had been a purebred, Russian wolfhound puppy, which she named Mishka; Mishka, too, went with Constance to the new place of residence on Camp Street. (Mishka would eventually become Constance's close companion, her protector. I see Constance so often in my memory now with Mishka at her side, Mishka's watchful eyes following her mistress's every movement, as if my mother were a child left in her care. I envied Mishka; I longed to learn the secret ways that would make my mother's white fingers touch my hair in conspiratorial affection, as they did that regal dog's.)

With Mishka in Constance's arms, the newlyweds went to live in Rand Calvert's half of the two-story, two-family, frame house he owned on Camp Street, a shabby old house on a shabby block, the place that would become my first home.

The waiter, Vallon, had brought our appetizers. I could see my father wasn't interested in his; he was waltzing his Crabmeat Maison around on his plate with his fork, while he gazed off in the direction of another table somewhere behind me. Suddenly he leaned forward in his chair.

"On our way out, I want you to glance at the last table near the door, and look at what's left of Phil Harris," he said in an undertone. "Remember when your cousins took you to see Phil Harris perform at the Blueroom, for your birthday? What were you then, nine? God Jesus, baby, then how old does that make Phil Harris now?"

"I would guess about two years younger than you."

"Very funny. I don't believe you're even concerned about poor old Phil Harris. You've got that 'don't bother me' look you were fortunate enough to have inherited from your father."

"I was thinking about Mama, about how she was before I was born."

He sat back again in his chair.

"It's too bad you couldn't have known her, Clay-Lee, the way she was then."

"But, Daddy, I feel as if I do, I do know her the way she was then. The way she was even before that, before she married you."

"How can that be? Don't tell me they're finally paying you something over at Tulane, and you've gone to the expense of hiring yourself a medium." He shook his head sadly. "The next thing I know, you'll be riding around in taxicabs."

"I didn't need to hire a medium, I just asked Felicity to talk with me about Mama. You're forgetting all those Friday-night dinners I had with Felicity."

"You're right. I forgot about Felicity for a minute." He added gallantly, "Possibly the only man in the State of Louisiana who knew Felicity and ever forgot her, even for a minute. . . . Felicity, God bless her."

He picked up his glass, saw that it was empty, and signaled again to Vallon, with his eyes.

"The City of the Dead"

WALKER PERCY (1916–1990)

Walker Percy was born in Birmingham, Alabama, the oldest son of Martha Phinizy and Leroy Pratt Percy. After his father's suicide when he was eleven and his mother's death two years later, Percy and his two brothers were adopted by their cousin, William Alexander Percy. Will Percy was a poet and author of the memoir *Lanterns on the Levee* (1941). His home in Greenville, Mississippi, was a literary haven in the delta, with visitors such as Carl Sandburg, William Faulkner, and Hodding Carter. Percy met Greenville native Shelby Foote and the two became lifelong friends. Percy graduated from the University of North Carolina and then Columbia School of Medicine with high honors, but contracted pulmonary tuberculosis in 1942. After several years of slow recovery from the illness, during which time he read widely in philosophy, psychology, and theology, Percy decided to give up medicine. In 1946 he married Mary Townsend, and the couple moved to New Orleans where he received instruction at Loyola for conversion to Roman Catholicism. Later they settled in Covington, Louisiana, but Percy continued to dine frequently at Galatoire's. According to Percy, "After writing two bad novels which I'm glad were not published, I sat down one day in New Orleans and began to write *The Moviegoer* and all of a sudden everything fell into place for me." *The Moviegoer* (1961) won the National Book Award. He wrote five other novels, including *The Last Gentleman* (1966), *Love in the Ruins* (1971), and *Lancelot* (1977). Percy is known as a "philosophical novelist," and his characters and themes deal with the problems of knowledge, faith, and the human condition. His nonfiction works include *Message in the Bottle* (1975) and *Signposts in a Strange Land* (1991), a selection of his uncollected essays, edited by Patrick Samway. The essay presented here, "The City of the Dead," was published in that volume.

The title is not quite ironic and only slightly ambiguous. It refers mainly of course to the remarkable cemeteries of New Orleans, true cities of the dead, and to a certain liveliness about them. But it also refers to my own perception of New Orleans as being curiously dispirited in those very places where it advertises itself as being most alive; for example, its business community and its official celebration, Mardi Gras. Compared with Dallas and Houston and Atlanta, New Orleans is dead from the neck up, having no industry to speak of except the port and the tourists—happily for some of us who wouldn't have it otherwise, unhappily for half the young blacks who are unemployed. As for Mardi Gras, boredom sets in early when Rex—"Lord of Misrule," as he is called, though he never quite looks the part, a middle-aged businessman—toasts his queen at the Boston Club, daughter of another middle-aged businessman. The boredom approaches deep coma at the famous balls, which are as lively as high-school tableaux. The real live festival of Mardi Gras takes place elsewhere, in the byways, in the neighborhood truck parades. As for famous old Bourbon Street, it is little more now than standard U.S. sleaze, the same tired old strippers grinding away, T-shirt shops, New Orleans jazz gone bad, art gone bad, same old $32 painting of same old bayou.

The cemeteries, true cities of the dead, seem at once livelier and more exotic to the visitor newly arrived, say, from the upper Protestant South where cemeteries are sedate "memorial gardens," or from New York City, where mile after mile of Queens is strewn with gray stone, a vast gloomy moraine. A New Orleans cemetery is a city in miniature, streets, curbs, iron fences, its tombs above ground—otherwise, the coffins would float out of the ground—little two-story dollhouses complete with doorstep and lintel. The older cemeteries are more haphazard, tiny lanes as crooked as old Jerusalem, meandering aimlessly between the cottages of the dead. I remember being a pallbearer at St. Louis No.1, one of the oldest cemeteries, stepping across corners and lots like Gulliver in Lilliput. The tombs are generally modest duplexes, one story per tenant, for good and practical reasons. It could actually accommodate an extended Creole family, for, given a decent interval when presumably coffin and tenant had gone to dust, the bones were shoved back into a deep crypt at the rear, room for one and all. After all these years a bothersome question of my childhood was answered: Where will people live when cemeteries take up all the space on earth?

They, the little cities, are liveliest on All Saints' and All Souls' Day when families turn out to fix up the family tomb, polishing or whitewashing the stone, scrubbing the doorstep for all the world like Baltimore housewives scrubbing the white steps of row houses. Not many years ago the lady of the house might be directing black servants in this annual housekeeping, as much mistress here of the dead as of the living at home. There are still iron benches in place where Creole ladies, dressed in the highest winter fashion, received friends all day. Even now, All Saints' and All Souls' have a more festive air than otherwise—should they not?—startlingly different from the unctuous solemnity of Forest Lawn. Crowds throng the tiny streets, housekeeping for the dead, setting out flowers real and plastic, perhaps regilding the lettering, while vendors hawk candy and toys for the children, and on All Souls' saying a not noticeably sad prayer or two for the dead.

Mark Twain once said that New Orleans had no architecture to speak of except in the cemeteries. As usual, he exaggerated, because the Spanish houses and their courtyards in the "French" Quarter and the little Victorian cottages, "shotguns," all over town are charming and unique. But on approaching New Orleans, one might well agree with Mark Twain. The major architectural addition in the past hundred years is the Superdome and the skyline looks like standard U.S. glass high-rises set like Stonehenge around a giant Ban roll-on. Not so in the cemeteries, where every conceivable style is rendered by taste or whim, from the simple two-storied "beehive" to toy Greek and Egyptian temples and even miniature cathedrals—to a small artificial mountain containing the mauseoleum of the Army of the Tennessee, General Albert Sydney Johnston atop, astride his horse and still in command. The great Texas general gazes at Robert E. Lee himself atop his column across town. It is easy to imagine a slightly bemused expression on the faces of these stern Anglo-Saxon commanders as they contemplate between them this their greatest city and yet surely the one place in the South most foreign to them.

"Relic"

ROBERT OLEN BUTLER (1945–)

Robert Olen Butler was born in Granite City, Illinois, and attended Northwestern University as an undergraduate, where he studied writing with Stephen Spender. After earning an M.F.A. in play-writing from the University of Iowa, he committed to a three year enlistment in the U.S. Army in 1969, and worked in a counterintelligence unit in Vietnam in 1971. After the war, Butler held various journalistic and teaching jobs, including editing his own investigative weekly newspaper, *Energy User News*, in New York from 1975-1985. In 1979 he began attending advanced creative writing courses at the New School for Social Research under Anatole Broyard. Butler published his first novel *The Alleys of Eden* in 1981, and it has been called one of the finest novels ever written about the tragic American experience in Vietnam. He continued to explore the theme of the clash of the American and Vietnam cultures in his novels, *Sun Dogs* (1982), *On Distant Ground* (1985), *The Deuce* (1989), and *The Deep Green Sea* (1998). In 1985 Butler accepted a creative writing post at McNeese State University in Lake Charles, Louisiana. One afternoon he sat down to write and took on the voice of a Vietnamese man in Lake Charles trying to understand his Americanized son. The story became "Crickets," which would be included in *A Good Scent from a Strange Mountain* (1993), his Pulitzer Prize-winning short story collection about displaced Vietnamese expatriates living in Southern Louisiana. The stories in the collection blend Vietnamese folklore and memories of the native land with American pop culture, including the following story, "Relic," told by a Vietnamese man living in the community of Versailles in New Orleans.

You may be surprised to learn that a man from Vietnam owns one of John Lennon's shoes. Not only one of John Lennon's shoes. One shoe that he was wearing when he was shot to death in front of the Dakota apartment building. That man is me, and I have money, of course, to buy this thing. I was a very wealthy man in my former country, before the spineless poor threw down their guns and let the communists take over. Something comes into your head as I speak: This is a hard man, a man of no caring; how can he speak of the "spineless poor"? I do not mean to say that these people are poor because they are cowards. I am saying that being poor can take away a man's courage. For those who are poor, being beaten down, robbed of rights, repressed under the worst possible form of tyranny is not enough worse than just being poor. Why should they risk the pain and the maiming and the death for so little benefit? If I was a poor man, I, too, would be spineless.

But I had wealth in Vietnam and that gave me courage enough even to sail away on the South China Sea, sail away from all those things I owned and come to a foreign country and start again with nothing. That is what I did. I came at last to New Orleans, Louisiana, and because I was once from North Vietnam and was Catholic, I ended up among my own people far east in Orleans Parish, in a community called Versailles, named after an apartment complex they put us in as refugees. I lived in such a place for a time. The ceilings were hardly eight feet high and there was no veranda, nowhere even to hang a wind chime. The emptiness of the rooms threatened to cast me down, take my courage. In Saigon, I owned many wonderful things: furniture of teak, inlaid with scenes made of tiles of ivory and pearl, showing how the Tru'ng sisters threw out the Chinese from our country in the year 40 A.D.; a part of an oracle bone from the earliest times of my country, the bone of some animal killed by ritual and carved with the future in Chinese characters; a dagger with a stag's antler handle in bronze. You might think that things like this should have protected me from what happened. There is much power in objects. My church teaches that clearly. A fragment of bone from a saint's body, a bit of skin, a lock of hair—all of these things have great power to do miracles, to cure, to heal.

But you see, though the Tru'ng sisters threw the Chinese out, just one year later the Chinese returned and the Tru'ng sisters had to retreat, and finally, in the year 43, they threw themselves into a river and drowned. And the oracle bone, though I did not know exactly what it said, probably dealt with events long past or maybe even foresaw this very world where I have ended up. And the dagger looked ceremonial and I'm sure was never drawn in anger. It would have been better if I had owned the tiniest fragment of some saint's body, but the church does not sell such things.

And here I sit, at the desk in the study in my house. I am growing rich once more and in the center of my desk sits this shoe. It is more like a little boot, coming up to the ankle and having no laces but a loop of leather at the back where John Lennon's forefinger went through to pull the shoe onto his foot, even that morning which was his last morning on this earth. Something comes into your head when I tell you this. It is my talent in making wealth to know what others are thinking. You wonder how I should come to have this shoe, how I know it is really what I say it is. I cannot give away the names of those who I dealt with, but I can tell you this much. I am a special collector of things. A man in New York who sells to me asked if I was interested in something unusual. When he told me about this shoe, I had the same response—how can I know for sure? Well, I met the man who provided the shoe, and I have photographs and even a newspaper article that identifies him as a very close associate of John Lennon. He says that certain items were very painful for the family, so they were disposed of and he was in possession of them and he knew that some people would appreciate them very much. He, too, is a Catholic. The other shoe was already gone, which is unfortunate, but this shoe was still available, and I paid much money for it.

Of course, I have made much money in my new country. It is a gift I have, and America is the land of opportunity. I started in paper lanterns and firecrackers and cay nêu, the New Year poles. I sold these at the time of T'êt, our Vietnam New Year celebration, when the refugees wanted to think about home. I also sold them sandwiches and drinks and later I opened a restaurant and then a parlor with many video games. Versailles already has a pool hall, run by another good businessman, but I have video games in my place and the young men love these games, fighting alien spaceships and wizards and kung-fu villains with much greater skill than their fathers fought the communists. And I am now doing other things, bigger things, mostly in the shrimp industry. In ten years people from Vietnam will be the only shrimp fishermen in the Gulf of Mexico. I do not need an oracle bone to tell you this for sure. And when this is so, I will be making even more money.

I may even be able to break free of Versailles. I sit at my desk and I look beyond John Lennon's shoe, through the window, and what do I see? My house, unlike the others on this street, has two stories. I am on the second story at the back and outside is my carefully trimmed yard, the lush St. Augustine grass faintly tinted with blue, and there is my brick barbecue pit and my setting of cypress lawn furniture. But beyond is the bayou that runs through Versailles and my house is built at an angle on an acre and a half and I can see all the other backyards set side by side for the quarter mile to the place where the lagoon opens up and the Versailles apartments stand. All the backyards of these houses—all of them—are plowed and planted as if this was some provincial village in Vietnam. Such things are not done in America. In America a vegetable garden is a hobby. Here in Versailles the people of Vietnam are cultivating their backyards as a way of life. And behind the yards is a path and beyond the path is the border of city land along the bayou and on this land the people of Vietnam have planted a community garden stretching down to the lagoon and even now I can see a scattering of conical straw hats there, the women crouched flat-footed and working the garden, and I expect any moment to see a boy riding a water buffalo down the path or perhaps a sampan gliding along the bayou, heading for the South China Sea. Do you understand me? I am living in the past.

I have enough money to leave Versailles and become the American that I must be. But I have found that it isn't so simple. Something is missing. I know I am wrong when I say that still more money, from shrimp or from whatever else, will finally free me from the past. Perhaps the problem is that my businesses are all connected to the Vietnam community here. There was no way around that when I started. And perhaps it's true that I should find some American business to invest in. But there is nothing to keep me in this place even if my money is made here. I do not work the cash registers in my businesses.

Perhaps it is the absence of my family. But this is something they chose for themselves. My wife was a simple woman and she would not leave her parents and she feared America greatly. The children came from her body. They belong with her, and she felt she belonged in Vietnam. My only regret is that I have nothing of hers to touch, not a lock of hair or a ring or even a scarf—she had so many beautiful scarves, some of which she wore around her waist. But if my family had come with me, would they not in fact be a further difficulty in my becoming American? As it is, I have only myself to consider in this problem and that should make things simpler.

But there are certain matters in life that a man is not able to control on his own. My religion teaches this clearly. For a rich man, for a man with the gift to become rich even a second time, this is a truth that is sometimes difficult to see. But he should realize that he is human and dependent on forces beyond himself and he should look to the opportunity that his wealth can give him.

I do not even know John Lennon's music very well. I have heard it and it is very nice, but in Vietnam I always preferred the popular singers in my own language, and in America I like the music they call "easy listening," though sometimes a favorite tune I will hear from the Living Strings or Percy Faith turns out to be a song of John Lennon. It is of no matter to a man like John Lennon that I did not know his music well before I possessed his shoe. The significance of this object is the same. He is a very important figure. This is common knowledge. He wrote many songs that affected the lives of people in America and he sang about love and peace and then he died on the streets of New York as a martyr.

I touch his shoe. The leather is smooth and is the color of teakwood and my forefinger glides along the instep to the toe, where there is a jagged scrape. I lift my finger and put it on the spot where the scrape begins, at the point of the toe, and I trace the gash, follow the fuzzy track of the exposed underside of the leather. All along it I feel a faint grinding inside me, as if this is a wound in flesh that I touch. John Lennon's wound. I understand this scrape on the shoe. John Lennon fell and his leg pushed out on the pavement as he died. This is the stigmata of the shoe, the sign of his martyrdom.

With one hand I cup the shoe at its back and slide my other hand under the toe and I lift and the shoe always surprises me at its lightness, just as one who has moments before died a martyr's death might be surprised at the lightness of his own soul. I angle the shoe toward the light from my window and I look inside. I see the words SAVILE ROW on the lining, but that is all. There is no size recorded here and I imagine that this shoe was made special for John Lennon, that they carefully measured his foot and this is its purest image in the softest leather. I am very quiet inside but there is this great pressure in my chest, coming from something I cannot identify as myself. This is because of what I will now do.

I wait until I can draw an adequate breath. Then I turn in my chair and gently lower the shoe to the floor and I place it before my bare right foot. I make the sign of the cross and slip my foot into John Lennon's shoe, sliding my forefinger into the loop at the back and pulling gently, just as John Lennon did on the day he joined the angels. The lining is made of something as soft as silk and there is a chill from it. I stand up before my desk and the shoe is large for me, but that's as it should be. I take one step and then another and I am in the center of my room and I stand there and my heart is very full and I wait for what I pray will one day be mine, a feeling about what has happened to me that I cannot even imagine until I actually feel it. I have asked the man in New York to look for another of John Lennon's shoes, a left shoe. Even if it is from some other pair, I want to own just one more shoe. Then I will put both of John Lennon's shoes on my feet and I will go out into the street and I will walk as far as I need to go to find the place where I belong.

"The Muse Is Always Half-Dressed in New Orleans"

ANDREI CODRESCU (1946–)

Andrei Codrescu was born in Sibiu, Romania, and now makes his home in New Orleans, which he calls "the most timeless city in the world." He was expelled from the University of Bucharest for criticizing the communist government and left his native country to escape the draft. Codrescu traveled in Europe before immigrating to the United States in 1966. His first book, *License to Carry a Gun* (1970), was followed by numerous volumes of essays, fiction, memoir, and poetry, including *The Blood Countess: A Novel* (1995), *Alien Candor: Selected Poems, 1970-1995* (1996), and *Messiah: A Novel* (1999). Codrescu is a regular commentator on National Public Radio, and his commentaries have been published in *Zombification* (1994) and *The Dog With the Chip in His Neck: Essays from NPR and Elsewhere* (1996). He has written and starred in *Road Scholar* (1993), a Peabody award-winning movie, and is a Professor of English at Louisiana State University in Baton Rouge. From 1983-1998 he served as the editor of *Exquisite Corpse: A Journal of Letters and Life* during the journal's time in print, and now edits *CyberCorpse*, the online "afterlife" of *Exquisite Corpse*. In his collection of essays, *The Muse Is Always Half-Dressed in New Orleans* (1993), Codrescu writes about the state of American life in the nineties with a displaced European's point of view. Included in that collection is the following title essay in which Codrescu writes about New Orleans from the point of view of a "nouveau native."

I live right near the Lafayette Cemetery where I like to take my friends from out of town for a cup of coffee and a quiet chat. No, you get the coffee *before* you go into the cemetery. Did you think they had waiters in cemeteries in New Orleans? Though, come to think of it, that would be very *N'awrleans*. (As we the nouveau natives have been taught it's pronounced.)

On the uptown side of Lafayette Cemetery, on Prytania Street, is the house where it is said that twenty-three-year-old F. Scott Fitzgerald wrote his first book, *This Side of Paradise*. He had the upstairs apartment, the one with the windows that look on the upraised graves. I can see him, coffee in hand, standing in his robe on the little balcony, wincing from last night's gin, looking down on the little houses of the dead, wishing he was one of them. "It's not so great on *this* side of paradise," he might have said, to no one in particular. No kidding. He hadn't even *met* Zelda yet.

The dead are buried aboveground in New Orleans because there is water less than five inches under the ground and anything you put in there floats off and rots. The rounded mausoleums at the Lafayette remind me of bread ovens: I think of the dead as loaves of bread quietly mummifying there under the blistering New Orleans sun. There is a flesh-troubling scent of sweet olive and night-blooming jasmine clinging to the crumbling bricks.

I took a great Polish artist named Wodycko here one afternoon. We sat on the grave of one Franz Caillou with our coffee, and he told me about a high school student strike he led in Warsaw in 1976. He took all his classmates to the Warsaw cemetery, and they studied history there from the gravestones. It was the true history of Poland, not the lies they were being taught in school. They looked up the heroes of Polish history who were forbidden by the Communists, and learned more in one day than they ever had in high school. That's not a bad idea for *any* school. If teachers brought their students to the cemetries instead of boring them to death in the classrooms, there would be a revival of interest in history. In New Orleans, certainly, cemeteries tell all the great stories because there are so many of them. There are more dead than living people here, and the dead are not all that dead.

Anyway, after Wodycko and I finished our strong black coffees, we went to the Commander's Palace restaurant to see if we could get in for lunch. Commanders' Palace, one of the world's best restaurants, is on the other side of the Lafayette from young F. Scott's digs. Usually, you need a reservation about three days in advance for Commander's Palace, but you never know.

"Absolutely not," said the pleasant young man in the foyer.

"But!" I exclaimed in despair, pointing to Wodycko, "Do you know who this is? It's Vaclav Havel, the president of Czcechoslovakia!"

The foyer boss looked us over doubtfully for a second, and then disappeared to consult with his boss. We fiddled with our souvenir sprigs of sweet olive, staring at the pictures of Victorian and Roaring Twenties New Orleanians on the walls. He reemerged shortly with his boss in tow. "Normally," the boss said, "we only do this for old New Orleans families and Hollywood stars. . . . but I'll make an exception this time. This way, Mr. Havel."

When we were seated before the large windows in the upstairs room, Wodycko said that he felt very privileged indeed. A huge live oak stood outside, big enough to live in.

He had the turtle soup. The turtle soup at Commander's is said to be over one hundred years old. They say that the turtle-soup pot has never gone out since the restaurant opened on these premises in 1888. One time, there was a fire and the first thing the cooks did was to take the turtle-soup pot outside. Then the building burned down. There is something indescribably comforting in knowing that you're eating from the same pot with your dead ancestors. The secret charm of old restaurants is precisely this sense of continuity: you sit down where someone sat one hundred years before you. They sat down, told a story, and died. Life goes on. Old cities soothe and ease the pain of living because wherever you are someone else was there before, had troubles worse than yours, and passed on. I don't see how people can inhabit spanking new suburbs without succumbing to terminal anxiety. We need the dead to make us feel alive. In New Orleans they're at it full time.

After we had our soup we strolled back up Prytania Street toward my house. I wanted to show Wodycko my fig tree, and to give him a bag of fresh, ripe figs to take with him to Warsaw where they've never seen figs outside a can.

We passed Bultman's Funeral Home on the way. The Bultmans buried anybody who's anybody in New Orleans for three generations. They are also art lovers and patrons. Frances Bultman, the family matriarch, died not long ago, leaving her art collection to the New Orleans Art Museum. The Museum honored her with a fabulous party at which the dying woman was lain on an elaborate catafalque-like divan as the best of New Orleans society and the art world filed by to pay their respects. Men gallantly kissed the puffy white hand that had deeded art to the city, and women curtsied in their fabulous gowns which in New Orleans are always a little more fabulous than elsewhere. A week later, Madame Bultman died and was on display in the foyer of the Bultman Funeral Home while the same people filed past once more, dressed in somberer hues, but still fabulous. A local *artiste* whispered that Frances looked much better than she did at the Museum where she had been (presumably) alive. Her granddaughter-in-law, Bethany Bultman, who wrote a book on table settings, whispered into the artiste's ear: "Of course she looks better, dear. . . . All her life she wanted tits. . . . I gave her some." Indeed. In death, the servant of Apollo and Thanatos shone in full-breasted splendor for her admirers.

At some point during her long life, Frances Bultman gave young Tennessee Williams a place to stay in an apartment at the back of the funeral home. Tennessee wrote *Cat on a Hot Tin Roof* there, and liked New Orleans so much he got his own apartment a short time later. The granddaughter-in-law, Bethany, is writing another book, too, on rednecks. "It's amazing," she told me, "rednecks are actually very nice people. I was always afraid of them, but now that I'm getting to know them, I find them very, very nice." Of course, the Bultmans have never buried a redneck, and rednecks couldn't afford to be buried by the Bultmans.

Wodycko wanted to know what time it was because he had a plane to catch in two hours. Neither one of us wore a watch. I pointed out the big clock in front of the Bultman Funeral Home.

It's one of the very few public clocks in New Orleans. The rest of them are also on funeral homes. In New Orleans, if you don't have a watch, you have to die before you can find out what time it is. But the real reason for the dearth of clocks is that time is not a big deal here. New Orleans time is approximate: nobody gets to parties for at least one hour after the official hour. Everything takes longer, even the simplest things. Buying a newspaper can take a half an hour if the vendor feels like telling you a story. Waiters may hang by your table, pencil in the air, for the space of several stories if you ask something too interesting. New Orleanians are great talkers and they consider time well spent and very relative if they remember something they want to tell you, or simply feel like commenting on the weather or the political climate (which is spicy in Louisiana, like the food.) Everyone is extremely well mannered, and manners take time to perform and to execute. Nor do stories get carelessly told. My students will invariably preface and footnote a tale while they tell it, and they have a great sense of timing. They may have difficulty spelling some of the words they use but they speak like angels, and for a long time.

Speaking of angels, the Lafayette Cemetery has some good ones, but the best ones are in the St. Louis Cemeteries 1, 2 and 3. Marie Laveau, the Queen of Voodoo, is buried in St. Louis No. 1, and there are always small sacrifices left on her grave: chicken feet, rooster's combs, half-drank hurricanes, cigars and panties. Lately, however, whole tourists have been sacrificed on Laveau's grave after dark, so it's not advisable to visit her during voodoo business hours. Marie Laveau herself is of somewhat doubtful authenticity (some have called her a popularizer and a money monger) but the spooky industry she's spawned is real enough: dozens of books, numerous movies, fetish crafts, sales of charms and amulets, and a great beer, Dixie's Voodoo Blackened Beer. Voodoo Beer, as it's known for short, is the thing to have as you stretch out on your porch.

I have a whole shelf of New Orleans books, and that's about one-hundredth of all the books about New Orleans. If you add all the books by New Orleans writers that are not necessarily about New Orleans you can fill a whole library. A local novelist once told me at a party, "No book set in New Orleans ever lost money." Now, I don't know if that's true, but there is something about New Orleans that makes writers happy. Parties, for one, where you can hear remarks like that. Richard Ford, the Montana short story writer, told me that he'd been living here secretly for two years because "I don't need to hang out with writers. These two streets by my house are enough." I knew exactly what he meant. New Orleans has enough characters in your immediate proximity to fill several books. And if you have the presence of mind—or the *kind* of mind—to remember things people tell you at parties you'll never run out of stuff. People—not just writers—are attracted to New Orleans because it's full of stories and listeners who have nothing better than to listen to them. There is a whole class of people here that my poet friend Tom Dent calls "people who never left." These are folks who come to New Orleans for a weekend visit, or for Mardi Gras or Jazz Fest, and then never go back. Their stories alone can fill a shelf.

The other day, I went down to the French Market to the tomato festival, and they were just about to crown the tomato queen—a young girl from some Louisiana parish—and up comes this older lady, about sixty-five, and she's wearing a big tomato around her hips, and these skinny legs with green stockings are sticking out of it. And she says to me: "Never mind *her*! (pointing to the young queen) *I'm* the real tomato queen! I been the tomato queen for twenty years now—ever since I left my husband and kids to come here on vacation—I never went back!" And then she said, "I'd love to stay here and chat with you some more, darling, but I've gotta see my other subjects. . . . I still have good legs, you know." And there are hundreds like her, sitting in bars that are really living rooms from the teens, twenties, thirties, forties, fifties, sixties, seventies and the eighties, just waiting to lay their stories on you. In most of America, probably because of television, stories are drying up. Not in New Orleans. They grow in abundance here, like the flowering vines, and the myrtles, the bananas and the figs.

Wodycko was himself beginning to feel that he ought to perhaps become one of the "people who never left." I gave him his bag of figs, and we had another cup of strong New Orleans coffee in my backyard by the pond. A golden-winged dragonfly buzzed a huge lily. Across the street, a half-dressed young woman with long, unruly hair was having her coffee on her balcony. She looked pre-Raphelite in the subtropical lassitude that began to envelop us. "It's the muse," said Wodycko. It was. He caught his plane back to Warsaw that afternoon, but he regretted it. He's written to me several times since. "I can't seem to leave New Orleans," he wrote, "it's as if a part of me still lives there."

I know what he means.

from *Crooked Man*

TONY DUNBAR (1949–   )

Anthony (Tony) Dunbar was born in Atlanta, Georgia, and grew up in Georgia and South Carolina. He attended Brandeis University and graduated in 1971, the same year that he won the Southern Regional Council's Lillian Smith Award for nonfiction for *Our Land Too* (1971). Dunbar spent seven years of his life (1964-1970) working with Southern civil rights and community development organizations, and dedicated seven more to the Southern Prison Ministry (1972-1978). His other nonfiction works include *Hard Traveling: Migrant Farm Workers in America* (1976), with co-author Linda Kravitz, and *Delta Time: A Journey Through Mississippi* (1990). Dunbar, a practicing attorney in New Orleans, is best known as the author of the popular Tubby Dubonnet mystery series. Dubonnet, a maverick criminal attorney in the Big Easy, loves his city, its fine cuisine, and a stiff cocktail. The series includes *Crooked Man* (1994), *City of Beads* (1995), *Trick Question* (1997), *Shelter from the Storm* (1998), and *The Crime Czar* (1998). Dubonnet tackles a difficult case in *Crooked Man* when his client Darryl Alvarez, who has been arrested for dealing drugs, hides one million dollars in his attorney's office before being murdered. In the following selection from the book, Dubonnet discusses the case while dining on "trout meunière amandine" at Galatoire's.

There's an off-track betting parlor on Bourbon Street near Canal. From the sidewalk you can't see what's inside because the windows are tinted dark like the sunglasses a lifeguard wears, but there's a neon sign outside to let you know the place is alive. Inside it is cool, clean, and green. There are little tables and chairs, a big television screen, and race results playing electronically on a board, like stock prices at a New York broker's office. There is a well-stocked bar, and waitresses come to the tables.

Outside the sun burned down, but inside Tubby was sharing a cocktail with Jason Boaz, the inventor. Both were watching the television screen on the wall, looking at the horses lining up at the gate. Tubby had ten dollars down on Peach Smoothie to place and another ten dollars on Trolley Car to win. The real live action was only a couple of miles away at the Fairgrounds.

People described Jason as lanky. He had a long, rugged face with a neat black beard. He wore heavy black plastic glasses that had never been in style. Today he had on a white shirt, a string tie, and baggy blue slacks, like a chemistry professor at some Midwestern college where they admire sloppiness. He was chain-smoking stiletto menthol cigarettes and partaking of Long Island Teas, a staggering combination of four white whiskeys and Coke.

The race started, and though neither man said anything they both leaned forward a bit because they had money on it. Jason had a bet on Rock 'Em, Sock 'Em. At the end, Rock 'Em, Sock 'Em took it. Peach Smoothie came in fourth, and Trolley Car retired limping. There were claps and moans, laughter and a half-hearted Bronx cheer from the other gentlemen and ladies spending money in the place.

"Attaboy," Jason yelled when his horse came in first.

"What did you have on him?" Tubby asked.

"Fifty bucks. I had a hunch and should have bet more. I could kick my self."

"Life is rough," Tubby said and crumpled his worthless tickets into the ashtray.

"See the jockey? That's Nicky Piglia's son." Tubby looked blank. "You know, Nicky Piglia. Has a po'boy shop, whatchacallit, yeah, 'Nicky's.' Out in Marrero. He serves a half and half that's, like, mammoth."

"Any relation to Roy Piglia, who got killed when Pan Am 282 crashed out in Kenner?" asked Tubby, remembering what was far and away his most lucrative case, the one that had made it possible for him to open his downtown office, start his practice with Reggie, and buy a new car. It was a bright-yellow BMW, and he gave it to his then-wife Mattie. She sold it after they got separated, and what did she do with the money?

"I don't know, maybe they're cousins. There's got to be about a million Piglias."

Another race was starting, and Tubby had a horse in this one, too. He was betting Shake and Bake to win, but the horse was stuck in Gate 4, not such a hot spot to be in.

"So Tubby, while I got your meter off, so to speak, you think it's worth me protecting my Porta-Soak and Mow?"

Tubby couldn't remember hearing about that one. "Tell me about it," he said.

"It's a neat idea. I thought we'd talked. There's a plastic water tank, like for one of those Super Soaker water guns, just bigger. And you pump that up. You strap the tank to your back. There's a tube comes out of the top with a spray nozzle, and while you mow your grass, or do anything that gets you really hot, you can give yourself a little shower or a light mist. It's adjustable."

Tubby lost his concentration on the race, which was just now beginning, and stared at Jason to see if he was serious. Jason wasn't giving anything away. He probably was. Jason's last idea had been for a shoe that circulated cold water around your feet. Ha. Ha. He had built a prototype and showed it around. He ended up assigning his patent to a Korean manufacturer for $418,000. Tubby had done the paperwork.

"Well, Jason, it sounds kind of clumsy. Why don't people just go inside and take a shower, or jump through a sprinkler? Anyway, who mows yards anymore?"

"Kids mow yards, and kids will like this. And college kids at the beach, they will like this. We make the tanks in orange, 'Day-Glo' green, crazy colors, you know, acrylics. They'll spray each other. They'll fill it with beer."

Tubby thought he could visualize that beach party. "Hell, of course you should patent it," he said.

"That's what I think."

"Get your drawings together, come by the office, and let's talk."

"Okay, why not. It might be a big payoff item."

"You got much left from the Cool Shoe?"

"Well, it's about a hundred dollars less for every hour I sit in here."

The horses came around the stretch. Shake and Bake first, then second, then third across the finish line.

"Like I said." Jason dropped his ticket into an empty coffee cup.

"Gotta run," said Tubby. "I got a lunch at Galatoire's."

"Hope you're not treating."

"No, this is a payback. Call me at work."

Tubby walked the two blocks to the restaurant. It was almost two o'clock, which was good timing for Galatoire's. There was no line.

"Good afternoon, Mr. Dubonnet," the head waiter said softly. "We will have a table in just a moment. Are you alone?"

"Mr. Chaisson is joining me," Tubby said. The dining room was narrow, and all of the tables were full. Old waiters, most of them familiar to Tubby, carried silver platters around, trailing fragrances of fish and garlic. No women servers distracted the diners.

Tubby was shown to a table against the wall beneath an ornate mirror. He ordered a gin on the rocks. His mind drifted over the things he was supposed to do that day. Then it settled for a moment on Jynx Margolis. Was there some chemistry there? It had been so long since he had dated anybody that he had forgotten how to read the signs. She was certainly appealing, in a good, clean, middle-aged fun kind of way, a nicely tanned and very fragrant kind of way. Problems did not weigh heavily on Jynx's shoulders. Marriage to her would be difficult, he imagined. She was irrepressibly self-indulgent and sort of an airhead sometimes. But who was talking marriage? Could she really find him attractive? Hard to tell with Jynx what was actually a magnetic field and what was simply her flirtatious nature. Maybe with her it didn't matter. She was a mystery to Tubby, a bit exotic. It was flattering having an exotic try to flirt with you.

Tubby was lost in thought when E. J. Chaisson came through the door. He was slight and dapper, combing his thin blond hair straight back to accentuate his large eyes and smooth, angular face, like a hungry street kid who had picked up good manners. He wore Italian suits from Rubenstein Brothers on Canal Street and always carried a cane or umbrella. Today it was a thin brown stick with an ivory handle that Tubby saw was a carved alligator, its tail curving around and gripping the wood. E.J. hung it with a flourish on the back of the empty chair between them.

"Tubby, I intended to arrive early and hold a table for you. Did you wait long?"

"Not at all. I've just ordered a drink. Join me." Tubby waved at the waiter.

"How have you been? A Sazerac, please," Chaisson told the man who appeared beside him.

"Busy, but that's what pays the bills."

"I've also been busy. I'm going into radio."

"Are you going to be explaining legal issues to the public?"

"That's certainly a good idea." His drink arrived. E.J. took a sip and nodded to show that it was agreeable. "No, I'm starting to advertise—in Vietnamese."

"You speak Vietnamese?"

"Heck no, but my yard man does. He's been working for me for a year, and one day we start to talking about what I do. He tells me, guess what, there's about twenty thousand boat people in New Orleans who he is related to, and not one of them knows an attorney."

E.J. grinned suddenly, showing his pointed white teeth, and winked. For emphasis he snapped a little bread stick from the basket the waiter put before him, stuck a scoop of fresh butter on the end, and waved it like a conductor's baton. "He's going to bring me clients. Plus interpret for them. If I take a case, he gets a piece of the action."

Tubby finished his drink. "The Bar Association won't like that." Tubby was an expert on things the Bar Association would and wouldn't like. He'd run several money-making ideas past its ethics committee, and each time had been advised to steer clear.

He was sensitive because of a problem he had had over the Pan Am crash. After Tubby had signed up one of the victims, a downtown attorney had complained that Tubby was hustling clients in the hospital. Tubby had explained, in a letter to the Bar, that the referral had come quite innocently from one of the physicians treating the poor man, a plastic surgeon named Dr. Feingold. Tubby also immediately stopped his check to the doctor, even though it was just a token of friendship. He heard no more about it from the Bar, but he had heard about the check from Dr. Feingold ever since.

"The thing is, you can't split your fees with a nonlawyer. It's unethical."

"Are you sure about that?" E.J. asked.

"Oh yeah, positive. Look it up in the rules."

"We didn't have to learn that stuff to pass the bar exam when I was in law school."

The waiter returned and took their orders. The oysters were salty, and E.J. ordered his *en brochette*. Tubby chose trout *meunière amandine*.

"Look," said Tubby, "there's ways around it. Why not just call your guy a paralegal and put him on a nice salary?"

"I don't think so," E.J. said sourly. "I'm afraid his appetite is a little bigger than that. He wants to be on the incentive plan."

"Send him to law school."

"Can't do that," E.J. said between bites of bread. "Then what would he need me for?"

"Okay, try this. Suppose you set him up an advertising company. Immigrants all love to own a company. Do you agree?" E.J. nodded. "He broadcasts advertisements in Vietnamese for your law office. You pay him according to the number of calls you receive from the ads. You have a gentlemen's understanding that, down the road, if the cases pay off he gets to raise his rates."

A peppered fillet, covered with sliced almonds, appeared before Tubby. He pricked it gently with his fork, and a puff of steam escaped, with it a light smell of daybreak and high tide at the beach. E.J. inspected his skewered oysters and bacon and inhaled with pleasure.

"Ah, this looks perfect," he crooned. "So you think that would be legal?"

"I don't see why not."

"Let me give it some thought. And I'll discuss it with Nyop. As you said, every immigrant likes to own a company.

"Like your grandfather."

"Actually, my great-grandfather," E.J. said, referring to the old Frenchman who had managed to acquire so much Vieux Carré real estate that it had taken his descendants four generations to work it down to the several blocks they now owned and leased at handsome rates. Unlike Tubby, who was originally from a hamlet called Bunkie, surrounded by sugarcane and rice plantations, and who had only landed in New Orleans because his father had gotten him into Tulane, E.J. was a pillar of New Orleans society. Never mind that several of his ancestors had been hung as outlaws by the Spaniards or the Yankees, E.J. paraded with the Krewe of Proteus, when it rode, and had flattered Tubby by inviting him to join. Tubby had declined because, at the time, he was privately too hard up for cash to pay the dues.

"How's your drug-smuggling case coming?"

"Okay. How did you hear about that?"

"I saw your name in the newspaper—the story about the bail hearing."

Tubby finished chewing a bite of fish, and stabbed a crisp slice of tomato. "There's not much for me to do. He got caught with the goods."

"Did they have a tip?"

"Oh, yes, but nobody is telling where it came from. The DEA field office down there was well prepared though they're still having to explain why all they caught was Alvarez."

"I've always thought it a little distressing how criminals turn each other in all the time. Where's the honor? Wouldn't it be terrible if professionals did that to each other?"

"We're slightly more reliable, I guess, but that's changing, too."

"A toast to the reticent nature of officers of the court everywhere. What do you think Alvarez was planning to do with the pot?"

"Sell it, of course," Tubby said. "For all I know he sells it out of the back room at Champs. Do you know Darryl?"

"Sure, I've eaten and imbibed a few at Champs. But it's a total surprise to me that he's in that league. So much pot must cost a lot of money."

"The police say its street value was in the millions. They didn't catch him with any cash, though. It probably left with the boat."

"Have you been over to Champs since his arrest?"

"No, but Darryl comes to see me. He was by yesterday."

"What's going to happen to him?"

"He'll probably go to prison for a while, unless he points the finger at someone else."

"Just what I was saying. Everyone feels this need to turn someone else in. They pass around guilt like a bottle of wine."

"Not Darryl. So far he's not talking, though he's sweating a little. I guess he's more like one of your professionals."

"Well, I have always appreciated discretion."

"You ain't never been in jail, *cher*."

"And I'm the second generation of my family with that distinction," Chaisson said with obvious pride.

from *Glass House*

CHRISTINE WILTZ (1948–)

Christine Wiltz was born and raised in New Orleans, leaving only for a two year period to complete her education at San Francisco State College. She held various jobs, including one as a bookseller at Maple Street Bookshop, before deciding to write a mystery. Wiltz succeeded and her first book, *The Killing Circle* (1981), introduced the New Orleans detective Neal Rafferty. Because the book was written from a male point of view, her publisher chose to use Chris Wiltz as the author name and did not release an author photograph. She published two more Rafferty mysteries, *A Diamond before You Die* (1987) and *The Emerald Lizard* (1988), also under the name Chris Wiltz. Christine Wiltz appeared as the author name for the first time on the jacket of her highly praised novel *Glass House* (1994). Her other works include the nonfiction book, *The Last Madam: A Life in the New Orleans Underworld* (1999). Wiltz decided to write the *Glass House*, which focuses on race relations in New Orleans, after the 1980 shooting of a white New Orleans policeman and its violent aftermath. In the author's note for the novel, Wiltz writes of "an inarticulable quality about life in New Orleans," that "has to do with the desire by people who live here to set themselves apart and do things their own way . . . ." In the following excerpt from *Glass House*, Thea Tamborella returns to New Orleans after a ten year absence on the occasion of the death of her Aunt Althea, who raised her after her parents were murdered in a grocery store holdup. Delzora, Althea's aging housekeeper and mother of Thea's childhood friend Dexter, welcomes her to the Convent Street mansion Thea has inherited from Althea.

After the body was taken away, Mr. Untermeyer and Delzora sat in the front parlor, she on the edge of the red brocade sofa, he on a side chair. He was solicitous, telling Delzora he hoped she hadn't undergone too much of a shock; telling her he would call Mrs. Dumondville's niece, who now owned the house; asking her if she would get it ready for the niece.

"It's ready," Delzora said, her hands folded in her lap. "I work here every day. I keep it ready."

Mr. Untermeyer cleared his throat. "I can't guarantee that Mrs. Dumondville's niece will keep you on," he told her in his genteel southern accent.

Did he think she was a fool? Why would he think she expected him to guarantee her anything? She said nothing to him, but she decided the policeman was more tolerable with his outright dislike than Mr. Untermeyer with his asinine concern.

At five o'clock, as was her habit, Delzora left work. She was picked up by the same young man who dropped her off every morning. He drove up in a gleaming white Cadillac with custom Continental kits built into the front fenders and spiked hubcaps that looked dangerous. He was wearing tight, bright-blue leather pants and a matching vest without a shirt on underneath it.

He opened the back door for Delzora as she came down the walkway in front of the house.

"Don't you never come pick me up again without no proper shirt on, Dexter, do you hear?" Delzora said to him.

"Yes, ma'am."

"You look like a pimp from the Quarters, all got up like that."

Dexter held the door for her silently while she settled herself like a queen on tomato-red crushed velour behind dark tinted windows. Then her carriage pulled out, traveling a stately ten miles an hour down Convent Street under a canopy of graceful oaks. Behind the oaks were the houses of the rich, set back from the clean street and surrounded by emerald-green lawns and artful landscaping. The white Cadillac was as out of place here as an Iowa prize pig on a stroll.

The canopy of graceful oaks was broken as the car reached the intersection of St. Charles Avenue. The avenue was the buffer zone between the very rich and the very poor. Across it the canopy resumed. A block farther the Convent Street Housing Project began.

Delzora didn't think about it because she'd been this way too many times before, but across St. Charles, Convent Street was darker. The houses on one side, the project units on the other, were set closer to the street and to each other; there were no green lawns for the sunlight to filter through oak leaves and sparkle upon. The oaks themselves were brooding and scary instead of graceful over here. They weren't so much a canopy as good cover—for crime, for poverty, for sadness, for the darker side of human nature. The droppings of the oaks fell to the street and were never swept away by the city or the residents. They stayed, messy, dank, and filling the air with the sweet odor of decay.

Delzora, her head resting against the velour, her eyes closed, knew when the car crossed St. Charles. From dense silence the Cadillac slid into the sounds of people on the street, kids shouting to each other over rap music blasting out of boom boxes, and across the street from the project, rhythm and blues coming in a wave from the open door of the Solar Club, a saxophone rift swinging out over the street and gone.

This continued for a while until there was another wide avenue, another buffer zone. The Cadillac could roll straight across New Orleans on Convent Street, through the inner city with its random and opposite elements that blend into a sort of symmetry, elements dispersed in a rhythmical flow of dark to light, sounds to silence, rich to poor, black to white. This is the rhythm of the city.

The taxi ride from the airport seemed overly long in the high-noon heat of August. At one point, traffic on the Interstate stopped altogether due, as it turned out, to an overheated car engine and two lanes blocked for resurfacing.

Even with the air conditioner full on, the backs of Thea's thighs were sticking to the black vinyl car seat. She pulled her short skirt down as best she could and rested her feet on the tips of her toes, her heels against the seat, to raise her bare skin off the hot plastic.

The cabdriver, a genial man with a large moon-round face, jowls beginning to sag, kept turning one ruddy cheek toward her as he talked. It had been a long time since she'd heard such a heavy New Orleans accent, nasal and lazy, not a hint of southern prettiness. He seemed to be complaining and apologizing all at once for the road conditions, speaking of potholes, politicians, payola, and tourists.

"Gotta keep the tourists comin, no argument there, but wit'out oil, everybody's a special-interest group these days, every pothole's got money-making potential, y'know?"

But Thea was too mesmerized by the city to be distracted by either the heat or the driver's patter. Her attention moved from one side of the expressway to the other, taking in hotels, office buildings, apartment complexes, restaurants, fundamentalist churches, lounges, stores, parking lots. Nothing looked particularly different, yet nothing looked quite the same either, still the helter-skelter trashiness of commercial suburbia, perhaps just more of it. She was eager to reach that rise not too far past the last Metairie exit, to come up over it and see the city dropped slightly below, the skyline of the old city, the real city, not the suburbs.

The driver cut into her anticipation. "Been to New Orleans before, miss?"

"I used to live here," Thea said. "Almost ten years ago." She didn't mention that she'd been to town since then, but only once, eight years ago, she and Michael together. She had wanted to make peace with Aunt Althea, but at dinner the first night Aunt Althea demanded to know if they were getting married.

Michael was arrogant. "Not this year. Probably not next year either."

Across the table Thea felt her aunt bristle. "Well, you're not sleeping together in my house," Aunt Althea said. "My house, my rules."

After that it was a contest of wills, Aunt Althea's and Michael's, with Thea's feelings trampled somewhere in between. They had gone back to Massachusetts after only three days.

"Long time," the driver said. "Lot's changed."

"I'm sure.

"Yeah, for one thing, since you been here the whole riverfront's different downtown, new aquarium, park, streetcar line right on the river. Casino's comin too."

"Oh, really?"

"Oh yeah, you can bet on it." He laughed heartily.

Thea smiled but she didn't join his laughter. They were coming up on the rise now. She leaned forward.

"For better or for worse, who can say. Won't hurt my business none, but it ain't gonna be any safer drivin a cab, that's for sure."

More of his face than one cheek was visible from this angle. His eyebrow was lifted and his eye darted from the road to her, waiting for her comment, but Thea fixed her gaze on the city that, as they got higher, was spreading out all around her. They rode above the trees and rooftops of uptown to the right; to the left were the high-rise buildings of downtown, and ahead, not just the one she remembered, but two bridges now stretching across the Mississippi. The taxi angled toward the St. Charles Avenue exit and approached her favorite landmark, the golden spire of St. John the Baptist, wet with sun. Thea's throat tightened and her vision blurred.

Her reaction startled her. She didn't like this city. There was too much squalor and chaos in it, decay and poverty were visible everywhere, neighborhoods jumbled, too much violence. She didn't like the people in New Orleans either. Their bonhomie was a smokescreen for their prurient curiosity, their politeness a wall of indifference to retreat behind. What they said was not what they meant; what they appeared to be was not what they were. Ultimately they were affected, narcissistic, dramatic. They used their nerves as their excuse. Michael called the people in New England tight-asses, but at least you knew where you stood with them, at least what you saw was what you got.

Thea had wanted to move away, and now that Althea's death had brought her back she had no intention of staying any longer than it took to sort through her aunt's personal things and put the house up for sale. Yet something was happening to her, something wholly unexpected. She realized that even though she didn't live here anymore, she'd come home.

The driver was saying something about getting a gun. "Don't make no sense not to protect yourself, y'know? Hard to believe things could get any worse, but that's what they say." He went on talking about casinos and crime.

They came down the off ramp and headed toward Convent Street. Thea's urge to cry was gone, her equilibrium restored, and she was anxious to see the house on Convent Street again, but as the driver was getting ready to turn she sprang forward and put her hand on his shoulder, interrupting his monologue. "Don't turn here."

He clicked his blinker off but said, "This's Convent Street, miss."

"I know, but I want you to take me somewhere else first." She gave him directions and the taxi cut across uptown New Orleans, traveling some avenues divided by medians, streets covered by oaks, then through treeless backstreets and into a quiet neighborhood. The houses looked as if they'd seen better days: torn screen hanging from one porch; the whole front of another house sinking, the steps separated from the rest of the structure; across the street, a badly rusted awning over a picture window. In contrast, there was a house with red geraniums growing in the front yard, another with its trim freshly painted a bold primary blue.

At a weatherbeaten white two-story building with large display windows to either side of doors set catty-corner to the street, she asked the driver to stop. He shifted in his seat to look at her, as if his big head couldn't turn on its thick neck any more than to show some cheek. Thea was noticing that the galvanized pole the grocery store's sign had hung from was still there, jutting out from the overhang above the doors. But there was no sign on it anymore, only the pole, and the windows as well as the glass on the upper part of the doors were blanked out by some white material, perhaps white paper on the doors, anonymous, no longer a store, impossible to tell if it was inhabited any longer. She edged closer to the car window to see the second floor. There were curtains upstairs.

She let out her breath, only now aware that she'd been holding it, and slid to her former position on the seat.

The driver, as if to answer the question evident in the arch of his eyebrows, said, "This used to be a grocery store."

"Yes, Nick Tamborella's Neighborhood Grocery," Thea said. "My father."

"Yeah? I use to live a coupla blocks over." He pointed back in the direction of Convent Street. Thea was holding her breath again, waiting for him to say something about the shooting, but he said, "I moved out to the Parish seventeen, eighteen years ago." He wouldn't remember; he'd been gone too long. She breathed. He said, "They broke in my house three times in a month, I said that's it. The only people would buy here anymore were the blacks. I said let em have it."

Thea remembered all the burglaries, she remembered people moving, times getting hard at the grocery, those times the only ones she could remember her parents ever arguing. Her mother wanted to leave; her father said there were no neighborhood groceries in Metairie. Her mother would suggest he work at one of the big supermarkets, he would be a manager in no time, and her father, in his hot-blooded Italian way, would strike his chest with his fist and shout, "Nick Tamborella works for no one!"

And then one afternoon the arguing was all over. Maybe the happy life she remembered living above this grocery store was over before that afternoon; it must have been over once all the fighting started. She didn't know, she couldn't remember that. What she did know was that one afternoon there were two gunshots. After that she had not returned to this neighborhood until today. She'd been—what was the word?—displaced; she'd been displaced ever since.

The cabdriver was shaking his head heavily. "Too bad," he said. "Used to be a good neighborhood."

He took Convent Street back across uptown, heading toward the river. When they got to the Convent Street Housing Project,

Thea did not notice that what she could see of the project looked better now than it had ten years ago or that most of the houses across from it looked worse. She was thinking that she hadn't seen this many black people all together in one place since her move to Amherst. They were sitting out on their porches or front steps to escape the heat inside their houses. Women in big blousy dresses fanned themselves with newspaper; the few pedestrians moved slowly. On the project side of the street, little kids in their underwear squealed as they ran in and out of the strong jet of water coming from an open fire hydrant. Just past this activity, across the street, the side the cab drove down, Thea saw the Solar Club. It was impossible not to notice: a midnight-blue stucco facade on a tall wood house, the old roofline visible toward the back, and over the arched doorway *Solar Club* written in neon script, hot-orange, flame-colored. She didn't remember it being there before.

Then the scenery changed, and moments later Thea was standing in the shade of the huge oak tree in front of Aunt Althea's house. Her house. She had always loved this house, the sheer size of it, its gabled roof, its wide, curving porch, the four long front windows, their moss-green shutters, and the front double doors with their tiny panes of leaded glass, gas lamps flanking them. It didn't seem to be as bright a white, its green trim not as crisp as it used to be, as Aunt Althea had always kept it, but that didn't matter right then. The sight of it, graceful and splendid, gave her joy.

She went up the brick walkway and rang the doorbell. Through the little leaded panes she saw several different Zoras running as fast as they could on their short legs.

Delzora was crying as she flung open the door. "Goodness, honey, is that you?"

The smell of the house reached out for her as Zora did. The smell was pure Aunt Althea, and until that moment she had not known how much she disliked it. It had a diminishing effect, diminishing her joy at the sight of the house, her happiness to see Zora.

"Look at you," Delzora said pulling back from their embrace, beaming up at her, though Thea herself was not a tall woman, "still a skinny ole thing, and you done cut off all your hair."

Thea's hair no longer hung past her prominent collarbones but was cut to her chin. She wasn't using it to cover herself anymore, with too-long bangs to hide her thick black eyebrows and, she had hoped, de-emphasize her too-large Roman nose, features identical to her father's and not at all like the light, bright, petite features on the girls at school, the girls Aunt Althea had so admired, the blonds she would point out and say, "Isn't that the prettiest girl you ever saw?"

Thea brought her bags inside and put them at the bottom of the stairway. "This house, Zora, it still smells the same. Like her."

"Everything here still be the same," Delzora said, assuring her. She closed the front door. "Where is your husband? How come he not be here with you?"

"Michael and I divorced last year."

"Lawd, honey, I'm sorry to hear that. You never tole your aunt?"

"I couldn't bear to. I couldn't bear to hear her say, 'Didn't I tell you?'"

Delzora shook her head. "God rest her soul, she weren't never slow to say I done tole you so."

"No, and it was hard enough, Zora, it was very hard."

"Well, don't you worry none, honey," Delzora said, taking two of Thea's bags and starting up the stairs with them, "everything gon be all right. You home now."

"Faubourg"

BRENDA MARIE OSBEY (1957–)

Brenda Marie Osbey was born and raised in the Seventh Ward of New Orleans. Both her mother and maternal grandfather were writers, so "writing seemed a natural form of expression," for Osbey. She began writing seriously while an undergraduate at Dillard University, and in 1980 she won the Academy of American Poets Loring-Williams Prize. Her first book, *Ceremony for Minneconjoux*, a collection of narrative poems about the people of New Orleans and the surrounding bayous, appeared in 1983. Osbey focuses on the lives of those she knows best, the Afro-Louisiana women, and sees her poetry as " a kind of cultural biography, a cultural geography." Her first book, as well as her next two volumes, *In These Houses* (1988) and *Dangerous Circumstance, Dangerous Women* (1991), are largely based in Tremé, the first suburb of the original city of New Orleans, which was settled in the 1710s by free blacks and is now a part of downtown New Orleans. In 1998 she won the American Book Award for *All Saints: New and Selected Poems* (1997), in which Osbey speaks through her Afro-New Orleans forbears, celebrating the ways the dead maintain a living presence in New Orleans. The poem presented here, "Faubourg," is a selection from *All Saints*. The glossary at the end of the book explains that "faubourg" means literally in French, "false town," and refers to any of the early, named suburbs and districts of New Orleans.

---

the faubourg is a city within the larger city
and the women walk in pairs and clusters
moving along the slave-bricked streets
wearing print dresses
carrying parcels
on their hips or heads.

within the small city of the faubourg
there is always work to be done:
rooms and yards and laundry to see to
and always some trouble
to be put to rest.
burdens to be shifted
from an arm to a hip
from a hip to the head.
there are children to be scolded and sung to.
there are wares to call out
to sell or buy or search for at market.
and along the narrow banquettes leading there—
a cook
a seamstress
a day's-work-woman to find or be found.
there are chickens to feel and buy
and get their necks wrung.
palm oil to buy and sell
palm wine
hot sweet potato pies.
And there are blues to be sung or heard
above the trees and rooftops
all hours of the day and night.

the dead must be mourned and sung over
and prayers told them to carry to the other side.
the dead must be chanted and marched to their tombs
and the tombs then tended and the dogs kept away.
yatta leaves must be dried and woven into belts and baskets.
rags must be burned in sulphur to ward off mosquitoes
and slave brick crushed and scrubbed across doorways.
there is love to be made
conju to be worked.

and quiet as it is kept
most anything can be done in the faubourg.

in such a city
what name is good for a woman?
in such a city
what good is any woman's name?

Acknowledgments

Special thanks to the following individuals and institutions for their assistance in making *Literary New Orleans* possible:

Faith Freeman Barbato, Thomas and Judith Bonner, Patricia Brady and the staff of the Historic New Orleans Collection, Violet Harrington Bryan, Bethany Bultman, Chester Chomka, City Archives of the New Orleans Public Library, Sarah Crofton, Joseph DeSalvo, Greg Deal, R. Roy Fausset, Richard Faussett, Deborah Foley, David Gold, Lisa Herman, Kenneth Holditch, Jazz & Heritage Foundation Archive, Susan Larson, Loyola University Special Collections and Archives, Cheri Marquette, Karen Anne Medlin, LouAnn Morehouse, Jennifer Patrick, Claire Reinertsen, Alan Robinson, Mary Price Robinson, Craig Tenney, Britton Trice, Tulane Manuscripts Department, Ursuline Convent Archives and Museum, Paul Willis, Anthony Zurowski, and many others, as well as the authors themselves.

"The Muse is Always Half-Dressed in New Orleans" from *The Muse is Always Half-Dressed in New Orleans* by Andrei Codrescu ©1993 by Andrei Codrescu. Reprinted by permission of St. Martin's Press.

"secret messages" from *Magnolia Street* by Tom Dent ©1976 by Thomas C. Dent. Reprinted by permission of the author's estate.

Selection from *Crooked Man* by Tony Dunbar ©1994 by Tony Dunbar. Reprinted by permission of Penguin Putnam, Inc.

Selection from *Mosquitoes* by William Faulkner ©1955 by William Faulkner, ©1927 by Boni & Liveright, Inc. Reprinted by permission of Liveright Publishing Corporation.

Selection from *The Annunciation* by Ellen Gilchrist ©1983 by Ellen Gilchrist. Reprinted by permission of Little Brown & Company.

Selection from *An Unfinished Woman* by Lillian Hellman ©1969 by Lillian Hellman. Reprinted by permission of Little Brown & Company.

Selection from "Hoodoo" from *Mules & Men* by Zora Neale Hurston ©1935 by Zora Neale Hurston and renewed. Reprinted by permission of HarperCollins Publishers, Inc.

"Faubourg" from *All Saints* by Brenda Marie Osbey ©1997 by Brenda Marie Osbey. Reprinted by permission of Louisiana State University Press.

Selection from *Shrovetide in Old New Orleans* by Ishmael Reed ©1978 by Ishmael Reed. Reprinted by permission of Lowenstein Associates, Inc.

Selection from *A Confederacy of Dunces* by John Kennedy Toole ©1980 by Thelma D. Toole. Reprinted by permission of Louisiana State University Press.

"The City of the Dead" from *Signposts in a Strange Land* by Walker Percy, edited by Patrick Samway, ©1991 by Mary Bernice Percy. Reprinted by permission of Farrar Straus & Giroux, Inc.

"Mornings on Bourbon Street" from *In the Winter of Cities* by Tennessee Williams ©1956 by Tennessee William and renewed. Reprinted by permission of New Directions Press, Inc.

Selection from *Glass House* by Christine Wiltz ©1994 by Christine Wiltz. Reprinted by permission of Louisiana State University Press.